Dancing with the Tsars

ROSS O'CARROLL-KELLY

(as told to Paul Howard)

Illustrated by

ALAN CLARKE

PENGUIN BOOKS

PENGUIN BOOKS

UK | USA | Canada | Ireland | Australia
India | New Zealand | South Africa

Penguin Books is part of the Penguin Random House group of companies
whose addresses can be found at global.penguinrandomhouse.com.

First published by Penguin Ireland 2018
Published in Penguin Books 2019

001

Copyright © Paul Howard, 2018
Illustrations copyright © Alan Clarke, 2018

The moral right of the copyright holders has been asserted

Penguin Ireland thanks O'Brien Press for its agreement to Penguin Ireland using the same design approach
and typography, and the same artist, as O'Brien Press used in the first four Ross O'Carroll-Kelly titles.

Printed and bound in Great Britain by Clays Ltd, Elcograf S.p.A.

A CIP catalogue record for this book is available from the British Library

ISBN: 978-1-844-88385-1

www.greenpenguin.co.uk

MIX
Paper from
responsible sources
FSC® C018179

Penguin Random House is committed to a
sustainable future for our business, our readers
and our planet. This book is made from Forest
Stewardship Council® certified paper.

For my Auntie Anne (Warren). With love.

Contents

Prologue

He's reading a book – and I mean that quite *literally*? He doesn't own a TV like normal people. Yeah, no, that'd be too obvious for Fionn. He's also listening to classical music. I can hear it from outside. Every so often he looks up from his book and sort of, like, smiles to himself, like he's just heard, I don't know, a note that he especially loves.

What a complete and utter jeb-end.

I'm watching him through the living-room window of the little gaff he's renting in Windsor Court, just off Stradbrook Road in Blackrock. It's, like, half-ten at night and he has the lights on and the curtains open, which means I can see in, but he can't see out.

I'm trying to see what book he's reading. I don't *know* why? I doubt if I'll have heard of it. I've read four books in my entire life – and three of them were Brian O'Driscoll's autobiography.

He picks up his phone. I'm guessing that Sorcha is ringing him because he suddenly looks at his phone and his face lights up, then he turns off the music using the little remote control. He's grinning like a butcher's dog. But his expression quickly changes once he answers and it's obvious that Sorcha is telling him that I'm on my way to see him, that she told me about the two of them having sex and that he's about to be subjected to a decking to end all deckings.

He hangs up, a big, worried look on his face, walks over to the window and looks out into the dorkness. Then he draws the curtains, which is a bit rude, so I take that as my cue to kick the front door down.

Yeah, no, I show it the sole of my right Dube, three times in quick succession – we're talking, Boomp! Boomp! Boomp! – and even though it doesn't actually open, there's definitely movement in it. Then I hear him gibbering away in the hallway, pleading with me not to hurt him.

'Ross,' he goes, 'it was one night. And we both agreed that it shouldn't have happened.'

That's what Sorcha said. Then she wanted the three of us to sit down and – direct quote – discuss it like mature adults. But that's not how I roll. Never will be. Ten seconds after she told me the news, I took off in the cor, with her following me in her old man's 2007 Hyundai Santa Fe.

I reckon, if I can get through this door, I'll have about five minutes to do whatever I want to the dude before Sorcha gets here. And that should be plenty of time. I kick the door a fourth time and this time I hear the sound of wood splitting.

'Ross,' Fionn goes, a note of definite fear in his voice now, 'we were working together twenty hours a day on the election. We shared a passion for the issues facing Dublin Bay South – a 3fe for Ranelagh, free Invisalign braces for mothers over forty, the restoration of the right-turn onto Ailesbury Road from Merrion Road northbound – and we confused those feelings for something else. It happens, Ross. It's called Campaign Sex.'

I'm there, 'She was my wife.'

And he goes, 'You were getting divorced.'

'That's irregordless. She's still my technically wife.'

'You'd been separated for nearly a year. She was free to be with whomever she wanted.'

Whomever? Okay, I'm not having that.

I kick the door again. This time it finally gives way and I move towards him with my right fist loaded and ready to deploy.

I go, 'This is called payback, Fionn – and it's pronounced fock you!' which is a really clever line that just comes to me in the moment.

But just as I'm about to deliver the punch, he surprises me by producing a small fire extinguisher from behind his back and he lets me have it full in the face. I'm suddenly, like, blinded by foam and that allows him to slip past me and out the front door, running like a cat on Hallowe'en night.

I manage to clear my eyes and I happen to notice the book he was reading on the floor of the hallway. *The Complete Dramatic Works of Samuel Beckett.* I told you. Haven't a clue.

Back outside I go. I can't see him anywhere, but then I hear a cor engine purring to life and I spot his silver Toyota Prius backing out of a porking space about fifty feet away from me.

I reach it just as he's completing the manoeuvre and I literally dive onto the front of the thing. So now I'm lying on the bonnet of a cor and I'm staring through the front windscreen at this so-called friend of mine who has committed the ultimate betrayal.

I'm there, 'We played rugby together!' trying to appeal to his sense of humanity. 'Rugby!'

I swear to fock, he goes, 'What does that even mean?' and I'm thinking, he's actually making it worse for himself here.

I'm there, 'It means we live by a code!'

And he's like, 'What code? Ross, you've slept with every girl-friend I've ever had.'

Which isn't true. There was that ginger girl with the Coca-Cola bottle lenses who he went out with when he was in Trinity. She wasn't nice at all. I only got off with her.

He goes, 'You slept with my sister and broke up her marriage. Well, for once I went with *my* urges. And do you want to know something?'

'Don't say it.'

'I loved it!'

'Get out of the cor or I'll smash this windscreen.'

'I loved every second of it! And so did Sorcha!'

'I don't want to hear it.'

'She said it was a change to be with someone who was a consid-erate lover!'

I hit the windscreen with my elbow but it just slides off.

He goes, 'She said she'd never been with anyone who was so concerned with *her* pleasure.'

What kind of a man talks that way?

I'm there, 'Open the door or – I swear to fock – I will smash . . .'

I bring my elbow down on the windscreen again – like it's an opposition player acting the dick in a ruck – and this time it actually cracks. I watch the shock register on the focker's face. One more blow and I'll be through it.

So he panics then and he puts his foot on the accelerator. He takes off – well, insofar as you *can* take off in a plug-in hybrid? – with me sprawled across the bonnet and holding onto the windscreen wipers for dear life.

Now *I'm* the one who's suddenly scared because the dude has obviously lost it out of genuine fear.

As he reaches the junction with Stradbrook Road, he slams on the brakes to try to throw me off, but I grab onto his wing mirror to stop myself falling, then I give the windscreen another bang with my elbow. This time it shatters in, like, a million pieces.

I suddenly hear a woman's screams. At first I think it must be Fionn, but it ends up being Sorcha, who has pulled up outside Dog Food Manor and is shouting, 'Stop it! Stop it!' out of the driver's window of her old man's cor.

I totally blank her. I can't believe she'd say that I wasn't a considerate lover.

I reach through the broken windscreen and I try to punch Fionn in the face, but he puts his foot down again and turns the wheel left and I have to make another grab for his wing mirror as he tears up Stradbrook Road towards the roundabout, with me hanging onto the front of his cor like Jason focking Bourne.

As we reach the end of the road, I try to aim another punch at him, but he pulls the wheel right this time and takes the round-about at, like, forty Ks per hour, with me scrabbling to stay on.

He's still trying to justify what he did, by the way. He's there, 'You didn't want her, Ross. If you did, you wouldn't have had sex with that woman in Glenageary.'

'It was technically Dalkey,' I go. 'It was on the border.'

Sorcha is suddenly driving behind us, beeping her horn, trying to get Fionn to pull over – except he *doesn't*? Instead, he storts doing circuits of the roundabout – five, I count – until, dizzy and feeling like I'm going to vom, I manage to finally reach through the smashed windscreen and rip his glasses from his face.

That ends up being the key play.

Instantly blinded, he leaves the roundabout, mounts the kerb and – with me still holding on for dear life – manages to slam the cor into a wall.

Luckily for him, I manage to roll clear just before the point of impact.

His cor ends up being totalled, and I'm talking totally totalled.

Sorcha porks and comes chorging over to us, going, 'Stop it! Stop it! Stop it!' although I suspect she's secretly flattered to have two men fighting over her.

I'm too focked to do anything, though. And so is Fionn. He opens the door on the driver's side and just falls out onto the grass. I'm lying about ten feet away, too sore and too tired to even move.

'What is wrong with you?' he goes.

And I'm there, 'Sorcha's pregnant. And she doesn't know which one of us is the father.'

1. Sorcha is Pregnant – and You Won't BELIEVE the Reaction!

Sorcha shows me to the spare room, where she keeps all the other old junk that she has no use for anymore. Her exercise bike. Her Pilates ball. Her collection of Davina McCall and Tracy Shaw exercise videos on VHS. The giant 'Sorcha' sign that once hung above her shop in the Powerscourt Townhouse Centre. All of the bridesmaid dresses she's ever worn. Her George Foreman Grill with the plug missing. Her old ghetto-blaster that only plays cassette tapes and the radio. Her mood boards from various decorating projects that she's planned over the years but then done fock-all about. The ice skates that she bought for her and Honor for a trip to the Smithfield Morket six or seven Christmases ago, which were never worn because Honor objected to sharing the ice with – *her* words? – 'a pack of focking skanks'.

I'm like, 'I'm not sleeping in here. No way.'

But Sorcha goes, 'That's all that's on offer, Ross.'

'What about your old pair's room?'

They're moving out tomorrow, by the way. Yeah, no, Sorcha was worried that the *dishormony* between her old man and Honor was – what was the phrase she used? – upsetting the happy equilibrium of her home?

The truth was that she feared what Honor might do to the dude.

'No,' she just goes. 'Mom and Dad are upset enough that I've asked them to move out without them having to watch you move your stuff straight into their room. You'd rub their noses in it.'

I'm there, 'I wouldn't rub their noses in it.'

I *would* rub their noses in it. I definitely would.

She goes, 'I want us to be clear as to the nature of our relationship now, Ross. You're only living here again for the sake of the children – especially Honor, who needs a strong male role model in her life. There's no *us* anymore. There's never going to be an *us* again – are we clear about that?'

I'm looking at her Pilates ball and remembering the fun we had with it the night she finished her two-week Certificate in Mediation course in the Smurfit Business School, then drank all that tequila. Jesus, the noises out of us – like two cows smelling death on the way to the slaughterhouse.

I'm there, 'I still think there's a chance for us.'

She goes, 'There isn't. It's over, Ross.'

'So am I allowed to bring girls back?'

'Excuse me?'

'I'm just wondering, if we are really finished, am I allowed to bring girls back?'

'Do you really need me to answer that question for you?'

From her body language, I'm guessing it's a no, but I'll run it past her again when she's in better form.

'One last thing,' she goes. 'I don't want any repeat of what happened tonight. I'm talking about you and Fionn. One of you could have been killed.'

I'm there, 'How could you do it, Sorcha? Him of all people?'

'You're *actually* going to lecture me,' she goes, 'on the subject of marital infidelity?'

'I just can't believe you'd lower yourself. Focking glasses.'

And that's when Honor suddenly sticks her head around the door. Midnight and she's still up. She sees me standing there and she goes, 'What are you doing here?'

I turn around to Sorcha and I'm like, 'Are you going to tell her the good news or am I?'

'Your father is moving back in,' Sorcha goes. 'He's going to be sleeping in this room and looking after you and your brothers while Mommy is doing the important work of the country.'

Jesus, she's only been appointed to the Seanad.

Honor's face lights up like I don't *know* what? Then she comes running at me and throws her orms around my waist, squeezing the basic life out of me. I actually laugh. I'm there, 'I knew you'd be happy. This way, I get to see my daughter every single day.'

'And your sons,' Sorcha goes.

And I'm like, 'Meh,' although I don't actually *go*, 'Meh'? I *actually* go, 'Hmmm.'

Honor's there, 'I'm so happy you're home. You're the only person in the world who actually likes me.'

'Hey, I more than like you,' I go. 'I think you're hilarious. The other good news, if you haven't heard it yet, is that Sorcha's old pair are moving out.'

'Oh! My God!'

'Tomorrow!'

'I was trying to think of ways to kill them and make it look like an accident. Like my grandmother did with that American man.'

Sorcha goes, 'Don't keep saying that, Honor. Fionnuala was cleared by an actual jury.'

And I'm thinking, yeah, a jury that didn't have all the evidence.

I'm there, 'Well, now you don't need to kill them, because they're focking gone-zo, the pair of them. Two dicks.'

Honor is suddenly looking around her with – it's not even a word – but a *quizzical* expression on her face? She's like, 'Are you sleeping in *here*?'

And I'm like, 'Yeah, no, this is going to be my room.'

She looks at Sorcha and goes, 'Why isn't he sleeping in your bed?'

She's a real daddy's girl.

Sorcha's there, 'It's complicated.'

'Is it because you're a frigid bitch?' Honor goes.

I laugh. She can be very funny – when you're not the one on the wrong end of it.

I'm like, 'Yeah, no, maybe you shouldn't speak to your mother like that.'

She goes, 'I'd say she's like Elsa in bed. The focking ice queen.'

'Honor, I said that's enough. Look, I'll tell you what, why don't you put your pyjamas on . . .?' and I hand her my wallet with my credit cords in it, '. . . then go online and buy yourself something nice.'

Oh, *that* does the trick! She hugs me again, then skips off to her room. Kids just need a firm hand. And then obviously money for stuff.

Sorcha goes, 'She really hates me.'

I'm there, 'I'm sure she doesn't. Deep, deep, deep, deep down.'

'Do you think she'll be upset when she finds out – about the baby?'

'Does Dermot Bannon like natural light?'

'I thought we might put off telling her for now. She's had – oh my God – *so* much upheaval in her life lately. I think we should wait until you've been back here for a few weeks, just so she feels safe and secure enough in her environment to take the news on board.'

She'll shit a kidney.

Sorcha goes, 'I'm going to have to tell my parents, though. Obviously – because my mom's, like, my best *friend*?'

I'm there, 'I can only imagine what your old man's reaction is going to be. His precious daughter. Make sure I'm there for that, will you?'

'I don't want you gloating.'

'I'm *going* to gloat. I'm warning you now.'

'I've asked Fionn to be here for one o'clock.'

'Fionn? Why does he need to be here?'

'Because he might be the father, Ross. He should be here when I tell my parents the news.'

I actually laugh.

I go, 'Hey, I'm already looking forward to it. I'm sure they're going to be very understanding.'

'You're *what*?'

Sorcha's old man's reaction is the exact same as the time we told him we were engaged.

'I'm going to have a baby,' Sorcha goes. 'I'm twelve weeks pregnant. And before you ask the obvious question, Dad, the answer is no, it's not going to affect the important work I have to do as one of *An Taoiseach*'s appointees to the Seanad.'

Sorcha's old man looks at his daughter like he thinks she's lost it. He goes, 'I wasn't going to ask that at all. I was going to ask how the hell you managed to get yourself pregnant?'

He obviously just assumes the worst – that *I'm* the father?

I'm there, 'Well, when two grown-ups love each other very much, they sometimes exchange a special kind of hug that can often result in –'

Sorcha gives me a look to tell me to shut up.

While this is happening, by the way, Brian and Johnny are kicking a – quite literally – *soccer* ball around the kitchen? They're shouting, 'Footbaw! Footbaw! Focking footbaw!' while Leo is telling us that we're all a pack of focktards and wankbottles and we're pretending that it's not happening because Sorcha is still convinced that totally ignoring their bad language is eventually going to make it stop.

Sorcha's old dear ends up having to sit down on one of their packing boxes. She obviously doesn't trust her legs. There's fock-all wrong with her tongue, though.

'Dorling,' she goes, 'you told us your marriage was finished. You said Ross was only moving back in for the sake of the children.'

I'm there, 'Well, buckle up, because you haven't heard the best bit yet,' and I'm just, like, staring at Fionn, wondering how Sorcha could have slept with someone who looks like that. I wonder did he take his glasses off when they did the deed or did he leave them on?

Sorcha just blurts it out like it's the most natural thing in the world. She goes, 'I don't know yet whether Ross is the father or not?'

Her old dear's bottom lip storts to quiver. I can tell she's already wondering how she's going to break this news to her mates in Glenageary Lawn Tennis Club. She goes, 'Whose baby could it be?' because the entire veterans mixed-doubles set-up are going to want to know.

Sorcha's old pair both look at Fionn then – the reason he's here becoming suddenly obvious.

'There's a chance,' the dude goes, 'that the baby is mine.'

Sorcha's old man goes, 'Yours?' and I can't help but notice that he doesn't seem altogether *displeased* by this news? He actually goes, 'I see,' and he looks at me and – *seriously?* – smiles.

Sorcha's there, 'It was the night that Gran passed away. I was in a bad place.'

'Stradbrook Road,' I go. 'Fionn *calls* it Blackrock, but it's actually more Monkstown Form.'

'I mean I was in a very fragile emotional state. Fionn and I had spent a lot of time working together on the election, hadn't we, Fionn?'

'That's right,' he goes.

'We were both passionate about the issues engaging the people of Dublin Bay South – a Fallon & Byrne for Sandymount, porking restrictions in Ballsbridge for any car with an engine size of less than two litres, a giant fan to blow the flue gas from the Poolbeg Incinerator towards Kilbarrack and Raheny – and we mistook that passion for something else.'

Fionn just nods. But I can tell from his face that he wants her. He's always wanted her.

'And you didn't use protection?' her old dear goes.

This, by the way, is definitely *the* most random conversation I've *ever* been involved in. Fionn's there, 'We did use protection. Look, I don't want to get into the ins and outs of it, but it must have slipped off.'

I laugh. 'Too big,' I go, 'for your little Smorties tube of a penis.'

He forgets I've seen him in the shower.

'And *him*?' her old man goes – meaning me. 'You're saying there's also a chance it's his?'

Sorcha's there, 'We were together on the night of the funeral. Again, I was all over the place emotionally.'

Her old man gives me a look. It reminds me of the way Sean O'Brien looks at you if you fock around with the seat settings in his Kia Stonic. He'll definitely kill me one day. Her old man, I mean. Sean O'Brien is a fan.

'Wait a minute,' her old man goes, suddenly remembering something, 'I thought we had him spayed?'

He's talking about the vasectomy that I *supposedly* had but actually *didn't*?

I'm there, 'Yeah, no, it didn't take – unfortunately for everyone involved.'

'What Ross means,' Sorcha goes, 'is that he didn't go through with it.'

He's like, 'Well, let's just hope and pray that the baby turns out

14

to be yours, Fionn. I'm not sure how desperately this planet needs any more of *his* progeny.'

And when he says it, I automatically look at Brian, who is eating the remains of this morning's porridge straight from the bin, then at Johnny, who is trying to push the prongs of a fork into an electrical socket, then at Leo, who is now shouting, 'Fock every last one of you wankers!'

They really have turned out to be rubbish kids. I take the fork from Johnny and I close the Brabantia.

'Anyway,' I go, fixing Sorcha's old man with a look, 'this is *our* problem to deal with? You two get on with your focking packing. I don't want you here for a minute longer than you have to be. Here, where are you moving, by the way?' because they haven't actually *mentioned* yet? Back to the Beacon South Quarter, I'm hoping, because I know how much they hated living there.

They end up just blanking me. *He* goes, 'I know I'm counting my chickens here, but I'm trying to imagine a combination of your genes, Fionn, and Sorcha's. You should take a test to establish the paternity.'

'It involves needles,' Sorcha goes, 'and I don't want to expose my *baby* to that. I've decided to wait until he or she is born. Until then, I'm going to concentrate on the important job that *An Taoiseach* has given me.'

Her old dear is far less happy than her old man. She stands up. She goes, 'You're burying your head in the sand, Dorling – the way you always do.'

Sorcha's like, 'Yeah, it's called getting *on* with things, Mom? I've got my maiden speech to write for the Seanad. Plus – there's probably going to be a lot of publicity about this – I'm planning to introduce a Private Members' Bill to ban all single-use, disposable coffee cups from both houses of the Oireachtas.'

'You're in denial, Sorcha. Have you thought for one minute about the impact this new baby is likely to have on your daughter?'

I go, 'We've decided to give ourselves a few weeks to pluck up the courage to tell her.'

Suddenly, the kitchen door flies open and Honor is standing

there, looking mad enough to kill us all with her bare hands. Which I wouldn't rule out.

She goes, 'What the fock is going on?'

I slip into self-preservation mode. I'm there, 'I don't know what your mother was thinking, Honor. She's claiming she was confused after her granny died, but I'm not buying it.'

Except Honor doesn't seem to *hear* me? She morches straight past me, as a matter of fact. Then she stares out of the kitchen window with this look of, like, horror frozen on her face. I walk over and I stand next to her. And that's when I realize that she's not talking about her old dear being pregnant at all. She's talking about the humungous Shomera at the bottom of the gorden.

I'm thinking, okay, when the fock did that arrive?

I turn around and I just, like, *glower* at Sorcha's old man. 'That's where you're moving to?' I go. 'Our back focking gorden?'

And he smiles at me and goes, 'Oh, you're not going to get rid of me that easily. I'm going to be around for quite some time – watching every misstep you make.'

The gaff is rammers. Half of Finglas must be crammed into Ronan's kitchen – we're talking all of Shadden's mates, then all the neighbours as well. Shadden's old dear, Dordeen, has spent the morning putting the entire contents of the frozen foods aisle from Lidl on the St Margaret's Road into a deep fat fryer, then arranged the results into greasy piles on paper plates.

Ronan and Shadden are celebrating their engagement. And this is what the Tuites call pushing the boat out.

Rihanna-Brogan, my – I still can't get used to saying this word – *granddaughter*, is sitting on my knee. 'Rosser,' she goes, 'can I have some money?'

Ronan hears it and he laughs. Four years old, bear in mind. I whip out a roll of fifties and I go to peel one off for her, except she ends up grabbing the entire wad from me.

Honor just stares at her little niece. I pick up on the fact that she's possibly jealous. I'm there, 'Don't worry. We'll go to an ATM on the way home and I'll get you a roll of fifties too.'

She goes, 'You focking better.'

You can't play favourites when it comes to your children.

'Footbaw!' Brian shouts. 'Me want watch footbaw!'

Except for the ones who love soccer. They can Foxtrot Romeo Oscar if they think they're getting anything.

Shadden's old man, the famous Kennet, appears then and goes, 'Theer she is – m . . . m . . . moy little p . . . p . . . p . . . princess!' and he picks Rihanna-Brogan up off my knee, throws her on his shoulders and storts galloping around the kitchen like a horse. He's actually good with her, and I'd be the last one to say anything nice about the stuttering focker.

Sorcha is talking to Shadden and one or two of her mates, trying to explain what the Seanad actually does.

I have to admit, I'm kind of curious myself.

'It plays an essential legislative role,' she goes, 'in determining the laws under which we *all* must live?'

They all just nod – not a focking breeze.

'Could you get me a medical keerd?' one of Shadden's mates goes.

See, that's real power in this port of the world.

Sorcha's there, 'No, I can't get you a medical cord.'

At which point the women all lose interest in talking to her. 'Ah, weddle,' one of them goes, 'as long as the muddy's good,' and then she sticks a plate under Sorcha's nose. 'Will you hab a gooey John?'

Sorcha's like, 'A what?' looking at the plate like it's got John the Baptist's head on it.

'A chicken gooey John. I lib on these things, so I do.'

Sorcha takes one, doing the whole Woman of the People routine, even though I once heard her describe frozen food as the top of a slippery slope that leads to heroin addiction and prostitution.

She turns around to Honor and goes, 'You look lovely today, Dorling.'

Honor just looks her up and down and goes, 'Yeah, like I *give* a fock what you think about anything?' and she walks off.

Sorcha looks at me and just smiles sadly. She goes, 'I couldn't ask them to move back to the Beacon South Quarter, Ross – they're my parents!'

And I'm there, 'Hey, I'm just worried about what Honor might do to them. As long as they understand that *we* can't guarantee their safety.'

I notice Ronan's mates, including Nudger, Gull and the famous Buckets of Blood, and I give them a nod to say hello.

Kennet decides to make a speech then. He goes, 'Birra hush, evoddy body. Ine just wanton to say a few w . . . w . . . w . . . w . . . w . . .'

'Woords!' one of the neighbours shouts. 'Huddy the fook up, will you, Kennet? Some of us hab bleaten woork in the morden.'

Everyone laughs. Even Tina, Ronan's old dear, catches my eye and smiles.

'Ine j . . . j . . . j . . . joost wanton to say,' he goes, 'tanks for cubben, t . . . t . . . tanks to D . . . D . . . D . . . D . . . D . . . D . . . Dordeen for p . . . p . . . p . . . prepeerdon alt the foowut and a happy engayug middint to my b . . . b . . . b . . . b . . . b . . . b . . . b . . . b . . . b . . .'

I check the time on my phone. This one could end up being a record.

'B . . . b . . . b . . . b . . . b . . . beauriful thaughter Shadden and her fiancé, R . . . R . . . R . . . R . . . R . . . R . . . R . . . R . . .'

'Ronan,' Dordeen shouts, putting us all out of our misery.

'That's reet,' Kennet goes. 'R . . . R . . . R . . . R . . . R . . . R . . . R . . . Ronan. Who Dordeen and me are veddy, veddy fond of, eeben though he's fadder's soyut of the famidy are alt s . . . s . . . s . . . s . . . s . . . s . . . sout ciders!'

Everyone in the room storts booing. It's easy to forget sometimes that *they* look down on *us* in pretty much the same way that *we* look down on *them*?

He goes, 'The only c . . . c . . . c . . . consodation, as I says to Dordeen, is that it'll be s . . . s . . . s . . . s . . . s . . . s . . . some soyuz of a wetton.'

Which presumably means *I'm* paying for it?

I notice Honor leading Rihanna-Brogan out of the room by the hand. I presume they're going upstairs to watch TV.

'And it woatunt be bleaten g . . . g . . . g . . . g . . . g . . . gooey

Johns that day,' Kennet goes, 'lubbly as thee are, D . . . D . . . D . . . Dordeen. In addyhow, to sum up, congratulayshiddens, Sh . . . Sh . . . Sh . . . Sh . . . Shadden and R . . . R . . . R . . . R . . . Ronan.'

Everyone raises their drinks and goes, 'Sh . . . Sh . . . Sh . . . Sh . . . Shadden and R . . . R . . . R . . . R . . . Ronan,' ripping the actual piss out of him.

'You're all a pack of fockholes!' Brian shouts. 'Fockholes, the lot of you!'

A minute or two later, I watch Ro go to the fridge and grab a stick of Heinemite and a can of something called – literally? – Skanderbeg, then he looks at me and nods at the back door. He obviously wants to talk, so I follow him outside to the gorden.

The rain has stopped.

He hands me the Heineken, then we sit down on their old sofa, which Ronan has been promising to get rid of ever since they bought their new sofa, which is about two and a half years ago now. He probably won't bother now. He'll wait for the thing to – I think it's a word – *decompose*?

I'm there, 'Shadden's old man seems to be under the impression that I'm going to be paying for the wedding. Where I come from, it's the bride's parents who stick their hands in their pockets.'

'On this soyut,' he goes, 'it's the fadder of the groowum.'

'Yeah, no, I thought that might be the case alright.'

'It's thradition, Rosser. Hee-or, Ine deloyrit to see you and Sudeka back togedder again.'

I'm like, 'Yeah, no, we're not properly together yet? It's separate rooms for now.'

'Ah, you'll woork yisser cheerm on her, Rosser. You two'll be alt lubbed up again afore you know it.'

'I don't know about that. It's just, well, this time it's not as simple as me waiting for her to come to her senses and forgive me.'

'What do you mee-un?'

'Look, keep this to yourself, Ro, because we haven't even told Honor yet.'

'What?'

'Sorcha's pregnant.'

'That's bleaten great newiz.'

'But she doesn't know yet whether I'm the father or not.'

'What? Sure who else could the fadder be?'

'Possibly Fionn.'

'Fionn? With the glasses?'

'Exactly. You've summed him up.'

'Moy Jaysus. That's some bleaten mess, Rosser.'

Shadden suddenly appears at the back door. 'Ro,' she goes, 'hab we addy mower of that Albanian bee-or?'

He's like, 'There's tree trays of it in the boot of me keer, Shadden. Ast your auld fedda to help you caddy them in,' and she focks off inside again.

I go, 'So it looks like *you're* still going through with it, then? Getting married, I mean?'

He's there, 'Of course Ine going troo wirrut. Shadden has her heert set on a New Yee-ors Eeb wetton.'

'New Year's Eve? Okay, that's plenty of time for me to hopefully change your mind.'

'You're apposed to be me best madden, Rosser. Doatunt be *throying* to get me to chayunge me moyunt.'

'I'm just not sure you're ready for marriage, Ro.'

'What makes you think Ine not rettty?'

'Well, firstly, you're still only nineteen. And, secondly, you've spent the last eight months riding half the Orts Block in UCD.'

'That's all oaber, Rosser.'

'Do you know how many times I told myself that lie?'

'It's norra loy. Look, Ine agreeyun wit you. The Eerts Block blew me moyunt. All them beauriful boords. I was like a choyult in a sweet shop, so I was. But the nobblety's arthur weerden off now. Ine retty to spend the rest of me loyf wit just one geerdle. And that geerdle is Shadden.'

'You better be sure, Ro. You don't want to end up like me.'

'You moytunt have been a veddy good husband, Rosser. But, in feerdness to you, you're a great fadder.'

And I just smile and think to myself, yeah, at least no one can question that. We clink cans. And, in that moment, I just happen to look up at the back bedroom to see Rihanna-Brogan blowing cigarette smoke out of the window. I know, as sure as I know my own name, that Honor is teaching my four-year-old granddaughter how to smoke.

I decide to just keep Ronan talking in the hope that he doesn't notice. I'm there, 'I still say it's in the family genes, though – the urge to cheat.'

He goes, 'Famidy genes, me boddicks. I can stop addy toyum I wanth. Which I hab now. Thrust me, Rosser, me days of hooerden around are wed and thrudy oaber.'

And it's at that exact moment that Shadden reappears. She's walking down the gorden towards us and she's holding – not a word of a lie – a bra. I notice Kennet walking a few feet behind her, a big serious face on him, then Tina, standing at the door, watching.

'Whose is this?' Shadden goes, dancing the thing up and down in front of his eyes.

Yeah, *wed and thrudy oaber*, my orse.

Ronan doesn't say shit. He's, like, lost for words. He's there, 'Er . . .'

Shadden goes, 'I ast you whose bra this is? I fowunt it in the boot of yisser keer.'

And suddenly I hear myself go, 'It's mine.'

Shadden looks at me, her eyes wide with surprise. She goes, 'Yoo-ers? Why have you got a bra in moy fedda's keer?'

I'm there, 'It belongs to, em – yeah, no – a woman. I asked Ronan to stash it for me.'

'A wooban?' Shadden goes. 'So a wooban you're sleeping wit?'

'Yeah, no, *slept* with? Past tense. Let's all move on. A New Year's wedding, by the way. That's exciting.'

But Shadden refuses to let it go. She's like, 'A wooban you slept wit behoyunt Sudeka's back?'

Ronan goes, 'Thee hab a maddidge of convedience – idn't that reet, Rosser? He's a free aichunt, so he is.'

Shadden looks at me with her eyes narrowed. 'That's because you desthroyut what you had. Why caddent you be mower like Ronan theer?'

I'm like, 'Ronan?'

She goes, 'He's hodest and he's loyult.' She drops the bra onto my lap and she goes, 'You'd wanth to steert growing up, Rosser. You reedy would.'

A few seconds later, little Rihanna-Brogan appears at the back door, standing next to Tina, crying her eyes out, vomit all down the front of her beautiful white dress.

'Ma,' she goes, 'Ine arthur getting sick, so I am.'

I stand up and I go, 'I think we might, er, head back to civilization.'

Sorcha is taking this whole maiden speech business very seriously. A bit *too* seriously, some might say? She's decided she's going to watch all seven seasons of *The West Wing* – for inspiration, I hear her tell her old man.

It's, like, half-nine on a Friday night and she's down in the Shomera with her old pair, watching Episode Two of Season One while I'm the one trying to persuade our children to go to sleep.

'Me want story,' Johnny goes, holding up a book.

I'm there, 'I've told you, I'm not reading that shit to you.'

It's a book about Sergio, the soccer-playing penguin, which Sorcha's old dear bought for him in Dubray this morning, despite me telling her that I'm trying my best as a father to wean them onto rugby.

Jesus, my old man kept me indoors with the curtains drawn for a month during Italia '90 just to make sure I didn't develop an interest in that ridiculous game. He stuck the TV in the attic and told me that I had a terminal illness and couldn't leave my room. That's love. But now I'm having to listen to this from my own children.

'Sergio!' Brian shouts. 'Me want Sergio!'

I'm there, 'I'm not reading that to you. As a matter of fact, Johnny, give me that book.'

I'm going to fock it in the bin once and for all. I try to grab it from him, except he holds onto it really tightly and storts screaming. Then Brian storts screaming and Leo goes, 'You're only a focking shitwaffle! You focking shitwaffle fock!'

This is what a Friday night looks like for me now. Seriously, I'd have been better off staying separated. I'd be pissed in Kielys of Donnybrook right now and this – without meaning to sound sexist – would be their mother's job.

In the end, I just decide, fock it, I couldn't be orsed with this. I don't care whether they go to bed or not. I just walk out of the room and lock the door. I'm leaving them to it. Leo gives the door a boot as I'm turning the key and goes, 'You focking, focking shitwaffle!'

I tip downstairs, thinking, I might actually have one or two cans in the fridge. And that's when my phone suddenly rings. It's Sorcha. Which is a bit random considering she's basically outside in the gorden. Of course she knows where I am so I've no choice but to *answer* the focking thing?

Her opening line is, 'Ross, can you come down here, please? I need to speak to you,' and she hangs up.

I'm straightaway thinking, okay, what fresh hell is this?

When I get down to the Shomera, I notice that *The West Wing* has been paused. The screen is filled with the face of Donna Moss.

I'm there, 'What's up?'

Sorcha goes, 'I've just had Shadden on the phone. She said Honor taught Rihanna-Brogan how to smoke.'

I always loved Donna Moss.

I'm there, 'Okay.'

'Okay?' Sorcha goes. 'Is that all you're going to say?'

'Jesus Christ, Sorcha, everyone in that focking house smokes. She was going to pick it up sooner or later.'

'She's four years old, Ross.'

'Well, Ronan wasn't much older when *he* storted?'

I notice that Sorcha's old dear is making coffee. I'm wondering is there a cup going.

'And this,' Sorcha's old man goes, 'is the strong male role model you thought your daughter needed?'

Sorcha's like, 'Dad!'

'I'm just making the point, Sorcha. Don't forget, this is the man who used your dead grandmother's mobile phone to send you text messages urging you to take him back.'

He has a way of making everything sound bad.

'Ross,' Sorcha goes, 'you need to speak to Honor. And you need to be firm with her.'

All of a sudden the lights go out in the Shomera. As a matter of fact, the TV goes off as well.

'Not again!' her old man goes. 'That's the third blackout this week!'

Her old dear's there, 'Electric Ireland keep saying it must be a fault in the way this thing is wired. The engineer said –.'

And suddenly there's a scream. Well, *two* screams: first, Sorcha's old dear, as she trips over a pouf, we're talking orse over proverbial tit; then Sorcha's old man, as a tray of boiling-hot coffees lands in his lap.

He's like, 'Aaarrrggghhh! Jesus, woman!'

She goes, 'I'm so sorry. I'll go and get some ice.'

He's still there, 'Aaarrrggghhh!' in absolute agony.

And I laugh, of course.

Sorcha just goes, 'Ross, get out! Go and speak to your daughter!'

Honor is looking out of her window down at the Shomera. She's like, 'Has the electricity gone again?'

And I'm there, 'Yeah, no, third time this week apparently.'

'I hate him.'

'Yeah, no, so do I. You know, I was actually wondering, do you not need planning permission to put something like that in your gorden?'

'No, I rang the planning deportment of Dún Laoghaire-Rathdown County Council and they said you didn't because it's not classified as an actual building.'

God, she really *does* hate him?

'Well,' I go, 'you'll be happy to hear that he's just been scalded by three mugs of hot coffee, which Sorcha's old dear happened to be carrying when the lights went out.'

She laughs. She's there, 'Oh my God, imagine if he needed, like, a skin graft operation!'

I go, 'Yeah, no, that'd be funny alright. Anyway, listen, there's something your mother wanted me to bring up with you.'

She's like, 'What?' already on the big-time defensive.

I'm there, 'Don't worry, you're not in trouble.'

'I'm not worried. I'm just asking what the fock is her problem now?'

'Okay, I'll just come straight out and ask you. Did you teach Rihanna-Brogan how to smoke?'

'Yeah? So what?'

'Shit. I sort of hoped you'd deny it. Yeah, no, it's just that Shadden rang. She's pretty upset apparently.'

'Everyone in that house smokes. She was going to pick it up sooner or later.'

'Hey, that's exactly what I said.'

'Shadden smokes like a focking chimney.'

'We think very similarly, me and you. We definitely do.'

We carry on looking out the window. They're watching *The West Wing* on Sorcha's laptop – obviously on, like, *battery* power?

I'm there, 'It'd be great, Honor, if you could possibly pretend to your old dear that I gave out shit to you, though.'

She's like, 'Why would I do that?'

'It would just make my life easier if she thought I was being a strong father figure to you.'

'Whatever. Oh my God, she's making such a big deal about that stupid focking speech.'

'She definitely seems to be full of shit alright.'

'She told me she wants me there to hear it.'

'It'd be a day off school, I suppose.'

'I told her to fock off. I'd rather pull my own back teeth out with a pliers.'

'That's another way of looking at it.'

'It's only the focking Seanad. It's like, oh my God, a year ago, Enda Kenny was trying to, like, abolish it – er, the man who actually *appointed* her?'

I laugh. I'm there, 'Is that true? Hang on, I thought it was the Taoiseach who appointed her?'

She goes, 'Enda Kenny *is* the Taoiseach?'

My ten-year-old daughter knows more about the world than I do. Jesus.

'Is he?' I go. 'Yeah, no, I wondered why his name was familiar.'

'She's banging on about this speech,' she goes, 'like she thinks anyone actually *gives* a fock what she has to say.'

'And meanwhile I'm having to make your breakfast every morning, drive you to school, phone out for the dinner, put the boys to bed. The focking *West Wing*. You wouldn't blame the girl.'

She moves away from the window and she lies down on her bed. She goes, 'So what's going on between her and Fionn?'

I sit down on the edge of the bed. I'm thinking, fock, what does she know? I'm like, 'What do you mean, Honor? Did you hear something?'

'Er, she's *constantly* on the phone to him? We're talking, like, ten times a *day*?'

'Yeah, no, he's going to be her Porliamentary Secretary or some shit.'

'Is she having sex with him?'

'Jesus Christ, Honor.'

'What? It's what everyone else is probably wondering. I mean, she's dumped you in the room where she keeps all the other shit she doesn't want anymore but can't bring herself to get rid of – her focking Wii Fit and her waffle iron.'

I'm there, 'It's complicated at the moment, Honor.'

She picks up the TV remote and storts flicking through the channels until she finds *The Late Late Show*. Up on the screen, Ryan Tubridy is going, 'Now, when we think of power couples, we think of Barack and Michelle Obama, Bill and Hillary Clinton, Brad Pitt and Angelina Jolie, even Jay-Z and Beyoncé Knowles. But my next guests can lay claim to being their Irish equivalents. *He* is the leader of New Republic, now the biggest political party in the Dáil, while *she* is a bestselling novelist who spent a year in prison for a crime she didn't commit and is now hoping to use the experience for positive ends . . .'

'Oh my God,' Honor goes, 'it's Granny and Granddad.'

I'm like, 'Switch the channel!'

Except she doesn't.

'Ladies and gentlemen,' Tubs goes, 'can you please put your hands together for Charles and Fionnuala O'Carroll-Kelly!'

Out they walk. No shame. *She* looks like she's been embalmed – obviously got botoxed this afternoon – while his wig looks even more ridiculous on TV than it does in real life.

The Camembert Quartet play George Michael's *Freedom*.

The two of them sit down.

Tubs goes, 'Now, I *say* celebrity couple – but you are, in fact, divorced, are you not?'

The old man goes, 'Yes, we were divorced, regrettably, after almost thirty years of marriage! But during Fionnuala's incarceration, let's just say certain – inverted commas – feelings were rekindled?'

Yeah, no, I caught them last week, bet into each other like two trains colliding. Let me tell you, seeing my old pair riding each other was not on the bucket list.

He goes, 'And now I'm happy to report that we are – as the social diarists would have it – an item again!'

The audience claps.

Tubs goes, 'You can hear the reaction! Charles, you've just had, well, it really was an amazing election for New Republic. A brand new political party, you finished with fifty-one seats, the largest party in the Dáil. How much does it hurt you that you are not the leader of the country today?'

The old man runs his hand through his hair slash wig and goes, 'Well, as I said to Hennessy Coghlan-O'Hara, my solicitor and long-suffering golf partner, after the Taoiseach managed to cobble together a government, "The ideological majority is more important than the parliamentary majority!" This time round, we didn't have the numbers to keep out Fianna Gael – or is it Fine Fáil – but I think the result was a clear message from the electorate that they are tired of the old parties who have governed this country – badly – since independence! And this deal between Enda Kenny and Micheál Martin, which was agreed for the sole purpose of excluding New Republic from government, represents only a temporary reprieve for two Civil War parties who no longer have any relevance in the Ireland of today!'

Tubs goes, 'Are you saying you still believe you will lead the country one day?'

'I will be Ireland's next Taoiseach, Ryan! And it will happen within the next three years!'

Again, there's more applause from the audience. He's always been very popular for some strange reason.

Tubs turns to the old dear then. He goes, 'Fionnuala, may I say you look fabulous tonight?'

She doesn't. She looks like a focking corpse. Seriously, the next time I see Tubs on Dún Laoghaire Pier, I'm going to throw him in the focking sea.

He's there, 'You've just gone through what must have been a harrowing ordeal – accused of murdering a man you loved, who was, in fact, your husband at the time. Tell me how difficult the last year has been for you.'

After a five-second pause for dramatic effect, the old dear goes, 'I can't, Ryan. Because I can't put it into words. And I'm saying that as someone who has sold more than seventeen million books worldwide and whose last novel was described by the wonderful Anne Enright as "no more or no less than the cover suggests". I don't have the words – though words doth be my stock-in-trade.'

Er, *doth be*?

'Oh my God,' Honor goes, 'her face doesn't even move when she talks.'

The old dear goes, 'I loved him, Ryan. As you said, I loved him very much indeed. To lose him was like losing half of myself. But to be accused of murdering him, well, that was like losing the other half of me. Because it meant I couldn't grieve him. In a way, it invalidated my sadness and my sense of loss. It stole twelve precious months from my life. And this wonderful man sitting beside me was the only person in the world who believed in my innocence.'

Hey, I went to visit her in prison a few times, and not always to take the piss. There's no shout-out for me, though.

Tubs goes, 'And now you're planning to use your profile as the victim of a miscarriage of justice in a positive way. Tell us about that.'

She's like, 'Well, since the day of my acquittal, Charles and I have been discussing how we might take this awful, awful thing that happened to me and make something good from it. So we've decided to set up a charitable foundation – a not-for-profit organization with the stated mission of strengthening the capacity of people in Ireland and beyond to meet the challenges of global interdependence.'

Honor goes, 'That sounds like a tax dodge.'

You don't spend as long as Honor has in the Mount Anville play-ground without picking up a bit of knowledge.

'I've already had a great many requests to make speeches,' the old dear goes, 'talking about my experience as a victim of injustice. I thought to myself, how can I use those speaking opportunities to benefit people in need? So I've come up with the idea of a founda-tion and I'm calling it "In the Name of Fionnuala O'Carroll-Kelly" or, if you like, "In the Name of FO'CK."'

'I want the legacy of this terrible experience to be my philan-thropic work. I want to use my fame to bring together the elites from the worlds of business, politics and celebrity to try to solve the problems of the world, with a special focus on issues regarding women and children, economic development, healthcare, Africa, AIDS, the environment and obesity, which I really can't abide. There's no excuse for it once you learn to exercise a bit of self-control.'

'It sounds like a very exciting initiative,' Tubs goes.

Seriously. In. The focking. Sea.

She's there, 'There is so much suffering in the world and we owe it to the next generation to do something to end it, Ryan. I have four grandchildren.'

I shout, 'You've got *five* grandchildren, you drunken grunt!'

'And before I let you go,' Tubs goes, 'they'll all be saying to me, "Why didn't you ask the question?" so I'm *going* to ask the question: are you two going to get married again?'

The old man goes, 'Well, things are in a state of flux at the moment!'

Yeah, I think, you're still married to someone else. I'm glad Helen is still in Australia – not here watching this.

'But right now,' he goes, 'we're enjoying the feeling of just being in – quote-unquote – love!'

The audience gives them a humungous round of applause.

Honor goes, 'So how did she get away with actually killing that man?'

I'm there, 'The jury didn't have all the evidence. Namely, the two-bor electric heater that she dropped into the bath to give the dude a hort attack.'

'Do you know where it is?'

'Er, no.'

'Oh my God, you *so* do!'

She's right. I found it last week, hidden in the nuclear fallout shelter at the bottom of the gorden, all blackened and burned. So I sort of, like, *re-hid* it? I don't know why. I just saw it and I acted. I pulled a few loose bricks out of the wall and stashed it in the cavity space behind it.

I'm like, 'Seriously, Honor, I've no idea what ended up happening to it.'

'Because if you did have it,' she goes, 'you could, like, totally blackmail her.'

She's so far ahead of me I've been pretty much lapped here.

I'm there, 'Blackmail her?' only realizing for the first time the actual value of the thing.

She goes, 'Isn't she going to inherit all of Ari's money now?'

'Yeah, no, two billion snots apparently.'

'That heater could send her back to prison. I'm just saying, she'd probably pay a lot of money for it.'

It's only, like, two days until Oisinn and Magnus are getting married. Two men. Getting married. To each other. And I'm totally cool with that. I'm so cool with it that I'm actually giving myself a big-time pat on the back here.

'You don't have to keep saying you're cool with it,' Oisinn goes.

I'm there, 'Er, I've only said it maybe three or *four* times?'

Magnus goes, 'But you undershtand, Rosh, that being cool with it meansh you shouldn't heff to keep shaying you are cool with it, yesh?'

Magnus is from Finland, which is the reason his accent is so random.

'Hey, whatever,' I go. 'I'm just making the point that I think it's great that in this day and age – blah, blah, blah.'

This is us in Kielys, by the way. They're having their last few pints as free men. I give Pat behind the bor the nod to say same again. Heineken all round, even though Magnus usually drinks Corlsberg. I won't allow it, though. I've already explained it to him: 'I'm happy to accept diversity, even embrace the thing, but there's still a line.'

And he respects that.

JP asks them how the plans are coming along. The actual ceremony is happening at the waterfall in Powerscourt, followed by a reception in Summerhill House.

'Itsh all goot,' Magnus goes. 'My parentsh are arriving in Ireland tomorrow, which ish ferry exshiteing.'

Oisinn hasn't even met them yet. Magnus's old man is some kind of executive in IKEA in Finland and his old dear is an actual – get this – *sex* therapist?

'Sho,' he goes, 'they are ferry much looking forward to meeting all of you. Let me jusht shay, they are lotsh of fun. For exshample, they shay to me, we will look after the cake, for the wedding, yesh? Sho my mother shends me a picture of the cake thish morning and guesh what? She hash made a large Daim Bar cake – you know like they sherve in the IKEA restaurant? Like I shay to you, they are lotsh and lotsh of fun!'

Yeah, no, I'll have to take his word for it.

Oisinn has something on his mind. I can tell. He goes, 'So we, er, also wanted to talk to you about your role in the day, Ross.'

I'm there, 'What do you mean? You still want me to be your best man, don't you?'

And – I swear to fock – the dude goes, 'No, I don't.'

I'm there, 'Yeah, some former teammate you turned out to be. What are you, scared I'll say something that might come across as, what's the word – homophobical?'

He goes, 'Let me finish, Ross. I don't want you to be my best man – because *we* want you to perform the actual ceremony. We want *you* to marry us.'

Jesus.

I actually burst into tears. And I haven't cried in Kielys since Isa Nacewa played his last ever game for Leinster the first time round.

I'm like, 'Dude, I don't know what to say.'

He goes, 'Well, you'd better prepare something because it's the day after tomorrow! We want you to do the introduction, talk a bit about us, all that. And we don't want any rugby references in it.'

'There'll have to be rugby in it.'

'I said no rugby, Ross.'

Magnus is a soccer goy, of course. He used to actually play the game professionally. Talk about lovers from different backgrounds. It's like that movie, *Romeo and Juliet*.

Christian arrives back from the reptile house.

'So,' he goes, still drying his hands on his chinos, 'I hear you and Sorcha are back together?'

I'm there, 'Not exactly. I'm back living in the gaff, but let's just say we're taking things slowly.'

'Hey, it won't be long before she sees what everyone else can see – you two are meant to be together.'

'I hope so, Dude.'

Christian is in cracking form, by the way – the happiest I've seen him in a long time. He's back with Lauren and the kids, he's off the drink and he's storting a new job next week, although he hasn't said what it is yet.

JP actually asks him. He's like, 'What's this job, by the way?'

'It's kind of in morkeshing,' Christian goes. 'It's a sort of ground-floor, front-of-operation, customer-facing role that's very, em, people-centric.'

I just shake my head. I'm there, 'All I can say is we must be finally back to where we were in 2003 because I didn't understand a focking word of what you just said!'

JP says the economy is definitely back. He goes, 'Have any of you heard of this new place – Linden Boulevard in Ranelagh?'

I'm like, 'No, what is it, a restaurant?'

'Yeah,' he goes, 'except they call it, like, a neighbourhood dining room. The theme of the menu is – I shit you not – survival rations.'

We're all like, 'What?'

'Everything on the menu,' he goes, 'has been inspired by a story of someone who was either stranded on a desert island, or lost at sea, or abandoned in the jungle, and what they were forced to eat to stop themselves from actually *storving* to death?'

Oisinn's there, 'And to think they said this country was finished.'

'It's all, like, clover and pine-needle salads,' JP goes. 'Women love it, of course, because you can eat pretty much anything on the menu and not put on weight. There's, like, a two-week waiting list to get a reservation for this place.'

I roll up my sleeve. 'Look!' I go. 'Goosebumps!'

Fionn decides to show his face then. Two hours late. The big entrance. I go, 'Nice of you to finally show,' and I make a big point of looking at my wrist, even though I'm not wearing an actual watch. 'We're already seven or eight pints down the road here. You focking lightweight.'

'Sorry,' he goes, 'I've been with Sorcha all day,' and he lets it just hang there.

He's got more front than Dollymount.

I'm there, 'What do you mean you were *with* her? Not *with* with?'

He goes, 'We've been working on her speech.'

I laugh. I'm there, 'Yeah? What season of *The West Wing* is she up to now?'

He goes, 'You know, this is what Sorcha was born to do, Ross. To lead. You could maybe support her instead of making snide comments all the time.'

Then he heads for the bor. The focking cheek of *him* – lecturing *me*?

I'm about to follow him to say something, but that's when Erika suddenly walks in.

God, she looks great. When *doesn't* she, of course?

I walk up to her and I go, 'Hey, Sis,' even though she hates me calling her that. 'Did you see the old man on *The Late Late Show*?'

She goes, 'I don't want anything to do with that man,' which is true – she hasn't spoken to him since Helen focked him out. 'What's going on between you and Sorcha?'

I'm like, 'Er, nothing. I've moved back into the gaff. Just to be a father to the kids. But it's separate rooms.'

She goes, 'Is she pregnant?'

I'm like, 'Pregnant?' trying to look shocked, even though I can actually feel my face turning red. 'What are you talking about?'

Shit, I keep looking over at Fionn. And she's definitely noticed that I keep looking at him as well because she has a look over her shoulder.

'I saw her in the Merrion Shopping Centre today,' she goes. 'And she looked really pale. What's going on, Ross? Why do you keep looking at Fionn?'

I'm there, 'I don't. I mean, I'm not. I'm just wondering why you'd presume she was pregnant just because she looked a bit pale.'

'She was in the pharmacy,' she goes. 'She was buying folic acid.'

The old dear is a sucker for the old traditions, especially the ones that involve alcohol. For as long as I can remember, going back thirty years and more, she's had lunch every Friday with Delma and the rest of her Foxrock Fanny mates in The Gables. And she always orders the exact same thing. The no-corb pasta alla vodka.

In other words, a pint of vodka.

Which means that, by three o'clock, she's usually observing another of her traditions – her Friday-afternoon drunk nap.

Honor actually looks up from her phone when she hears me taking the right-turn onto Westminster Road. She's like, 'Where are we going?'

Yeah, no, I've just collected her from school.

I'm there, 'We're calling into the old dear's gaff. I just need to, em, collect something. Something I forgot to take with me when I moved out.'

She's like, 'Yeah, whatever,' and then she goes back to her phone.

I end up nearly missing the filter light. Some woman behind me in a red Ford Ka beeps her horn. Out of the window, Leo shouts, 'You shouldn't even be on the road, you stupid focking pigmutt!'

They're like sponges at that age. They take everything in.

Sixty seconds later, I pull into the old dear's driveway. I don't bother knocking on the door. I just walk around the side of the gaff, then tip down to the bottom of the gorden, looking over my shoulder the entire time.

I let myself into the – yeah, no – nuclear fallout shelter and switch on the light. I walk over to the port of the wall where I removed the bricks before. I put my fingers in the cracks and I manage to ease them out of the wall again. I stick my head into the hole and I use the torch on my iPhone to get a proper look.

It's still there. I put my orm into the wall, up to the shoulder, reach down, grab the little handle and pull it out. Then I head back to the cor. I whip open the boot, drop the heater in there, then I slam it shut and breathe an actual sigh of relief.

I hit the road again.

Honor doesn't say shit until we're back on the dualler and driving through Cabinteely. Then, out of the blue, she goes, 'Did you get it? The two-bor electric heater, I mean.'

And I'm there, 'Trust me, Honor. The less you know, the better.'

I'm watching Fionn shooting the shit with Oisinn's soon-to-be in-laws, we're talking Kristoffer and Hedvig, who are totally buying into his act. He's going, 'I was telling Magnus, I'm actually something of a Finophile myself.'

A Finophile? I will smash his glasses – and then they will be broke.

Hedvig – who's an absolute ride, just to give you a mental picture – goes, 'You heff vishited Feenlend?'

And, of course, Fionn can't resist going, 'Three times actually. The first time was about fifteen years ago. I was doing a bit of travelling around Eastern Europe and I got the ferry from Tallinn across to Helsinki.'

'Yesh, ish a beautiful croshing,' Kristoffer goes. 'Ish ferry, ferry nyshe.'

'Well, that was the beginning of my love affair with your country. I actually bought a Lada while I was there and I drove up as far as Kokkola. I even brought the cor back to Ireland with me!'

I remember that. The thing was basically a biscuit tin on wheels.

And he used to drive around in it in the middle of the day with his headlights on. 'It's actually how they drive in Finland,' he'd go, sounding delighted with himself. I eventually took a shit in the boot, underneath the spare wheel. He could never figure out where the smell was coming from, but it got worse and worse until he was eventually forced to sell the thing for scrap.

I think he got forty quid for it in the end.

Hedvig – she actually looks like Belén Rueda except with boxier calves – thinks he's great, of course. A lot of people are fooled by him.

'Vell,' she goes, 'you musht shtay wish ush the neksht time you come to Feenland wish your femily.'

And I watch Fionn's eyes drift towards Sorcha, who happens to be on the phone to her old pair, checking that the triplets are okay.

I don't say anything. I've got my duties to carry out.

It's a cracking day for an outdoor wedding. Oisinn looks so – I'm just going to come out and use the word – *handsome* in his black tux? I say it to his face as well. And he goes, 'Thanks. And thanks again for doing this.'

I'm like, 'Hey – the pleasure is mine, Dude,' then I spot Magnus walking towards us. He's wearing a white tux and looking – hey, I'm calling it – very handsome as well.

I'm there, 'Do you want to get storted, gays? I mean goys?'

Okay, I need to calm the fock down.

Magnus looks at Oisinn and goes, 'You are shure you shtill want to do thish?'

Oisinn laughs. 'More than anything in the world,' he goes.

I'm there, 'Then it's on! It's on like LeBron!' and as I say it, I pull my pages out of my inside pocket.

'Remember,' Oisinn goes, 'no rugby.'

And I just give him a wink.

I tell everyone to take their seats. There's, like, one hundred and twenty of the things, borrowed for the day from the new IKEA order-and-collection centre in Carrickmines. I'm pretty sure I mentioned that Kristoffer is a big shot in the company.

I'm actually kacking it a little bit, having not had a drink all morning.

But then I'm suddenly staring out at this, like, sea of smiling faces, in the beautiful sunshine of – let's call a spade a spade – County Wicklow, and I realize that everyone wants me to do well here. I look at Oisinn's old pair – who are big, big fans of mine – sitting in the front row. Then I'm looking at Magnus's old pair, sitting on the other side of the aisle. Hedvig is smiling at me. I think she has a definite thing for me.

I'm looking at Sorcha, who's absolutely glowing, then Honor, sitting beside her, texting away on her phone. Then I'm looking at Erika, who looks fantastic, and I'm not saying that in a creepy, *incesty* sort of way? I'm just saying I love her hair when it's that length and I also love the way her holy grails are bursting out of that low-cut dress. I'll leave it at that.

Then I'm looking at Christian, JP and – yeah, no, fock *him* – Fionn and I'm thinking about all the things we've been through together with Oisinn and I'm thinking, this is going to be a day to remember.

Oisinn and Magnus are standing on the red corpet at the other end of the aisle. They're, like, whispering in each other's ears, exchanging their few last words as two single dudes. I nod at the string quartet, then the music storts up – we're talking *Dance of the Flowers* by Something Tchaikovsky – and they stort walking towards me, holding hands and grinning like two – what's the phrase? – cheddar cats?

Thirty seconds later, they're standing in front of me and I go, 'Ladies and gentlemen,' and I can hear the actual nerves in my voice, 'we are gathered today to celebrate the marriage of Oisinn Wallace and Magnus Laakso-Sigurjónsson.'

Magnus gives me a smile and a nod to tell me that I got the pronunciation very nearly right.

I look down at the speech that I spent twenty minutes this morning preparing. The first line is, 'Marriage is a bit like rugby. You have to be committed. You have to accept that you might not always score. And there are times when you'll inevitably find yourself playing away from home.'

But in the end I don't read it. I end up just standing there, trying to think of something to say, something from the hort.

I can nearly hear people thinking, 'Er, what's this? The legendary Ross O'Carroll-Kelly lost for words? This is a definite first!'

A good, like, thirty seconds pass without me saying shit. There's just the sound of the waterfall and birds singing. Then I look at Sorcha and suddenly I'm not angry with her for having sex with Fionn. I'm actually remembering the last time she was pregnant with the triplets. We bought three flatpack cribs from IKEA in Ballymun and tried to put them together ourselves one Saturday morning when I was still a bit pissed from the night before.

And that's when the words just come.

'When you buy something from IKEA,' I go, 'it says Self-assembly on the box. But self-assembly doesn't mean it assembles itself. *You* have to put it together, following the steps patiently. And in that way, I suppose, IKEA furniture is a bit like marriage.'

I'm staring at Sorcha and she's staring back at me, obviously thinking, wow!

I'm there, 'What you walk away with is not the finished orticle. You have a lot of work to do when you get it home. And sometimes you look at what you've ended up with and you think, "Okay, this is not what I thought it was going to be like."'

I can see people – including Oisinn and Magnus – looking at each other, thinking, 'What a time for him to have one of his deep-thinking days!'

I'm there, 'Have you ever noticed how everyone else's IKEA furniture always looks perfect? Well, that's only from the outside. The truth is that no one's is *actually* perfect. Everyone who puts together anything from IKEA ends up with bits missing or bits left over.'

I'm suddenly losing Magnus's old man. He turns to Fionn, who's sitting behind him, and goes, 'Thish ish not sho – if you follow the shteps correctly.'

Of course, Fionn agrees with him, trying to make me look bad.

'The thing about marriage,' I go, 'is that it might not be made from proper wood. It might be only, like, MDF. But if you put it together properly – making sure you do all your screwing correctly – there's no reason why it shouldn't last you for a lifetime.'

38

There ends up being a round of applause at the end. It's just, like, *spontaneous*?

Then we continue with the ceremony. One of Magnus's mates reads a poem by some Russian dude who is apparently Magnus's favourite poet, then Erika reads a passage from *The Bridges of Madison County*, which is apparently Oisinn's favourite book.

I suppose the signs were there if we'd wanted to see them.

Then we do the exchange of promises and Oisinn and Magnus kiss each other and I pronounce them – literally – husband and husband.

It's a definite moment. There's no doubt about that.

Of course, all anyone can talk about when it's all over is my speech. There seems to be general agreement that it was vintage, vintage Ross O'Carroll-Kelly.

Afterwards, there's, like, a champagne reception before we all head for the hotel for the actual *meal* bit? Honor walks over to me and goes, 'Can I have a drink – as in, an *actual* drink?'

And I'm like, 'We've had the conversation about alcohol, Honor. You can have it when you're fourteen and not before that.'

Then I spot Sorcha, standing on her own, so I tip over to her. I go, 'I had a word with Honor. I don't know if I mentioned. About giving Rihanna-Brogan that cigarette. I gave her a serious, serious talking-to. Ask her if you don't believe me.'

She goes, 'You don't get a pat on the back for doing the right thing as a parent, Ross.'

'Fair enough. You look lovely, by the way. I don't know what you thought of my speech and my point about marriage being like the cribs we bought for the triplets, but that line was intended for you. What I was trying to say was that you can't just get fed up working on them, fock them in a skip, then go to Mamas and Papas in Dundrum to buy three ready-made ones for two Ks a pop. Even though that's what we *did* actually do?'

'Ross –'

'What I'm trying to say is that I don't care that you're pregnant by possibly him. I still want you back. I want to be a proper husband to you this time.'

'Fionn and I have decided to try to make a go of it, Ross.'

I'm, like, stunned. Understatement. My entire body goes cold. I go, 'Excuse me?'

She's there, 'This isn't the time or the place to have this conversation, Ross.'

'I disagree. What do you mean, you and Fionn have decided to try to make a go of it?'

'Just that, Ross. He told me how he feels about me and I'm prepared to open myself up to the possibility that maybe I feel the same way about him.'

And that's when Fionn – I swear to fock – walks over to us and goes, 'What's going on?'

I'm like, 'Oh, yeah – what happened to, "We shared a passion for the issues facing Dublin Bay South"? What happened to, "We confused those feelings for something else"?'

I can see one or two people, including Erika, looking over, wondering what we're whispering about.

He looks at Sorcha and goes, 'You told him?'

She's like, 'Yes, I told him.'

I'm there, 'You said it was just Campaign Sex. That's a direct quote.'

He goes, 'I'm in love with her, Ross.'

'I should have killed you that day on Stradbrook Road.'

'I've always loved her.'

'You don't even know yet that the baby is yours.'

'Whether it is or not, I want to be with her. And eventually, yes, I would love to marry her and spend the rest of my life with her.'

It's at that exact point that Magnus's old man arrives over and decides to stort pulling me up on elements of my speech.

'You shay that our furniture is jusht medium denshitty fibreboard,' he goes, 'but do you alsho know that thish shubstance ish glued under heat and pressure to produshe a building material of shuperior strength that ish guaranteed never to warp?'

I hold up my hand and I go, 'Sorry, we're having a private conversation here. Will you shut the fock up about MDF?'

Magnus – standing a few feet away – is like, 'Hey, Rosh, what ish the matter?'

I look Fionn straight in the eye and I go, 'That's my still technically wife you're talking about.'

Sorcha goes, 'You're making a scene, Ross.'

A lot of people are suddenly getting interested. Chloe and Amie with an ie especially. Even Honor is looking at something other than her phone for once. I just decide, fock it, though. Let it all come out.

I stare at Fionn and I'm there, 'Remember that Lada you bought to drive to focking Koka Kola? Do you know what the smell was? I took a dump in the boot. It was under the spare tyre – that's the reason you couldn't find it.'

Fionn's there, 'You're making a fool of yourself, Ross. As if your IKEA speech wasn't embarrassing enough.'

I throw a punch at him, which ends up missing by about three postcodes. Then Fionn hits *me* with a punch – a very lucky punch, it has to be said – which just so happens to deck me. And suddenly we're rolling around on the grass, throwing digs at each other and calling each other every name under the sun.

We end up having to be pulled aport. Christian and JP grab me, while Oisinn and Magnus grab Fionn.

Hedvig goes, 'Why are you fighting on thish day of all daysh?'

And I'm there, 'Butt out of it, you total smoke show.'

Oisinn's like, 'Can you two not just set aside your differences for one day?'

And I go, 'There's something you don't know. There's something none of you know.'

Fionn's there, 'Ross, keep your mouth shut. That's what we agreed.'

But I can't. Not anymore. Because it's killing me.

Sorcha goes, 'Ross, this isn't how we want Honor to find out!'

And Honor's there, 'Er, find out *what* exactly?'

'Sorcha's pregnant!' I go.

Sorcha puts both of her hands up to cover her face. And, in that moment, I know that she may never forgive me for this.

There's, like, gasps all around us, then silence, except for the sound of Chloe going, 'I focking said it the second I saw her orse in that dress!'

Then Honor goes, 'Excuse me?'

'It's true,' I go. 'Your mother's pregnant. And there's a fifty-fifty chance that the father is that four-eyed focker there.'

2. What Happens to Ross Will Make Your Jaw Drop!

'Footbaw!' Brian goes.

This is while I'm fixing the boys their breakfast.

I fire straight back with, 'Rugby!' because I've decided that I owe it to them as their father to try to teach them the difference between right and wrong.

'Footbaw!' Brian goes again.

And I'm like, 'Rugby! Leo, eat your mashed banana.'

'Fock you,' Leo goes, 'you focking orseclown!'

'Come on, eat up.'

'Focking orseclown! Focking focker!'

I'm like, 'Johnny, you eat up too!' except he's in his own little world as usual, singing a little song to himself. 'Come on, Johnny, bananas are good for you. They'll help you grow up big and strong when you're playing –'

'Footbaw!' Brian goes.

I'm like, 'Rugby!'

'Focking footbaw!'

'Focking rugby!'

Sorcha walks into the kitchen. She goes, 'Why is everyone shouting?'

Those are literally the first words she's spoken to me since the wedding on Saturday.

I'm there, 'Yeah, no, I'm just trying to set a good example for my children. One of us has to, I suppose.'

She goes, 'What does that mean?'

'No, I'm just imagining what it's going to be like for them growing up. Their father in the spare room, their mother's lover in her bed.'

'Fionn isn't *in* my bed, Ross.'

'Yet.'

'You can't blame *me* for the break-up of our marriage.'

'This just feels like a horsh punishment, that's all.'

'I told you the rules when you moved back in. Our marriage is finished. I'm quite entitled to be with whoever I want.'

'Pack of bullshit!' Leo goes. 'Pack! Of! Bullshit!'

I stick the spoon in his mouth.

Sorcha's there, 'I don't care how upset you were, Ross, that isn't how I wanted our daughter to find out that she was going to have a little brother or sister.'

I will never, ever forgive Fionn for this. And I am genuinely a very forgiving person, especially when it comes to anyone who plays – or has played – rugby. Rob Kearney is a prime example of what I'm talking about. Whenever we run into each other, it's always the same. We spend the first five minutes pushing and shoving each other, making threats and saying hurtful things about one another's schools. Then it's suddenly forgotten and we're hugging it out and laughing and joking and talking the common language of the people's game.

It actually happened a few weeks ago in the Homeware Deportment in Brown Thomas. Rob was returning an Aeroccino Plus Milk Frother to the Nespresso store because it was stainless steel and he'd decided to make the colour theme for his kitchen vanilla cream. I'd popped in to use the jacks – a shit-and-run, as I said to the dude in the coat and the top hat as he held the door open for me. I saw Rob as I was reaching the top of the escalator, shouted something slanderous about Clongowes, then the next thing anyone knew, he had me in a headlock and the girls working the Rimowa Luggage concession stand were literally running for cover. By the time the security staff made it up to the third floor, we were sitting in The Restaurant, sharing an Italian Antipasti Platter for Two, Rob was telling me what a genuine loss I was to the game and I'd agreed to take the milk frother off his hands for exactly what he paid for it.

One word . . .

'Footbaw!' Brian goes.

And I'm like, 'The word is rugby, Brian. Definitely rugby.'

But with Fionn, it's different. There's a line, even for people who

44

soldiered together on the field of play. And he well and truly crossed that line.

Sorcha goes, 'You ruined Oisinn and Magnus's wedding day.'

She's at the sink washing out an empty Sheridan's fig and apple compote jor. I have no idea why and I don't ask.

I'm there, 'I'd hordly say I ruined it. Everyone had a good time once we got to the hotel.'

'Well, you ruined it for me,' she goes. 'Do you have any idea what it felt like to have everyone whispering about me behind my back?'

'Hey, you're lucky you're a woman – because they were saying shit to *my* actual face. Specifically, how does it feel to have a wife who's pregnant with a baby that might not be yours?'

'I stopped being your wife the day you went to Dalkey and had sex with that –'

'Focking slut!' Leo goes, letting me down in a big-time way.

The back door opens and in *he* walks. Her old man. Doesn't knock or anything. He walks in wearing his dressing-gown and slippers. He's there, 'Dorling, can I use the kettle?'

And I go, 'No, you focking can't. And don't call me Dorling.'

He ignores this, fills the thing with water, then switches it on.

Sorcha's there, 'Oh my God, is the electricity gone again?'

'Since nine o'clock last night,' he goes. 'They're sending another one of their so-called engineers this morning. Honestly, we're at the end of our bloody well tether.'

I'm there, 'You've some balls coming in here complaining, considering you're getting it for free.'

He gives me a serious filthy, the skint focker.

He goes, 'And that's how you break the news to your daughter that her mother is going to have a baby, is it? In front of a crowd? While brawling on the ground like a common thug?'

This is a man, can I just say, who's never watched a full rugby match in his life?

He turns to Sorcha then and goes, 'How are you feeling?'

She's there, 'I was a bit sick this morning. I don't know if it's the pregnancy or if I'm just nervous about my speech tomorrow.'

'Never mind – at least you'll have Fionn there. Oh, it's wonderful to see you two making a go of it, Sorcha. Your mother and I have always liked him.'

I end up having to stand there listening to this.

Sorcha goes, 'Well, we're taking things slowly for now.'

He's there, 'Those flowers in the living room. They were from him, I take it.'

'White and yellow roses, yes. Can you believe he actually remembered they were my favourite flowers?'

'It's lovely to see you so happy at the moment.'

That's a definite dig at me.

'Well,' she goes, 'I'm going to go into the Seanad this morning just to collect the keys to my office. Fionn thinks I should maybe stand in the chamber and try to visualize myself addressing the House.'

He goes, 'That's an excellent idea, Dorling.'

I go, 'Hey, *we'll* definitely be there tomorrow. Obviously not Honor. I'm talking about me and the boys.'

Her old man's like, 'Don't you dare bring those three into the Upper House of the Oireachtas. It's bad enough *you* going around making a public spectacle of yourself without having them effing and blinding in the public gallery.'

'They won't be effing and blinding.'

'Fock you,' Leo goes, 'you focking fock!'

I pick him up and I'm like, 'Come on, boys, out to the cor. We're going to take your sister to school.'

Sorcha's old dear is suddenly shouting her mouth off in the gorden. She's going, 'Edmund, it's back! The electricity is back!'

And I'm there, 'You heard the woman. You can fock off back to your little shack now. There's no other reason for you to even be here.'

Out into the hallway we go. I shout up the stairs to Honor. I'm like, 'Okay, Honor, let's hit the road!' but there ends up being no answer. It's only when I take the boys outside that I discover she's already sitting in the front passenger seat, her nose stuck in her phone as usual.

I put the boys in the back and we hit the road.

'I've just given *him* a mouthful of abuse,' I go as we're heading up the Vico towards Dalkey. 'I told him he had some balls complaining about the electricity constantly going when he's not even putting his hand in his pocket for it. The prick.'

Honor would usually take that as her cue to launch into a rant about the slow death she'd like to treat him to. But she doesn't say shit.

She's obviously still not talking to me.

I try to keep the conversation light and breezy. I'm there, 'I'm going to pop in to see your grandmother this morning. I've decided to definitely blackmail her. How much do you think I should ask for – to hand over the heater, I mean?'

Again – nothing.

Then, about five minutes later, out of the blue she goes, 'Why didn't you tell me?'

I'm like, 'Tell you? Tell you what?'

'You knew she was pregnant and you didn't focking tell me.'

'Look, I've only known for just over a week. And, to be honest, I was struggling to get my head around it. Still am, to be fair.'

'So when were you planning to let me in on your little secret?'

'Whenever we plucked up the courage. We knew you'd probably go apeshit.'

'I thought we were friends.'

'What?'

'You're always saying, "It's me and you, Honor. It's me and you against the world."'

'I'd love to believe that. I genuinely would.'

'Well, friends don't keep secrets from each other.'

'Oh, Honor –'

'You focking lied to me. I actually *hate* that you're my father.'

'You don't mean that.'

'I do. I wish you were dead – like *her*. And her parents. And that focking baby she's carrying.'

The old man is pushing champagne on me at, like, eleven o'clock in the morning.

'It's a celebration!' he tries to go. 'Young Honor must be terribly excited, is she?'

I'm there, 'She's, em, still processing it. Is that the proper word?'

He refills my glass.

He goes, 'Oh, she'll get used to the idea! You see if she doesn't! Another little sister or brother for her!'

I'm there, 'You haven't heard the full story yet.'

'Well, all I know is I'm going to be a grandfather for the – what are we up to now? – *seventh* time?'

'It might not be mine.'

Oh, that rocks him back on his heels. He goes, 'Might not be yours? In what way?'

And I'm there, 'In the same way that Ronan isn't Sorcha's son and Erika isn't the old dear's daughter.'

'Well, whose baby could it be, then?'

'It turns out she had sex with Fionn.'

'Fionn? Your friend –?'

'Former friend.'

'– with the –?'

'With the glasses, yeah. They're, like, boyfriend-girlfriend now.'

'But I thought you'd moved back in?'

'To look after the kids.'

'Good Lord!'

'You said it.'

'Speaking of Erika,' he goes, topping up his glass, 'how is she?'

I'm there, 'She's fine. She wants fock-all to do with you, though.'

'I realize she's angry that things didn't work out between her mother and me! But it doesn't mean she's not still my daughter! Or that Amelie isn't still my granddaughter!'

'Well, you've seen the last of both of them, from what Erika's saying. You look like shit, by the way. I'm just stating that as a fact.'

'I'm not surprised! Your mother and I have been working night and day on her foundation!'

'Her foundation? She usually just slaps that on with a spatula.'

'I'm talking about her charitable foundation! Non-profit – quote-unquote!'

'Oh, that.'

'We've invited submissions, Ross! We're looking for various causes around the world that might need her help! Your mother has created one of these famous Facebooks pages, asking, "What In The Name Of FO'CK Do *You* want?" Which is very clever, you'd have to agree!'

'Whatever.'

'There's one charity she's already decided to help! A very worthy cause, I think we'd all agree! They're all about landmines, Ross! Isn't it wonderful to see her so determined to make something good from the terrible injustice that was done to her?'

He genuinely believes she had fock-all to do with Ari's death.

I'm there, 'And now she's going to get her hands on all his moo. How much is it going to be – just as a matter of interest?'

He goes, 'I don't think your mother has even thought about the money.'

I actually laugh in his face. I'm there, 'Yeah, my focking hole. Two billion squids is what everyone seems to be saying.'

'It won't be anything like that,' he tries to go. 'Ari wasn't nearly as wealthy as the prosecution suggested. I think it's something in the order of forty million dollars!'

Okay. So the heater has to be worth, what, half of forty million? You do the math. I'd need a calculator.

At that exact moment, she steps into the kitchen. Seriously, the woman could sniff out alcohol from one end of Brighton Road to the other. She pours herself a glass of champagne – not a flute, by the way, an actual slim Jim.

I decide to just act normally around her. I notice a bit of stubble coming through her make-up just above her top lip.

'God, is it Movember already?' I go. 'It comes around quickly, all the same, doesn't it?'

She just blanks me.

The old man goes, 'I was telling Kicker about this landmines crowd you've decided to help, Fionnuala! But it turns out he has some wonderful news of his own!'

I'm there, 'We don't know if it's wonderful news yet.'

'It seems that young Sorcha is pregnant!'

'There's a very good chance that it isn't mine.'

We're some focking family when you think about it.

She doesn't respond either way. Or maybe she does but her face doesn't move because of all the walrus spunk she's had injected into it in an effort to hold back time.

The old man goes, 'Where are the triplets, by the way?'

I'm like, 'I left them outside in the cor. They're too annoying.'

'You left them in the cor? On a hot summer's day?'

'Hey, go outside if you want to see them. And – yeah, no, good point – maybe open the window a crack as well.'

Off he goes to see them, leaving me alone with the old dear. I knock back the rest of my drink.

'Where is it?' she instantly goes.

I'm like, 'What are you talking about?'

'You know perfectly well what I'm talking about, Ross.'

'Oh, you mean the two-bor electric heater that was in the nuclear fallout shelter?'

'It's mine and I want it back.'

'It's just I remember you saying very clearly in court that you'd never owned a two-bor electric heater. Which means you lied under oath. Which means the jury that let you off were missing one vital piece of evidence.'

'I didn't kill Ari.'

'Maybe I'll ring the Gords and tell them I found it.'

'Look, there is a very simple explanation for why I had that heater. I bought it for Iryna – you remember that Ukrainian char-lady that I had?'

I remember her alright. Iryna the Cleaner, we used to call her.

She's there, 'She used to complain about the cold in the utility room when she was doing my ironing. So, like I said, I bought that heater for her. As an act of kindness. Although I ended up regretting it, of course. Do you know she swore at me when I took the money out of her next wage packet?'

I'm there, 'Stop changing the subject.'

'I'm telling you the truth, Ross. Then, one day, the washing machine leaked and water got into it. And that's the reason I hid it – because I knew that if the Gords found it, they would put two and two together and come up with –'

'The truth.'

'I can't go back to that prison. I shan't.'

'That's what I wanted to hear.'

'What's it going to cost me?'

'Do you mean, What In The Name Of FO'CK Do *I* Want?'

'I'm presuming it's money.'

'You catch on fast.'

'How much?'

'A million snots.'

'A million euros? I'm not giving you a million euros.'

'You seem to be forgetting something. One phone call to the Feebies and you won't see a focking cent of that money. As a matter of fact, you'll spend the rest of your days behind bors.'

'Can you give me some time? To think about it?'

That's what she has the cheek to ask me.

'Hey,' I go, 'it's a lot to take in. Which is why I'm going to give you till the end of the week to say yes.'

Brian and Leo are gobbing on the inside of the window of Sorcha's office, then cheering their spits on as they race each other towards the floor.

I definitely shouldn't have brought them. You can tell that's what Sorcha's old man is thinking.

He turns around to Fionn and goes, 'If the baby does turn out to be yours, Fionn, we should put its name down for a good school.'

Yeah, St Columba's is *his* idea of a good school. I'm just making the point.

'And what if it turns out to be mine?' I make the mistake of going.

The focker makes a big point of looking at the triplets, then goes, 'Well, there's no sense in throwing good money after bad, is there? Do technical colleges still exist?'

I refuse to take the bait, though. I'm determined not to ruin this day for Sorcha. She's outside, by the way, pacing the corridor, practising her speech by reading it to herself in a sort of, like, angry whisper. It's how she always prepared for debates back in her Mount Anville days.

Johnny has now joined Leo and Brian in gobbing on the glass. I'm there, 'Goys, maybe don't do that,' but they carry on anyway. If I had to put a positive spin on it, I'd say it shows that the competitive instinct is strong in them.

Sorcha steps back into the office. 'Okay,' she goes, 'I think I'm ready.'

Her old man puts his orm around his wife's shoulder and goes, 'Our daughter is about to address the Upper House of the Oireachtas! What a day this is!'

Fionn kisses Sorcha on the lips. In front of me. He goes, 'We're all so proud of you, Sorcha. Remember, this is what you were born to do.'

She's there, 'Thanks, Fionn.'

Leo suddenly grabs Johnny by the back of the neck and smashes his head into the window. Johnny storts wailing and Sorcha ends up losing it with me. She goes, 'Ross, can you please deal with that?'

Her old man's there, 'I don't know why he insisted on bringing them. As matter of fact, I don't know why he's even here himself.'

And Fionn – I swear to fock – goes, 'Sorcha, it *would* be great if you could focus on what you're going to say to the House and put all these extraneous matters out of your mind.'

That's all we are now. Her husband and her children. Extraneous matters.

When Johnny finally stops crying – and bleeding – we all head for the chamber. Sorcha isn't ready for the shock that awaits her when we get there.

The place ends up being empty.

She's like, 'Oh my God, did I get the wrong day or something?'

But Fionn's there, 'No, it's definitely a Tuesday. The House is supposed to be sitting.'

Sorcha's old dear goes, 'But where are all the senators?'

It's straightaway obvious that Sorcha has made way too big a deal of this so-called job she's been given.

I'm there, 'It looks like this Enda Kelly or whatever he's called was royally ripping the piss out of you.'

Fionn tries to be the hero of the hour, of course. He goes, 'Well, I, for one, would still like to hear what you have to say,' even though she's going to be basically talking to herself.

Sorcha nods and goes, 'Okay,' and she takes her seat on the floor of the House, while the rest of us head for the public gallery – which *also* happens to be empty?

Sorcha's old man goes, 'It's still a proud, proud day for our family,' but he's fooling no one and I let him know that by laughing out loud and shaking my head.

Down on the floor, Sorcha knocks back a mouthful of water, clears her throat, then storts. She goes, 'It is both an honour and a privilege to stand here today as one of *An Taoiseach*'s nominees to Seanad Éireann, the Upper House of the Oireachtas.'

She really pronounces the 'ock' in *Taoiseach* as well. It reminds me of a September night in Renords back in the day, when I crashed the wrap porty for *Up for the Match*. The two Seoiges were trying to impress me by out-Gaeilgeoiring each other and I went home with half a pint of phlegm in my hair.

God, I loved that night.

Sorcha's old pair look at each other and they just smile like the whole thing *isn't* an anti-climax?

'I want to take this opportunity,' Sorcha goes, 'to thank *An Taoiseach* for entrusting me with this important, important responsibility and I promise to repay his faith by serving my country to the best of my ability.'

'Ask! My focking! Hole!' Brian suddenly shouts.

I put my hand over his mouth.

Sorcha tries not to let it knock her confidence.

'From the time I was a little girl,' she goes, 'one of my actual heroes was Mary Robinson. I've always been proud to be able to say that we had exactly the same alma mater – in other words, Mount Anville. It was her election as President of Ireland in 1990 that instilled in me the firm belief that anything is possible in life if you work really, really hord and go to a good school.'

'Shut your whore mouth!' Leo shouts.

Shit. I use my other hand to try to shut him up then.

'As I became older, I storted to find out more and more about her career in politics, including all of the speeches she made here, in Seanad Éireann.'

Brian bites my hand and I end up having to pull it away.

Sorcha goes, 'I started to read all about the amazing, amazing work she did in this chamber, campaigning for such causes as the legal availability of contraception.'

Brian goes, 'Shut the fock up and give your focking arse a rest!'

Fionn looks at Sorcha's old man and goes, 'She's doing great.'

They always considered him son-in-law material.

I'm there, 'Yeah, no, it's a pity there's no one here to hear it, isn't it?'

Sorcha goes, 'It was Mary Robinson who made me actually care about the work that goes on in this chamber, which is why it genuinely upsets me when I hear people say that it's just a talking shop, or a social club for politicians who are either too old or too unlikeable to be democratically elected.'

And that's when – I swear to fock – a woman walks in and storts Hoovering the corpet. Seriously. She storts Hoovering the actual corpet.

Sorcha's old man shouts, 'Turn that blasted thing off!'

The woman shouts, 'Soddy?' because she can't hear him over the sound of it.

The dude points at the thing with a big angry face on him and the woman takes the hint and knocks it off.

'How dare you switch on that confounded thing?' he goes. 'Can't you see that the House is sitting?'

She's there, 'Thee usuaddy doatunt mooyunt me Hoobering while they're thalken. I've anutter job to go to at fowur o'clock. I clean the office of the Director of Corpordut Enfowurce Muddent, so I do.'

He goes, 'My daughter is in the middle of making her maiden speech!'

She looks around her with a bewildered look on her face. She's like, 'To who?'

He goes, 'Into the historical record of this chamber!'

The woman looks at Sorcha for the first time. She's like, 'Hab you much mower?'

'About three-quarters of a page,' Sorcha goes.

The woman's there, 'I'll wait so,' and she *does* end up waiting? She sort of half stands and half sits on a desk with her orms folded impatiently in front of her while Sorcha goes back to her speech.

'I want to help make Seanad Éireann relevant again,' she goes. 'I want people to look at Seanad Éireann and be proud of this chamber. I want to do that by –'

And then she suddenly stops. She looks around this humungous, empty chamber and she realizes that she's basically just gabbing away to herself.

'You're talking out of your focking hole,' Leo shouts.

Then – shit! – I see her eyes filling up with tears. She sighs and folds up her speech. I've seen Sorcha upset many, many times over the years. I remember once she stopped talking to me for three days when I told her I thought Phoebe was the Jar Jar Binks of *Friends*.

But this is more than just sadness. It's, like, resignation. It's like, What's the point in even carrying on?

All those *West Wing*s. Jesus.

That's when Fionn, again, tries to be the hero of the hour. He goes, 'Where do you think you're going?'

She looks up at the public gallery. She's like, 'This lady is right. There's no one here. She might as well get her Hoovering done.'

I'm actually thinking, yeah, no, fair enough – it's a good point.

But her old man goes, '*We're* here!'

And then Fionn's like, 'Exactly! We've waited a long time for this day – and we'd very much like to hear what you have to say!'

'Shut the fock up,' Leo shouts, 'and give your focking hoop a rest.'

But I watch Sorcha suddenly smile. And she looks at Fionn the way she used to look at me back in the day. And her face suddenly fills with – I don't know – *resolve*? She opens her speech and she goes back to reading it.

She's there, 'I want to make Seanad Éireann relevant again. I want to do that by taking the lead on important issues that affect the lives of our citizens and those living in the world beyond. I wish to give notice that it is my intention, in the current lifetime of this House, to introduce a Private Members' Bill that will have the effect of banning all single-use coffee cups from both houses of the Oireachtas by the year 2056. I really believe this is achievable. In the meantime, we, as politicians, should demonstrate our commitment to saving the environment by using – and being seen to use – alternatives to traditional disposable receptacles for our hot drinks.'

She opens up her Valentino tote and she whips out that Sheridan's fig and apple compote jor I saw her rinsing out yesterday morning.

'One of the ways we can do this,' she goes, 'is by *upcycling*? This is what I'm planning to use when I buy a takeaway coffee in future. It's actually an old compote jor, but it also serves perfectly well as a reusable coffee cup, even though the glass can become so hot that it's pretty much impossible to pick it up. This problem can be easily surmounted by gluing little pieces of felt to the glass to serve as heat-resistant finger grips, as I have done here.

'This is the kind of imagination that we, as national leaders, need to demonstrate if we are to bequeath a planet worth living on to our children – and to our children's children.'

'Ask! My focking! Orse!' Brian shouts.

Sorcha goes, 'The Stone Age didn't come to an end because we ran out of stones. It came to an end because we discovered better and more efficient ways of actually *doing* things?

'In conclusion, I just wanted to say that I am very much aware of what a privilege it is to be asked by *An Taoiseach* to serve as a member of this House. I intend to do so in a way that honours the service of previous well-known members, but especially the amazing, amazing Mary Robinson. *Go raibh míle maith agaibh. Agus beannacht Dé libh.*'

God, I miss Renords.

We give Sorcha an unbelievable reaction. And it has to be said that I definitely end up out-clapping Sorcha's old pair and also

Fionn – who's always had, like, women's hands? He shouts, *'Go h'iontach!'* obviously trying to compensate. *'Go h'iontach! An-mhaith! An-mhaith!'*

It's as our applause dies down that I realize there's someone in the chamber who's, like, still *clapping*? I look across and I spot her standing in the doorway. It's Muirgheal Massey, the Deputy Leader of the old man's porty. She's hated Sorcha's basic guts ever since losing to her in the contest for Head Girl of Mount Anville all those years ago.

I've heard people say that only elephants and Frank Sinatra hold grudges for longer than Mounties.

Still clapping, she goes, 'Wow, Sorcha!' except obviously meaning it sorcastically? 'You promised all those years ago that you were going to change the world! And look at you doing it now – one coffee cup at a time!'

Sorcha tries to say something back, but she's suddenly drowned out again by the sound of the Hoover.

Oisinn and Magnus aren't pissed off with me at all. I swing into their aportment in Rathgor and I manage to catch them just before they leave for Hawaii on their honeymoon.

They're actually more worried about me, and I'm just going to come out and say fair focks to them.

Magnus goes, 'I heff to shay, *I* wash very shurprished to hear thish newsh that Shorcha ish pregnant – perhapsh wish another mansh baby. Sho God knowsh how *you* musht have felt, Rosh.'

I'm there, 'This is all good shit for me to hear, Magnus. Because Sorcha was under the impression that I might have put a possible *dampener* on your day?'

Now it's Oisinn's turn to give me a boost. He's like, 'You didn't put a dampener on anything. We had a great day. I have to say, though, I'm pretty surprised at Fionn. You don't do something like that to a former teammate.'

'My point exactly – we played rugby together.'

Even though I tried it on with most of Fionn's girlfriends over the years. And slept with Christian's old dear, of course.

The doorbell rings and Magnus goes outside into the hallway to answer it. It ends up being his old pair. It turns out they're dropping them to the airport.

In they come. Kristoffer and Hedvig. I think I already mentioned that *he* works for IKEA and *she's* a total focking ride. They end up being totally cool about what happened as well.

I go through the motions with the whole, 'Look, I'm sorry if anyone was upset by my actions and blah, blah, blah.'

But Kristoffer goes, 'Itsh quite alright, Rosh. That wash a lot for you to heff to keep to yourshelf, yesh? Your wife, she ish pregnant with thish other mansh baby?'

'Possibly,' I go. 'We don't know for sure yet. And anyway we have an open relationship.'

'Open?' he goes.

And I'm like, 'Well, open slash over.'

He nods.

'Alsho,' he goes, 'you shay you do a shit in thish mansh car?'

This point seems to have stuck in his head, for some reason.

I'm like, 'Yeah, no, that was a rugby thing. If you understood the game, you'd know where I was coming from with that one.'

Again, he just nods.

Hedvig's there, 'Well, perhapsh you should alsho apologishe for what you shay to me?' although she doesn't *seem* too pissed off.

I'm there, 'What did I say to you again?' because I genuinely can't remember.

'You shay to me, "Butt out" and then you call me – what wash thish? – a shmoke show?'

I laugh. I remember now. I'm there, 'Yeah, no, a total smoke show.'

Oisinn goes, 'That's a compliment, Hedvig.'

She's like, 'You shay itsh a gute thing?'

I'm there, 'A very *gute* thing.'

She smiles – delighted with herself. I have a definite way with people.

Kristoffer's there, 'He's shaying he finds you attrective, Hedvig!'

'Sho,' Magnus goes, 'we better leave – otherwishe we will mish our flight.'

I turn around to Kristoffer and I go, 'So when are you heading back yourselves?'

He's there, 'We heff deshided to shtay for a lidl while. Perhapsh a few weeks. I have shome holidaysh due to me and alsho we would like to trevel around a lidl bit and find out shome more thingsh about thish country.'

I'm like, 'I wouldn't bother your holes. There's not a lot to see once you go outside Dublin. I wouldn't want to mislead you.'

'Well, we have heard there ish beautiful partsh in the wesht of Ireland. We heff deshided to Airbnb our way around the country.'

'Hey, it's up to you. I'm just warning you in advance. Anyway, I better hit the road myself. I left the kids outside in the cor. Although don't worry, I left the window open a crack this time.'

I'm pretty sure I left the window open a crack.

I tell the goys to have a great time in Hawaii and I give them both a big hug. Then I tell Kristoffer and Hedvig to enjoy checking out the rest of Ireland, even though I know they won't, because it's shit. I give *them* both a hug as well. Fock it. One for everyone in the audience is my attitude.

And it's fine. It's *all* fine.

Except something totally random happens when I'm hugging Hedvig. And I'm definitely not imagining this. She basically grabs a handful of my orse.

Ronan rings me while I'm driving into town. He goes, 'Stordee, Rosser? How's she cutten?'

I'm there, 'She's cutting very well, Ronan – don't you worry about that. What's the crack?'

'Ine joost arthur been talken to Shadden, so I am.'

'Yeah? Has she finally forgiven Honor for teaching Rihanna-Brogan how to smoke? Even though I'm surprised at you raising a tout.'

'She's caddemed down alreet.'

'She overreacted. I think she'd admit that, looking back.'

'Ah, hopefuddy Rihatta-Barrogan getting sick will purr her off ebber smoken again in the long terdum. Mire eeben end up thanken Hodor wooden day in anutter few yee-ors.'

'Well, hopefully she'll be back talking to *me* by then.'

'What do you mee-un?'

'Yeah, no, I, er, broke the news to her about Sorcha being pregnant with possibly Fionn's baby. She had a total shit fit with me.'

'She blayumt you? It's not your foddult, Rosser.'

'She's angry with me for keeping it from her. She said she hates that I'm her father and she wishes I was dead.'

'Moy Jaysus.'

'Usually you've to wait until they're sixteen before they hit you with lines like that. It's all ahead of you, Ro.'

Miracle of miracles, I manage to find a porking space on Stephen's Green. I take the boys out of the cor and put them in their stroller, still chatting to Ronan on the old Bluetooth earpiece. I head for, like, Kildare Street. Yeah, no, I forgot to mention, Sorcha forgot her work diary this morning – she's got, like, total baby brain at the moment – and she asked me to bring it into town for her. Which, by the way, I'm more than happy to do, even though it's clearly a job for Fionn – *as* her focking secretary.

'In addyhow,' Ronan goes, 'the reason Ine rigging is me and Shadden have been thalken about vedues.'

I'm there, 'Vedues?'

'Yeah, wetton vedues.'

'Oh, wedding venues!' Sometimes it takes me longer than other times, but I always get there in the end.

'She's arthur foyunten a hothel that she veddy much likes the look of – and we'd lubben you to look arrit wirrus.'

'That's very nice of you, Ro.'

'Especiady seeing as you're paying for it.'

'I forgot about that. By the way, whose bra was that in the boot of your cor?'

'Dudn't mathor.'

'I would say it very *much* matters?'

'Her nayum's Belintha.'

'Belinda?'

'That's reet – Belintha. She's a boord in me class. It was a wood-off, Rosser.'

'Another one-off. They're certainly stacking up, aren't they?'

'In addyhow,' he goes, trying to change the subject, 'we're looking at this hothel tomoddow morden. Kennet and Dordeen are godda be cubbin wirrus as well.'

'Here, where is it, by the way? You haven't said yet.'

'Clodden Teerp Cast Doddle.'

'Sorry?'

'Clodden Teerp Cast Doddle.'

'Go again.'

'Clodden Teerp Cast Doddle.'

'Go again.'

'Clodden Teerp Cast Doddle.'

'Keep going.'

'Clodden Teerp Cast Doddle.'

'Still not getting it.'

'Clodden Teerp Cast Doddle.'

'Still not getting it.'

'Clodden Teerp Cast Doddle.'

'One more time.'

'Clodden Teerp Cast Doddle.'

'One more time.'

'Clodden Teerp Castle Doddle.'

'One more.'

'Clodden Teerp Castle Doddle.'

'Last time.'

'Clodden Teerp Cast Doddle.'

'One more.'

'Clodden Teerp Castle Doddle.'

'One more.'

'Clodden Teerp Cast Doddle.'

'Again.'

'Clodden Teerp Cast Doddle.'

'Again.'

'Clodden Teerp Cast Doddle.'

Eventually, I'm just like, 'Look, I have to go here, Ro,' because I spot Sorcha standing outside Leinster House. 'Just text it to me, will you?'

He's there, 'Gayum ball.'

'Try it one last time, though.'

'Clodden Teerp Cast Doddle.'

'Again.'

'Clodden Teerp Cast Doddle.'

'No, like I said, just text it to me.'

We both hang up.

Sorcha is delighted to see the kids. She's all, 'Hello, boys!' giving them hugs and kisses and all the rest of it. Nothing for me, of course. Fionn probably wouldn't allow it. She just takes the diary from me and goes, 'How do you think they're coping, Ross – with their mother working full time in politics?'

Leo's there, 'Fock you, you dirty focking maggotfock!'

I'm like, 'You can see for yourself, Sorcha, they're fine. And I'm fine as well, by the way?' because I'm definitely warming to the role of the stay-at-home dad. 'We dropped Honor to school this morning, then we popped into D. L. Kids, although we were asked to leave after fifteen minutes because one or two parents objected to the swearing.'

'Pack of fockers!' Brian goes.

Sorcha smiles except in a *sad* way? 'I do feel guilty,' she goes. 'This is the painful balancing act that I heard Michelle Obama talk about in an interview with Oprah. You want to spend every minute of every day with your children, but you also want to bequeath to them a better world.'

I'm like, 'Er, yeah, I suppose so. I'm glad they were there to hear your speech the other day.'

She goes, 'Are you sure it was okay? It wasn't too wishy-washy, was it?'

'In places. But, overall, it was definitely easier to follow than some of the speeches I've heard you make.'

Sorcha suddenly puts her hand over her mouth. For a second, I think she's going to spew.

I'm like, 'Are you okay? Do you need to sit down?'

She's there, 'It's just nausea. I'll be okay in a . . . Okay, maybe I *do* need to sit down?'

She walks up to the dude at the Leinster House security gate and goes, 'Is it okay if my husband comes in with the children? I'm just feeling a bit –'

Husband. At least she's still acknowledging that.

The dude, seeing how pale she looks, just nods and through the gates we go. We head for this bench in the sort of, like, forecourt in *front* of the building? We both sit down.

I'm there, 'You had pretty bad morning sickness with Honor, I seem to remember. *And* the boys.'

I'm wondering is that a sign that the baby is possibly mine? I don't know is the answer.

'Fionn thinks I've been overdoing it,' she goes.

I'm there, 'Whose baby do you *think* it is? I'm talking about deep, deep down, who do you think is the father?'

'For the hundredth time, Ross, I don't know. Oh my God, you're as bad as my dad. We're all going to have to wait to find out, okay?'

All of a sudden, pretty much at the same time, we both become aware of this, like, humungous scrum of people milling around in front of the actual Leinster House building. It's my old man that I recognize first. You couldn't focking miss him with the wig, of course, even in a crowd of other fat men in their fifties and sixties. Then I spot a dude with a camera, standing on top of a stepladder.

Sorcha goes, 'They're obviously doing the official photograph. New Republic's fifty-one TDs. I still love your dad, even if he's a Fascist. Did you see that tweet he put out this morning about introducing a travel ban on people from Laois?'

I'm there, 'Is there a place called Laois?'

'It's a county. In the middle of Ireland.'

'That seems a bit random.'

'Well, random or not, it's obvious that your father still believes the way to build his power base is to demonize minorities. I genuinely believe his policies are dangerous – and that's not me being a bitch. As a matter of fact, I was half thinking of using my position as a senator to speak out against, not only the danger of single-use coffee cups, but also New Republic's brand of populist hate-mongering.'

'Yeah, if you can squeeze it into your schedule, you maybe should.'

I hadn't actually realized it until now but all of the old man's TDs look exactly the same. It's basically just fifty overweight, middle-aged men, plus the infamous Muirgheal Massey.

She's standing at the front of the grouping, next to the old man, while several of her – I suppose – porty colleagues are quite openly groping her and making sexist comments about women and how they should be at home making dinners and babies.

'Oh my God,' Sorcha goes, obviously copping it the same way I do, 'please don't tell me that *that's* the future of Irish politics.'

'Pack of pricks!' Leo shouts, speaking for us all. 'Pack! Of! Focking! Pricks!'

Muirgheal must hear this because she looks over and spots us across the forecourt. She steps out of the frame and tips over to us – all smiles.

She goes, 'Oh! My God, Sorcha! Congrats!' and it's straightaway obvious that she's being a wagon.

Sorcha's like, 'Congrats on what? My speech?'

'Well, that – *not* so much! But Chorles said you were pregnant!'

'Yes,' Sorcha goes, 'I haven't officially announced it yet.'

Muirgheal looks at me and goes, 'You must be thrilled, Ross?'

I'm there, 'Er, I am actually, yeah.'

'Although I hear there's a chance it's not yours.'

I'm like, 'Why don't you fock off, Muirgheal?'

Sorcha goes, 'No, it's fine, Ross. I'm not going to be publicly shamed by anyone. Yes, Muirgheal, there's a chance that the father is Fionn de Barra. We are officially together now. As you know, he and I spent a lot of time together during the General Election campaign. We developed a passion for the things that mattered to the people of Dublin Bay South – a law requiring Donnybrook Fair to put handles on their paper bags, legislation to ban greyhound racing and other working-class sports from areas like Ringsend and Harold's Cross, a clear statement from the government on where Terenure ends and where Dublin 4 begins – and, yes, it's developed into something stronger.'

Muirgheal fake-smiles her and she's like, 'Of course, being *only* a senator, you've plenty of time to be going around getting pregnant and having babies. You couldn't do it if you were an *elected* public representative.'

Sorcha's there, 'Muirgheal, can I ask you a question? Do you find that kind of behaviour acceptable?'

'What are you talking about?'

Across the forecourt, one of her porty colleagues grabs his crotch and shouts, 'The Dáil member is upstanding!' in our general direction.

The others all laugh.

'That,' Sorcha goes. 'The way they're talking to you. The way they were groping you just a second ago. You know you don't have to put up with that – as, like, a woman?'

Muirgheal's like, 'Oh, puh-lease! We don't all see ourselves as victims, Sorcha.'

I'm suddenly thinking about Hedvig grabbing my orse yesterday.

'But you *are* a victim,' Sorcha goes, 'whether you know it or not.'

Muirgheal's like, 'Yeah, maybe that's why I'm in the actual Dáil and you're in the Seanad!'

Sorcha looks at me, then back at Muirgheal. 'There's nothing wrong with being in the Seanad,' she goes. 'It plays an essential legislative role in determining the laws under which we all must –'

Muirgheal's there, 'Oh, come on, Sorcha! It's a consolation prize. It's like when you run for Head Girl and you don't win and they make you the Chairperson of the Yearbook Committee.'

Which is actually what happened to Muirgheal. Like I said – elephants and Frank Sinatra.

She goes, 'I mean, don't you feel guilty, Sorcha?'

Sorcha's there, 'What's there to feel guilty about?'

'Er, you're a mother of four children. With another one on the way. And you're missing them growing up – for *what* reason, remind me again?'

'Enda Kenny thinks I have a vital role to play in politics.'

'Er, reusable coffee cups? Sorcha, people are laughing at you.

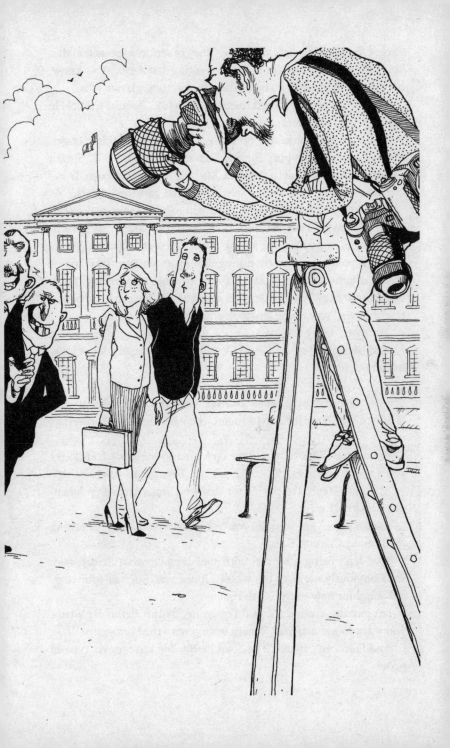

Except the cleaning staff, of course. They're seriously pissed off that you stopped that woman from Hoovering last week. You know, they're threatening to go on strike? She has to work two jobs.'

My phone beeps. It's a text message from Ro. Clontorf Castle! He was trying to say Clontorf Castle!

'Well, if you must know,' Sorcha goes, 'I'm still confident of getting cross-porty support for my Private Members' Bill. Simon Coveney brings a flask to the Dáil. Micheál Mortin has been drinking his coffee out of the same soup tin for the past three years.'

But Muirgheal's there, 'And, meanwhile, back in the real world, I'm the Deputy Leader of the Opposition. And when this government falls, I'm going to be sitting at the Cabinet table. And you'll still be a political irrelevance, pregnant by either your husband or your Parliamentary Secretary, making speeches to an empty chamber about things that no one gives a fock about. Face it, Sorcha, you might as well stay home and look after your children.'

'Fock off!' Leo goes.

And Muirgheal's there, 'And God knows they need a lot of looking after.'

They're already there when I arrive – we're talking Ronan and Shadden and little Rihanna-Brogan, then Kennet and Dordeen as well.

Kennet has the balls to pull me up for being late as well. He looks at his watch and goes, 'T . . . T . . . T . . . Toyumt do you calt this?'

And I go, 'Yeah, I'm paying for this wedding. I'll turn up whenever the fock I want.'

Ronan goes, 'Ah, weddle, you're hee-or now, Rosser,' meaning the famous Clontorf Castle.

Shadden's being a bit *cool* with me? Despite what Ronan said, she's obviously *not* over the whole Honor teaching her four-year-old daughter how to smoke thing.

I'm looking around me and I'm going, 'Is this definitely where you want to get married? What's wrong with the Shelbourne?'

And Dordeen's there, 'The Sheddle Burden idn't for *eer* type of people.'

She's not wrong there. She's wearing – I shit you not – pyjama bottoms. She's a focking disgrace. And she's got a body on her like a laundry bag stuffed with moose meat.

'In addyhow,' Shadden goes, 'the Sheddle Burden caddent cathor for the number of guests we hab cubben.'

And I'm like, 'Okay, how many guests have you got coming?' bracing myself for the news of how much this is going to cost me.

'Sebben hundordid,' Ronan goes.

I'm like, 'Seven hundred? You're nineteen years old. You haven't even *met* seven hundred people.'

And Kennet goes, 'A lorra them are f . . . f . . . frents of me and D . . . D . . . D . . . D . . . D . . . D . . . Dordeen,' and he pulls out what's obviously a list of names.

I might have guessed. The second I said I'd pay for it, he'll have seen it as a chance for a reunion with every focker he ever shared a cell with since he was fourteen years old.

There's music on in the reception of the hotel. A piano and violin version of a song that I sort of *half* recognize?

'Ah, Jaysus,' Dordeen goes, 'I lub this bleaten song, doatunt I, Kennet?' and then she storts actually singing it, going, '*Cos you make me feelt, you make me feelt, you make me feelt like . . . a . . . natur . . . doddle . . . wooban!*'

Fock's sake.

Eventually, the wedding planner arrives to talk us through the arrangements. She introduces herself to us. Her name is Corrina and if I had to compare her to someone it would have to be Nadine Lustre, except she's from somewhere down the country and has a very slight, outward-turning squint, which I find quite cute.

She's there, 'So what kind of wedding do yee fellas want?'

Yee fellas.

I wish I got off with more women from the country.

'Sometin veddy faddency,' Dordeen goes. 'Like sometin you'd seen on the tedevision. *Downtoorden Abbey* or one of them. No expedense speert.'

I'm like, 'Hang on a second –'

'And not forgethin a f . . . f . . . f . . . f . . . faree bar,' Kennet goes.

69

'I doatunt waddent addyone putting their hant in their bleaten p . . .
p . . . p . . . p . . . pockets.'

'Yeah, until the end of the focking night,' I go, 'and it's time to
pay the bill. Then you'll presumably have yours in b . . . b . . . b . . .
b . . . bleaten mine, you stuttering f–'

Dordeen actually *turns* on me then?

She goes: 'Hee-or, your sudden ast eer thaughter to maddy him –
not the utter way arowunt. It shouldn't be costing us a peddy.'

I'm like, 'Yeah, that's not how it works on the Southside.'

'Nud of us keers how it woorks on the sowt soyut. Your sudden
is veddy lucky to get a geerdle like eer Shadden. The bleaten cheek
of you to be pudden faces evvy toyum you're ast to take out your
bleaten waddet.'

Kennet goes, 'We waddent yisser b . . . b . . . b . . . best funk shid-
den roowum, Corrina. Best of evvyting, mattord of fact. F . . . F . . .
F . . . Flowerts. Lights. M . . . M . . . Music.'

Corrina's there, 'What about food?' looking at Ronan and Shadden. 'What kind of food were yee thinking of?'

'Just make shewer there's loawuts,' Dordeen goes, staring
straight at me. 'The deardor, the bethor.'

I look at Ronan, but he's not even following the conversation.
He's just, like, staring at Corrina – I swear to fock – pretty much
drooling?

I'm like, 'What about you, Ro? Do you have any thoughts?'

He's there, 'Soddy?' suddenly snapping out of it.

'I'm just wondering did you have any opinions about this wedding? You're supposedly getting married on New Year's Eve – I
don't know if you remember that?'

'No,' he goes, 'Ine easy, Coddina. Whatebbor Shadden waddents.'

Corrina goes, 'Look, I'll just go and get my menu book, then I'll
talk yee through some of the options.'

'I'll t . . . t . . . t . . . t . . . t . . . ted you what,' Kennet goes. 'Gib us
foyuv midutes. I neeyut a c . . . c . . . c . . . cigordette.'

'Jaysus, Ine gaspon meself,' Shadden goes, then she stands up, as
does Dordeen, and the three of them head outside, followed by
Rihanna-Brogan, going, 'Mammy, cad I hab a cigordette?'

I'm going to be blamed for that. I just know it. I turn around to Ronan to say the same thing to him, except he goes, 'Ine joost going to the jacks. Ine boorsting hee-or. Be back in a midute, Rosser,' and off he goes, leaving me on my Tobler.

I whip out my phone and I send Honor one or two texts. I'm just like, 'Hey, Honor, I'm here with the Tuites! Dordeen is wearing pyjamas! Over to you!'

Usually, she'd hit me straight back with something hilarious to say to the woman, but this time I get nothing. And it actually breaks my hort. We were such good friends. When she's not talking to me, life just feels – I don't know – *shit*?

Then this, like, weird feeling comes over me. Just this sudden sense that something is not right. It's like when you leave the house and you can't shake the feeling that the cleaner left the iron plugged in.

I stand up and I head for the reception area. And that's when I notice Ro locked in deep conversation – with the famous Corrina.

She doesn't look happy, by the way.

I hide behind a pillar and I listen to the conversation. *She's* going, 'I can't believe you're asking me that.'

And *he's* there, 'Ine oatenly looking for yisser phone number. I think you're lubbly.'

Oh, fock.

Corrina's there, 'But yee're getting married, sure. I'm about to explain the menu options to your fiancée for your wedding day.'

He goes, 'Ine not maddied *yet*, but.'

He's got the gift of the gab, in fairness to him.

'But yee're engaged,' she goes.

And Ronan – oh, Jesus – slips his orm around her waist and he goes, 'That ditn't stop you checken me out, but. I saw you – unthressing me wit yisser eyes, wha?'

And that's when Corrina – not before time – hits him the most unbelievable slap across the face.

So it's, like, Saturday morning and I'm in the gorden, trying to interest the boys in a rugby ball and I might as well be trying to teach economics to pigeons.

I'm going, 'Just pick it up, Brian,' because I'm still hoping he's going to be my inside-centre. 'At least give it a try. You might like the feel of it.'

'Ask! My focking! Hole!' he goes. 'You stupid focking thunderfock.'

I go over and pick the ball up myself, stopping only to give him a little shove in the back – the kind the referee never sees – and he falls on his snot. He'll hopefully think better of me for it.

Sorcha and her old man are sitting on the patio a few feet away, enjoying the morning sun. Sorcha is telling him about Muirgheal. About what she *said* to her? And about all those other TDs trying to grab her and telling her that she should be at home making dinners.

He goes, 'It's always been the same for women in this country, Sorcha. They've always been treated like second-class citizens.'

He's drinking coffee from his famous 'World's No. 1 Dad!' mug.

Sorcha goes, 'But why does it have to be like that?'

He's there, 'I saw a lot of the same thing in the Law Library, Dorling. Unfortunately, it's a man's world – we just deign to let women live in it.'

'But Muirgheal is entitled to be treated with the same respect as any other politician. There's just, like, so much sexism in the world. I was saying to Fionn last night that *someone* needs to raise awareness of it?'

Brian picks himself up off the ground and calls me a focking clownhole fock. I tell him *he's* the focking clownhole fock.

I look around for the other two. Leo is busy. He's lying on his side, kicking the bricks holding up the Shomera. So I put the ball in Johnny's hands instead. I swear to fock, he doesn't even notice.

I can't tell you how much of a failure I feel as a father.

'Well, why not you?' Sorcha's old man goes.

Sorcha's like, 'What do you mean?'

'What do you think I mean? Someone needs to raise public consciousness about the issue of the lack of gender equality in the world. I'm asking, why not Sorcha Lalor?'

He doesn't call her Sorcha O'Carroll-Kelly, by the way – he never did.

'Oh! My God!' she goes.

He's there, 'Women's rights could be your calling, Sorcha – just like the rights of our gay citizens was Mary Robinson's.'

'Oh my God, I think I've got an actual idea!'

'I thought you might!'

'What if I arrange an International Gender Equality Hour? I pick a certain time on a certain date and I ask everyone in the world to stop whatever they're doing at that time and reflect on the lack of opportunities for women in the world today?'

'I think you've found your cause, Sorcha! And, if you don't mind my saying, what a wonderful way to make the Seanad relevant again!'

'I can't wait to tell Fionn!'

Sorcha's old dear steps out of the Shomera. She goes, 'The electricity's gone – again!'

He's like, 'This is getting beyond ridiculous! They said the last time that the problem was fixed!'

Sorcha goes, 'Oh my God, Mom, this man here – your actual husband – has just helped me come up with an idea to try to highlight the lack of gender equality in the world.'

She's there, 'That's wonderful, Dorling.'

'I'm going to organize an International Gender Equality Hour. Oh my God, it could become, like, an *annual* thing, where hopefully, eventually, everyone in the world will stop and reflect on issues like the gender pay gap, the glass ceiling, the fact that nine out of ten people in the boardrooms of major companies across the world are men. Oh my God, I have to ring Fionn!'

I'm standing there, listening to this, while spinning the ball in my hands. I make the mistake of going, 'An hour's a very long time, though, isn't it?'

Sorcha's there, 'What do you mean?'

'To be thinking about one specific thing. I'm just saying that an hour is a very long time.'

Her old man goes, 'Maybe an hour is a long time for someone with your attention span.'

I decide not to say anything back. I turn around to Sorcha and I go, 'Could you look after the boys? I have to pop out for an hour.'

She's like, 'Where are you going?'

'To see my old dear. There's something I have to, er, talk to her about.'

'Don't be long. I want to stort work on this thing today.'

I walk into the house, through the kitchen, then into the hall-way. And that's when I spot Honor, standing on a chair with her head in the fuse box.

'Oh my God, it was you!' I go.

She gets an actual fright. She ends up nearly falling off the chair. She's there, 'You focking scared me!'

I'm like, '*You're* the reason the electricity keeps going in the Shomera.'

She goes, 'Have you got a problem with that?'

'Honor, I can't believe you would do something like this –'

'I don't give a shit what you think.'

'– without involving me.'

'What?'

'It's driving him mad, Honor. The pair of them. They keep ring-ing the ESB or whatever they're called now, dragging engineers out here and giving out yords to them.'

'Are you saying you think it's funny?'

'I'm saying I think it's hilarious!'

I watch that little hord face of hers suddenly soften. Two words. Positive. Feedback.

She goes, 'What I've been doing is pulling the fuse out, then replacing it with one that doesn't work, just in case he checks the box. Then as soon as I see the engineer pull up outside, I put the working fuse back in.'

I'm like, 'So that's why they can't find out what the fault is!'

'Do you think it's good?'

'It's so good,' I go, lifting her down off the chair, 'it's actually a bit disturbed. So are we friends again?'

'Friends don't keep secrets from each other.'

'I'd do anything to get back in your good books, Honor. I genu-inely would.'

She suddenly bursts into tears. 'I'm scared,' she goes.

I just take her in my orms and I hold her tight. I'm like, 'Scared? What are you scared of?'

She goes, 'What if the baby is yours?'

'And why does that scare you? You don't want it to be Fionn's, do you?'

'Because it might change things – between us.'

I hold her at orm's length and I look into her sad little eyes. I'm there, 'Er, you've got three brothers, Honor. Has that stopped you from being my number one favourite?'

'That's different,' she goes. 'They're idiots.'

'They *are* idiots.'

'You don't like them as much as you like me.'

'I definitely thought they'd be more rugby.'

'What if it's a little girl, though? You might love her more than you love me.'

'Okay, *how* is that even possible?'

'Because she might be nice. She might be nice in the same way that I'm horrible.'

'Oh, Honor.'

'I know I'm horrible. I'm horrible and I'm dark and I'm mean.'

'Hey, can I let you into a little secret?'

'What?'

'I've been pissing in Sorcha's old man's favourite mug for about a year now.'

She bursts out laughing – we're talking, like, proper uncontrollable laughter.

I'm there, 'I do it pretty much every time I have a few drinks on me. I take it out, piss in it, dry it using kitchen roll, then I put it back.'

She goes, 'Oh! My God!'

'Have you ever thought that you being horrible is one of the things I most love about you?'

'No. You gave out to me for teaching Rihanna-Brogan how to smoke.'

'That was more your mother's idea than mine. I actually thought it was funny.'

'Did you?'

'What, a four-year-old girl smoking? Who wouldn't find that hilarious!'

'I also taught the triplets all the swear words they know.'

'And one day we might look back on that and think it was funny as well. I'm nearly sure of it. Look, not everyone gets our sense of humour, Honor. That's the main problem.'

'So you're saying you prefer me being horrible?'

'I'm saying I love you the way you are.'

She dries her little eyes with her hand. Then we suddenly hear the sound of tyres on the gravel outside. 'That'll be the ESB,' she goes. 'I better put the fuse back in.'

And I'm there, 'You do that. I'll be back in hour. I'm just going to blackmail your grandmother.'

I ring the doorbell, but there ends up being no answer, which is weird because the old dear's Lexus NX is porked in front of the gaff and so is the old man's Merc.

I'm thinking, they'd better not be having sex again. Whatever o'clock it is on a Saturday morning. They're a focking disgrace.

Then I think, actually, no – it's a scorcher of a day – maybe they're in the back gorden, so I tip around the back of the house and that's exactly where I find them.

I laugh out loud as I take in the scene.

The old dear is wearing – I shit you not – a black stab vest and a clear plastic visor, the kind of thing that a welder would wear, except this doesn't just cover her eyes, it covers her entire face.

The old man is adjusting the straps on it, presumably to tighten it, while looking up at the sky and going, 'What time is the chap coming? I think there's to be cloud later this morning.'

At first I'm wondering is it some kind of, I don't know, kinky sex game? But then I spot the photographer. He's the same dude who was in front of Leinster House the other day, taking the pictures of the old man and his – I know this is possibly rich coming from me – but *sexist* mates?

The old man spots me and goes, 'Look, Fionnuala, it's Kicker!

Now don't you try to draw me into a debate about my comments on the people of Laois!'

I'm there, 'I'd never heard of Laois until last week.'

'It's where you'll find some of the laziest, most criminally minded –' and then he suddenly stops. 'He's only gone and bloody well drawn me in, Fionnuala! Incorrigible! That's the only word for you, Ross!'

I notice there's, like, various lamps and umbrellas arranged around the bamboo area of the gorden.

I go, 'Okay, what the fock is this?'

The old man goes, 'We're doing some publicity shots – for your mother's foundation brochure.'

She's sort of, like, eyeing me – another, possibly, made-up word – *warily*?

I'm there, 'So why is she focking dressed like a posh RoboCop?'

'I think I mentioned to you, Ross, that one of the charities she's decided to help is involved in clearing landmines, IEDs and the other awful, awful debris of war.'

'That's right,' she goes, then she tilts her head to one side and flutters her eyelashes. The full Diana.

I'm there, 'Oh my God, you are so full of shit.'

'Oh, it's a wonderful organization,' the old man tries to go. 'They're involved in demining projects all over the continent of Africa! And not only demining but also weapons and ammunition disposal and stockpile management! There's a lovely phrase on their website, Ross! Something about working with aid and development partners to create a safe and secure something-or-other and help prepare the way for long-term something-else! It might have been stability or something of that colour!'

The old dear's phone all of a sudden beeps. She looks at it. 'It's Thato,' she goes. 'He's at the front door.'

Off the old man focks to answer it.

The photographer storts fiddling with the lights and the umbrellas, leaving me and the old dear on our Tobler.

I laugh because I suddenly *cop* something?

I'm there, 'Is that supposed to look like Africa?'

'I'm too busy to visit at the moment,' she goes, 'to see first-hand the wonderful work they're doing on the ground.'

'Jesus, I remember you buying those bamboos from Woodies in Sandyford.'

'Also, I think I'd find Africa too depressing.'

'Of course you would. There wouldn't be an O'Brien's off-licence on every street.'

'No, rather than swanning around these countries, which are full of AIDS and God knows what else, I decided that my time would be better spent here in the developed world, using my profile to raise money from corporations, foreign governments and private donors to help ease the suffering in all these desperate, desperate parts of the world.'

'Yeah, great talk, *Mom*! Now, pleasantries over – have you given any thought to what I said the last time I was here?'

'What *did* you say?'

'Yeah, don't act the innocent. You know what I'm talking about. I want a million squids for that heater.'

'You see, the thing is, Ross, Ari wasn't as wealthy as I originally thought.'

'Still wealthy enough to justify offing him, though.'

'He only left me about one million dollars.'

'It was forty million, according to the old man.'

She looks away. It's game, set and match and she knows it. She goes, 'Fine.'

I'm there, 'Sensible woman. Go and fetch it. Then I'll go and get the heater for you.'

'I don't have it yet. It could be six months before I see anything.'

'Six months?'

'That awful granddaughter of his –'

'Who, Tiffany Blue?'

'Yes, she's still determined to fight me for it. She's threatening to go to court to ensure I don't get a cent of Ari's money.'

'Not my problem.'

'Please, be reasonable.'

78

'You're going to be back sharing a landing with the Scissor Sisters before the weekend is over.'

I go to walk away.

She's like, 'Wait! Please, Ross! I can give you some money now. We'll call it an advance until this business with Ari's granddaughter is sorted out.'

'How much are we talking?'

'I think there's about five thousand euros in the safe.'

'Is that all?'

'It's not a lot, I know.'

'Okay, we'll call it a down-payment. You've just bought yourself another six months of freedom. But if I don't get my money by the end of the year, then I'm turning you in.'

All of a sudden, the back door opens again and out the old man steps, followed by this dude who's – look, I'm just going to come out and say it, even though it makes me a racist – but *black*?

He's on crutches, I notice, and wearing a full-leg plaster cast. And I laugh, because I suddenly realize how I know the name Thato. He's the little South African baby who was adopted years ago by the daughter of Delma, one of the old dear's friends. And now he's all growed up. He played Junior Cup for King's Hospital this year and he had a medial collateral ligament tear, which is presumably why his leg is banjoed.

I'm there, 'I don't focking believe this. You're going to pretend that he stepped on a mine?'

The old man puts his orm around Thato's shoulder and goes, 'It's a day's work for the chap, Ross! Plus he gets to help those who are still living on the continent that he was fortunate enough to escape! Isn't that right, Thato?'

The old dear looks at me nervously and goes, 'I'll just, em, get that for you, Ross.'

I'm there, 'Be focking quick about it as well.'

Into the gaff she goes.

Thato's like, 'Hey, Ross, how the hell *are* you?'

I'm like, 'Yeah, no, life couldn't be better, Thato. Bad luck, by the

way. I'm talking about the Junior Cup. I thought you'd a definite chance this year.'

'Thanks, Dude. It was just one of those things. A freak accident.'

'Yeah, no, Delma rang the old dear and asked me to have a word with you, as someone who overcame disappointment to achieve everything I achieved in the game. But in the end –'

I couldn't be focking bothered.

I'm there, 'I sort of forgot.'

He's like, 'Hey, it's cool.'

The old man goes, 'If you want my advice, Thato, you'll rest that leg for a year, then come back stronger for the Senior Cup.'

The old dear takes her focking time. She leaves us there talking rugby for about, like, twenty minutes, before she reappears at the back door. She gives me a nod.

I say goodbye to Thato, call the old man a knob, then I head into the house. She hands me a massive wad of notes.

I'm there, 'It's all in there, is it?'

She goes, 'Five thousand euros. I counted it myself.'

'Good.'

'Ross, I really would do anything to stay out of prison.'

'Hey, that's music to my ears.'

Ten seconds later, I'm out of there. I stort the cor. I feel genuinely great. Out onto Torquay Road I go, then down through Foxrock Village, fanging an orange filter light as I take the turn onto Westminster Road.

I'm cruising along at a fair old speed. I decide to take the money out and count it after all. I'm holding the wheel and I'm trying to pull the wad out at the same time and I suddenly notice that the light at the end of Westminster Road is red.

I slam my foot on the brake, except nothing happens. As in, the brakes don't *work*? I actually close my eyes as I plough through the light and onto the actual dual-carriageway. For a second or two, I think I've had a miraculous escape. I open my eyes and stort to pull the wheel to the right, and that's when a cor smashes into the side of me.

I'm suddenly sent into a mad spin, turning round and round as I cross the second carriageway and I'm listening to the sound of glass breaking and metal grinding and I'm getting the whiff of petrol and burning rubber and I'm thinking about Honor and how will she survive in that house without me and I'm thinking about the old dear saying that she'd do anything to avoid going back to prison.

And that's the last thing I remember before everything turns suddenly black.

3. When You See What's on This Menu, You Won't Want to Eat Again!

It's Sorcha's voice that I can hear. Above the beep, beep, beep of the presumably *life*-support machine?

She's going, 'The hope is that it'll become, like, an annual event, kind of like Earth Hour, where people all over the world will stop what they're doing and reflect on the lack of gender equality in the world today.'

Then I hear Honor go, 'Er, my dad is in an actual coma here.'

I'm thinking, am I? Am I *actually*?

'He's not in a coma,' Sorcha goes – so apparently not. 'He's just unconscious. The doctor said he's not in any danger.'

The old man must be here too, because I hear him go, 'Thank God for airbags, eh?'

My ribs feel pretty bashed up, in fairness to them.

Honor's like, 'Everything doesn't always have to be about you, though.'

Sorcha's there, 'Chorles asked me what was on my political agenda for the next few months and I answered his question.'

'Well it all sounds terribly exciting!' the old man goes. 'That's one in the eye for the people who say the Seanad is nothing more than an elitist talking shop, totally and utterly detached from the reality of people's everyday lives, eh?'

'Thank you, Chorles. Can I take it you'll be taking port?'

'Taking port?'

'I've invited all of the other porty leaders to Honalee to observe the hour together in a show of political ecumenism. They're hopefully all coming. We're talking Enda Kenny, Micheál Mortin, Brendan Howlin, Gerry Adams –'

'You've invited Gerry Adams . . . to Killiney?'

'Yes, because I'd love this to be a cross-porty issue. You know, when I set up the International Gender Equality Hour account on

Twitter, I got followers from Fianna Fáil, Fine Gael, Sinn Féin, the Labour Porty –'

I can feel Honor's breath on my face. She's saying in my ear, 'Wake up! Daddy, wake up!'

She's the only one who seems to *give* a shit that I'm lying here in a jocker?

The old man's like, 'What date is it happening, did you say?'

'A week on Saturday,' Sorcha goes. 'It's on from, like, midday. For one hour. And I think you, of all people, should make an effort to be there.'

'Me of all people?'

'Chorles, only one of your fifty-one porliamentary porty members is a woman. The rest are all upper-middle-class, privately educated, white men in their fifties and sixties.'

'Well, *I* would put that down to coincidence rather than – inverted commas – sexism!'

God, he's a dick.

'*And*,' Sorcha goes, 'I should have brought this to your attention at the time, but I noticed a few members of your porliamentary porty acting in an inappropriate way towards Muirgheal.'

He's like, 'Inappropriate, you say?'

'They were groping her, Chorles. And making disgusting comments. Women politicians want to feel valued for the contribution they make, not objectified by a bunch of dirty old men.'

'Steady on, Sorcha! That's the Opposition front bench you're maligning!'

'And *you're* their leader, Chorles. You owe it to them to set an example and you can do that by coming to Honalee with the other porty leaders on the day.'

'Well, I shall see if I can make it out there for at least part of it! I would point out, however, that this thing is happening in the week of the Brexit referendum! I expect I'll be much in demand that weekend as the leader of the only mainstream party that believes Ireland's future lies outside the European Union!'

Sorcha laughs. She's like, 'You don't genuinely believe the people of Britain are going to vote to leave Europe, do you?'

Jesus Christ, I'm thinking. If I'm not in a coma now, I will be in about sixty focking seconds. That's the reason I end up opening my eyes.

Honor goes, 'Daddy!'

It's honestly the happiest I've seen her since I showed her a video clip of Beyoncé getting her hair caught in an electric fan.

She goes, 'You're alive!'

She throws herself across the bed. Jesus, my ribs are sore.

I can't believe how calm Sorcha and my old man are. They're taking it very much in their stride. *He* goes, 'Welcome back to the land of the living!'

I'm like, 'Where am I?'

Sorcha's there, 'You're in St Vincent's Hospital.'

I'm like, 'Private?'

She goes, 'Public.'

And I'm there, 'Honor, go and get my clothes, will you?'

The old man is having none of it, though. 'Stay put, Kicker, at least until the doctor checks you over! You've got quite a bit of bruising!'

I'm like, 'What the fock happened?'

'Are you saying you don't remember?'

'No . . . Fock, I actually *don't*?'

'There you are, then! It looks like it's another one of your famous concussions!'

'Shit.'

'You were in a car crash, Kicker!'

'A cor crash? Seriously?'

Sorcha goes, 'On the dual-carriageway. You drove through a red light at the bottom of Westminster Road like I'm always telling you not to do. And you were hit by a Škoda Octavia.'

'Jesus!'

'You're lucky to be alive.'

'Shit – can I just ask –?'

'Don't worry,' Sorcha goes, 'the other driver wasn't hurt at all.'

I was actually going to ask how my *cor* was?

Honor goes, 'The cor was a total write-off, though.'

Fock. At least someone has their priorities right.

The old man's there, 'Your mother sends her best wishes!'

I'm like, 'Oh, right. How's she doing these days?'

'Are you saying you don't remember being in the house today?'

'Is that why I was on Westminster Road?'

'Yes, indeed! We were doing a photo shoot for your mother's foundation brochure!'

'Shit, I don't remember even being there!'

'Well, you were! In all your bloody well glory!'

And that's when Erika appears in the ward.

I'm there, 'Now *there's* a sight for sore eyes slash ribs!'

She spots the old man standing next to the bed and goes, 'I'll come back later.'

The old man goes, 'Nonsense, Erika! I was about to leave anyway! How's that lovely granddaughter of mine?'

But Erika just goes, 'It's none of your business. I told you, I have nothing to say to you,' and the old man takes the hint and focks off.

Erika sits on the edge of the bed. She looks fantastic. She's wearing – yeah, no – shorts. Sister or not sister, she has incredible legs, if that doesn't sound too weird?

She's like, 'What happened?'

I'm there, 'I don't remember. Apparently, I fanged an orange light –'

'A red light,' Sorcha goes.

'– at the bottom of Westminster Road and I got ploughed by a focking Škoda Octavia of all things.'

Sorcha goes, 'Come on, Honor, let's go and find the doctor and we'll see can we bring your daddy home.'

Off *they* fock then, leaving me and Erika alone. And I end up just blurting it out.

I'm like, 'She tried to kill me, Erika.'

Erika goes, 'What? Who?'

'My old dear. She did something to my cor.'

'You're babbling, Ross. Sorcha's just gone to get the doctor.'

'Erika, I'm telling you the truth. She did something to the brakes. That's the reason I went through that red light.'

'Why would she try to kill you?'

'Because I have the goods on her. I have the two-bor electric heater that she dropped in Ari's bath.'

Her mouth falls open. She's like, 'Are you serious?'

And I'm there, 'I'm not a liar, Erika. Well, I am a liar, but I'm not lying in this case.'

'So why haven't you gone to the Gords with it? Jesus, Ross, she could stand trial again.'

'She's my mother. That still means something.'

'That's bullshit. You hate that woman more than anyone.'

'Yeah, no, cords on the table, then – I was hoping to blackmail her for a million yoyos from Ari's money. It wasn't even my idea. It was actually Honor's.'

She just shakes her head, as if to say, Hey, that's the Rossmeister – don't ever change.

'You stupid focking idiot,' she goes.

I'm like, 'Okay, I know what I am, Erika.'

'If she killed her second husband in cold blood, do you really think she'd have any qualms about killing you?'

'Yeah, I did actually.'

'Then you're a fool. The woman is psychotic.'

'Hey, I've been saying it all my life.'

'What about him?'

'Who?'

'Dad. Do you think he had anything to do with it?'

'No.'

'Are you sure?'

The truth is I'm not. And she can see that realization in my face.

She goes, 'Where is it now? The heater!'

I'm there, 'It's stashed. In the room where Sorcha keeps all her old rubbish. Her juicer and her video recorder and her Nintendo Brain Trainer. And me.'

'Get up. We're going to get it.'

She picks my clothes up off the chair and drops them on the bed. She's like, 'Come on, get dressed.'

I hop out of the bed and I stort throwing my clothes on.

I'm there, 'What are we going to do with it?'

She goes, 'What do you think we're going to do with it? We're going to bring it to the Gords.'

Sorcha and Honor arrive back. Sorcha goes, 'I can't find the doctor.'

I'm like, 'Doesn't matter. I'm signing myself out. There's fock-all wrong with me.'

'Er, aport from the fact that you can't remember anything that happened?'

'Hey, you heard the old man – I've had more concussions than I've had hot women. My head always clears eventually.'

She's there, 'Fine. Erika, would you give Ross and Honor a lift back to Killiney?'

I make the mistake of going, 'Why, where are you going?'

And she's there, 'I'm having lunch with Fionn. Oh my God, he's so sweet, Erika! He's bringing me to the Bad Ass Café in Temple Bor, where we used to go back in 2003, when we morched against the invasion of Iraq.'

Erika goes, 'How, em, romantic.'

And I'm thinking, Yeah – puke!

Some dude on the news is saying that British Prime Minister David Cameron has urged voters to remember the peace and stability that European unity has helped bring to the continent since the Second World War when they come to vote on whether or not they should remain a part of the European Union.

I reach across Erika – God, those legs! – and I switch the radio off. She goes, 'Ross, I was actually listening to that.'

I'm like, 'Why? It's not going to affect us, is it?'

She just shakes her head and goes, 'If what you don't know can't hurt you, then you are focking invincible.'

I don't even understand that, which means the joke is actually on *her*?

'Okay,' Honor goes, 'is anyone going to tell me what the fock is going on?'

She's sitting in the back.

I'm there, 'Your plan to blackmail your grandmother unfortunately backfired, Honor.'

She's like, 'What?'

'Yeah, no, she tried to kill me.'

'Are you saying she did something to the cor?'

'She must have focked with the brakes or something. I put my foot down to stop at the lights and fock-all happened.'

Honor goes silent for a long time. She was cool with the idea of her grandmother killing a complete stranger. But killing me – that's crossing a line.

She's like, 'What are you going to do?'

I'm there, 'What do you think I'm going to do? I'm going to give the heater to the Feds. Let *them* deal with her.'

'You're talking about going to the Gords?'

'She belongs in prison, Honor.'

'But what about the money?'

'Honor, the woman just tried to kill me.'

'Sofa King what? Man up, will you?'

'What do you mean?'

'You could still get the money out of her. You just have to be cleverer than she is.'

Erika takes the turn onto the Vico Road. 'Honor,' she goes, 'your grandmother is a psychopath. She killed her husband and she's just tried to kill your father.'

I'm like, 'Hang on, Erika, let's hear her out. What are you saying, Honor?'

She goes, 'Do you know what you could do with that money? You could buy a house and put Sorcha's stupid focking parents in it!'

'I'm not buying them a gaff,' I go.

'Somewhere shit. Like Terenure.'

'Okay, I like the way you're thinking.'

'I'm saying, don't just give up.'

'But what if she tries to kill me again?'

'She won't. I've got an idea.'

'Okay. Shoot.'

'You put the heater in one of those storage places. Then you write a letter to be opened in the event of your sudden death or disappearance, telling the Gords where to find it.'

Erika goes, 'Honor, you watch far too much TV.'

I'm there, 'She's right, though. Not if I get my hands on the evidence and put it in a safe –'

Oh, shit.

We all say the same as Erika takes the turn into the driveway.

We're all like, 'Oh, shit!'

Because the old dear's Lexus NX is porked outside the gaff.

Honor's like, 'I'll go.'

And I'm there, 'No, you won't,' doing the whole protective father thing. 'Leave it to me.'

I get out of the cor and I walk up to the door. I'm actually *shaking*? So badly, in fact, that it takes me a good thirty seconds to put the key into the lock to let myself in. But in the end I manage it.

Into the hall I creep, listening out for her. Then I hear her voice coming from the kitchen. She's obviously talking to Sorcha's old pair about her foundation because I hear her go, 'If, by talking about my own experiences as someone who has suffered unnecessarily, I can persuade governments and corporations to help the victims of these awful, awful landmines, then the time I spent in prison will not have been in vain.'

I tiptoe up the stairs, then slip quietly into my room. I look under the bed. It's still there. I reach under and I pull it out.

But the sense of, I don't know, relief that I feel doesn't last long. A few seconds later, I hear the old dear coming up the stairs. She's shouting down at Sorcha's old pair, going, 'Yes, Ross asked me to bring one or two things into the hospital to him.'

He goes, 'Sorcha just phoned and said he'd signed himself out.'

But she just blanks him. She's like, 'I'll just be a few minutes.'

I'm looking around me, thinking, okay, where the fock am I going to hide? I'm about to dive under the bed with it when I hear something suddenly hit the window. It's a pebble. I walk over to the window and I open it. Honor is standing below.

I'm there, 'She's coming up the stairs, Honor.'

She goes, 'Drop it out of the window.'

She's so smort. She definitely didn't get it from me.

I'm like, 'Do you think you can catch it?'

She's there, 'Of course I can catch it!'

I drop it and she *does* catch it! Now *that* she *did* get from me?

'Give it to Erika,' I go, 'and tell her to get the fock out of here.'

I close the window. Literally five seconds later, the bedroom door opens and I'm suddenly standing face to face with the woman who tried to murder me this morning.

'Oh,' she goes, 'you're –'

And I'm there, 'Alive?'

'I was going to say home. Your father said you'd been in a terrible accident. He said the car was a complete write-off.'

'Yeah, no, thanks for your concern.'

'I was about to go to the hospital to see you.'

'Yeah, nice try. So how did you do it?'

'I have no idea what you're talking about.'

'Did you cut my brakes or something?'

'Don't try to blame me, Ross. How many times have we all warned you about driving through that light when it's red?'

I hear Erika's cor drive away.

'You won't find it,' I go. 'And don't say, "Find what?" because you know very well what I'm talking about. It's gone to a safe place. The price has gone up to five million – or else I'm sending it to the Gords.'

'What exactly *is* Brexit?' I go. 'It's just the whole world seems to be suddenly banging on about it.'

Everyone just, like, rolls their eyes, as if not knowing makes me somehow *stupid*?

It's actually little Ross Junior who ends up telling me. It turns out he's learning about it in school. 'The Unithed Kingthom,' he goes, 'ith going to dethide nektht week whether to thtay in the European Union or leave.'

Seven years old. Smort kid – if also a bit strange.

I'm there, 'Thanks, Ross. That's all *anyone* had to say. It's quicker than everyone sighing and throwing their eyes up to the focking sky.'

I'm still none the wiser, by the way. I thought it was about Britain. Where the fock – and actually *what* the fock? – is the United Kingdom? And while we're at, would someone mind explaining to me what actually *is* the European Union and since when has it been a thing?

'It's not going to happen,' JP goes. 'There's more chance of Donald Trump becoming the next President of America.'

Everyone laughs. Seriously, I must stort watching the news – just to be able to follow the conversation when it happens to be *not* about rugby?

We're in the back gorden of Christian and Lauren's place in Booterstown, by the way. They're having, like, a borbecue – unofficially, it's to celebrate them being back together again, which I'm actually delighted about, even though Lauren wouldn't be my number one fan.

As if to prove my point, she walks up to me, holding the giant Optimus Prime robot that I brought for Ross Junior – and which, by the way, he's barely even *looked* at? She goes, 'Who brought this?'

And I'm like, 'It was me. Although I notice he still hasn't taken it out of the box – er, a *bit* ungrateful?'

'What have I told you about buying presents for him?'

'Hey, I know it's not his birthday, Lauren, but he's my godson. I like to spoil him.'

'I'm talking about you buying him gender-normative toys?'

'Gender –?'

'Toys for boys! Why do you always buy him toys specifically for boys?'

Every conversation in the gorden stops. All the girls are looking at us over the top of their Aperol spritzes, while the goys all look at their feet.

I'm there, 'I hate to point out the obvious, Lauren, but he *is* actually a boy.'

Little Ross Junior decides to hang me then. He goes, 'What my Mom ith trying to thay, Roth, ith that I thon't like roboth and thuper heroth and thoth typthe of thoys. I actually prefer to play with dollth.'

I'm there, 'I'm not buying you dolls.'

'I love dollth. I have thixty-theven dollth.'

'I repeat. I am not buying you dolls.'

I'm not buying you anything, in fact, you little focking Judas.

Lauren goes, 'Ross, go and play with the other children and let the grown-ups talk.'

She's talking to Ross Junior, rather than me. It says a lot that I have to point that out.

Off he goes. Lauren shoves the robot into my chest and goes, 'Here, take it. And stop trying to impose society's ignorant and out-dated gender roles on my son.'

When the storm has passed, everyone returns to their drinks and their conversations. I tip over to Christian, who's manning the actual grill – flipping the burgers and blah, blah, blah – and I go, 'Rather you than me, my friend,' and I'm saying that as someone who was originally happy to see them get back together.

He's there, 'Hey, I'm sorry, Ross. You know how protective Lauren is of him.'

'Yeah, no, whatever. She's never been a fan of mine. I just rub her up the wrong way.'

He goes, 'Hmmm,' and doesn't even *try* to contradict me?

'Do you remember the time she went to stay with that Erasmus friend of hers in Germany and when she came home she insisted that everyone took their shoes off before they went into your house?'

'Yeah, you told her to fock off, Ross – on her own doorstep.'

'And I'd do it again, Christian. It was focking ridiculous. I said it to her: "You're not in *Rothenburg ob der Tauber* now. The Dubes stay on." How's the job going, by the way?'

'Good.'

'What exactly are you doing again?'

'It's kind of hord to explain –'

'Hey, I don't give a fock one way or the other. I was only making conversation with you.'

While I'm talking to him, I'm watching all of the kids play-ing together. We're talking Honor and the triplets. We're talking

Christian and Lauren's Oliver and little Ross Junior. We're talking JP and Chloe's Isa. We're talking Erika's Amelie. I sort of, like, smile to myself.

I'm there, 'It's nice, isn't it? Seeing all our kids playing together?'

He smiles and nods, then goes, 'I still can't get my head around, well, you know –'

He means Sorcha being pregnant by possibly Fionn, except he doesn't want to say it.

I'm there, 'I can't either. Maybe it'll only sink in when she storts showing.'

'And they're, like, together now?' he goes. 'As in, like, a couple?'

'They're giving it a go apparently.'

'Well, for what it's worth, I told him that I thought what he did – sleeping with Sorcha, especially when she was vulnerable –'

'And still married to a former teammate.'

'– exactly – was bang out of order. I told him I'd prefer if he didn't come here today.'

'Hey, that's nice to hear. Thanks, Dude.'

After about twenty minutes of catching up, I do the whole mingling thing. I tip over to where the women are sitting around a big round table on the patio.

'So,' Amie with an ie is saying to Sorcha, 'how are you, you know, doing?'

She means how's the pregnancy going? And I can tell from the way Chloe's ears prick up that it's obviously been the subject of a lot of discussion.

'Fine,' Sorcha goes. 'Just a bit of morning sickness, which I've had with all of mine.'

It's obviously not what they wanted to hear because Sophie turns around then and goes, 'I mean, do you have *any* idea who the father is, Sorcha? As in, who do you think it is in your hort of horts?'

And Erika – in fairness to her – goes, 'Why don't you mind your own focking business, Sophie?'

Lauren changes the subject by asking Sorcha how the plans for this International Gender Equality Hour are coming along.

Sorcha goes, 'Absolutely amazing, Lauren – that's if Likes on Facebook and Retweets on Twitter are any kind of *barometer*?'

Lauren says she's shared literally everything that Sorcha has posted about it and she knows at least four girls who are going to be doing it.

Amie with an ie goes, 'Can people do things *while* they're thinking about the lack of gender equality in the world?'

Sorcha's there, 'What's so important that it can't wait?'

'Well, I was going to get my eyebrows threaded that Saturday. I was thinking, if I made the appointment for exactly the same time, I could think about it while I was sitting there in the chair. Two birds with one stone.'

Erika obviously can't listen to any more because she stands up and says she's going to go and check on Amelie. I walk down to the bottom of the gorden with her.

I'm there, 'Do you still have it?' and I'm obviously talking about the heater.

She goes, 'No, I focking sold it on Done Deal, Ross.'

I'm there, 'Okay, I'm *presuming* that's sorcasm?'

'It's still in the boot of my cor.'

'Yeah, no, cool – don't leave without giving it back to me.'

'Ross, you need to go to the Gords.'

'I'm not going to the Gords. I went online – well, Honor did – and she's found this self-storage place. It's just off the M50 in, believe it or not, Santry.'

She doesn't get a chance to tell me what she thinks because that's when Fionn decides to show his face. I'm there, 'What the fock is *he* doing here? Christian said he was told to stay away.'

He rushes over to the table where the girls are all sitting. Sorcha's there, 'What's wrong, my love?'

My love? For fock's sake.

He's out of breath, by the way. Like he used to be on the rugby field after, like, twenty minutes of play.

'I'm sorry,' he goes, 'I've been trying to ring you for the past hour.'

She's there, 'I have my phone on silent. What's going on?'

'There's a clash of dates.'

'What are you talking about?'

'The International Gender Equality Hour. Midday next Saturday. Which is the same time as the International Fashion Influencers Summit at the RDS.'

'The *what*?'

'It's like the Web Summit except it's for, well, style and lifestyle bloggers. It's a huge deal apparently.'

Amie with an ie goes, 'Oh my God, yeah, Lydia Elise Millen and Blair Eadie are coming here for it. *And* the Blonde Salad, I *think*?'

Fionn's there, 'I'm wondering should we maybe change the time of International Gender Equality Hour?'

Sorcha's like, 'Excuse me?'

'I was going to suggest maybe bringing it forward to ten o'clock in the morning?'

'Change the time of International Gender Equality Hour? To accommodate a summit for fashion bloggers? Are you *actually* serious?'

She sounds genuinely disgusted. It's good to see *him* under pressure for once?

He goes, 'Sorcha, it doesn't make any sense to go up against them.'

She's like, 'There'll *be* no competition, Fionn. I think we'll find out next Saturday that women are far more interested in gender equality than they are in clothes.'

I watch Chloe, Sophie and Amie with an ie exchange dubious looks. And that's when I suddenly hear a bump behind me. Lauren screams and goes running past me. When I turn around, it turns out that little Ross Junior has fallen flat on his face.

'Ross!' she goes, turning him over. 'Ross!'

Christian rushes over to him as well.

It looks like *I'm* going to have to finish cooking the burgers? I actually don't mind. I pick up the tongs and I stort turning them on the grill while Sorcha and Chloe and JP and one or two others ask if they can help. With Ross Junior, I mean. It's pretty obvious to everyone that I've got the burgers under control.

I go, 'What happened?' just to let people think I actually care.

I watch Christian's nose suddenly twitch a bit, then he looks up and he's there, 'He's drunk.'

'Jesus,' Lauren goes, 'he's plastered.'

Christian's going, 'Ross! Ross, can you hear me? Ross, please, wake up!'

Lauren storts looking around her, going, 'Who was it? Who gave my son alcohol?'

And my eyes automatically drift over to Honor, who's sitting on the swing chair a few feet away, texting, with a little smile playing on her lips.

Ronan leaves me a voice message to say that he and Shadden are going to see a band tonight in the Broken Orms in Finglas which they think could end up being their wedding band.

They're called *26 Plus 6 Equals 1*, which should actually be a clue as to what kind of band we're talking about.

'They're on at noyun o'clock,' he goes, 'and me and Shadden would lubben if you could be theer to see them wirrus.'

The two of them are already there when I arrive – sitting at the table nearest the front. They're both like, 'Howiya, Rosser?' and then Kennet arrives back from the bor with a pint for himself, going, 'What k . . . k . . . k . . . kepp you, Rosser? They're about to cub on stayuch.'

Ronan is wearing a sort of vest, presumably to show off the names of the Easter Rising mortyrs, which are tattooed on his upper orm.

I pull up a stool and I sit down. 'Hee-or,' Ronan goes, 'are you alreet, Rosser?' because he can see I'm a little bit stiff in my *movements*?

I'm there, 'Yeah, no, the old ribs are bit bashed up. I had a bit of an incident in the cor the other day. I'm actually alright.'

Speaking of bruises, though, I notice that Ro has a humungous one on his neck.

The band comes on – there's, like, a massive tricolor hanging behind them – and they launch into the first number.

Eermurt keers and tanks and guddens,
Came to take away eer suddens,
But evody madden must stadden behoyunt,
The medden behyount the woyer.

Ronan claps along and stamps his feet and bellows out every word of the song. Shadden smiles, but I can tell from her face that this isn't exactly the kind of music she had in mind for the biggest day of her life.

The band race through the first half of their set – shit that 'the Brits' did to us figures in pretty much every song, even though the singer is only about twenty and definitely not old enough to have experienced any of the things he seems so worked up about.

The interval arrives and the band goes off to take a break.

Shadden turns around to Ro and goes, 'Yeah, not a bleeden chaddence.'

Ro's there, 'Thee do utter stuff as weddle, Shadden. Thee do one or two songs by *The Scarript.*'

'I doatunt want to be listodden to rebiddle songs on me wetton day. It's bad enough you habben them in the house alt the toyum.'

Her and Kennet then pop outside for a smoke – seriously, how long did they think they were going to keep Rihanna-Brogan off them? – leaving me and Ro sitting there.

He goes, 'Doatunt woody, Rosser – she'll cub arowunt to the idea.'

I'm there, 'They'd certainly make it a memorable reception. So how did you get that bruise on your neck?'

It's a hickey. Take it from someone who's had plenty.

At the exact same time we both go: 'Paintball.'

Well, *he* pronounces it, 'Payuntbalt.'

And I laugh. Because paintball was what I always told Sorcha when I had a hickey.

'A few of us went out to cedebrate fidishing eer exaddems,' he tries to go.

And I'm like, 'And you went paintballing? What exams were you celebrating, Ro – your focking Junior Cert?'

'Ine tedding the troot, Rosser.'

'What was her name?'

He goes silent for a good sixty seconds then.

I'm there, 'Ro, there's an old phrase I love that says you can't shit a shitter. I saw that Corrina in Clontorf Castle slapping you across the chops.'

Eventually, he goes, 'Her nayum's Dodder.'

I'm like, 'Dodder? Like the river?'

'No, Dodder!'

'Donna? Are you trying to say Donna?'

'Yeah. Dodda.'

'She must have some set of teeth on her. That's some mork she left on you.'

That's when he just blurts it out. He goes, 'I think Ine a sex addict, Rosser.'

I actually laugh.

He's there, 'Ine seerdious. I caddent stop thinking abourrut – morden, arthurnoon and neet. It's on me moyunt the entoyer toyum.'

I'm like, 'That's because you're nineteen, Ro. It's supposed to be. That doesn't make you a sex addict.'

'Ine about to maddy a beauriful geerdle –'

'You could definitely do worse.'

'– the mutter of me little priddencess. And Ine playin arowunt behoyunt her back. That's why Ine saying there's sumtin depinitely wrong wit me.'

'You can't go on like this, Ro. Paintball. Bras in the boot of your cor. It's only a matter of time before Shadden stops giving you the benefit of the doubt.'

'I neeyut to learden to conthrol it, Rosser. I neeyut to go somewhere – somewhere there's no good-looken boords.'

'Would you consider transferring to DCU?'

'Rosser, I neeyut your help. The bleaten giddult is kidden me, so it is.'

And as the band take the stage again, I realize what I have to do. It's my duty as his old man to stop him making the biggest mistake of his life. And I don't mean booking *26 Plus 6 Equals 1* for the wedding reception. I mean I have to stop him getting actually married.

Some dude on the radio says that the United Kingdom has voted to leave the European Union and that British Prime Minister David Cameron has resigned as a result.

I switch off the radio.

'The news is so focking boring,' Honor goes.

I'm there, 'I hate it. I'd actually ban it.'

We're back in the old minibus, by the way, just until I can get myself a new set of wheels. And we're on the M50 – we're talking me and Honor in the front, and the three boys in the back – on the way to the famous Santry, with the two-bor electric heater in the boot.

I'm there, 'Thanks again – for helping me with this.'

Honor goes, 'It's better than going to school.'

Yeah, no, I gave her the day off. Hey, it's Friday and her summer holidays stort in a week or two anyway.

Primary school is a waste of everyone's time, let's be honest.

I'm like, 'I was thinking, afterwards, we might hit town. Buy you something in BTs. Maybe take the boys to the Disney Store.'

Yeah, no, Johnny has gone mad into *Moana*, this Disney cortoon about some princess from, I don't know, Tonga, or Samoa, or one of those third-tier rugby countries. I wouldn't mind but he hasn't even seen it yet – it's not in the cinemas until Christmas, although the toys are already in the shops. They're not shy when it comes to picking your pocket, that Disney crowd.

Still, the way I see it is, at least it's not soccer.

The traffic, by the way, is bomper to literally bomper. Some dude in a silver Fiat Multipla drives for about half-a-mile in the hord shoulder, then storts indicating, looking to pull into the lane in front of me, but he can fock right off if he thinks that's happening.

I say it as well. Just in the cor. 'You can fock right off if you think you're getting in front of us.'

I keep inching forward every time there's a gap in front of me and the dude is spitting nails. He's trying to catch my eye, because he obviously wants to vent, except I'm pretending I can't see him. He winds down his window and tries to say something to me, but I make sure to keep staring straight ahead.

I've got, like, the back window open. And, out of the blue, Leo storts giving him dog's abuse. 'You can fock right off if you think you're getting in front of us!' he goes.

Me and Honor crack our holes laughing. I look to my left and the dude is just, like, stunned.

Brian's like, 'Where did you get your driving licence – in a focking raffle?'

Honor goes, 'Oh my God, that is *so* funny, boys!'

And I'm there, 'It is – it genuinely is,' even though, deep down, I'm also wondering what kind of kids can't grasp the basics of rugby but can pick up road rage in an instant.

After a few minutes, for no apparent reason, the traffic storts moving freely again. I put my foot down and lose the dude. Brian gives him the finger out the window as he becomes just a speck in my rearview mirror.

We pass exits for places like Palmerstown, Blanchardstown and The Naul and I suddenly feel like one of those explorers in the olden days, who feels like he might drop off the side of the Earth at any minute.

Honor goes, 'Can you bring me to the RDS tomorrow?'

I'm like, 'What's on at the RDS?'

'There's, like, a summit for fashion influencers. I want to meet Sincerely Jules.'

'Shit, that's the thing that's kicking off at the same time as Sorcha's, I don't know, *equality* thing?'

'So?'

'RTÉ are sending someone out to the gaff. She's invited all the politicians. Enda Kenny. Something Howlin. Gerry Adams –'

'And how does that affect us?'

'She said she wants us all to be there – observing it as a family.'

'It sounds to me like the girl wants it every way. She wants you to be her husband but only when it suits her.'

'That's a good observation, Honor. That's a very good piece of analysis.'

Safety First Santry ends up being this humungous warehouse of a place. The manager dude who comes out to meet us ends up giving us the company spiel. They provide a secure, discreet and non-judgemental service to private citizens who wish to secure their valued possessions in a state-of-the-ort, purpose-built vault for reasons they don't want to know.

Which sounds pretty much good enough to me. Honor asks him three or four questions, though, which he answers to her satisfaction, then she nods at me as if to say, This place will do.

We follow the dude down the corridor. He's got a ring of keys on his hip like a prison officer. I'm carrying the two-bor electric heater, while Honor is pushing the boys in their stroller.

The dude shows us into this, like, vault, then he checks out the size of the bag and points out a locker to me. He goes, 'What about 1333042759?'

I'm like, 'What do you think, Honor?'

'Yeah, that's fine.'

He finds the right key and he opens it. I put the heater in and the dude doesn't ask what's in it, even out of curiosity. He just slams the door shut and locks it.

Brian goes, 'Fock you, dickslop.'

Again, the dude doesn't even bat an eyelid. A non-judgemental service is right.

Ten minutes later, I've paid up and the dude has given me a printout of my box number and my password. It really is that simple. Five minutes after that, me and Honor have put the boys back in their cor seats and we're on the road again, then five minutes after that I'm taking the junction for town.

Since we're getting on so famously, I decide to bring up the delicate matter of what happened at Christian and Lauren's borbecue.

'Honor,' I go, 'can I ask you a question?'

She's like, 'It depends what it's about.'

She's nobody's fool, in fairness to her.

I'm there, 'Did you give alcohol to little Ross Junior?'

She doesn't answer one way or the other. She just goes, 'Are you accusing me?'

I'm like, 'No, I'm not accusing you.'

'Did *he* say I gave him alcohol?'

'No, he can't remember a thing about it. And I'm not surprised. He was the drunkest person there. And that's saying something given the way I was putting them away.'

'He fell on his face.'

'Yeah, no, I watched him.'

'Are you saying you didn't find that funny?'

'He's only seven years old, Honor. They had to pump him out at the hospital.'

'Why is it funny when Rihanna-Brogan smokes a cigarette but it's not funny when Ross Junior drinks half a bottle of wine?'

'I can't answer that, Honor. It's sometimes hord to put your finger on why one thing is funny and another thing *isn't* funny? But I wouldn't be any kind of father if I didn't ask you if you had anything to do with it.'

'I didn't pour it down his throat if that's what you're wondering.'

'Hey, I've asked you the question and you've answered it. Job done.'

'Instead of giving me a hord time, Lauren needs to be asking *herself* questions? As in, what the fock was she thinking, leaving all that alcohol lying around with children playing nearby – oh my God – totally unsupervised? Maybe she needs to examine her own failings as a parent.'

'The word hypocrite comes to mind.'

'*And* she was a wagon to you.'

'She *was* a wagon to me.'

'How focking dare she have a go at you in front of all those people just for buying her son a present?'

'Hang on. Honor, are you saying you did it to defend me?'

'You're the only one who ever sticks up for me.'

'That's because I think you're great.'

'Well, I was thinking, fock you, Lauren, that's my dad! And you're being a complete orsehole to him just because he's not bright enough to argue back!'

'That's a nice thing for me to hear, Honor. *He* hung me out to dry as well, can I just point out?'

'Little focking crybaby.'

'*I have thixty-theven dollth!*'

'All *I* did was suggest he see how much of it he could knock back.'

'He made his own choice. That's what it's beginning to sound like to me.'

'Isn't his dad an alcoholic?'

'Excellent point. He was certainly murder for the sauce for a while there. I was the one who actually got him off it.'

'So maybe the problem is genetic?'

'A lot of things are certainly storting to add up.'

'That might have occurred to Lauren if she wasn't so busy trying to humiliate my dad in front of, like, sixty people.'

'Hey, I'm sorry I ever doubted you, Honor. Okay, let's go hit the Disney Store!'

The second we reach the shop, the boys stort going literally ballistic. Inside, they can see Maui – or, more specifically, some dude walking around in a giant fat suit with a humungous fake head on top.

'Maui!' Johnny shouts. 'Maui! Maui! Maui!'

Johnny is the quiet, sensitive one.

Leo is the opposite. He's looking at Maui like he wants to kill him. He's going, 'Look at this focking shitbutler!'

I'm actually laughing as I let them out of the stroller and the three of them tear into the shop like animals released from a trap.

I do the whole responsible parent thing of waiting at the door to make sure they don't wander out onto Grafton Street. That's my responsibility. Whatever damage they do while they're in the shop is Disney's tough shit. And anyway, Honor can be trusted to look after them like she looks after us all.

I'm standing there for, like, thirty or forty seconds when all of a sudden some bird tips over to me and goes, 'Hi, how are you today?'

They're very *like* that in the Disney Store? They come up to you and they're all, 'Hey, who are you shopping for today?' and I sometimes end up having to go, 'Would you ever *bibbidi-bobbidi* back the fock off?'

But this time I don't say it because I can't help but notice that the woman is wearing a grass skirt and a boob tube – and she has *the* biggest venti lattes I have ever seen.

And I've seen plenty.

She goes, 'Who are you shopping for today?'

And I'm there, 'Well, I'm here with my daughter and my triplet sons.'

'Oh my God!' she goes. 'That is *so* cute.'

She sounds like she might be American.

I'm there, 'Yeah, no, thanks. That's them over there, kicking the shit out of whoever's in that Maui costume.'

She turns around and she has a look. They've surrounded him like feral dogs.

Johnny is hugging him from behind, Brian is biting his leg and Leo is just repeatedly booting him in the shins, going, 'You focking, focking prick!'

Honor looks at me across the shop as if to say, Is this funny?

See, kids just want to know where the boundaries are. I give her a thumbs-up and she smiles.

I hear Honor then tell Brian to try to get the focker down on the ground where they can do some proper damage to him. The woman goes, 'They've, er, certainly got a lot of energy.'

'Yeah, no, they're focking thugs,' I go. 'I only bring them in here because you're one of the few shops that doesn't chorge for breakages. I'm Ross, by the way?'

She's like, 'I'm Moana,' and then she laughs. 'Oh my God, I spend so much of my day in character that I've convinced myself that I *am* her!'

'Your name *isn't* Moana, I'm presuming?'

'No, it's Jaila.'

I'm trying to think who she looks like so that I can describe her. I suppose she looks like Moana, because that's who she's been made *up* to look like? She's got a wig of thick black hair and more fake tan than you'd see at a Loreto on the Green Past Pupils Networking Breakfast.

I'm there, 'It's nice to meet you, Jaila. You sound like you're from the States.'

'I am,' she goes. 'I'm from New York.'

'I love New York.'

'Well, I'm from Rochester. It's Upstate.'

'The Windy City!'

We hear this sudden crash. The boys have managed to bring Maui down, sending a display of *Stor Wors* toys crashing to the floor along with him. The dude is lying on his back, struggling to get up – except he *can't*? Because Leo is kicking him in the head, Brian is booting him in the nuts, and Johnny's teeth are clamped so tightly around his ankle that I think his jaw might have actually locked.

Jaila goes, 'Perhaps I should go and assist my colleague.'

I'm there, 'Ah, he'll be fine. They're only really attacking him out of fear. Tell me a bit about you. What are you doing in Ireland?'

'Well,' she goes, 'this job is only, like, part time. I'm actually studying in Trinity.'

I'm like, 'Do you mean Trinity College?'

'Er, yeah.'

'So brains *and* beauty. Do you mind me asking, do you have a boyfriend?'

She laughs. She goes, 'Oh! My God! I cannot believe you're hitting on me in my place of work!' although she doesn't sound like she's going to take it up with Human Resources.

I'm there, 'Hey, I'm single, in case that's what you're worried about. As in, I'm not actually *with* their mother anymore?'

'Oh,' she goes, seeming to genuinely mean it, 'that's too bad.'

'Hey, she's with another dude now. A geek. But we're still determined to be the best parents we can possibly be for the sake of our children. We don't want them to grow up damaged.'

I hear Honor shout, 'Pull his head off, Leo! Pull his focking head off!'

I turn around to Jaila and I go, 'So would you be interested in maybe going out some time?'

She goes, 'Out? Do you mean for, like, dinner?'

That's students for you. Always looking for a free feed.

She goes, 'Hey, have you heard about this amazing place in, like, Ranelagh – is that how you pronounce it? – and it serves, like, survival rations with a gourmet twist?'

'I have heard about it. It sounds absolutely disgusting. A sure sign that the economy is back.'

'I'd love to try it.'

'I'll ring up and see can I get us a table. Are you free tonight?'

'Absolutely!'

I ask her for her number and she storts rhyming off her digits to me.

And that's when I hear Honor go, 'Oh! My God!'

I look over to see that Leo has pulled the head off the poor focker in the Maui costume. And Oh! My God! is right. I can't actually speak. I can't even move. Not even to stop Brian jumping on his chest. Because I recognize the dude in the fat suit as well as I recognize my own face.

It's Christian.

I've found a box of Sorcha's old mix tapes amongst her junk. I pull one out just randomly and I look at the track listing. It's all *Leave Right Now* by Will Young and *The Closest Thing to Crazy* by Katie Melua and *Beautiful* by Christina Aguilera.

Yeah, no, her taste in music was always up her hole.

The cases, I notice, have all got, like, dates on the side – we're talking August 1998, we're talking September 2002, we're talking April 2005 – and that's when I suddenly realize that these are Sorcha's Splitting Up With Me tapes.

Jesus, there's, like, one here for every single time I broke her hort over the years. And there must be, like, seventy of the focking things.

I find her old tape-recorder – she always refused to use the phrase 'ghetto-blaster'. I plug it in and stick in a tape.

The song that comes on is *Save the Best for Last* by Vanessa Williams, which I suddenly remember is an alright song. I always liked that line, 'Sometimes the snow comes down in June, sometimes the sun goes round the moon,' although, now that I think about it, it actually sounds like total horseshit.

There's a knock on the door. Honor sticks her head around the door and goes, 'I've got something for you.'

I'm like, 'Come in,' which she does. She hands me a piece of paper. It ends up being a letter that she's typed up. I give it the old left to right.

It's like, '*In the event of my death or disappearance, please recover this item from a vault in Safety First Santry. Box number and password on the receipt attached. It is the two-bar electric heater that my mother, Fionnuala O'Carroll-Kelly, used to murder Ari Samuels by dropping it in his bath to give him a heart attack. She knows that this item is in my possession and she has made an attempt on my life, which I took seriously enough to keep this heater as insurance.*'

I'm there, 'This is amazing, Honor. Is bar not spelt with an o?'

She goes, 'No, it's spelt with an a.'

'I'll take your word for it. You're the one doing well at school.'

She's suddenly listening to the song – Vanessa Williams commenting on the sun, the moon and other matters she clearly knows fock-all about. She's like, 'Oh my God, *what* the fock are you listening to?'

I'm there, 'I found a box of your old dear's mix tapes. What are we going to do with this letter, by the way?'

'Well, first,' she goes, 'you need to sign it. Then you need to give it to someone for safekeeping.'

'Erika.'

'Good idea.'

'Do you want to maybe stick a P.S. on the end about how I want to leave my Rugby Tactics Book to Leo Cullen?'

She just gives me this, like, *withering* look, then she walks out of the room.

I decide to give Christian a quick ring, mainly to check is he okay. He answers pretty much straightaway. I'm there, 'Dude, I'm sorry again – about my kids kicking the shit out of you? You're not, like, hurt, are you?'

He goes, 'It's mostly bruises – and bite marks. I quit, by the way.'

'What? Why did you do that?'

'It's about the fifth time I've been attacked by children in the past week. There was something about the suit that frightened them. I couldn't take it anymore.'

'What are you going to do for bread?'

'Lauren's old man is going to give me a job.'

'Hennessy?'

'Yeah, serving writs.'

'Dude, that shit's dangerous.'

'It's not as dangerous as working in the Disney Store, believe me. By the way, I hear you've got a date for tonight.'

I'm there, 'Free agent, Christian. Sorcha's moved on – so why shouldn't I?'

'Jaila's nice.'

'Yeah, no, she's great. Actually, I probably should stort getting ready. I managed to get a reservation for that Linden Boulevard place. Someone cancelled.'

'The place that serves the survival rations? It sounds revolting.'

'There's more to a restaurant than whether or not the food tastes nice. I'm glad we haven't forgotten that. I'll talk to you soon.'

When I've hung up, I throw my eyes over the letter one last time. Then I grab a pen and right at the bottom I write: 'P.S. Please pass on my famous Rugby Tactics Book, which contains all my thoughts about the game, to Leo Cullen, c/o the RDS, Ballsbridge, Dublin.'

'I'm thinking of having the Antarctic Snow with Cherry Labello to start,' Jaila goes, 'followed by the Toothpaste on a Bed of Wattle Signalgrass.'

The menu is, like, *genuinely* hilarious? Next to every item, there's a little story about some dude who managed to stay alive for ten weeks lying face-down on a piece of driftwood in the Pacific, or some bird who spent five weeks wandering around the Sahara Desert and somehow still survived, or some dude who got his orm trapped under a rock during a landslide and somehow lived to tell the tale. And then it explains how each tale of heroism inspired the dish beside it.

I'm there, 'Yeah, no, I was looking at that Snow myself. Imagine having to chew your own hand off at the wrist – the poor focker.'

She looks fantastic, by the way, even if she looks fock-all like the girl I chatted up in the Disney Store. It turns out she was blonde under that black wig and she's about fifty shades of brown paler than when I last saw her. And obviously she's wearing more clothes. A grass skirt and a boob tube wouldn't be the thing to wear for a night out in Ranelagh, even in a restaurant that promises – what did it say on the website? – a 'relaxed, informal dining experience'?

The waitress arrives over. Jaila orders – like she said – the Snow, followed by the Toothpaste. And I'm like, 'Can I ask about the Protein Bor?' because it's literally the only thing on the menu I would even *consider* eating?

The waitress goes, 'The Protein Bor is actually for two people. It's, like, to share.'

'Oh, I see that now,' I go, looking at the little tale of woe beside it. '*Gonzala and Rosario Pinares –*'

'It's also a three-course thing.'

'*– were missing for three months in the Andes.*'

'We bring you a tiny bit of it for your starter, then a bigger piece for your main course, then what's left of it for your dessert.'

'You know what, I think I'll just go for the Snow as well, followed by – let me see – the Bonjela Three Ways.'

I close the menu and hand it back to her. Like I said, it's not like I'm even going to eat it.

Jaila goes, 'And can we get some water as well?'

'Stagnant or toilet?' the waitress goes.

We're both like, 'Stagnant.'

Then off she focks.

I'm there, 'People have obviously got more money than sense again. I suppose we should be happy about that as a nation.'

She goes, 'My friend said they used to do this, like, BYO thing, where they actually let you drink your own urine. Although I think they had to stop for, like, health reasons.'

113

I'm like, 'Do you know did they chorge a corkage fee for that?'

She laughs. 'Oh my God,' she goes, 'you are *so* funny.'

I'm there, 'Hey, sometimes lines just come to me and I say them out loud. That's how it works.'

Jaila makes most of the running in terms of the conversation:

'What do you do for a living?'

'Have you ever done anything for a living?'

'What was your major in college?'

'Is Sports Management an actual thing?'

'Seriously?'

'Are you a movie person or do you prefer, like, box sets?'

'What box sets have you seen recently?'

'Do you like reading?'

'What's the best book you've ever read?'

'Who's Brian O'Driscoll?'

'Are you a cat person or a dog person?'

'Can you cook?'

'What's your favourite thing to cook?'

'Do you have, like, a pet peeve?'

'Are you a coffee person or a tea person?'

'Are you a morning person or an evening person?'

'Do you have a man-crush?'

'Is that the same Brian O'Driscoll that you mentioned before?'

This goes on for, like, the best port of twenty minutes – being asked question after question. It's like I've gone to the chemist and asked for Solpadeine.

Our food eventually arrives. I don't bother eating my storter. I just play with it using my spoon until the snow melts, then, when Jaila goes for a slash, I tip it into a plant pot beside me. It's the same with the Bonjela Three Ways, which turns out to be Mouth Ointment, Teething Gel and Cold Sore Cream on a nest of Dock Leaves with Rainwater Jus. I wait until Jaila isn't looking, then I use my napkin to mop the entire plate clean, then I go, 'Wow!' just to make her think that I ate the focking thing.

Eventually, much to my relief, our plates are cleared away and the meal – so-called – is finally over. I'll tell you something, they might be serving up storvation rations, but they're not afraid to chorge. We're talking a hundred and twenty focking snots!

In honour of International Gender Equality Hour tomorrow, I decide to do the feminist thing and I let Jaila pay.

Hey, if she wants to eat snow and toothpaste, good luck to her. I'm not sticking my hand in my pocket for the privilege.

Then she suggests going back to her gaff for a drink.

She lives in an aportment on Pearse Street, which turns out to be actually nice. She's sharing with another American bird who's studying something or other and a Lithuanian bird who's studying – I don't know – something else.

She tastes of Colgate and the dry porridge oats with a spoonful of Bovril that she had for dessert. She's some kisser, it has to be said. Jesus, she could stick her head in your laundry basket and separate your whites from your colours with that tongue of hers.

Of course, I'm not going to reveal any more details than that. If people want filth, they can read one of my old dear's books.

All I will say is that it's not long before we're rolling around the parquet floor and she's taken off her top and her bra and I'm getting stuck into her nunga nungas with the excitement of a child attacking the drink refill station in Nando's. And that we end up finalizing the deal with her sitting on top of me, with her head thrown back, her jaw unhinged and her eyes spinning.

And sixty seconds after that, we're both fast asleep.

I wake up with a horrible feeling of something or other.

'What time is it?' I go, because I can't find my phone?

Jaila rolls over and checks hers on the nightstand. She's like, 'It's twenty past eleven,' and then she sort of, like, nuzzles into my neck. 'Last night was – oh my God – so amazing!'

'Thanks,' I go. 'Hang on, did you say twenty past seven?'

'No, I said twenty past eleven.'

'Oh, fock!' I go, throwing back the covers. 'Oh, fockety, fockety, fock, fock, fock!'

She's like, 'What? What's wrong?'

'It's International Gender Whatever the Fock? It's in, like, less than an hour.'

She's like, 'It's what?' obviously having never heard of it.

I stort picking my clothes up from the floor. 'Where the fock is my phone?' I go, because it's not in the pocket of my chinos when I pull them on.

She goes, 'What's this International Gender thing?'

I'm there, 'It's a thing my wife – sorry, my ex-wife – is organizing. RTÉ are possibly sending Samantha Libreri. Sorry, can you help me find my phone?'

'Hold on,' she goes. 'I'll call your number.'

Which is exactly what she does.

A few seconds later, I hear a voice go, 'Tommmy Booowwweee!!!' and I'm thinking, okay, either my phone is under the bed or Ryle Nugent is.

Jaila gets down on her hands and knees to look under there while I continue throwing on the old threads. She suddenly stands up and she's got my phone in her hand. Ryle is still going, 'Tommmy Booowwweee!!!'

I actually recorded him saying it one night in The Chophouse on Shelbourne Road. And let me tell you, he loved being asked. He's since done them for hundreds of people I know – including Tommy Bowe himself. He *could* chorge for it, but he doesn't. That's Ryle for you, as he often says himself as he's telling you to put your money away.

Anyway, everything is fine – I'm seconds away from getting out of here – until Jaila just happens to look at my screen. And that's when it all storts to fall aport.

'Who's Venti Lattes?' she goes.

I'm there, 'Sorry?'

'You have me in your cell phone as Venti Lattes.'

'Do I? That, em, seems definitely random alright.'

She's like, 'Is that a reference to my chest?'

And I make the mistake of going, 'Okay, cords on the table, yes, it is,' thinking the girl might take it as a compliment and hopefully move on.

But that's when, without any pre-warning, she focks my phone across the room at me. It hits me smack on the forehead and bounces onto the floor. I bend down to pick it up. In the time it takes me to stand up again, Jaila has crossed the floor and swung her hand at me, connecting with the left side of my head.

All of a sudden, all I can hear is the sound of ringing in my head. The last person to hit me in the ear like that was a borman in Flannerys in Limerick when I ordered a Jack Daniel's and Coke and asked for a swizzlestick.

Jaila storts going totally apeshit then, calling me every name under the sun. Then she picks up a chair and I'm thinking, okay, Rossmeister, it looks very much to me like this date is coming to an end.

I manage to slip out of the room just as the chair smashes against the door. I head down the stairs, still buttoning my shirt, then I tip outside onto Pearse Street.

I look at my phone. The screen is cracked and it's half-eleven. But then I spot a taxi passing and I stick my hand in the air New York style. He pulls up and I hop in. I tell him Killiney and then I go, 'Put your focking foot to the metal, will you? I have to be there by twelve o'clock.'

'Twelve o'clock today?' he goes.

He's one of those. Thinks he's Peter Kay.

He's like, 'There's no chance of that, my friend. The roads are at a standstill.'

I'm there, 'What?'

'There's some fashion thing on in the RDS.'

'Oh, shit.'

'Said on the traffic news they're expecting up to two hundred thousand people there today.'

That means Sorcha is going to be in an even *worse* mood?

I'm there, 'Just get me there as quick as you can – with the minimum focking chat out of you as well.'

The dude ends up being as good as his word. As in, we don't make it for twelve. I end up racing into the house at twenty-five past.

I meet Honor in the hallway.

She goes, 'You know you've got a big bruise on your forehead?'

I'm there, 'Yeah, no, long story. Just tell me, what kind of form is your old dear in?'

'Not good. No one's turned up. I told her to go fock herself in front of Samantha Libreri.'

'Samantha Libreri's here, is she?'

God, even *saying* 'Samantha Libreri' puts me in an instantly good mood.

Honor goes, 'No one is doing her stupid equality thing anyway. Everyone's at the RDS.'

I'm there, 'I know. I just passed through Ballsbridge. The traffic was focking murder.'

'When are *we* going? I want to meet Sincerely Jules.'

'Just let me show my face here first.'

Then into the living room I go.

Honor was right. There's no sign of my old man. No sign of that dude Whatever He's Called Kenny. No sign of Gerry Adams. The only people who are there are Sorcha, her old pair, Fionn and the boys, who've been dressed up in little dungarees and flat caps – a blatant attempt by Sorcha to make them look cute for the cameras.

'Look at this focking cocknugget!' Leo goes when he sees me.

Sorcha's old man takes one look at me and goes, 'Nice of you to show your face,' like a focking schoolteacher would.

I notice Fionn subtly smile.

I'm there, 'Sorry I'm late, Sorcha. The traffic in Ballsbridge was murder. Samantha, how the hell are you?'

Samantha smiles at me. There's always been a rapport there.

I sit down on the sofa next to Sorcha. I can feel the TV camera pointing at me, so I try to look like I'm thinking about the lack of gender equality in the world right now by tutting and shaking my head and rolling my eyes and sighing.

Sorcha goes, 'So where the hell have you been?'

That's how actually angry she is. She says it in front of everyone. I'm tempted to point out the obvious – that she doesn't *get* to ask me shit like that anymore? But before I get a chance to say anything,

Brian's there, 'Why don't you all fock off, you pack of focking spunkmonkeys!'

The cameraman looks at Sorcha and goes, 'Can you stop them swearing like that?'

But Sorcha's there, 'We've actually decided, as co-parents, not to create taboos around certain words in case it increases their *appeal*?'

'It's just we've been filming for more than half an hour and we haven't got anything we can broadcast.'

'Fock you,' Leo goes, 'you focking cockdwarf fock!'

But Sorcha can't get over the fact that I didn't come home last night. Again, she goes, 'I asked you a question, Ross – where were you last night? And why have you got a bump on your head?'

I'm there, 'That's none of your actual business.'

She goes, 'Excuse me?'

It'd probably make great TV if it wasn't for the fact that Brian and Leo have gone into effing and blinding overdrive and there's basically not two seconds of footage that wouldn't have to be bleeped out.

'Focking pack of focking shitfock pigs!' Brian is going.

And Leo's like, 'Fock every last one of your cockdwarf fockdogs.'

Sorcha goes, 'You were supposed to be back here for ten o'clock last night. I want to know where you slept last night?'

I'm there, 'If you must know, I was on a date.'

Let me tell you something – there is no worse feeling in the world than having Samantha Libreri looking at you in a disappointed way. It actually crushes me.

Sorcha's there, 'You were on a what?'

I'm like, 'Don't try to fool Samantha and the rest of the nation with your co-parenting bullshit.'

'Excuse me?'

'You don't get to be all judgy of me – considering you're the one who's possibly pregnant by your Porliamentary Secretary there.'

Every jaw in the room just drops.

I think it's fair to say that it's not the successful event that Sorcha hoped it would be.

She points at me and goes, 'How dare –' but she doesn't get to finish her sentence because the *electricity* suddenly goes off?

The cameraman turns to the sound dude and goes, 'We've lost power.'

I love my daughter. I love my daughter more than anyone or anything in the world.

Samantha's like, 'Okay, let's just write this off as a wasted morning.'

And I'm there, 'Er, if it's okay with you, Sorcha, I'm going to take Honor to the RDS.'

4. *This Speech by Sorcha Will Give You Goosebumps!*

Erika is putting stickers on paintings when we walk into the gallery.

She's definitely surprised to see us.

I go, 'Hey, Sis, how the hell are you? We were just passing.'

She looks . . . okay, I'm not even going to go there. Other than to say I can actually *see* her ninny pies through the fabric of her light cotton dress.

Honor holds up her Brown Thomas shopping bags to show her what an amazing father I am.

Erika goes, 'Er, wow – look at all the stuff your daddy bought for you!'

Honor's there, 'It came to two and a half grand!'

Erika looks at me. 'That's a lot of money,' she goes, 'to spend on a girl of ten.'

I'm just like, 'Thanks, Erika,' and I go to let the boys out of their stroller.

Erika's there, 'Oh, no, you don't, Ross. I don't want them running around the gallery. There's a lot of valuable –'

But I'm like, 'Hey, it's cool. They know how to behave themselves.'

'You dirty focking cockmonkey!' Leo goes, as he climbs out. 'Dirty focking cockmonkey fock!'

Honor's there, 'I'll look after them,' then off they go.

I turn around to Erika and I'm like, 'Actually, there *is* a reason I called in here this morning? You might call it an *arterior* motive?'

I produce the envelope.

She goes, 'What is that?' looking at it but not wanting to actually touch it.

I'm there, 'It's a receipt for the safety deposit box where I stashed the two-bor electric heater. And a letter to the Gords, explaining where they can find it. You'll see I've written on the front that it's only to be opened in the event of my death or disappearance.'

She goes, 'Ross, I don't want any part of this.'

'I also threw a line in to say that I want Leo Cullen to have my Rugby Tactics Book.'

'I think you're making a big mistake.'

'There are things in there that could help him, Erika.'

'I'm not talking about your stupid focking book. I'm talking about you blackmailing your mother. You know what she's capable of, Ross. She's already tried to kill you once.'

'That's why I need you to keep this letter safe. Seriously, Erika, my life could depend on it.'

'I don't want anything to do with it,' she goes. 'I don't want anything to do with *her* and I don't want anything to do with *him*.'

I have no choice than to put the letter back into my pocket while Erika goes back to stickering pictures and changes the subject. She goes, 'I heard you ruined Sorcha's International Gender Equality Hour.'

That's the nice thing about Erika. You can talk to her about anything, especially if it involves pain or humiliation for someone else.

I'm there, 'I wouldn't say I ruined it exactly. To be honest, I was more angry with myself for making Samantha Libreri think the worst of me.'

'It serves Sorcha right,' Erika goes. 'And I'm saying that as her best friend. She has a boyfriend when it suits her. But when RTÉ is sending the cameras around to the house, she wants her husband there playing happy families with her.'

'*She* said that just because our marriage is over doesn't mean we're not still a family.'

'And what about Fionn? Is he part of the family now as well? Sorry, I'm being a bitch.'

'Hey, keep it going. It's one of the things I've always loved about you. That and your, you know, chest.'

She suddenly stops stickering. She goes, 'I'm sorry, Ross, but what the fock are the two of them thinking?'

This is the first time since the news broke that Erika has

genuinely opened up like this. It's only just occurring to me that she must be nearly as pissed off about this pregnancy as *I* am? She was, like, engaged to Fionn – and she's one of those girls who expects her exes to remain single forever, then to die at the end of a lonely life, calling out her name with their final breath. And here's this – let's not forget – glasses-wearing geek, who she obviously had to lower herself to even be with in the first place, suddenly all loved up with her best friend, who's possibly pregnant by him.

That kind of shit is not good for Erika's brand.

I'm there, 'I forget how hord it must be for you as well.'

'It's not hord at all,' she goes. 'I didn't want Fionn. She's welcome to him.'

She's lying.

I'm there, 'Hey, the whole thing is focked up, Erika. You know she's got her twelve-week scan tomorrow and she wants me *and* Fionn to be there? I mean, talk about *awks* much?'

She goes, 'Do you want her back? It's a serious question.'

'It's irrelevant. She's with him now.'

'Say if it doesn't work out, though?'

I'm there, 'Hey, I'd give anything for things to be the way they were before,' meaning her at home bringing up the children and me, you know, carrying on behind her back. 'But I genuinely don't know how I'd cope if we got back together and the baby turned out not to be mine.'

She goes, 'Do you still love her?'

'I suppose. But then I found all these mix tapes in a box in the junk room.'

'Sorcha and her mix tapes.'

'She has one for every time I broke her hort over the years.'

'She used to make me listen to them every time we were in the cor together.'

'Vanessa Williams. Talking out of her hole.'

'I can't believe she actually kept them.'

'Anyway, I've been listening to them, thinking, would I have cheated on her as many times as I did over the years if I genuinely loved and respected her?'

'That's unusually self-aware for you.'

'And then I look at Ronan. He's supposed to be marrying Shadden, yet he's trying it on with every girl who makes eye contact with him these days. He's about to make exactly the same mistake I did.'

She doesn't comment on this either way. She goes, '*He* was on the radio this morning,' and from the way she says it, it's obvious she's talking about the old man.

I'm like, 'What was he banging on about?'

'He was telling Sean O'Rourke that the people of Britain have demonstrated the spirit of Churchill in resisting Germany's efforts to achieve in peacetime what they failed to achieve in two world wars.'

'Jesus. Do you have any idea what any of that means?'

'He said if he becomes the next Taoiseach, he's going to take Ireland out of the European Union.'

'That's, em, a bummer.'

A change suddenly comes over Erika's face. 'Give me that letter,' she goes.

I'm like, 'I thought you didn't want anything to do with it.'

'Just give me the letter. I'll keep it safe.'

I whip it out of my pocket and I hand it to her. She puts it into the drawer of her desk.

At that exact moment, Brian picks up a painting that was leaning against the wall, goes, 'You focking, focking dickbagel,' then he smashes Leo over the head with it. Leo's head goes straight through the actual canvas. It's like something from a funny movie.

Brian and Johnny burst out laughing. Me and Honor actually laugh as well. Erika not so much.

I'm there, 'We, er, better split.'

'That painting was on sale for five thousand euros,' she goes.

And I'm like, 'Another sign that the economy is definitely back!'

The sonographer looks like she could be Deepika Padukone's slightly less attractive older sister and I'm saying that as a compliment to the girl, even though I'm picking up on hostile vibes from her.

'Other than me,' she goes, 'there are only two people permitted in the room and that's the mother and the father of the baby.'

All me and Fionn can do of course is just stare at each other.

'I've got this,' I go. 'You can fock off home.'

And the woman turns around to him and she's like, 'I'm sorry – you and Sorcha can catch up later on,' obviously taking him for the gay bezzy mate. 'She'll have a photograph to show you and everything!'

I actually laugh.

It's Sorcha who ends up having to put the woman straight. She's like, 'This is my husband – but we're actually separated – and this is my current portner. One of them is the father of my baby, but at this stage, we don't know which.'

It seems to come as a definite shock to the woman if her *face* is anything to go by? She clearly hasn't been working in Holles Street long. You'd have to wonder is she cut out for it?

'Oh,' she goes. 'In that case, you'd both better stay.'

She closes the door behind her and switches off the light. She nods at the bed and goes, 'If you wouldn't mind taking off your shirt and hopping up on the bed there.'

She's talking to Sorcha. I think that goes without saying.

'So how have you been doing?' she goes, drawing the curtain around her and leaving me and Fionn on the other side.

Sorcha's there, 'I've had a bit of morning sickness. Plus I've been – oh my God – *so* tired in the last few weeks. Although that's possibly more to do with work than with my pregnancy.'

The woman's like, 'Do you have a stressful job?'

'Yes, I'm actually a senator.'

This is followed by a good thirty seconds of total and utter silence.

Eventually, Sorcha goes, 'It *is* actually a stressful job, you know?'

And the woman's like, 'Yes, I'm sure it is.'

'I'm just wondering why you pulled a face then, when I mentioned that I was a senator?'

'It's just I thought they'd abolished that place.'

'Well, they didn't.'

'Was there not a vote or something?'

'There was a referendum. And 51.7 per cent of the Irish people decided that the Upper House of the Oireachtas *was* of value and was worth actually keeping.'

The woman obviously couldn't be orsed arguing the toss because she pulls back the curtain and tells me and Fionn to make ourselves comfortable. There's only one seat. I'm the quickest to react and I manage to swing my orse onto it before Fionn has even properly seen it.

I laugh. I'm there, 'You were always slow from a standing stort.'

Sorcha is lying on the bed with her belly exposed. She's really storting to show now and it's the first proof any of us has that she isn't making the entire thing up.

'Okay,' the sonographer goes, nodding at the TV screen just in front of me, 'are you ready to see your baby for the very first time?'

I'm quietly congratulating myself on getting the best view in the house when, out of the corner of my eye, I notice that Sorcha and Fionn are holding hands and sort of, like, smiling at each other, looking all loved up. She wants it to be his baby – that much is obvious. They even exchange a little kiss.

'This might feel cold,' the woman goes.

And I'm thinking, it does, believe me. But it turns out she's talking about this, like, pink *gel* shit? She squeezes some onto Sorcha's belly, then she really storts rubbing it in.

Again, the gel.

'The purpose of the twelve-week scan,' she goes, 'is to determine whether your baby is healthy and growing as it should be. But, like I said, you will also get to see the baby for the first time and you'll be able to see that its organs, bones, limbs and muscles are all in place.'

'If it's Fionn's,' I go, 'it definitely won't have muscles. That question will probably be answered for us today, then.'

Fionn doesn't rise to it. It's very, very hord to provoke the focker. Unlike Sorcha, who is clearly still smorting from the sonographer's comments about the Seanad being basically a waste of everyone's time. She carries on trying to make a point, even as the sonographer picks up the little hand-held gadget and puts it down on her gel-smeared stomach.

'The other reason I'm tired,' she goes, 'is because I was organizing the International Gender Equality Hour. I was actually the main person *behind* it?'

The woman – I swear to fock – goes, 'The what?'

'Are you saying that you – as a woman – didn't do anything to mork the actual moment?'

'When was it?'

'It was last weekend. It was midday on Saturday.'

'That'll explain it, then. I was at that fashion thing in the RDS. My daughter is a big Sincerely Jules fan.'

Suddenly, up on the screen comes a black-and-white image of just this, like, blob. But the longer I stare at the blob, the more it storts to resemble something I actually recognize, something – I don't know – human. I can make out the head, then a leg, then an orm.

I feel my eyes fill up with suddenly tears.

I'm staring at it, thinking, does it look more like me or more like Fionn? Even though I know deep down that it doesn't look like either of us. But I'm thinking, yeah, no, the shape of the head is certainly the same as mine.

'The good news,' the sonographer goes, 'is that everything looks normal at this stage. I'm getting a good, healthy heartbeat. The limbs are forming nicely.'

Sorcha, by the way, isn't even *looking* at the screen? She's still banging on about last weekend's bullshit non-event, as if in denial about what's going on here. She's there, 'Are you *seriously* telling me that *you* – presumably an *educated* woman? – chose to go to a conference of fashion bloggers rather than observe an hour of silent reflection to highlight the struggles of women throughout the world for parity of esteem?'

You can see that Sorcha is highly offended.

'Like I said,' the woman goes, 'I didn't hear anything about it. Do you want to maybe look at the screen? That's your baby there.'

Sorcha looks at the screen, but she doesn't express an opinion one way or the other.

I turn my head and I steal a sideways look at Fionn. His eyes are just, like, fixed on the screen. And they're streaming with tears. And I can tell that he's thinking exactly the same thing as me. He's in love with that little shape on the screen and he wants that baby to be his every bit as much as I want it to be mine.

Honor says she wants to learn the Chorleston. This comes, like, totally out of the blue. And, like any responsible father, whenever my daughter expresses an interest in anything, I'm straightaway suspicious.

I'm like, 'Why, Honor? What's the angle here?'

She goes, 'There's no angle.'

'Why bother, then?'

'I just want to learn how to do it. It's, like, my favourite dance on *Strictly*.'

'Really? I thought you only watched *Strictly* to see someone fall during a lift and seriously injure themselves.'

'Yeah, that was at the beginning. Now I actually *like* it?'

'Random.'

'And anyway, Mom's always saying I should find an interest. She says I can't spend the entire summer trolling Niall Horan and Danny O'Donoghue on Twitter like I did last year.'

'Where are you going to learn this dance, Honor?'

'Dalkey Town Hall. There's classes on Thursday nights.'

'Hey, I don't mind dropping you off and collecting you.'

I swear to God, her face just – I don't know – collapses in on itself.

'I'm not looking for a lift,' she goes. 'I want you to be my dance portner.'

I actually laugh. I'm like, 'Me? I can't dance.'

'You can learn,' she goes, 'same as me.'

'Not a focking chance. I'll drop you off and I'll wait for you in – yeah, no – Finnegan's.'

'Daddy, please!'

'Could you not ask one of your friends, Honor?'

'I don't have any friends.'

'What?'

'Er, I *don't* have any friends.'

'I thought that was just a figure of speech. You must have one or two.'

'Okay, when is the last time you saw me go on a play date? When is the last time you even heard my phone ring?'

Jesus. I don't know is the answer to both of those questions.

She goes, 'I told you, Dad. Everyone hates me except you.'

In that moment, my hort breaks – I swear to fock – right down the middle.

'Okay,' I hear myself go, 'I'll learn the Chorleston with you.'

She's like, 'Really?'

'Really.'

She throws her orms around me and sort of, like, hugs my neck.

All of a sudden, I hear a cor outside in the driveway. I walk over to the window and I look out. It ends up being the old dear's Lexus.

'Honor,' I go, watching her get out of the cor, 'why don't you go and make us a couple of cappuccinos?'

She's there, 'The milk frother doesn't work.'

I turn away from the window.

'What,' I go, 'the one I bought off Rob Kearney?'

She's like, 'Yeah, it's never worked. That's why he wanted to get rid of it.'

'He told me it was because it didn't match the colour theme of his kitchen.'

'It was probably just out of warranty and you were the first sucker he ran into.'

'Focking Clongowes,' I go, shaking my head. 'And I'm saying that as someone who despises them and yet respects them enough to still look out for their results every time they play.'

There's a ring on the doorbell. 'Who's that?' Honor goes.

I'm there, 'Yeah, no, it's my old dear.'

'Is that why you were trying to get rid of me?'

'Look, it's for the best. The woman is dangerous.'

But she still follows me out to the front door.

'That's why I'm not leaving you alone with her,' she goes.

I feel genuinely sorry for anyone who can't see how sweet my daughter can sometimes be.

I'm there, 'Thanks, Honor.'

I open the front door. The old dear is standing there, looking like Meryl Streep being slowly poisoned. I'm like, 'What do you want, you gin-addled skeleton?'

She goes, 'Hello, Ross. Hello, Honor.'

Honor's there, 'Hi,' standing between us, making sure the old dear doesn't try anything.

I'm there, 'You heard me. What do you want?'

She goes, 'I have a peace offering for you.'

I'm like, 'What kind of peace offering are we talking?' and that's when I notice a second cor turn into the driveway from the Vico Road. It's a brand-new Audi A8 – we're talking black, we're talking 161D, we're talking even nicer than the one I wrote off.

The old man is behind the wheel. He storts tooting the horn when he sees us, driving around in circles.

Honor runs over to him, leaving me alone with the old dear. I don't think I'm in any immediate danger – I hope.

I'm there, 'What's this – a guilty offering?'

'For the last time,' she goes, 'I didn't do anything to your brakes.'

'Yeah, like you didn't kill Ari.'

'I didn't kill Ari!'

'Peace offering or not, I still want my five mills. That's unless you want me to ring the Feds and tell them where to find the murder weapon.'

'You'll get your money when my inheritance comes through. Then I want that item that you stole from me returned.'

'You mean the two-bor electric heater you used to murder a man?'

'I did nothing of the sort. It's just I can see how a barrister might try to twist it to his advantage.'

I look over her shoulder. Honor is sitting in the driver's seat of my new cor. The old man is showing her how the push button ignition works but her legs aren't thankfully long enough to reach the pedals.

The old dear goes, 'Where is it? Just as a matter of interest?'

I'm there, 'Somewhere you'll never find it.'

'You gave it to that sister of yours, didn't you?'

'I'm saying nothing.'

'Erika.'

'Like I said, it's somewhere you won't get your hands on it.'

She stares at me for a good twenty seconds. Then she goes, 'Anyway, I just wanted to drop your new car off before I left for the airport. I'm going to Moscow.'

I wouldn't give her the pleasure, of course.

'Moscow?' I go. 'I've never even heard of it.'

I have actually heard of it – I just don't know what country it's in.

She's like, 'It's in Russia,' as if reading my thoughts. 'I've been asked to give a speech at a human rights conference. In front of five thousand people, Ross!'

I'm there, 'Like I said, I've never even heard of the place. You could be making it up for all I know.'

The old man leaves Honor behind the wheel of the cor and walks over to us then. He goes, 'A brand-new set of wheels! What do you think, Kicker?'

And I'm there, 'You missed me saying thank you and if you think I'm going to say it again, you can fock off.'

'You told him about your trip to Moscow, did you, Dorling?'

'Yes, she told me. I found the whole story really, really boring.'

'The "Justice in Chains" conference organized by the Human Rights Advocacy Commission, if you don't mind! It seems like we've all got something to celebrate today!'

'What are *you* celebrating?'

'Of course, you won't have heard the news yet! Well, you remember that Hennessy and I submitted a tender to build and operate a private prison on Lambay Island for people who don't pay their water charges?'

He was elected to the Dáil on the strength of his *opposition* to water chorges – a fact he seems to have conveniently forgotten.

I'm there, 'Yeah, you're a total hypocrite – you know that?'

'I am happy to tell you,' he goes, 'that at ten o'clock this morning we received the news that we were successful in the process! The

Department of Justice and the Office of Public Works have chosen Hennessy and me to develop and run a prison colony on Lambay Island for the kind of people who don't want to pay for bloody well anything! You are looking at the first Governor of Aquatraz!'

I feel ridiculous.

Yeah, no, I'm standing in Dalkey Town Hall with Honor and a bunch of – I'm not lying to you – old-age pensioners, waiting for Mrs Leonard, our dance teacher, to show her face.

I'm like, 'Honor, what the fock are we doing here?'

She goes, 'What do you mean?'

'All these old people. Jesus Christ, it's like the focking cast of *The Best Exotic Marigold Hotel* in here. Could we not find a class with people our own age in it?'

'Mrs Leonard is the best Chorleston teacher in, like, the whole of Ireland.'

The woman eventually arrives. *She* ends up being old as well and not in a Judi Dench kind of way. She introduces herself to us, then she goes around the room, asking each of us to say who we are and why we're here. I stand there listening to all these tales of woe – 'I'm seven years widowed this Christmas and my daughter thought I should get out and meet people' or it's like, 'I'm a martyr to me nerves and the doctor said it might help with my anxiety' – until it's finally my turn and I go, 'Yeah, no, I'm Ross O'Carroll-Kelly. I can't dance for shit and I've basically been dragged here tonight against my will.'

No one seems impressed with my introduction.

Then it's Honor's turn and she's there, 'I'm Honor O'Carroll-Kelly and I'm the one who actually dragged him here.'

Everyone laughs. People always love Honor. At the very beginning.

She goes, 'The reason I dragged my dad here is because he's my best friend in the whole world and the only person who never, ever judges me, no matter what I do.'

Everyone goes, 'Aaawww!!!'

It's lovely alright. Of course, I feel like nearly going back and changing my own answer now, except it's too late.

'Okay,' Mrs Leonard goes, 'let's talk about this wonderful dance step we've all come here to learn. The Charleston is a popular dance because it allows for a range of variations and improvisations. In recent years, both the 1920s and Swinging Charleston styles have been popularized by television shows such as *Strictly* and *Dancing with the Stars*, which I'm sure you all watch!'

Of course they focking do. They're old people.

'Tonight,' she goes, fiddling with a portable CD player, 'I want to find out a little bit more about you as individuals, your sense of timing and rhythm and your range of movement. I'm going to put on some music and I want to see you all dance. Forget about the Charleston for now. I just want you to allow your body to respond to the music as it would if you heard it in a nightclub.'

It's a long time since any of this crew was in a nightclub.

She puts on the CD and it ends up being *Mambo No. 5*, a song that always reminds me of my glory days in Club 92, especially the line, 'A little bit of Erika by my side', although that was obviously before I found out she was a blood relative.

So we all stort dancing and I end up being surprised by the standard. It turns out a lot of these old people can definitely move. Mrs Leonard is walking among us going, 'Excellent! Good movement! Careful of your hip, Maggie!'

She's obviously very impressed with Honor because she goes, 'You've done ballet! I can tell!'

And Honor, grinning from ear to ear, goes, 'I *have* done ballet! *And* tap!'

And Mrs Leonard goes, 'I think you're going to be wonderful at the Charleston!' and Honor's face lights up.

Anyway, this continues for about twenty minutes. She plays various other songs, including *I Gotta Feeling* – wouldn't you focking know it? – by the Black Eyed Peas, then she eventually tells us all to sit down and take a break.

She goes, 'I just want one person to stay standing because I want to show you all something.'

I'm already thinking how proud I am of my daughter. But Mrs Leonard looks at me and goes, 'Ron – is that your name?'

I'm like, 'No, it's Ross. As in, Ross O'Carroll-Kelly?'

It breaks my focking hort – Dalkey used to be a rugby town, but it's sadly becoming more and more GAA. You often see Dublin flags flying on the main street. If that had happened ten years ago, they'd have burned Cuala to the ground.

She goes, 'I'm going to put this song on again and I want you to dance just as you've been dancing for the last twenty minutes or so.'

She sticks it on again: *I Gotta Feeling*.

So I stort doing what I would call my *thing*. And – I swear to fock – the woman storts criticizing me in front of my daughter. 'Okay,' she goes, 'what are you doing with your feet?'

I look down.

I'm there, 'Er, not much.'

'Not much is right,' she goes. 'You're barely moving them. You're just shuffling your weight from one to the other.'

'That's how I've always danced.'

'The only thing you're really moving is your shoulders. And you're moving them rather *too* much.'

I look over at Honor. I can tell she's embarrassed for me.

I'm like, 'Hey, no offence taken.'

'And what's happening with this hand?' Mrs Leonard goes. 'Why does it look like you're gripping a vertical hand rail?'

'That's the hand that'd usually be holding my pint.'

'Your pint?'

'Of Heineken. You said to dance like we were in a nightclub.'

'Do something else with that hand – definitely not that.'

I put it down by my side. A few seconds later – shit – it automatically pops up again. She pushes it back down and she goes, 'If I have to tie it down, I will! Now, what's happening with your face? What kind of mood are you trying to convey with that expression?'

'I suppose flirty.'

'Flirty?'

'I call it Blue Steel.'

'And the women go for that, do they?'

'They used to – back in the day.'

'Okay, stop!'

So I stop.

'Now,' she goes, turning to Honor and the OAPs, 'I asked Ron to demonstrate how he dances because it is the exact antithesis of the Charleston. Heavy-legged. Full of fear. Minimal movement below the level of the shoulders. And a complete absence of –'

'Heineken!' some old dude shouts – obviously fancies himself as a focking comedian.

Everyone laughs.

Mrs Leonard goes, 'I was going to say joy! But Heineken too, yes!'

I'm thinking, no focking way. I'm not going to be a figure of fun for a bunch of old people. They've got Francis Brennan for that.

'Okay,' Mrs Leonard goes, 'now we're going to learn the rudiments of the Charleston. I would suggest that anyone who needs to empty their bladder should do so now.'

There's a stampede for the jacks, of course.

Me and Honor are left just sitting there on our Tobler. I actually reach for my jacket. I'm about to tell her that I couldn't be focking bothered with this bullshit anymore – I said I'd give it a go and that's what I've done – but that's when she turns around, totally out of the blue, and goes, 'What was it like, Dad?'

I'm there, 'What was what like, Honor?'

'I know you went for the twelve-week ultrasound the other day.'

'Oh – em, it was fine, I suppose.'

'What did it look like?'

'It was, I don't know, small – hord to make out.'

'And what did you think? When you saw it? Were you excited?'

'We still don't know if it's mine yet, Honor. It's fifty-fifty.'

'Did it look like it might be a girl?'

I'm there, 'Like I said, it was very difficult to properly see any –' and then I suddenly stop. Because I cop it – why she wants me to do this Chorleston thing in the first place. She's, like, trying to make a connection with me.

I put my orm around her shoulder and I go, 'Honor, you really have nothing to worry about. I'm not going to love this kid more than I love you – because that would be impossible.'

She shrugs in, like, a sad way. She's there, 'I just thought if we had, like, a shared interest, then even if suddenly you're all about this baby, me and you would still have this.'

I'm actually on the point of tears. All the old folk stort to drift back from the jacks. Mrs Leonard's there, 'Now, are we all ready to learn the Chorleston?'

And I stand up and go, 'I was born ready!'

My old man still hasn't shown his face. Me, Ronan and Kennet are in Suited 'n' Booted in the Northside Shopping Centre in Coolock, getting fitted for our suits for the supposed wedding.

And – yeah, no – like I said, there's still no sign of him, even though he's supposed to be a groomsman.

The dude doing the actual measuring takes one look at my waist and goes, 'Thirty-four?'

And I'm like, 'Thirty-four? You cheeky focker – I'm a thirty-two?'

'T . . . T . . . T . . . T . . . T . . . Toorty-two,' Kennet goes. 'Ast me bleaten howult!'

Ronan laughs. The two of them.

I'm there, 'I'm a thirty-focking-two – end of conversation.'

The shop dude hands me the thirty-two trousers with a Scooby Dubious look on his face.

Me, Ro and Kennet disappear behind the curtain.

I'm there, 'Where the fock is *he*, by the way? As in my old man?'

I whip off my chinos.

'He's arthur thexten me,' Ronan goes. 'Says he's rudding a few midutes late.'

I'm there, 'Some focking groomsman he's turning out to be. Letting you down already and the wedding still five months away.'

The shop dude sticks a shirt through the flap in the curtains. 'Fourteen-and-a-half-inch neck,' he goes.

Ronan's like, 'Moostard,' and he takes it from him. 'Cheerlie'll be hee-or, Rosser. Your ma was gibbon some speech at some humid-den reets conference in Moscow and he's arthur been watching it loyuv on the webcam.'

I step into the trousers and I pull them up. Jesus Christ, they won't zip up. They're too focking tight. Of course, everyone has to make a big song and dance about it.

Kennet goes, 'What am I arthur t . . . t . . . t . . . t . . . teddon you. Toorty-two – says I, norra a bleaten ch . . . ch . . . chaddence!'

The shop dude looks at me bursting out of the things like Peter O'Mahony throwing on Simon Zebo's clothes for the crack.

'You might even need a thirty-six,' he tries to go.

I'm there, 'Your sizes obviously run small.'

I notice Ronan stort to unbutton his shirt, then he suddenly hesitates. He's like, 'Hee-or, Kennet, you woultn't moyunt popping outsoyut and seeing is Rosser's auld fedda on the way, would you? He dudn't know this peert of towun. He moyt be bleaten lost.'

Kennet goes, 'Yeah, norra botter,' then off he focks.

Ronan unbuttons his shirt, then takes it off and I can instantly see why he was so keen to get his future father-in-law out of the way.

His entire body is covered in scratches.

He must notice that I'm staring at him because he goes, 'It was a cat, Rosser.'

And I'm like, 'What cat? It must have been Scor out of the focking *Lion King*, was it?'

They're all over his front, all over his back.

I'm there, 'No wonder you wanted Kennet out of the way.'

He goes, 'I doatunt waddent anutter leckshotter,' as he throws on the dress shirt.

'I just don't want you to make the same mistake I did. I've realized it recently, Ro, listening to Sorcha's old mix tapes. I should have never got married. I wasn't mature enough.'

'How can you say sometin like that? If you hatn't of maddied Sudeka, there'd be no Hodor. There'd be no Brian, Johnny or Leo.'

'And I couldn't imagine a world without Honor. But she's the only decent thing to come out of my marriage – and obviously I have to throw in a mention for, like you said, the boys. But, Ro, I cheated on Sorcha literally hundreds of times. And I realize now – listening to the likes of Katie Melua and Will Young – that I hurt her so much. And now I'm getting my just desserts. I'm living under the same roof as her while she's riding one of my friends and she's quite possibly pregnant by him. If it turns out to be *his* baby, he'll probably want to move in. It's a focked-up situation. And Sorcha's right – I created it. You don't want that, Ro.'

'That's godda be the end of it, but. Ine not godda be doing the doorty addy mower.'

'Who was she? Am I allowed to ask?'

'It dudn't mathor. A boord off me roawut is alls you neeyut to know.'

'Does Shadden know her?'

He doesn't answer me.

I'm there, 'Is she a *friend* of Shadden's?'

He goes, 'She's one of her berroyut's mayuts.'

'Jesus Christ, Ro!'

'Ine arthur saying to you I doataunt want a leckshotter.'

'I'm saying I've *seen* her bridesmaids. They're horrific-looking. For fock's sake, Ro, if you're going to risk everything, at least make sure the girl is a looker.'

The shop dude sticks the thirty-six-inch trousers through the curtain. I put them on, even though I know they're going to be way too big for me.

They end up fitting me perfectly.

I'm there, 'What if Shadden finds out?'

He goes, 'She woatunt, Rosser. Lorrayunt woatunt say athin.'

'Lorrayunt. Jesus, Ro.'

'What's wrong with Lorrayunt?'

'These names. I don't want to come across as a snob. Anyway, another one-off, was she?'

'She's the last, Rosser.'

'I'm sure she is.'

'Ine arthur been talken to Nudger.'

Nudger is his mate – although it'd be more accurate to describe him as his kindly, petty-criminal neighbour who took Ronan under his wing when he was just a kid.

I'm there, 'What does Nudger have to say?' because he's always tried to keep him on the straight and narrow.

'He says I hab to learden to conthrol it,' he goes. 'Me sex thrive, he's talken about.'

'And how does he propose you do that?'

'Using meditayshidden.'

'Medi –?'

'– tayshidden. Nudger's a Buddhist, Rosser.'

I actually laugh.

'A Buddhist?' I go. 'Doesn't he have, like, fourteen convictions for assault or something?'

'He leardened it insoyut, so he did. He hasn't dudden a sthretch for yee-ors since he leardened the eert of self-conthrol.'

'And you think *you* can learn it?'

'Ine arthur downloaten a load of bleaten Tibetan manthras, Buddhist chaddents, all sorts. Thee woorked for Nudger. You remember what he used to be like, Rosser. Floy off the handoddle for addy bleaten reason. Throwing digs and all the rest. Not addy mower.'

I'm there, 'It's worth a try, I suppose.'

The old man finally decides to show his face. He sticks his ridiculous head through the curtain and goes, 'Sorry I'm late, chaps! I've just been on the radio, debating with young Varadkar about the advantages of Ireland leaving the European Union!'

Ronan goes, 'Doatunt woody, Cheerlie – you're gayum ball, so you are.'

Through the curtain he comes. He's got a rolled-up something – possibly a *map*? – tucked under his orm.

He goes, 'Kennet said he'll be back in a moment! He's outside having one of his world-famous cigarettes!'

I'm there, 'What's that under your orm? It looks like a map.'

'Not much gets past you!' he goes, blowing smoke up my orse. Most things get past me. 'That's precisely what it is! A map of Lambay Island!'

'Lambay Islunt?' Ronan goes.

'That's right, Ronan! Mister Hennessy Coghlan-O'Hara BL and my good self have had our tender accepted! We are going to build a prison!'

He hands Ronan the map.

'A priddon?' Ronan goes, unrolling it.

'That's right!' the old man goes. 'It's for people who refuse to pay for their water! Even though I'm against water rates – New Republic's position is clear on that!'

'Aquathraz,' Ronan goes, feasting his eyes on the thing. 'Ah, it's veddy exciting, Cheerlie, me owult flower.'

The old man's there, 'We're hoping to have the thing completed by the spring of next year! Then we can start filling it up with the likes of Paul Murphy and his ilk! People *Before* Profit? *Before* Profit, Kicker! The gall of these people!'

Ronan goes, 'Ah, no, no, no,' like he's spotted – I don't know – some *flaw* in the plans? It turns out that he has.

He goes, 'You doatunt wanth the windows of the cells to be vidible from the mayun land, Cheerlie.'

The old man's like, 'Really? Why not?'

'In case shams steert signaling – wit their keer headlights. Sending messages to feddas insoyut. Ine talking about Mowerse Coawut.'

'Good Lord, I never thought of that!'

'That's basic, Cheerlie. You'd wanth to turden the cell block arowunt a-hunthrit-and-eighthy degreeyuz so's the winthows face out into the sea. And you habn't enough geerd towers hee-or.'

'Not enough gord towers?'

'Not be a long sthretch. A priddon of this soyuz, you'd want seben or eight. One theer, one theer, one theer – and definitely one theer. Jaysus, that whole soyut of the island is veddy badly expowused, so it is.'

The old man looks at me with a big smile on his face – like he's watching, I don't know, a rabbit ironing or something.

'Ronan,' he goes, 'what are you doing for the summer?'

Ro's like, 'Nuttin, Cheerlie. Ine arthur fidishing me foorst yee-or exaddems, as you know.'

'Hennessy and I have been talking about hiring a security consultant! To advise us on how to make the prison secure to the point of being un-bloody-well-breakable! Well, who better for that job, Ronan – than you?'

Ronan's little sex addict face lights up. I can instantly tell what he's thinking. It's, like, the answer to all his problems. Somewhere there are no women. Somewhere he can do his chanting and his mantras. He's there, 'Cad I *lib* on the islunt, Cheerlie?'

The old man goes, 'Good Lord, I'm not sure it's absolutely necessary to *live* there, Ronan! No, there'll be boats bringing construction workers back and forth all day!'

'No,' he goes, 'if Ine godda do it, I'd wanth to stay theer evoddy neet.'

It's, like, ten o'clock in the morning and I'm trying to get the boys dressed for the day. We're supposedly heading for Dundrum to buy Honor a feather boa for our Chorleston class. I'm trying to pull Brian's little Leinster jersey over his head except he's having *none* of it?

'Me want that one!' he goes, pointing at his Manchester Soccer Club one, which Sorcha's old dear bought him for his birthday. She bought one for each of them, in fact. I keep focking them out but they keep rescuing them from the bin.

I'm there, 'We've already been through this. You can wear those things in the house. But no son of mine is going to Dundrum in a soccer jersey. Say if we ran into Drico coming out of the Bose shop like we did last time? It'd break his focking hort. And you supposedly named after him?'

'Fock you,' Brian goes, 'you focking shitpigeon fock!'

Leo, I noticed, has managed to take off his own Leinster jersey and he's trying to pull his Manchester Soccer Club one over his head, except it's on *backwards*?

I think it's fair to say they're not going to win any Young Scientist of the Year prizes, these three.

I'm like, 'Leo, I said no.'

Johnny, by the way, is wandering around the room, staring at the ceiling, going, '*La la la la la, la la la la la, la la la la la lala lala lala . . .*' which sounds very much to me like *Loving You* by Minnie Riperton, Track Three on Sorcha's September 2000 Breaking Up With Me mix tape.

'Focking wanker!' Brian goes, as I manage to get the Leinster jersey over his head, then I pull his orms through it and I pull it down over his little Ned Kelly. 'You focking wanking fock!'

In other words, it's another normal morning in the O'Carroll-Kelly house. That is until the moment Honor bursts into the room and goes, 'There's a feminist in the kitchen!'

I'm there, 'Just open the door, Honor, and it'll fly out again.'

'Okay, did you actually hear what I just said?'

'Er, not really, no. Your brother was calling me a focking wanking fock. You said there was something in the kitchen?'

'A feminist.'

'A feminist? Okay, how did one of those get in?'

'Er, my so-called *mother* let her in?'

'Jesus.'

'Dad, you need to do something. You should hear the way they're talking.'

'What way are they talking?'

'Just all – I don't know – *angry*.'

'Okay, you take over here – don't let them wear those Manchester soccer things. As a matter of fact, stick them in a black bag, will you? I'll weigh it down with rocks and fock it in the sea later on.'

I tip downstairs. Even from the hallway, I instantly realize what Honor was talking about. I hear a woman's voice go, 'I told this asshole straight out. I was like, "My friend happens to be non-binary girl adjacent – do you know how focking ignorant that comment is?"'

I hear Sorcha go, 'Oh my God, good for you!'

'Of course, he was all, "Hey, I'm sorry if I offended anyone." And I tweeted straight back. I was there, "*If* you offended anyone? That's a total non-apology. Don't you lay your heteronormative oppression on me, you neomasculinist asshole."'

I'd recognize that voice anywhere. I push the kitchen door. She's sitting next to Sorcha at the free-standing island.

'Croía Ní Chathasaigh!' I go.

A little bit of background might be called for here. Croía Ní Chathasaigh was a friend of Sorcha's in UCD. She was actually the hooker on the UCD women's rugby team, Vice-Captain of the Irish

Debating Team and auditor of the LGBT society. And while, deep down, she probably admired me as a rugby player, she was no fan of what I would call my overall act.

As a matter of fact, I would go so far as to say that Croía hated my basic guts and was very vocal in her opinion that Sorcha should dump my cheating orse and find someone who recognized what an amazing person she was. They actually stayed good friends right up until the day that me and Sorcha got married, then I neither saw her nor heard her name mentioned ever again.

I'm like, 'How's it going, Croía?' because I can't help being a people person. 'Are you still playing women's rugby?'

She doesn't answer me. She just goes, 'Speaking of neomasculinist assholes . . .'

I'm there, 'Hey, I was only making conversation – going through the phases.'

'I'm not playing *women's* rugby. I'm playing rugby.'

'With a bunch of other women, though?'

'I see you're still an essentialist asshole, then.'

This is how it always was between us. We're talking open, open hostility.

I always had a thing for her, though. I always said she looked like Zoë Ball if Zoë Ball didn't give a shit about her hair. But, unfortunately, she always had a thing for Sorcha.

I'm there, 'What the fock are you doing in my kitchen anyway?'

Sorcha opens up her laptop and goes, '*I* invited Croía around, Ross.'

'It's just you haven't heard from her since – whatever it was – two nights before the wedding, when she rang you and said you were making a massive, massive mistake by marrying me.'

And Croía goes, 'I'm sorry, was I wrong or something?'

Sorcha's obviously filled her in on our current relationship status.

'Croía and I reconnected on Twitter,' Sorcha goes. 'She retweeted all my posts about the International Gender Equality Hour. Then I read her feminist blog, which described it as "necessary". So I DM-ed her to say I'd love to hear her thoughts about why we failed to get people to engage with it?'

'The reason is simple,' Croía goes. 'It's because the male patriarchy was never going to allow it to succeed.'

Sorcha's like, 'And the fact that most women seemed to care more about some fashion bloggers summit.'

I think that sonographer really touched a nerve with her. I stort getting the breakfast ready for the boys.

'That's what I'm focking talking about,' Croía goes. 'A conference for women who've been duped into believing that they have to conform to traditional male notions of beauty. Males like Ross there.'

I put the porridge into the microwave. I'm there, 'What do you mean by males like me?'

'I mean misogynists,' she goes.

'Misogynists? What do they do again?'

'They hate women.'

'I don't hate women. I love women. I think I've proven that. We can talk numbers if you want.'

'You know, I'm going to bake a loaf of bread using my vaginal yeast, then every time a man says he actually loves women, I'm going to force it down his focking throat.'

'This is all good stuff,' Sorcha goes, tapping away at the keys. 'I mean that thing you were saying about women feeling they have to live up to men's expectations of how they should look.'

Croía goes, 'Stop typing for a minute, Sorcha. I want to say something. Can I be straight with you?'

Sorcha *does* stop typing? She goes, 'Oh my God, Croía, please do. You're someone whose opinion I – oh my God – always, always valued.'

'You have turned out to be a major focking disappointment to me.'

'*Excuse* me?'

'Not just me. A lot of girls in our class feel the same way.'

'In what way have I disappointed you?'

'We all looked up to you so much. We used to say, that girl can do anything she puts her mind to – she'll be Ireland's first woman Taoiseach if that's what she wants.'

'I suppose I went down the retail route for a while.'

'You opened a focking clothes shop.'

'*And* I was a success at it! Oh my God, Croía, I would have thought you of all people would have described that as empowering!'

'You ran and hid. You know, I used to pass the shop sometimes. I'd look in the window and see you, I don't know, putting a focking bikini on a dummy and I'd think, there she is – the great feminist leader we all talked about.'

'I also got married and had children, Croía.'

'Then one day, a few weeks ago, I saw that you'd been appointed to the Seanad. And I was talking to – do you remember Eithne Fennelly?'

'Oh my God, we nearly set up a Women's Rights in the Islamic World Society together, except we had a huge row over whether banning the burqa was an act of feminist liberation or yet another effort to restrict the rights of women to wear whatever they wanted, then she ended up getting glandular fever and missed so much college she had to repeat Second Year.'

'Well, I did a post-grad in Gender Studies with her – and I said to her on WhatsApp, "Hey, you'll never guess who's back!"'

'And it was me?' Sorcha goes.

Croía's like, 'Yeah, it was you. Well, it was someone who looked like you. I watched your maiden speech on Oireachtas TV and I couldn't believe what I was hearing.'

'They've found single-use coffee cups inside the digestive systems of baby polar bears, Croía.'

'Fucking coffee cups. I mean, you told me what Muirgheal Massey said to you. Hey, Muirgheal is just your typical gender-normative Basic Bitch. But she was right. That shit is so far beneath you.'

The microwave pings. The porridge is ready.

'Well, I also tried to do something for gender equality,' Sorcha goes, 'and no one was interested.'

Croía's like, 'That's because you're not properly woke.'

'I would have considered myself *reasonably* woke?'

'You didn't even sell it like you believed in it. You just declared it a day – like Arthur's Day, or National Fish and Chips Day, or Pride – and hoped everyone would just go along with it.'

'What else could I have done?'

'First, you've got to reorient people's political compasses. Remind women that they are living in a patriarchal society that is set up for the benefit of men, most of them white assholes.'

'And how do I do that? Are you talking about maybe storting a blog like yours?'

'You don't need a blog. You have an even bigger platform. I'm talking about using your position as a member of the *Seanad* to point out certain uncomfortable truths about the imbalance between the sexes in Ireland. For instance, Sorcha, have you ever noticed that the Irish word for women is an anagram of "man"?'

I ask the obvious question. I'm there, 'What's an anagram?'

But I end up just being ignored.

'Oh! My God!' Sorcha goes. 'I've never thought about that before.'

I stort spooning the porridge into bowls.

'And doesn't it bother you,' Croía goes, 'that there are basically *no* major streets in Dublin City Centre named after women?'

Sorcha's there, 'Oh my God, I hadn't thought about that either. But, now that you say it, yes, it does actually bother me.'

'There's a Pearse Street and a Connolly Street. Er, where's Marki-evicz Street?'

'Oh my God, it actually *really* bothers me?'

'These are the kind of issues that you have to remind women about to engage them. *Then* you can ask them to set aside an hour to consider the lack of gender equality in the world.'

The doorbell rings. Sorcha doesn't stir and I take the hint that she wants *me* to answer it? I'm suddenly remembering the influence that Croía always had over her. If she spent even an hour in the girl's company, she was definitely less inclined to put up with my bullshit.

Out I go.

It ends up being focking Fionn.

I go, 'Yes?' treating him like some random caller offering to power-hose the cobblelock.

He goes, 'Stop being an idiot, Ross.'

'What is this, a booty call?'

'I want to talk to Sorcha.'

'Yeah, this is my home, Fionn. It's where my children happen to live. If you want to have an affair with my still legally wife, you can conduct it elsewhere.'

He just pushes past me into the gaff. I follow him down the hallway to the kitchen. I try to trip him once or twice by kicking his feet together.

'Sorcha,' Fionn goes, 'I've got some news –' and then he stops and he's like, 'Oh, hello,' and it's pretty obvious that he's never met Croía Ní Chathasaigh before.

She fixes him with a look that suggests she doesn't think much of him, then she goes, 'Okay, let me guess – the boyfriend?'

Sorcha's like, 'Yeah, sorry, Croía, this is Fionn. He's also, like, my Porliamentary Secretary?'

'Yeah, just what we focking need,' Croía goes. 'Another cisgender white male to help us fight for the cause of women's rights!'

No one knows what to say, especially Fionn, who seems in genuine shock.

Sorcha goes, 'Er, Fionn, what is it you wanted to tell me?'

He's there, 'Yeah, I don't know if you got my text earlier but Simon Coveney said he was really moved by your speech in the Senate and that he's planning to recycle a jam jar for use as a coffee cup.'

Before Sorcha can even open her mouth, Croía goes, 'Is it just me or has it suddenly become very Let's Compare Focking Penis Sizes in this room?'

I laugh. I love seeing Fionn put under pressure.

Sorcha goes, 'Croía thinks I should drop the whole reusable coffee cup thing, Fionn, and concentrate solely on feminist issues.'

He tries to go, 'You're going to need something more than feminism if you're going to engage with the voters of Dublin Bay South.'

Croía doesn't even look at him. She goes, 'Sorcha, I have a dream.'

And Sorcha's there, 'I'd definitely love to hear it, Croía.'

'I dream of a world in which women are not only equal to men – they're better in every conceivable way. I dream of a world in which women aren't the oppressed – they're the actual oppressors, giving men some well-deserved, karmic payback for the way they've treated women for centuries. I dream of a world in which men are acknowledged as the weaker sex – physically, intellectually and emotionally. I dream of a world in which the CEOs of all of the world's major companies and all of the heads of state of the world's leading countries are women. I dream of a world in which it's men who are frightened to walk the streets alone at night. I dream of a world in which it's men who earn less money, own less of the world's land and wealth, and are forced into unfulfilling roles involving domestic jobs such as the raising of children.'

'Oh my God,' Sorcha goes, 'I think I'm going to cry. Croía, I would like to hire you as my special adviser.'

Fionn's there, 'Er, do I not get a say in this?'

Croía'a like, 'Sorry, Sorcha, I feel like I'm trapped in a focking Matrix of Male Domination here. I can't be around this many men.'

Sorcha goes, 'Er, okay, let's go up to the living room to talk some more. Fionn, could you bring us two cappuccinos?'

It's hilarious listening to him being spoken to like a *proper* secretary? Croía and Sorcha fock off out of the room and I watch him – still in shock – faff about with the Aeroccino for about ten minutes without bothering to tell him that it's focked.

He's the supposed genius.

Eventually, he goes, 'What's wrong with this thing?'

And I'm there, 'Clongowes is what's wrong with it.'

'I don't know what that even means.'

'It means the next time I see Rob Kearney, *he's* the one who's going to be in a focking headlock. Although five minutes later – if past performance is anything to go by – I'll be sharing some kind of charcuterie platter with the focker and telling him my ten favourite moments from his career in reverse order – even doing a little Ryanair trumpet blast before I reveal my Number One. Sometimes I envy people who don't love rugby. Although I know that's crazy talk.'

There's, like, silence between us then. And I don't know why – maybe I feel sorry for him – but I end up going, 'I saw your face. That day at the hospital.'

He smiles at me and goes, 'And I saw yours.'

'There's no feeling in the world like it, is there? Seeing it for the first time. I had it with Honor, of course. And the boys.'

'I know it's stupid, but when I was looking at that tiny little thing on the screen, I was wondering did it look like me or did it look like you?'

'That *is* a bit thick alright. I'm surprised at you.'

I walk over to the kitchen door and I shout upstairs to the boys that their breakfast is ready.

Fionn's there, 'No offence, Ross, but I really hope it's my baby.'

'I do too,' I go. 'Hope it's *my* baby, I mean?'

Honor tells me that I'm definitely improving, although I'm sure she's only saying it to make sure I come back again. 'My pint hand keeps popping up,' I go. 'It's, like, an *automatic* thing?'

We're in the cor, driving home from our dance class.

She's there, 'We could, like, incorporate it into our routine.'

I'm like, 'What do you mean by that, Honor?'

'As in, it could be, like, your *thing*? Ross O'Carroll-Kelly performs the Chorleston while holding a full pint of Heineken – and he doesn't spill any of it!'

I laugh. I'm there, 'I could definitely manage that. Bear in mind, I've fallen on my face while holding a pint of the Wonder Stuff and managed not to lose a drop. Mary in Kielys often tells the story.'

I pull up in front of the gaff and I kill the engine.

She storts smoothing out her feather boa across her legs. She goes, 'You're not thinking of giving it up, are you?'

I'm there, 'Of course I'm not thinking of giving it up!'

I am thinking of giving it up. Even though I know it'll break her hort. One or two more classes, I reckon, then I'll make some shit up about an old rugby injury coming back to haunt me.

If in doubt, blame Jerry Flannery.

'Because you'll get better,' she goes. 'Oh my God, do you want to watch Sophie Ellis-Bextor and Brendan Cole do the Chorleston on *Strictly*? It's one of my favourite dances – oh my God – *ever*?'

I'm like, 'Er, yeah, no, you go and set that up on the laptop and I'll definitely have a look at it.'

She hops out of the cor and skips into the house. I'm just open-ing the door on my side when my *phone* all of a sudden rings? At first I think it might be Ronan – yeah, no, he moved to Lambay Island this morning and it's his first night sleeping alone in the portacabin that will be his home for the summer.

I don't recognize the number, though. It's like Eben Etzebeth – long and foreign-looking. I end up answering it anyway.

I'm there, 'Hello?'

There's a woman's voice on the other end. She goes, 'Hey, ish that Rosh?'

I actually laugh.

'Okay,' I go, 'I know it's *one* of the Seoiges – but which one? Here, give me a few bors of *Wagon Wheel*.'

The woman goes, 'No, Rosh, thish ish Hedvig – the mother of Magnush, yesh?'

Again, I laugh, because I suddenly recognize her voice and I'm remembering the last time we met – her grabbing my orse like she was testing an avocado for ripeness.

I'm there, 'How the hell are you? How's the trip around Ireland going?'

She goes, 'Well, we are beck in Dublin now.'

'What did I tell you? There's really fock-all worth seeing beyond the Loughlinstown roundabout.'

'No, thish ish not sho. We drove the entire Wild Atlantic Way – we shaw many, many amashing thingsh.'

'We'll have to agree to differ.'

'And now we are beck in Dublin – for jusht one more week. We are shtaying in an Airbnb housh in Monkshtown.'

'See, Monkstown – that's what I consider the *real* Ireland?'

Suddenly, she storts talking in this, like, flirty voice. 'And sho now,' she goes, 'there ish shomeshing thet I wish to shay to you.'

I'm there, 'Hey, *shay* away, Hedvig.'

'Sho when we are driving, I am thinking about you, yesh?'

'Okay.'

'I am especially thinking about what you shay to me – I am total shmoke show.'

150

'I stand by it. For your age.'

'And I heff to shay to you, I find thish very – how to shay? – flattering, yesh?'

'Hey, you grabbed my orse.'

'Thet ish my way of shaying to you that I think you are alsho total shmoke show – yesh?'

'Hey, I'm not looking for an apology.'

'That ish gute becaush I am not shaying shorry. Ash a matter of fact, I am wondering if you would like to come to the housh thish evening?'

You can probably imagine me. I'm smiling like it's the first day of the Six Nations Championship.

I'm there, 'You want me to go there? To the house?'

She's like, 'Yesh.'

'Okay, I'm trying to think of a delicate way to put this. Are you inviting me over for, like, definite sex?'

'Definite shecks?'

'As in, I'm not interested in spending the night looking at slides of your focking holiday – all the amazing things you supposedly saw. Cross-eyed children driving their drunken parents home from the pub on a tractor. Shit like that. I want to know if you're talking about us having guaranteed sex?'

'Yesh, I'm talking about ush heffing guaranteed shecks.'

I slam the door of the cor and I stort the engine. 'I can't believe I'm asking this,' I go, 'but what about your husband?'

She's there, 'My hushband ish cool with thish.'

'Seriously?'

'Yesh, we are very – how to shay? – open-minded. Kristoffer ish heppy wish whatever makesh me heppy, yesh?'

'I wish there were more husbands in the world like him. I genuinely do. What's the address?'

She gives it to me and I tell her I'll be there in fifteen minutes. Or ten if I break the speed limit, which I'm suspecting I probably will.

I stick the cor into reverse and that's when I notice Honor standing on the doorstep, holding her laptop. I open the window.

She's like, 'Where are you going?'

I'm there, 'I, er, have to go somewhere.'

'I thought we were going to watch Sophie Ellis-Bextor do the Chorleston? And then I was going to show you Georgia May Foote.'

I look at her little face and I decide that I can't let her down. Then I think about it for a few seconds longer and I decide, fock it, I can.

I'm there, 'I'll only be an hour or so,' including the commute.

I turn the cor around, point it in the direction of Monkstown, then off I go.

The gaff is on Trafalgar Lane – we're talking *proper* Monkstown here? Hedvig opens the door and the first thing I notice is that she's still in her civvies. To be honest, I *was* expecting, I don't know, a negligee or something.

She just goes, 'Oh, hello there,' like I'm there to collect the focking census form.

I'm like, 'Okay, I'm beginning to wonder whether something might have been lost in translation here. We are definitely, *definitely* going to do this? And by *this*, I mean –'

She grabs the front of my Leinster jersey and pulls me into the house. I suppose that answers my question.

She storts leading me down the hallway towards the kitchen.

'Would you like to heff a dreenk?' she goes. 'There is shome vodka and alsho I think there ish shome cansh of Budweisher in the refrigerator.'

I don't even dignify that with a response – other than to grab her around the waist from behind and go, 'I wouldn't drink that focking piss if I was dying of thirst!' as I spin her around.

I stare into her eyes, then I throw the lips on her.

She lets out a little squeal of delight. I'm a genuinely good kisser. She holds up her end, in fairness to the woman. She puts her hands on my chest and pushes me backwards against the wall – sucking on my lips like it's her mission to drink all the colour from my face. I slip my two hands up the back of her Scandi-noir-style knitted sweater and I manage to unfasten her bra with an efficiency she definitely appreciates.

And there I'm going to leave the story in terms of details of who did what to who and for how long because my reputation as a gentleman means way too much for me to go revealing secrets for anyone else's cheap thrills.

All I will say is that, after helping her out of her jumper and jeans, I end up throwing her over my shoulder and carrying her in a fireman's lift up one flight of stairs to a sort of mezzanine level, where I feel a slight tweak in my lower back from an old Facet Syndrome injury I picked up against Gonzaga back in the day, and I lay her down on this, like, upholstered, faux-antique lovers' chair, where we remove the rest of our clothes while I'm waiting for the twinge to pass. Then I carry her up the remaining stairs to the bedroom.

She's going, 'Not sho fasht, Rosh. We heff all night.'

Anyway, after a few minutes of back and forth – and some very choice language out of her mouth for a woman of her age – I suddenly hear the front door slam, then the sound of footsteps on the stairs.

I'm like, 'Shit!'

I stand up.

She goes, 'What ish wrong?'

I'm there, 'Er, your husband's coming up the stairs,' and I'm suddenly as limp as an empty verruca sock.

My inner GPS takes me over to the window and I look out, trying to estimate the drop to the ground.

She laughs. She goes, 'What, now you are all of a shudden shy?'

I'm like, 'Shy?'

The bedroom door opens and there's Kristoffer, removing his shirt. He goes, 'Hey, thatsh not fair – you cannot shtart without me!'

I'm like, 'Hang on, what the fock are *you* doing here? What's going on?'

'Thish ish Kristoffer?' Hedvig goes. 'He ish my hushband!' and she says it in, like, a *defensive* way?

I'm there, 'I know he's your husband. I thought it was just going to be me and . . . Jesus Christ!'

I step past the two of them onto the landing, then down the stairs, gathering up my clothes as I go. They follow me, Kristoffer with his shirt off and Hedvig in the total raw.

He storts going, 'When my wife ashked you to come here tonight, what did you think?'

I'm there, 'I thought the obvious. I thought I was in. With her. I didn't know you were focking . . . swingers.'

He goes, 'But you shay to ush you heff an open marriage.'

'Meaning it's open to certain things – specifically, me being with other women. I didn't say I was open to that carry-on.'

Hedvig goes, 'I'm shorry, Ross. When I phone you tonight, I shay to you to come for shecks and you shay to me, "What about your hushband?"'

'I meant was he going to be out of the house?'

'Thish you did not make clear.'

'So, what, you automatically assumed I wanted to –? Jesus Christ!'

'You shaid you wished there were more hushbands out there like Kristoffer.'

'I didn't mean it in that way!'

Kristoffer goes, 'Shtay for a drink, Rosh. I think there are shome Budweishers in the fridge. Perhapsh in a little while you will feel differently.'

I'm there, 'Hey, I'm not into either of those things,' not knowing which I'm more insulted about. 'Even if you said Heineken, I don't think I'd –'

And that's when there's a ring on the door. Kristoffer – bare-chested and with no shame whatsoever – goes to answer it.

I'm like, 'What the fock do you think you're doing? That could be anyone.'

But he opens the door anyway and I'm suddenly hearing Magnus's voice, going, 'Hey, Dad, we thought we'd shurprishe you!'

But it's not Kristoffer and Hedvig who are about to get a surprise.

Then in they walk, we're talking Magnus, followed by – oh, holy focking shit! – Oisinn. You can see the confusion on both their faces as they watch me pull my Leinster jersey over my head.

Oisinn actually laughs. He's like, 'Ross, what are *you* doing here?'

And Magnus must know about his old pair and their – let's just say – *tendencies*, because he goes, 'Aha! Rosh, I did not know you like thish type of thing!'

I'm there, 'I don't! I don't like it! It was crossed wires, that's all!'

Hedvig goes, 'He thought I wanted to have shecks with jusht him!' and she says it like that somehow makes *me* the deviant? 'Then when your father walked in, Rosh wanted to jump out the window!'

Oisinn cracks his hole laughing. 'Okay,' he goes, 'I'm going to need a minute or two to process this.'

I head for the door, turning back only to give him a serious filthy. I'm there, 'Dude, this *never* focking happened, okay?'

Another speech?

Sorcha is on the phone to Fionn and that's exactly what she says.

'Yes,' she goes, at the same time picking up her Saint Laurent tote, 'I'm going to make another speech. In about an hour's time.'

That's two in the space of a month. It does seem a little bit 'look at me' – although I'm smort enough *not* to point that out?

Unlike Fionn obviously.

'You're asking me what it's about?' Sorcha goes, sounding like her 'tude towards him has definitely changed. 'It's about toxic masculinity, Fionn, and the role that straight white men have played in creating a world that despises women.'

And, of course, my first reaction is, oh my God, I can't miss this.

No sooner is Sorcha out the door than I'm straight up the stairs to wake Honor and the boys. I'm going, 'Come on, get dressed – we're heading into town.'

'Fock you,' Brian goes, 'you focking pissmidget fock.'

I'm like, 'Yeah, whatever,' throwing the covers off him. 'Come on, let's get you dressed.'

Honor suddenly appears at the door. She's like, 'What's going on?'

I'm there, 'We're heading into town. Your old dear's about to make a speech.'

She goes, 'Another one?'

'I know, it's insane. But I heard her giving Fionn a hord time on the phone and I just know it's something I have to hear. Help me get these three dressed, will you?'

Brian goes, 'You focking, focking pissmidget fockbag fock.'

Literally one hour later, we're running down Kildare Street, me pushing the stroller in front of me and Honor chasing after me, going, 'What's this speech even about?'

I'm there, 'I don't know. Toksvig vascularity. Something like that.'

'Toksvig? Is she talking about *Sandi* Toksvig?'

'Possibly. I'm just as much in the dork as you are, Honor. I just heard her mention that people like Fionn have created a world that despises women and I thought, okay, this is something I definitely need to hear.'

Into the building we go. I flash my old Blockbuster Video cord at the dude on security and he just nods as we fly past him. The chamber – again – ends up being basically empty. Fionn and Croía are sitting in the public gallery and they both turn around when we bundle our way in. Croía actually rolls her eyes and goes, 'Okay, I'm suddenly suffocating on the testosterone in here.'

Poor Fionn *already* looks beaten down by her?

Sorcha is just getting to her feet as I'm sitting down. She definitely doesn't seem as nervous as the last time – as in, the pages in her hand aren't shaking and her voice is clear and confident.

She's like, 'Today, I want to discuss an issue that I believe is the most serious issue facing the planet today –'

'People who put ordinary rubbish in the green bin,' I go.

'I'm talking about institutionalized gender inequality.'

'*She's* changed her tune,' I go.

Croía turns around and shushes me.

Sorcha goes, 'It is sadly everywhere. Whether we like it or not, we live in a world that is anti-women. We live in a world where casual misogyny is the norm. We live in a world where to be a woman is to be a second-class citizen, a status that is reinforced every day in everything from the gender pay gap to our healthcare policy to the language used by men when they talk about women.'

'Shut your focking mouth,' Leo suddenly shouts, 'you stupid focking cow!'

Croía – I swear to God – turns around and says to him in the most vicious way, 'You shut *your* focking mouth, you evil little instrument of the patriarchy!'

Leo shits himself. And I mean that quite literally. I hear him squeeze out a fort – and, from the sound of it, and the subsequent smell, it's obvious there was follow-through.

It does the trick, though. There isn't a peep out of any of the boys after that. Never mind speechwriting, we should hire this woman as a nanny. She's like a permanently pissed-off Mary Poppins.

Sorcha goes, 'Men will never know what it feels like to live in a culture that demeans and dehumanizes them in such a way. To live in a world where prejudice is normalized. For thousands of years, straight white men have existed in safe spaces where the subordination, objectification and belittling of women is the norm. We see it everywhere and at all times. It's in the harassment that women face every day of their lives by the most privileged group in society. It's even enshrined in our national language. Does it not strike anyone else as odd that the Irish word for women – *mná* – is an anagram of man?'

Mná. That's so random. Although I wouldn't know if that was true, not having a word of the language myself. Sometimes, when I'm at an ATM and I'm asked if I want to do the transaction in English or Irish, I'll occasionally choose Irish in a fit of – I don't know – patriotism. And I always end up regretting it. The last time I did it, I somehow managed to change my pin number and apply for a small business loan for an agricultural project in Wexford.

'I have decided to dedicate my time in this house to calling out misogyny wherever I see it,' she goes. 'To ask, for instance, why are there virtually no streets in this city named after women? Why have none of the many, many women who have made such a vital contribution to this state been honoured by having a street named after them? It can only be down to chauvinism and toxic masculinity.'

Oh, shit – the cleaning woman suddenly walks in, carrying the Hoover. She plugs it in.

Sorcha turns around to her and goes, 'If you switch that thing on – God help me – I will break your focking fingers!'

Croía goes, 'Well said, Senator! She's just another willing dupe for the hypermasculine overlords who consider women good for nothing except domestic servitude!'

The woman focks off. She can sense that the mood in this place has changed.

Sorcha goes, 'I intend to dedicate my time in this chamber to getting men – including our politicians – to interrogate their attitudes and check their privilege.'

That's when my *phone* all of a sudden rings? I get a serious filthy from Croía but I end up answering it anyway because I can see from the screen that it's Erika ringing.

I go, 'Hey, sexy! How the hell are you?' and I step outside into the corridor. 'I'm in town, by the way. Sorcha's making another – believe it or not – speech. You'd love it. Men are getting it in the neck.'

But there's something wrong. I can hear it straightaway.

'That evil focking bitch!' she goes.

I'm there, 'I wouldn't go that far, Erika. It's just another fad that'll hopefully pass.'

She's like, 'I'm talking about your mother,' and that's when I realize that she's crying.

'Her?' I go. 'What's going on, Erika? What's she done?'

And she goes, 'She burned my focking gallery to the ground.'

5. Twitter Responds to This Shocking Comment by Charles!

There's, like, fire engines porked half the length of Duke Street – we're talking four or five of the things. And there's hundreds of people standing around, staring at the blackened building that was once my sister's ort gallery. The fire is out but there's, like, a rancid smell of wet ash in the air and people are speculating about what happened, saying that someone apparently broke in at four o'clock this morning, after disabling the alorm, turned the place over, obviously looking for something, then torched it afterwards.

The firemen are packing up their hoses. Their work here is done.

I manage to find Erika among the throng of people. She's standing there with her make-up all over the place. She's got one of those aluminium blankets wrapped around her shoulders – presumably for the shock – and Oisinn and Magnus are standing either side of her, telling her that, hey, at least no one was hurt.

I suppose they've lost their business as well. Gaycation Ireland had their offices upstairs.

I tip over to them, not one hundred per cent sure how welcome my presence is going to be. That question ends up being answered pretty much straightaway. 'This is your focking fault!' Erika goes, pointing at me. 'I told you to go to the Gords.'

I'm wondering – possibly selfishly – whether the letter is still safe? I decide not to ask, though.

I'm there, 'We don't know for definite that it *was* my old dear, Erika? She's actually in Moscow at the moment – the one in Russia.'

Erika goes, 'It was her. I know it was her.'

Honor goes, 'I'm so sorry, Auntie Erika,' and she throws her orms around her.

I'm there, 'Okay, I know I'm being a selfish wanker asking this question, but did she manage to find the letter?'

Erika's there, '*That's* what you want to know?'

'It's a simple yes or no question.'

'No, she focking didn't find the letter,' Erika goes, except she basically spits the words at me.

I breathe a definite sigh of relief, as she pulls it out of her jacket pocket and practically throws it at me. She goes, 'I told you I didn't want anything to do with it and now I've lost my focking gallery.'

I end up apologizing as I stuff the thing into my pocket.

Of course, who arrives on the scene then – oh, for fock's sake! – only Hedvig and Kristoffer. I can barely even look at them, although they seem to have *literally* no shame?

Kristoffer goes, 'Magnush – what hash heppened?'

Magnus is there, 'Right now, it looksh like arshon. Shomebody broke into the building in the early hoursh, ranshacked the plaish, then shet fire to it.'

'They are shertain of thish?'

'I shpoke to the Chief Fire Offisher. He shays that shome kind of acshelerant wash ushed, which shuggestsh that it wash shtarted deliberately.'

'Well, thenk God that nobody wash injured – that ish all I can shay!'

As it happens, him and Hedvik are on their way to the airport. They're heading home today – and good riddance is all I can say. The country will be a safer place without the likes of them two wandering around, with their swinging act.

'If you want ush to shtay,' Hedvig goes, 'we can change our ticketsh.'

Magnus is like, 'No, no, itsh all gute. We can work from the housh until we shubmit the inshurance claim. We will be fine. Like you shay, the important thing ish that everyone ish okay.'

Hedvig's there, 'Okay, sho we will shay goodbye now,' which is what they end up doing. 'Goodbye, Oisinn. Goodbye, Erika. I am sho shorry thish hash happened. Goodbye, Rosh.'

I keep my head down. I'm like, 'Yeah, no, see you,' unable to even make eye contact with them.

'Shorry again,' she goes – this is in front of, like, everyone, including my children, 'about our lidl mishundershtanding, yesh?'

I can see Erika thinking, okay, what's she talking about?

Oisinn goes, 'Are you not going to give them a hug, Ross?'

I'm like, 'Nope,' my head still down.

He laughs.

Then off the pair of them go to the airport – like I said, the streets will be safer with them gone.

I'm like, 'Fock's sake, Oisinn.'

He goes, 'I'm only ripping the piss, Ross. I'm not going to tell anyone.'

'You better not.'

'I gave you my word, didn't I?'

Ronan's been on the island for, like, two weeks now and I've basically heard nothing from him aport from the occasional text, which is why I decide to pay him a surprise visit.

There's, like, boats leaving every twenty minutes from a place called Portrane. I stick the name into the satnav and I hit the M50.

I'm passing the exit for Dublin Airport when I get a text message from JP to say that Sorcha is going to be on the radio with Pat Kenny, so I flick through the presets until I hear the dude's voice.

He's going, 'Why are there no streets in Dublin named after women? That's a question that my next guest asked recently in the Seanad and, in doing so, prompted a lively debate on social media about the apparent lack of recognition for women on the map of Ireland's capital city. Senator Sorcha Lalor, thank you for joining us in the studio today.'

She's there, 'Yes, thank you for inviting me.'

'Now,' he goes, 'I have to admit that this is something I hadn't thought a lot about until this week. But when I read the extracts that you tweeted from your speech, I must admit, I started to wander around Dublin City Centre in my mind – and I realized you were absolutely right! Just about every street *is* named after a man. Many of them deserving men, I should add. But there are a great many deserving women who haven't been similarly recognized. Does that surprise you?'

'Well, first of all, you don't get a pat on the back for acknowledging that women are just as deserving as men of having streets named in their honour. But to answer your specific question, no, Pat, it doesn't surprise me at all, given the casual misogyny that's existed for centuries at the heart of our social and political culture.'

'So you're saying that this state of affairs – where we have virtually *no* streets in the centre of Dublin named after women – has been arrived at due to a sort of unthinking sexism, if you will?'

'Yeah, thank you for *bropriating* my words, Pat. How about *I* say what I mean and we trust that I'm articulate enough to make myself understood by your listeners?'

Oh, shit.

He's there, 'Of course, I didn't mean any –'

'Because,' she goes, '*if* you'll allow me to speak, what you did just there is typical of the Male as Norm principle that governs just about everything in this mancentric world in which we live, from the politics of inter-gender conversation to town-planning, which is what you've invited me – *as* a woman – on your show to talk about.'

Pat's there, 'Er . . .'

I actually feel sorry for the dude.

'Yes, it's a fact,' she goes, 'that for hundreds of years our civic leaders – almost exclusively male, by the way – have ignored the role that women have played in Irish public life while overstating that played by men. The map of Dublin is simply a reflection of the misogyny that pervades in our society. It's why Grafton Street is named after a man. It's why O'Connell Street is named after a man. Pearse Street, Henry Street, Nassau Street are all named after men. Westmoreland Street, Parnell Square are named after men. Even Temple Bar is named after a man.'

Pat goes, 'There is – I *should* point out in the interests of balance – a *Mary* Street.'

'Which was named after the *Virgin* Mary,' Sorcha goes, 'a typically misogynistic conception that seeks to deny the mother of

Jesus Christ her sexual identity – not to mention control over her own fertility.'

There's one or two nuns in Mount Anville who won't enjoy hearing this. She used to be a minister for the Eucharist.

'As I said at the top of the item,' Pat goes, 'there has been a lot of discussion of this subject on social media – various people suggesting the names of deserving women who haven't been recognized. Do you have any thoughts in that regard?'

She's there, 'Well, what I want to know is why there is no street named after – just some of the names I've found through a simple Google search – Hanna Sheehy-Skeffington, who founded the Irish Women's Franchise League and was instrumental in getting women the vote? Why is there no street named after Dorothy Stopford Price, a doctor whose work saved hundreds of thousands of lives from tuberculosis? Why is there no street named after Lady Gregory, who was a vital figure in the Irish Literary Revival?'

'Of course, there are many women in history –'

'It's interesting how we always refer to it as *history*, Pat? Why do we never call it *herstory*?'

'Well, the first three letters of the word are not *actually* a gender-indicative prefix.'

'Yes, thanks for that, Pat. Maybe if you stopped manterrupting me, I might be able to finish the point I was trying to make.'

'Sorry, go ahead.'

'Oh, you're giving me permission to speak, are you? I've received your man-date?'

'You were going to make a point, Senator – we're running out of time on this item.'

'My point is that we live in a patriarchal world that values the contributions of men above the contributions of women. Lack of recognition, lack of respect, lack of esteem are things we've had to put up with through our – yes, Pat – *herstory*. And it's something that I intend to consistently highlight in my capacity as a member of the Upper House of the Oireachtas.'

Pat goes, 'We're getting a huge number of texts in on this subject – almost all of them supportive. Amanda in Douglas says,

"Pat, can you please tell that woman that she is a breath of fresh air and just what politics in this country needs."'

'Thank you, Amanda.'

'John in Laytown says, "Thank you, Senator Lalor, for raising this important issue. I've been saying it for years. There are a great many Irish women who have done heroic work who should be recognized by having streets named after them, including Mary Robinson, Christina Noble and Sister Stanislaus Kennedy. This is something that our political leaders urgently need to put right."'

'Yeah, I don't need a *man* to validate me, John.'

'And Francis in Waterford, says, "It's wonderful to hear such an enlightened feminist voice on the radio. If there were more senators like Sorcha Lalor, there wouldn't be any case to be made for abolishing the place."'

'If Frances is a woman, then thank you, Frances. If Francis is a man, I find that comment frankly patronizing.'

'Senator Sorcha Lalor, thank you for joining us on the programme. It's a subject I'm sure we haven't heard the last of.'

It's, like, lunchtime when I step off the boat onto the island. The place is a real mess. There's, like, cranes and JCBs and bulldozers and mountains of muck everywhere. And there's men in hord hats shouting at each other in possibly Polish, although, knowing my knowledge of the world, they could be from the west of Ireland.

There's no sign of my son, though.

I walk nearly the full way around the island, calling out his name, going, 'Ronan? Ronan? Ro?' and I suddenly feel like that bird at the end of the new *Stor Wors* movie – the one who *looks* like Keira Knightley but *isn't* Keira Knightley? – wandering around in the middle of nowhere, trying to find Luke Skywalker.

I can't even ring him because I left my phone back in the cor.

I'm on the point of giving up when I find the little beach. It's on, like, the farthest part of the island from the mainland, sheltered in a little, I don't know, *cove*? I remember him mentioning a beach on the phone. As I clamber down this little cluster of rocks, I spot his tent – the black one with the giant cannabis leaf on the side – in the distance.

As I make my way down the beach towards it, I stort to hear the chanting. It's like, 'Hooooooocha . . . Desoootaaaaa . . . Channn-nahhhhhhhh . . . Cooolalaaa . . . Sleeeeeeee . . . Raaaacchaaaa . . . Meeeeenaaahhh . . . Loooooooolaaahhh . . .'

I pull back the flap of the tent and there's two of them in there – Ronan and the famous Nudger, his guru. They're both sitting cross-legged, surrounded by burning candles and joss sticks, their palms turned upwards, their eyes shut tightly and their iPod buds in their ears.

And they're going, 'Ahooooaaahhhhh . . . Ooooommmmm . . . Waaaallllaahhhhhh . . . Keeeeeeeena . . . Soooooooonaaaahhhh . . . Ungaaaaaaarrrrr . . . Chinhoooooohaaa . . . Rannnaaaaa . . . Beeeeeee . . .'

At the top of my voice, I go, 'Ormed Gordaí – come out with your hands in the air!'

That's when I see Nudger's true Buddhist credentials. He jumps up with his fist already cocked, ready to punch me into a ten-year coma.

I literally scream.

I'm like, 'Nudger, it's me – it's the Rossmeister!' and he manages to stop himself from decking me.

Ronan goes, 'You're arthur frightening the Jaysus out of us! You should have thexted if you were cubbin.'

I'm there, 'Yeah, no, I thought I'd surprise you.'

'You ceertainly did that,' Nudger goes, 'I nearly bathored you theer, Rosser.'

I'm like, 'It's great to see you both so chilled out. How's Blodwyn?'

Blodwyn is his girlfriend. A petty criminal – slash shoplifter – from Wales. I rode her once.

'She's all good,' he goes. 'She's expecting eer foorst.'

I'm like, 'She's pregnant?'

'That's reet. A little geerdle. Tree muddents to go.'

'That's great news. Fair focks, Nudger.'

I turn around to Ronan then. I'm like, 'And what about you? How's it all going here?'

He's like, 'It's going moostard, Rosser. Ine lubben the woork. Ine arthur finding seben or eight creases in Cheerlie's pladdens alretty. I caddent believe he was godda put the bleaten dock that close to the exersoyuz yeerd! And then Ine doing the Buddhist chanten tree toyums a day – idn't that reet, Nudger?'

Nudger nods and storts rolling a joint.

'And is it, like, working?' I go.

Ronan's there, 'I habn't had sex in two weeks.'

'I should hope not. You're on an island with a bunch of Polish construction workers.'

'Polish? They're alt from Duddygall, Rosser!'

'Donegal? Jesus. Well, you know me, Ro – everyone who's not from South Dublin sounds exactly the same to my ears. The point I'm trying to make is that, well, you wouldn't be having sex given that there's no actual women on the island.'

'The thing is, but, I habn't eeben had a wank, Rosser. Two weeks – and I habn't pult meself off once.'

'Hey, that's, er, great news.'

I know they say we're too quick to praise our children these days but I still say it anyway.

I'm there, 'I'm proud of you, Ro.'

He goes, 'It reedy woorks, Rosser. The chanten, the sitar music, the meditayshidden, the little birra hash that Nudger brings oaber. Ine arthur learden how to switch off me libeetho, so I am. Ine cured, Rosser.'

'That's good news for you – and for Shadden obviously.'

'Ine saying to Nudger, he should be doing this for a libbon. Imagine how much thee'd pay for a serbice like this oaber in Hoddywoot! Alt them fiddum steers with their bleaten sex addictions, wha?'

Nudger smiles modestly, then lights up. He takes two blasts off the joint, then passes it to Ronan.

Out of the blue, I go, 'Ro, can you do me a favour?'

He's like, 'What koyunt of a fabour?'

I'm there, 'Can you look after something for me?' and I whip out the envelope. 'It's not a major deal or anything.'

I hand it to him and he reads what I've written on the front.

'*To be opent in the event of moy dett or thisapperdance*,' he goes. 'What the bleaten hell is going on, Rosser?'

I'm like, 'Yeah, no, it's probably nothing to worry about. There's a chance that my old dear tried to kill me recently, although she claims that's just me being paranoid. She also possibly burned down Erika's gallery. That's kind of my insurance.'

'Insurdance?'

'Just keep it somewhere safe, Ro. And if I turn up dead, just give it to the Feds.'

'That'd be touten, Rosser.'

'Then give it to Erika to give to the Feds. Just keep it safe, will you?'

He folds it in two and sticks it in the back pocket of his jeans.

'Hee-or,' he goes, 'I was godda rig you today in addyhow, Rosser – to talk about the stag.'

I'm like, 'The stag?'

'Ine getting maddied. I hab to hab a Jaysusing stag.'

'I know, but is that not, I don't know, tempting fate? I mean, you're a recovering sex addict?'

'Doatunt woody. Long as I stick with the programme, I'll be foyun.'

He offers me the joint, but I shake my head, so he passes it back to Nudger instead.

I'm there, 'So where are you thinking in terms of? What about Borcelona?'

Ro's like, 'Where?'

'Borcelona.'

'Are you trying to say Barsiddle Owner?'

'Er, that's what I *did* say? Borcelona. Yeah, no, I was on two or three stag weekends there – back in the old Celtic Tiger days. It's an incredible city – *full* of culture, apparently – even though I saw fock-all of it.'

'I've no inthordest in Barsiddle Owner, Rosser.'

'What about Scotland, then? We could go to see that soccer team you love. The Glasgow Celtics. Well, obviously, *I* wouldn't go to the match. I'd drink in one of the local pubs.'

'No inthordest, Rosser.'

'Or have you thought in terms of an Irish stag? What about Kilkenny? I was at a few stags in Kilkenny after the recession hit. It's actually a surprisingly cosmopolitan town. A real melting pot. We met hens from Liverpool, hens from Manchester, hens from Newcastle, hens from Birmingham –'

'Estepona, Rosser.'

'What?'

'That's where Ine habbon me stag.'

'It's on the Costa del Soddle,' Nudger goes.

I'm there, 'The Costa del –?'

'Soddle. You to fly into Madaga – it's not feer from theer.'

'Okay – and why there specifically?'

Ronan goes, 'It's where they're *alt* libbon. The Hedgehog. The Rabbit. The Stoat. The Breadman. The Milkman. The Door to Door Salesman –'

I'm there, 'Are these all criminals you're naming?'

'The Axe. The Machete. The Samurai Sword –'

'I'll take that as a yes.'

'Mad Eddie. Mad Freddie. Mad Frankie. Mad Johnny. Drunk and Disorderly. Assault and Affray. Grievous Bodily Heerm and his young fedda, Actual. All these feddas have been dribbon out of Arelunt, Rosser, by the Criminoddle Assets Budeau. And Estepona is where thee've ended up.'

'You want to spend your stag weekend sitting around watching a bunch of criminals?'

'That's reet.'

'Why don't we just check into a B&B on Gordiner Street and look out the window?'

Nudger laughs, in fairness to him.

'Veddy fuddy,' Ronan goes. 'These are all me heerdoes, Rosser. I woorship these feddas like you woorship Rodan O'Garda and the utter lad –'

I'm like, 'Who?'

'Brian O'Thrisk Coddle. I just want to see it, Rosser.'

'Why do you need to see it? You've got your books, your news-paper cuttings, your *Love/Hate* box set.'

'Because it's all cubbing to an end. They're thalken about clean-ing irrup – the entoyer coast. Putting feddas behoyunt beers, seizing all the doorty muddy. A lot of me childhood heerdos are already retoyerden to Dubai. But there's something magic about Estepona. I just want to see it before it all chayunges.'

I remember Sorcha used to say the same thing about Cuba. The ancient cors. The absence of McDonald's and Storbucks. Everyone smoking and dressing like it's the 1970s. I used to tell her to imagine Skerries on a really hot day. I think that's what helped her get it out of her system. But Ronan won't be so easily discouraged.

'It's like Camedot,' he goes, 'for Irish criminoddles. Make the booking, Rosser. Ine thinking August. Joost a small crew. You, me, Nudger, Buckets, Gull, Anto, Kennet and Dadden. And Cheerlie, of course!'

Nudger offers him the joint but Ronan shakes his head, puts his buds back in his ears, then a few seconds later, he's back going, 'Haalaaahhhhh . . . Booooonnnnnaaaahhhhh . . . Saaallllaaahhhh . . . Taysaaaaaahhhhh . . .'

Erika tells me to meet her in Sophie's at The Dean at midday. No reason given. Just meet her there, she says – alone. And don't be late.

She's already sitting at the table when I arrive.

'You're late,' she goes.

I'm there, 'Only a few minutes,' as I lean down to air-kiss her.

She's there, 'Yeah, okay, once on each cheek is more than enough, Ross. Jesus Christ, it's like being licked by a Saint Bernard.'

She's in terrible form. Which I suppose is *understandable*?

I'm like, 'You look fantastic – and I don't mean that in a weird way.'

She goes, 'Whatever.'

'Are you wearing tights or are they your actual legs?'

She doesn't answer me one way or the other.

I sit down and I stort looking at the menu. I go, 'I love this place. So do the boys. Honor used to take them outside there and they used to spit off the roof. Then the manager asked me not to bring them anymore. The eggs Benedict is nice, by the way.'

She goes, 'I'm not here to eat.'

'I probably shouldn't fill up too much either. I've got – believe it or not – *dancing* later on? Did Honor tell you we're learning the Chorleston?'

'We're here to meet someone, Ross.'

'Meet someone? Who are we meeting?'

At that moment, I look up to see my old dear making her way across the floor of the restaurant. I'm actually too in shock to even come up with something horrible to say to her by way of a greeting.

I say that to her as well. I go, 'If I'd known we were meeting you, I would have had a line ready.'

She's there, 'How lovely to see you! To see you both!'

Erika doesn't say shit and the old dear instantly picks up on her hostility because she sits down and storts looking at the menu to avoid making eye contact with her. She goes, 'I've heard the ceviche of seatrout is excellent.'

Erika – straight out – goes, 'I know it was you. I know it was you who burned down my gallery.'

The old dear's mouth drops open – it's like we're staring down the throat of the monster from *Cloverfield*. 'Burned down your gallery?' she goes. 'What are you talking about?'

'You're not a good liar, Fionnuala. I mean, you *should* be a good liar – given that your face never moves.'

I laugh. I wish *I'd* come up with that.

The old dear goes, 'Charles mentioned that there'd been a terrible fire and that you'd lost –'

'I lost everything,' Erika goes.

'But no one was hurt. Isn't that the important thing?'

She storts looking around her for a waitress, going, 'I wonder could the chef make me a penne alla vodka?'

Erika keeps staring her down. She goes, 'It was you, Fionnuala.'

The old dear looks her in the eye for the first time. 'I don't know what the hell has gotten into you two. I've got Ross accusing me of interfering with his brakes, now you're accusing me of arson. I wasn't even in the country. And, by the way, neither of you has asked me how my speech in Russia went. The answer is very well. Four major corporations have decided to make substantial donations to my charitable foundation. And I've been invited to speak at an even bigger conference in Minsk next month.'

Erika goes, 'I'm not saying you did it yourself. You paid someone.'

'You're as bad as each other, you two. Why would I have done such a thing?'

'To cover up a burglary.'

'A burglary? Oh, this is getting more and more ridiculous.'

I decide to throw my thoughts into the mix. 'You thought Erika had the two-bor electric heater,' I go. 'The one you used to murder a man.'

She's there, 'We've been through this, Ross. I was acquitted by a jury –'

'A jury who knew fock-all about any heater. As a matter of fact, you denied ever owning one.'

'I knew, if the Gords got their hands on it, how they would try to make it look. Even more so now, given that I'm planning to sue them for wrongful arrest and malicious prosecution. They'd use this to try to put me back inside.'

Erika goes, 'And you would go to any lengths to stop that happening.'

'Look, Ross has this *item* we're all talking about in his possession. We have a deal that when my inheritance from Ari's estate comes through, I will give him some money and he will give me –'

I'm there, 'The murder weapon.'

'– this electrical appliance that certain parties would love to get their hands on, yes.'

Erika goes, 'You did it, Fionnuala. You burned down my gallery and I'm going to find the proof.'

The old dear gives her one of her famous shit-munching smiles.

'Erika, I know you're sad that things didn't work out between your mother and Charles. He simply mistook his feelings for her. It was nostalgia more than anything – a romantic trip down memory lane. Please don't punish *me* for that.'

The waitress arrives to take our order. The old dear stands up.

'I've rather lost my appetite,' she goes.

Erika's like, 'Me too.'

And I'm there, 'Well, I'm still storving. I think I will have the eggs Benedict after all. And could you do me a side order of maple candied bacon?'

Erika stares the old dear down and goes, 'You and Charles have made an enemy of me, Fionnuala. I'm going to destroy you – *and* him.'

'That's it,' Mrs Leonard goes, 'remember the basic steps from the last day. Left foot goes back, then forward. Right foot goes forward, then back. This is how we're going to start every week.'

She storts walking down the line, inspecting us all, going, 'Very good, Breda. Try to keep those steps the same size, Aidan. The object is to finish on the same spot. You're heading for Dalkey Dart Station. Left foot goes back, forward. Right foot goes forward, back. Excellent, Honor. Excellent as always.'

She stops in front of me. 'Now,' she goes, 'what's going on here?'

I continue doing the steps.

She's there, 'You look like you're bursting for the toilet.'

I'm like, 'I'm doing it the way you said.'

'Swing your foot outwards – in an arc. Unstiffen those legs. And swing from your hip. Now, everyone, we're going to add a little kick to the step. Remember this from the last day? It's left foot back – like a rock step – kick forward, then step. Right foot, kick forward and, as you do, pull that knee up and reach it back to take the step. Then do it all over again. Rod, what on Earth are you doing?'

She's talking to *me*, by the way? Yeah, no, my pint hand has popped up again. She goes, 'Those hands shouldn't be doing anything except following the natural swing of the step. Put it down, Rod! Put it down!'

I suddenly stop what I'm doing. I'm there, 'There's way too much to remember.'

She goes, 'What are you talking about? We covered this in the last class. This is what we do to warm up.'

I turn around to Honor and I go, 'I'm sorry, Honor, I can't do this.'

She's there, 'Dad, you can't give up.'

I can see the devastation on her little face, but I still go, 'I can and I am,' and I head for the door. Embarrassingly, I notice that I'm still carrying my imaginary pint. 'I'll wait for you in Finnegan's.'

Two minutes later, I've filled that hand with an *actual* pint? The pub is empty on account of it only being ten past six.

Bored, I whip out my phone and I check my Twitter feed. I notice that the old man tweeted something this afternoon. It's like, 'No street or public monument named after Constance Markievicz? What about the Red Cow Roundabout?'

I laugh, even though I have no idea what it even means. I notice he's only got, like, two Likes, one Retweet and one comment (a 'lol') for it. I think about Liking it, but in the end I decide not to give him the pleasure.

Suddenly I notice that there's someone standing next to me. I'm expecting it to be Honor, but when I turn to look, it ends up being – believe it or not – Mrs Leonard.

She goes, 'I've been teaching dance for more than fifty years. And in that time, I can tell you, I've seen more than a few hissy fits.'

I'm there, 'Yeah, no, Dalkey – I can only imagine.'

'But this is the first time I've ever run after someone who walked out of one of my classes.'

'You're wasting your time – that's if you're looking for me to go back.'

'I did it this time for two reasons. First, I can't bear to watch that beautiful little girl's heart breaking?'

I end up having to actually ask. I'm there, 'Can I just check, do you definitely mean Honor?' because – honestly – I'm the only one who *ever* talks about her in that way.

'Yes,' she goes, 'I mean Honor. The other reason is because she's good. I mean, she's very, very good. One of the best I've ever seen.'

I'm there, 'That's great. I'll support her all the way.'

'She doesn't want to dance unless you dance with her.'

'I *can't* dance. I think we've established that fact.'

'Everyone can dance. It's just your mind is elsewhere.'

'There's a lot of shit going on in my life at the moment.'

'Like what?'

'You don't want to know.'

'Yes, I do.'

'Okay. I think my mother tried to murder me recently and my wife is pregnant – possibly by one of my friends.'

'Oh, boo-hoo! The great dancers – do you think they never had troubles? Of course they did. But they used their mental pain as energy. Let me ask you a question, did you ever play a sport?'

I roll my eyes and I shake my head.

She goes, 'Have I said something ridiculous?'

I'm like, 'Yes, Mrs Leonard, I played a sport. I was a rugby player. And I was a pretty big deal around here.'

'All my sons played rugby in school.'

'What school?'

'St Michael's College.'

'So not at a high level, then?'

I have to get my digs in. That's what an unbelievable competitor I still am.

She goes, 'And, as all of my boys discovered, if you can play rugby, you can dance.'

I'm there, 'I personally don't see the connection.'

'In rugby, you learned about angles, didn't you? You learned about timing, knowing the right moment of release. You learned about space and lines of movement.'

'Accidentally, as port of the process, yeah.'

'That's all dancing is! These exercises I'm showing you are no different from the set-pieces you learned on the rugby field.'

'Well, why can't I do them, then?'

'Did you get a skip pass right the first time you did it?'

'No.'

'Someone dropped the ball, yes?'

'Presumably.'

'But you did it again and again and again and again. If knowledge is the treasure, then practice is the key.'

This weird – I swear to God – *feeling* comes over me? The only way to describe it is that it feels like there's suddenly a presence in the room. I'm wondering did I drink that pint too quickly?

She's like, 'What's the matter?'

'Yeah, no,' I go, 'you *sounded* like someone there. A priest – the greatest man I've ever met – who had a massive, massive influence on me. He used to say, "Winners are not people who never fail – they're people who never quit."'

'He sounds like a very wise man.'

I sit there for a few seconds without saying shit. I think deep down, we both know I'm going back.

'Look,' I go, 'I'm not sure your method of coaching is going to get the best out of me.'

She's there, 'What method is that?'

'Telling me how shit I am in front of everyone else. Warren Gatland tried that approach back in the day and I ended up being lost to the game. Tony Ward has described me as one of the greatest losses.'

'So how should I handle your talent, Rod?'

'By boosting me. By telling me that I'm great all the time. You could also stop calling me Rod. Seeing as the name is Ross.'

'Ross? Why did I think it was Rod?'

'Because you know nothing about rugby. I mean, you sent your kids to Michael's, for storters.'

'Shall we go back to class, then . . . Ross?'

Two minutes later, we walk back through the door. Honor's face – I can't even begin to describe the delight on it. She doesn't say anything. She just smiles at me with, like, tears in her eyes. I take my place in the line beside her.

'Okay,' Mrs Leonard goes, 'let's try it to music,' and she puts on this tune – it's real, like, *olden* days music? – and she goes, 'Okay, left foot goes back, forward. Right foot goes forward, back,' and I suddenly discover that I can do it.

As in, I'm *actually* doing it – as in, like, *properly*?

And Mrs Leonard smiles at me and goes, 'Excellent, Ross! See? Now you're getting it!'

Ronan rings me at, like, eight o'clock in the morning, going, 'What's the stordee, Rosser?'

I'm like, 'Are you in some kind of trouble?' because I'm still basically asleep and I've literally never had a conversation with my son this early in the morning.

'No,' he goes, 'it's moostard, Rosser. Ine arthur doing me mentoddle exercises for the modern, now Ine about to steert woork for the day. Ine doing a fuddle snag list for your auld fedda. I think he's godda need a geerd house on the soyut of the islunt facing the mainlanth – to stop unathordized landens.'

I'm like, 'Is that what you're ringing to tell me?'

He laughs. He's there, 'Soddy, Rosser, no – Ine just wondorden how the pladdens for the stag are cubbing on?'

I'm like, 'They're coming on very well, Ro. I've booked us into the Four Green Fields Hotel slash Aportments in Estepona.'

'Ah, nice wooden, Rosser. Supposed to be a great spot.'

'Nine of us. I also booked us all onto a flight from Dublin to Malaga. And, just so you know, I'm arranging a few, you know, activities for us.'

'What koyunt of actippities are we thalken?'

'I'll leave that as a surprise. How are you getting on with, well, you know . . .'

'Ine fuddy cured, Rosser. It's a combinashidden of the chanting and meditayshidden and the woork that your ould fedda's arthur gibbon me. Ine beerly thinking about sex.'

'At all?'

'The weekends are diffordent. I doatunt do addy of me exercises. I go howum to Shadden and we're at it all bleaten Saturday and all bleaten Suddenday, so we are.'

'Yeah, you don't have to tell me everything, Ro.'

'Riding like goats.'

'That's great news.'

There's suddenly a ring on the doorbell, followed a few seconds later by another, which means no one is answering the door, so it looks like I'm going to have to do it as per focking usual. I tell him I'll give him a shout later, then I hang up and head downstairs to answer it.

It ends up being Croía. There's no greeting, by the way. She doesn't even wait to be invited in. She just brushes past me into the hallway, going, 'Sorcha? Are you here? Sorcha?'

She finds her in the kitchen. I follow her because I'm kind of curious as to why she's calling to the door at – like I said – eight o'clock in the actual morning.

'Did you see what he focking tweeted?' she goes.

Sorcha's there, 'No – who?'

'Charles O'Carroll-Kelly – that unreconstructed neomasculinist asshole.'

Sorcha looks over Croía's shoulder at me.

I'm there, 'Hey, you can say what you like about him. I was just going to make myself a coffee.'

I switch on the old Nespressso. I'm going to make myself an old Clooneycino.

'He called Constance Markievicz a cow,' Croía goes.

Sorcha's there, 'He called her a *what*?'

'Actually, a *red* cow. Which I presume is a reference to her being a Communist. He wrote, "No street or public monument named after Constance Markievicz? What about the Red Cow Roundabout?"'

'Oh! My God!'

'He said that about Constance focking Markievicz! I mean, can you focking believe this guy?'

'That is, like, *so* disrespectful to her memory! Ross, where's my laptop?'

I'm there, 'I left it on the island there.'

She sits down, opens it and storts tapping away on the keys. Croía stands behind her, looking over her shoulder.

I'm there, 'I presume he was just joking. Or drunk. Hordly anyone Liked or Retweeted it, if *that's* any consolation?'

'Oh,' Croía goes, 'that's okay, then. I mean, it's perfectly fine for men to use that kind of language to characterize women as long as it's just banter – is that what you're saying?'

'No, I'm just saying that's what his defence is going to be.'

I take out the Aeroccino, more out of habit than anything, then I remember and I fock it in the bin. I decide to make the froth with the battery-powered milk whisk. I can't keep hating Rob Kearney forever. Leinster will be back playing in a few weeks and this will all seem so unimportant.

'Here she is,' Sorcha goes, straightening the screen on her laptop, suddenly all business. *'Constance Markievicz was an Irish Sinn Féin and Fianna Fáil politician, revolutionary nationalist, suffragette* – oh my God! – *and socialist. A founder member of Fianna Éireann, Cumann na mBan –'*

'Focking typical,' Croía goes. 'Even the brave women who fought as Volunteers had to be called a name that sounds like, Come on, the man!'

'*– and the Irish Citizen Ormy, she took part in the Easter Rising in 1916, when Irish republicans attempted to end British rule and establish an Irish Republic. She was sentenced to death – but this was reduced on the grounds of her sex.*'

'Denying her the martyr's fate to which she was entitled – just because she was born with a vagina.'

'Listen to this, Croía. *On 28 December 1918, she was the first woman elected to the British House of Commons, though she did not take her seat and, along with the other Sinn Féin TDs, formed the first Dáil Éireann. She was also the second woman in the world* – in the actual world! – *to hold a Cabinet position when she became Minister for Labour of the Irish Republic from 1919 to 1922.* Oh my God, she was amazing!'

'Look at her posing with the gun there. She was *such* a badass bitch, as well.'

'Are we allowed to say bitch?'

'*We* are. Men aren't.'

'Oh my God, I can't believe that *this* is the woman that Charles referred to as an actual cow.'

'You have to call him out, Sorcha.'

'Me?'

Croía goes, 'You were the one who raised the issue of street names in the first place. This asshole is trying to trivialize it,' and she hands Sorcha her mobile phone. 'Read the second comment underneath his tweet.'

Which is what Sorcha *then* does? She goes, '*Only a senator could have the time and energy to dedicate to shit like this!* Oh! My God!'

'And Charles actually liked that comment.'

'This isn't just an attack on – what was her first name? – *Constance* Markievicz? This is actually a personal attack on me.'

'It's what men do, Sorcha, when they feel that their hold on power is threatened. You've got to put out a statement.'

'I'm opening Word as we speak.'

Ten seconds later, she goes, 'Ross, what's this file you've created? Grievous Bodily Harm. Dangerous Robbie Folan. Fat Frankie Maher . . .'

I'm there, 'It's just a few notes I took for Ronan's stag weekend.'

At the mention of the word stag – I don't think I'm imagining this – Croía looks at me like I'm a pulled pube in her Edamame salad.

I'm there, 'There won't be any strippers or titty bors or anything like that if that's what you're wondering.'

Sorcha goes, 'Do you need me to save this file, Ross?'

'Of course I need you to save it. That's my plan of action for the weekend.'

Croía goes, 'Okay, first of all, you have to mention how deeply offensive his comments were to women. And how many women would find them triggering . . .'

That's when Sorcha's old pair walk into the kitchen from outside. Jesus Christ, they might as well be back living here for all the time they spend in the gaff.

'Electricity's gone again,' her old man goes. 'That's the second time this –' and he suddenly stops because he sees Croía standing behind their daughter, basically telling her what to write.

He goes, 'Oh, hello, Croía. We haven't seen you in a long time.'

'Well,' Croía goes, 'it may come as a surprise to you that I don't cease to exist just because I'm not being observed by a man.'

It's hilarious. For once in his life, the dude doesn't know what to say.

Sorcha's old dear goes, 'Sorcha mentioned that you were back on the scene. She said you helped her with her speech – the one where she said those things about Our Lady.'

Croía goes, 'The virgin birth is a male invention and a libel on womanhood. And anyway, I think Sorcha said a lot more than that in her speech.'

Sorcha looks up from the laptop and goes, 'Chorles attacked me on Twitter, Dad. He called Constance Markievicz a cow, then someone else said that I must have little enough to worry about if I thought the lack of streets named after women was an actual issue.'

I finish whisking the milk. I'm thinking, do you know what? I probably would have done the same thing if I'd been in Rob Kearney's position. He's a great goy and I'd genuinely consider him a friend.

'No woman should be referred to as a cow,' Sorcha goes. 'I'm going to demand a public apology.'

Croía's there, 'We want more than an apology, Sorcha. He should resign.'

Sorcha thinks about this for a few seconds, then goes, 'You know what? You're right. If Charles O'Carroll-Kelly thinks it's cool to talk about women in that way, he is not fit to hold public office.'

Sorcha continues tapping away at the keys. I can see her old pair both staring at Croía. I can tell that they're not keen on her.

He actually tries to change the subject. He goes, 'Did you, em, take your folic acid this morning, Dorling?'

But before Sorcha gets the chance to answer, Croía goes, 'Yeah, subtle reminder there, Sorcha, that your real purpose on this Earth is to be a focking receptacle to carry around a baby for a man.'

Sorcha's old man is just staring at her, with his mouth open. But I'm there thinking, I'm actually storting to *warm* to this girl?

Honor says she has something for me.

I'm there, 'What is it?'

She hands me a box and just, like, shrugs, all embarrassed.

I'm like, 'No, seriously, what is it?' because you never know with Honor. It could be a dead animal.

She's there, 'Open it!'

Which is what I do. It ends up not being a dead animal. It ends up being a hat. Not an ordinary hat either. It's an actual fedora.

She goes, 'It's for dancing.'

She takes it out of the box and she puts it on my head.

'Oh my God,' she goes, 'you look *so* cool!'

I'm like, 'Really?'

She leads me over to her full-length mirror.

I laugh, then I tilt it slightly. I'm there, 'It does actually suit me! Thanks, Honor!'

She goes, 'I just wanted to say thank you – for not giving up.'

'That's down to Mrs Leonard explaining it to me in, like, rugby terms. And obviously not wanting to disappoint you.'

'Well, I just want you to know that I'm grateful, okay?'

I give her a big hug.

I don't want to tempt fate by saying this, but I genuinely feel that Honor has turned a corner in terms of her behaviour – and that's mostly down to me. Whatever happens long term between me and Sorcha, I think she'll look back on her decision to let me move back in as a definite turning point.

I don't know *what's* going to happen to the other three, though. I think they're lost to me.

Brian is suddenly standing in the doorway. 'You're a focking wanker!' he goes.

I'm just like, 'You're the wanker, Brian.'

'Why don't you fock off?'

'I've a better idea – why don't *you* fock off?'

'You focking shitwaffle fock!'

'Here, Brian, I saw Leo earlier – and he was flushing your Match Attax cords down the toilet.'

Oh, that brings him to his senses. He runs off down the landing, looking for his brother. A few seconds later, I hear a bump, followed by the sound of them killing each other.

I shut the door to drown it out.

'Hey,' Honor goes, 'do you want to practise that side lift that Mrs Leonard showed us?'

And I go, 'Yeah, actually – good idea.'

I straighten my hat in the mirror. Then we're just getting ready to stort when my phone all of a sudden rings. I answer it and it ends up being the old man.

'I'm looking to speak to your good lady wife!' he goes – and from his tone, it doesn't sound like it's for a catch-up.

I'm there, 'Why are you ringing me? I don't really have anything to do with her anymore.'

'I've tried her mobile and it's switched off!'

'That's because she's over at her boyfriend's house.'

'What is she trying to do to me, Ross?'

'What are you talking about?'

'She's called for me to resign because of a joke I made about Constance Markievicz!'

'Yeah, no, you called her a cow. I saw your tweet.'

'She shot an unarmed policeman in Stephen's Green!'

'Sorcha?'

'No – Constance Markievicz!'

'Yeah, no, I was going to say it doesn't sound like something Sorcha would do.'

'There are worse things I could have called her than a cow! But now I'm being attacked on social media! People are calling for me to stand down as the leader of New Republic! I've got celebrities saying I'm disgusting! Who's Vogue Williams, by the way?'

'She's on TV. She's someone I fancy in a major way.'

'Well, *she's* the latest to throw in her two cents' worth! I've got the Women's Council of Ireland condemning me! I've got SIPTU saying my comments are deeply sexist and offensive to all women! Some of the party's biggest donors are demanding that I consider my position! Even Hennessy is coming around to the view that I should make some sort of qualified apology! He's drafting something for me right now!'

'Like I said, me and Sorcha just live under the same roof. I can't control her.'

'I've got important work to do, Kicker! Ireland – more than ever – requires a strong opposition and I'm having to deal with this bloody well nonsense!'

I'm there, 'Hey, I've got important shit to do myself,' and I just hang up on him.

Honor cues the music. Then she goes, 'Ah one, ah two, ah three . . .'

Christian has a black eye. It's a real beauty as well. It's, like, swollen to the size of a peach and he can barely see out of the thing.

I'm there, 'Whoa!' turning his shoulders to get a better look at it. 'Who did that to you?'

We're in Kielys, by the way. The usual Friday-night thing.

He goes, 'Hennessy has me doing repossession cases. Tractors and form machinery.'

'Jesus!' I go. 'Surely the Disney Store was a better option?'

'He's giving me the most violent cases. He hasn't forgiven me for breaking up with Lauren in the first place. This is payback.'

I order him a Ballygowan – although I suspect it won't be long before he's back on the drink.

'Anyway,' he goes, 'it's not the biggest worry we've got on our plates right now.'

I'm there, 'What do you mean?'

I love the way he can open up to me. That's what a best friend is for.

He goes, 'Little Ross has been wetting the bed.'

I'm there, 'Jesus. He's a bit old for that shit, isn't he?'

'Yeah, it storted a few months back. Remember the borbecue – when he drank all that wine?'

'I do, yeah – the little focking dipso.'

'Well, it storted around that time. Lauren thinks something might be troubling him. Like he's keeping something in.'

Shit. I think I know what that might be.

I'm there, 'It sounds to me like Lauren's talking out of her hole, Christian.'

'She wants to take him to a child psychiatrist.'

183

'I don't think there's any need. I genuinely don't.'

'Ross, he's wetting the bed four or five nights a week.'

'Well, have you thought that maybe it's Lauren's actual fault?'

'What do you mean by that?'

'I just think she's over-mothered that kid. And I'm saying that as his godfather. *Thixty-theven dollth!* No offence, Dude. And the focking bollocking she gave me when I bought him a Transformer.'

'You don't think that's the reason, do you?'

'It's not natural. Then *you're* coming home every night from God knows where with your face all bashed up. It's no wonder he's wetting the bed.'

'Do you think that could be the reason?'

'I think that it's one of the reasons – between that and the other thing. Lauren raising him like a girl.'

'I'm always on at her about that. Telling her that she's overprotective of him. I mean, his little brother beats him up!'

'I always let my boys fight. Shut the door and leave them to it – that's my approach. Let them find their place in the hierarchy.'

'Lauren still thinks he's repressing something.'

'Definitely don't take him to a child psychiatrist, though – the reason being that I genuinely don't think there's any need. Genuinely.'

Oisinn and Magnus arrive then – the two of them all smiles, like they've got some joke that only they're *in* on?

Christian says he was sorry to hear about the fire.

Oisinn goes, 'Hey, it's cool, we didn't really lose anything that wasn't insured. All of our information was in the cloud.'

Magnus is there, 'Sho now we are jusht working from the apartment until we find shomewhere shuitable to move to.'

Oisinn goes, 'Even though there's barely room to *swing* a cat in there! Do you get it, Ross?'

I feel my face definitely redden. I'm there, 'I don't know what you're talking about. But whatever it is, I think you should drop it.'

Magnus laughs. He goes, 'Right now, we are planning for the firsht *Brokeback Mountain*-themed shtag weekend. Itsh going to be lotsh and lotsh of fun.'

Yeah, no, he said the same thing about his old pair.

I decide to change the subject. I'm there, 'Did you see Christian's eye? Hennessy has him repossessing equipment from, like, formers.'

Oisinn pulls a sore face. 'Yeah,' he goes, 'I was going to ask where you picked that up. Your father-in-law must really hate your guts.'

Christian's there, 'He does. But, hey, it's a job.'

Oisinn goes, 'Oh, well – it's all *swings* and roundabouts! What do you think of that one, Ross?'

Christian looks at me for an explanation. I just shrug. I'm like, 'Yeah, no, I have literally *no* idea what he's talking about? Total tumbleweed moment, Oisinn.'

JP and Fionn eventually show their faces. Fionn looks like shit, I'm happy to say. It's obvious that the honeymoon period between him and Sorcha is over and they're at that point of the relationship where they're discovering all the things about each other that piss the other one off.

I'm there, 'You don't look well. I'm not saying that to be a dick.'

He doesn't respond either way – just gets his round in. I'll give him that. He always gets his round in.

I'm there, 'Unusual for you – getting your round in, I mean.'

We've sort of become separated from the rest of the crew.

I'm there, 'You're not with Sorcha tonight, no?' and I know he's not because she's decided to spend some quality time with the kids – trying to persuade Honor to talk to her while the boys call her every dirty name under the sun.

He goes, 'No, I'm, er, a bit of a spare wheel at the moment.'

I'm there, 'Is that a reference to Croía?'

He nods. 'She's certainly a big influence on Sorcha,' he goes, 'isn't she?'

I'm there, 'They were bezzy mates in UCD. Croía was a kicker – did you know that? In *women's* rugby.'

'No, I didn't.'

'Although don't *call* it women's rugby in front of her. She was actually very good. For a woman.'

'That's something I haven't heard yet. Which surprises me, given that Sorcha talks about her twenty-four hours a day. I'm sorry, I'm just feeling like a bit of a gooseberry at the moment – at least in political terms.'

'What the fock are you talking about?'

'It's just Croía wants Sorcha to increase the pressure on your old man over this Constance Markievicz thing.'

'She *was* actually a cow – that's according to him. A total one.'

'That's not the point. Look, the language he used *was* offensive to women. I'm just not sure it's a resigning matter.'

'Fock him. And I'm saying that as his son. He deserves everything he gets.'

'Look, Croía is very driven. And she has her own agenda. But there's not much compassion in her. She's very much ideology over human feeling.'

'Hey, *he's* been a dick ever since he put that wig on his head. You've seen that yourself.'

'I just think that demanding his resignation – it's not proportionate to the offence. There has to be room for people to make mistakes in life – especially when they apologize for them, which Charles has done.'

'Just so you know, Hennessy wrote that statement for him.'

'Whether he did or not, I think that should be the end of the matter. Unfortunately, I lost that argument. Sorcha's challenging him to a debate now and Croía is prepping her for it. I made my position clear today and, well, Sorcha asked me to leave.'

'Look, this is just typical her, Fionn. She's always looking for gurus. I remember back in the Celtic Tiger days, she used to go to some – I can't believe I still remember this word – *Jainist* guru, who had a place where the Cookbook Café is now in Glasthule. He used to cover her body in chickpea dip and she'd sit for an hour listening to his wind chimes, then pay him a hundred snots. She'll eventually see through Croía like she saw through Bismillah.'

He just nods, then pushes his glasses up on his nose. After a few seconds of silence, he goes, 'She's really starting to show, Ross.'

I'm there, 'I know. I was looking at her this morning, thinking, people are going to stort commenting soon on how fat she's getting.'

'I asked her when she was going to announce it, but she said Croía thinks the patriarchy will use it to undermine her.'

'Jesus.'

'I think, at some level, Sorcha is still in denial about even being pregnant.'

'We both saw it, Fionn. She's definitely not making it up.'

Over his shoulder, I suddenly spot Erika walking into the pub. I go, 'Excuse me for a second.'

Over to her I tip. I'm like, 'What are you doing here? Where's Amelie?'

She goes, 'My mom is looking after her.'

'Helen? She's home from Australia?'

'Yes, she's home from Australia. I need to talk to you about something.'

'Okay, what? Am I allowed to tell you that you smell great?'

'What was Fionnuala doing in Russia?'

'It was some conference, wasn't it? Human rights or some shit?'

'A human rights conference? In Russia? Does that not seem odd to you?'

'You know me, Erika. There's very little going on between my ears. Especially when it comes to, like, world events.'

'I tried to find out something about it. I went online. I couldn't find anything about a conference in Moscow. *Or* in Minsk, where she said she was going next. What's that charity she was talking about?'

'Something to do with landmines. In Africa. Although she refuses to actually go there. The photographs for the brochure were taken in the back gorden in Foxrock. The dude who supposedly lost his leg actually played Junior Cup for King's Hospital. He got a medial collateral ligament tear.'

'There's something going on, Ross. Something big. I'm going to get to the bottom of it.'

Just as she says this, the bor is suddenly filled with what sounds like *Disney* music? I know the tune from listening to it with possibly Honor when she was a baby. I'm thinking, what the fock have they put on in here? Then I happen to look over to where the goys are standing – we're talking Oisinn and Magnus, Christian, Fionn and JP – and they're all just looking at me, laughing their heads off.

I'm like, 'What's the crack?'

And Oisinn goes, 'It's from *The Jungle Book*, Ross! You must know it! *King of the Swingers!*'

They all crack their holes laughing. And it's straightaway obvious that he's told them what happened.

Erika goes, 'What's that about?'

'Ah, it's nothing. I got propositioned – by Magnus's old pair.'

'His old *pair*? What, the two of them?'

'She's a sex therapist, Erika. She's very much anything goes.'

Erika laughs. It's nice to see.

I'm there, 'I turned up at the gaff. We storted to get down to brass tacks. Then *he* walked in, unbuttoning his shirt.'

That's when Erika *really* laughs. And all the goys stort singing, '*Now I'm the King of the Swingers – oh, the jungle VIP . . .*'

'Let me assure you, Cathal,' the old man goes – he's talking to Cathal Mac Coille, the dude from *Morning Ireland* – 'I am anything *but* a misogynist!'

I'm trying to remember some of the jokes that I've heard the old man and Hennessy tell each other over the years. Jokes about women drivers. Jokes about women golfers. Jokes about women judges.

If I can think of one, I'm definitely going to text the programme.

Sorcha goes, 'Chorles, you made a comment that was deeply, deeply offensive to all women. It was also disrespectful towards one of the most heroic figures in Irish herstory.'

The old man's like, 'In Irish *what*?'

I'm listening to this in the kitchen while getting the breakfast ready for the kids.

'Herstory,' Sorcha goes. 'Except you probably know it as history – the male-written narrative, which I'm happy to say is being revised by people like me and the thousands of other women who are standing up and asking why women have been expunged from the story of Ireland?'

'Look, I've apologized for what I said! I think that should be the end of the matter!'

Cathal Mac Coille is straight in there. He goes, 'How sincere *was* that apology, Charles, given that we know you had several major financial donors – including, I read this morning, the Chordata Hotel Group – threatening to withdraw support for the party?'

He's there, 'I'm certain my daughter-in-law can attest to my sincerity, Cathal, having known me for the best part of twenty years! As I said in my statement, I accept that I may have been a little loose in my use of language in relation to Mrs Markievicz! And naturally I'm sorry if anyone was offended by those words!'

Sorcha goes, 'We don't want to hear you re-read your statement, Charles. You were asked whether or not your apology was sincerely meant, especially given this minimizing language you use – I should say *manamizing* – where you say *if* people were offended by what you said, like you consider their response to be unreasonable or even hysterical.'

'Well, I *do* consider it unreasonable and I *do* consider it hysterical to suggest that Charles O'Carroll-Kelly is in some way misogynistic! I *very* much enjoy the company of women! I've *employed* women, for heaven's sakes! When a lot of others in this country wouldn't have!'

'Mostly as receptionists, from what I gather. Not in positions of actual power.'

'I'm talking about the 1970s, Sorcha! Women didn't want that kind of thing back then!'

'So now you're an expert in what women want, are you? You must have extraordinary intuition – especially given that you don't spend a lot of time around them.'

'What in the name of Hades is that supposed to mean?'

'Well, you don't really have any women in your porty, do you?'

'No women? The Deputy Leader of New Republic is a woman! A bloody fine woman! And a very able one too!'

'Can I just cut in here, Cathal, and mention that this is something I called Chorles out on quite recently? I was standing in the forecourt at the front of Leinster House when the New Republic porliamentary porty was having its official photograph taken. It was – *as* Charles said – one woman, plus fifty white, cisgender, middle-aged, Irish men.'

'Democratically elected!' the old man goes. 'Let's not forget that!'

'While they were having their photograph taken, I watched several of them either groping or attempting to grope Muirgheal Massey. They were staring at her bottom and they were grabbing at her breasts.'

'Well, I wasn't aware of that!'

'Yes, you were aware of it, Chorles, because I brought it to your attention at the time and you said she didn't seem to mind it too much.'

'I'm not sure if those were my exact words!'

'They were also shouting disgusting things at her, which you must have heard because you were standing right next to them and I could hear them from fifty feet away.'

Cathal Mac Coille goes, 'Charles, did you hear those comments made?'

The old man's there, 'I may have done, yes! But it was banter, Cathal! The type of thing that chaps do when they get together and there's an attractive lady in the company!'

Cathal Mac Coille goes, 'I think it's fair to say, Charles, that not all men behave that way.'

Sorcha's like, 'They do if they're members of New Republic, Cathal. It's the most patently sexist political organization in the country. I said that to Chorles the day I invited him to spend International Gender Equality Hour in my house. But, unfortunately, he couldn't find the time in his schedule.'

The old man ends up suddenly losing it with her. I can hear his chair scraping back and him suddenly getting to his feet. He goes, 'I'm in the business of opposition! I don't have time for this! This is a silly-season story! I made a slightly off-colour joke. I have apologized to the late Mrs Markievicz and to anyone who decided to take offence at it! And, as far as I'm concerned, that is the end of the matter!'

But as I listen to him storm out of the studio, I get the definite sense that it's not going to be.

Honor says she's going to miss me. I remind her that I'm only going to be gone for, like, three nights. She says it's going to feel like three weeks and I just think to myself, I cannot believe the change that has come over this girl since I moved back home.

She's literally like a different kid.

'That stupid focking prick,' she goes, meaning Sorcha's old man, 'and his sappy bitch of a wife are going to be looking after us while you're away.'

I laugh. She's genuinely hilarious.

I'm there, 'The time will fly, Honor. I just want to give Ronan a proper send-off. And possibly persuade him not to get married.'

'I focking hate Shadden,' she goes.

'Yeah, no, I have to admit, I've definitely cooled on the girl since she rang your old dear, telling tales on you.'

Mrs Leonard walks over to where we're sitting. The class has just ended. I'm grabbing a breath and Honor is changing out of her dance shoes.

'Excellent work today!' she goes, making a point of looking at me. 'Now we've no class for the next two weeks. But make sure to keep practising that Lindy Hop, okay? What is it, Ross?'

I'm there, 'Rock, step, kick, step, back – aaand – rock, step, kick, step, kick, kick back – aaand – rock, step!'

'Well remembered,' she goes. 'Just keep saying it in your head until it's second nature.'

She's great, Mrs Leonard. I'm just thinking, if only Warren Gatland had understood me like she understands me – well, it could have changed the course of Irish rugby history. Slash herstory.

Honor goes, 'Have a great holiday, Mrs Leonard. See you in two weeks.'

A few minutes later, we're sitting in the cor, heading home. Honor is doing a finger-dance on the dashboard, going, 'Rock, step, kick, step, back – aaand – rock, step, kick, step, kick, kick back – aaand – rock, step!'

She checks her Twitter feed then. She's like, 'Oh my God, everyone is talking about Granddad!'

I'm there, 'My old man, you mean? Yeah, no, he thought this thing was going to go away but it obviously hasn't.'

'Who's Constance Markievicz anyway?'

'I've no idea. I don't think anyone in the country had heard of her until about a week ago.'

'Apparently, SIPTU has said its members will withdraw all services to New Republic's Molesworth Street headquarters from midnight tonight unless he resigns.'

'I have to say, I feel very nearly sorry for him.'

'Oh my God, Meryl Streep has described his comments as unacceptable.'

'Meryl Streep? The actress?'

'Yeah.'

'What the fock does it have to do with her?'

'She obviously heard about it on Twitter. It also says that the Gords are investigating whether calling a woman a cow might constitute a hate crime.'

We eventually arrive back at the gaff. There's, like, a black Toyota Highlander in the driveway that I don't instantly recognize. I just presume it must be Croía's and she's here to talk about how they can keep up the pressure on the dude.

Except when we walk into the house, there ends up being a surprise waiting for us. Or actually an *ambush*?

Sorcha is standing at the kitchen door. She goes, 'Can you two come down here, please? I want to talk to you about something.'

Down we go. Out of the corner of her mouth, Honor's like, 'What do you suppose this bullshit's about?'

I'm there, 'No idea.'

But I do when I see the line-up in the kitchen. We're talking Sorcha's old pair, sitting on one side of the table, looking all serious. Then, on the other side, Lauren and Christian.

I already know deep down what this is about. But I still try to bluff my way out of it. I'm there, 'Which one of you two is driving the Toyota Highlander? How would you rate it in terms of driveability?'

Neither of them answers.

Sorcha goes, 'Lauren and Christian have come here today to talk about a very serious matter.'

I'm there, 'Let me be the judge of that. What's on your minds?' still hoping against hope that it's something else – that maybe Ross Junior has grown tired of dolls and decided he wants the Transformer after all.

It's Sorcha's old man who goes, 'Christian and Lauren here say that Honor gave their little boy alcohol.'

I'm there, 'That's rubbish. What actual evidence is there?'

Christian can't even look me in the eye.

I'm there, 'I'm surprised at you, Dude, coming here with a horse-shit story like that. We played rugby together.'

Honor – no fear in her whatsoever – totally wrong-foots me by going, 'It's not horseshit. I told him to drink it. Half a bottle of wine.'

I look at her as if to say, what the fock are you doing?

Lauren glowers at her and goes, 'Why would you do something like that?'

She's there, 'Because you were being a focking bitch to my dad. He bought your son a present – because he's kind. And you couldn't even say thank you. It's not his fault that the kid is a focking sissy.'

It's a lovely thing for me to hear. I just smile at her.

Then I hear Sorcha go, 'Ross, did you *know* about this?'

And I'm looking at Honor – and thinking about what she just said – and I realize that I can't lie.

'No,' I go, 'this is genuinely the first time I'm hearing about . . . okay, actually – cords on the table? – I *did* know.'

Christian *is* suddenly able to look at me. 'So that's why you tried to persuade me not to send him to a child psychiatrist?' he goes.

Lauren just shakes her head. She's going to definitely add this to her list of reasons to hate me. That's the type she is. She keeps score. She's there, 'My son has been wetting the bed because *she* threatened him that she would hurt him if he told anyone.'

Honor goes, 'That kid needs to toughen up. He's a focking wuss – and he can't hold his drink.'

She's not wrong, but I'm wondering is this the wisest gameplan here?

Sorcha's old man goes, 'So this is the strong role model you felt your daughter needed, Sorcha? This is the father who was going to have a stabilizing influence on your daughter?'

Honor goes, 'Why don't you fock off back to your wooden shack, you bankrupt prick? And bring your fat-legged wife with you?'

She has a point, in fairness. Sorcha's old dear has thighs like Edwin Maka. I'm not sure this is the time to bring it up, though.

Sorcha's old man goes, 'These two are as bad as each other, Sorcha.'

Honor's there, 'Do you know why the electricity keeps going off in your so-called Shomera? Because I keep pulling the fuse out! Dad, tell them what you did to his favourite mug!'

I'm there, 'I'm not one hundred per cent sure how it'd help the situation, Honor.'

Sorcha's like, 'Honor, you're grounded. For the whole of next term. That means no more Dundrum. And no more dancing.'

Honor goes, 'You're not going to stop me from dancing, you stupid focking bitch.'

She's like a South Dublin Billy Elliot – except with a filthy mouth.

Sorcha's there, 'I can stop you and I will.'

And that's when suddenly Croía bursts into the kitchen, going, 'We got him, Sorcha! We focking got him! Charles O'Carroll-Kelly just stepped aside as the leader of New Republic!'

6. The Windows of This Car were Steamed Up. Wait Till You See What's Inside!

So I'm heading for the airport and I swing by Foxrock to collect my old man, except the front gorden is swarming with journalists and photographers. I end up having to fight my way to the front door. They're all shouting, 'What do *you* think of Constance Markievicz?' and 'Do you think it's right to call any woman a cow?' and 'Are you prepared to resign from whatever it is you do for a living?'

I let myself in using my key and I meet the old man in the hall-way. He's still in his dressing-gown at, like, three o'clock in the afternoon. Unshaven as well, with his hair slash wig all over the place.

He goes, 'You saw the hyena pack outside, did you?'

I'm there, 'Why don't you ring the Gords? They're basically trespassing.'

'I'm not sure how quick they'd be to respond to an emergency call from this house – given that your mother is suing them for malicious prosecution.'

'Go and get dressed. We're heading for the airport.'

'Airport?'

'Yeah, no, it's Ronan's stag weekend.'

'I'm not going anywhere, Kicker. I'm sure the little chap will understand.'

'Come on, a few days in Estepona could be just what you need.'

'It's a living nightmare, Kicker. I'm getting abuse online. Abuse on the phone. I can't sleep. I can't drink. I can't smoke.'

'It'll all die down, I'm sure, now that you've stepped down.'

'Not *down*, Ross. I've stepped *aside* – pending an internal discipli-nary investigation. It was Muirgheal's idea. She thought it might take the heat off for a few weeks. She also put out a wonderful state-ment saying that Charles O'Carroll-Kelly was far from a misogynist and that he's always given women an opportunity to advance.'

I laugh. I'm there, 'Yeah, *one* woman – who happens to be Muir-gheal herself.'

He goes, 'I gave your wife an opportunity too. I was the one who talked her into running for election in the first place. Come with me. Hennessy is down in the study.'

So that's where we end up heading.

The dude is helping himself to a glass of XO from the decanter. When he sees me, the first thing he says is, 'What the hell is wrong with that wife of yours?'

I'm there, 'She's not really my wife anymore. Not in the sense that I have any control over her.'

'You could try talking to her. Bring her into line.'

'Trust me, I'm the last person in the world she wants to talk to right now.'

He points at the old man – *while* still looking at me? – and goes, 'She's destroyed a good man. I hope she's pleased with herself.'

The old man sits down in his ormchair in the corner. His dressing-gown is only loosely tied. He puts his feet up on the leather ottoman and I end up seeing way more of the dude than I ever wanted to see.

He's like, 'Sorcha didn't destroy me, Old Scout. *I* destroyed me.'

'I still say we should put out another statement,' Hennessy goes. 'You could say you're an old dinosaur trying to learn new ways, while acknowledging the valuable role that Constance Markievicz played in Irish history and the fact that she's not bovine in any way. You've listened to the community, you're prepared to work on any prejudices you might have, and you're determined to do better in the future.'

'No, I think Muirgheal is right. There's too much anger out there. My only hope is to sit on the sidelines for a few months, then come back a chastened man.'

'And what about all these other women?'

Whoa!

I'm like, 'Er, *what* other women?' because this is definitely news to me.

The old man goes, 'A woman I interviewed for a job back in 1968 said on Twitter that I called her "Sweetheart" during the course of the interview. Another woman said I put my hand on the small of her back as I opened a door for her in the Royal Hibernian Hotel in 1976.'

I'm there, 'Jesus!'

'We don't know what else they're going to throw at me. The best thing I can do is to disappear from public view for a few months, then come back claiming to be a changed man.'

I'm there, 'You could possibly do with having a shower. You seriously smell.'

He goes, 'I will. Your mother's arriving home tonight – I don't want her to see me like this.'

I'm there, 'By the way,' remembering my conversation with Erika, 'what exactly is she doing in Russia again?'

He goes, 'She's speaking at a human rights conference – about how it feels to be the victim of injustice. You know what? I might even join her on the circuit after this.'

'How does it work, though?'

'How does what work?'

I can feel the weight of Hennessy suddenly *staring* at me?

I'm there, 'This foundation of hers.'

He goes, 'Well, they pay her to speak about her experiences and the good she's planning to do in the world. Then various corporations and philanthropists and businessmen contribute money to her portfolio of charitable causes.'

'It's just that Erika said that the Russians aren't, like, *into* human rights? She said it wouldn't be big over there.'

'Don't talk to me about that girl. I heard what she said to your mother. Accused her of burning down her gallery, if you don't mind. Have you ever heard the likes of it, Hennessy?'

He looks about as unhappy as I've ever seen him.

I'm like, 'Why don't you take that stupid wig off?'

He's like, 'I beg your pardon?'

'You heard me. Be honest, you haven't had one good day since you put that thing on your head.'

'That's not true.'

'Seriously, you were happily married – to Helen. You had the love and respect of your daughter and your daughter-in-law. You had all your grandchildren around you. People actually liked you. You became a dick basically from the moment you found that wig in Helen's attic. What good is it to you now? Go on – take it off.'

He looks at Hennessy, who just shrugs.

The old man walks over to the mirror above the fireplace. He takes a long, hord look at himself – as if taking a mental *picture*? – then he takes a firm grip on the wig, one hand either side of his head.

He goes, 'I'm using a very strong adhesive. I think the only way to do it is to give it a good, firm –' and I suddenly hear this ripping sound, then him going, 'Ouuuch!'

He stays standing in front of the mirror for a good twenty seconds, staring at himself, the wig now in his hand. Then he turns and he faces us – the old Chorles O'Carroll-Kelly again.

He goes, 'What do you think?'

I'm there, 'A definite improvement.'

I look at Hennessy, still nursing his brandy. He's got, like, tears spilling from his eyes. He goes, 'Jesus, Charlie, I miss you already.'

Kennet calls the air hostess as she's pushing the drinks cort past.

'Hee-or, Love,' he goes, 'it's b . . . b . . . b . . . b . . . bleaten roastin in hee-or, so it is. Is there addy chaddence of opening a w . . . w . . . window?'

The entire plane laughs like it's the funniest thing anyone has ever said.

Ronan is sitting in front of me, next to Nudger. He's kneeling on his chair, talking to me over the back of his seat. He goes, 'He's a bleaten cadickter, isn't he?'

No, he's a focking idiot, I think.

I don't say that, though. I go, 'Yeah, he sort of *is*, I suppose?' just trying to keep the peace.

Being called a 'cadickter', I know from experience, is the Q Mork for working-class people who fancy themselves as comedians when travelling abroad. Kennet has already achieved it and we're not even in the air an hour. I hope it'll encourage him to maybe shut the fock up for the rest of the weekend. Unlikely, though.

'Where's Buckets of Blood?' Ronan goes, because that's who *I'm* sitting beside?

I'm there, 'He said he was gasping for a cigarette. He was going to see could he take the battery out of the smoke detector in the jacks.'

'Jaysus, he's been thrun off how meddy playuns for doing that?'

He steps into the aisle, then takes Buckets of Blood's seat beside me. He's there, 'You're veddy quiet, Rosser.'

I'm like, 'Yeah, no, I'll definitely loosen up when I've had a few drinks. There's just one or two things happening at home.'

'Cheerlie? It's a pity he couldn't make it, Ross, but I toalt him I wondertherstand. You caddent say athin these dayuz.'

'That seems to be the way things are going. Then Honor's in trouble again.'

'Hodor? What's she arthur doing now?'

'Nothing. Well, very little. You know Christian's eldest lad – Ross Junior?'

'The fedda with the dolls?'

'Yeah, that's him. That's exactly him. Well, Honor sort of got him drunk.'

'Moy Jaysus.'

'To the point where he had to be pumped out.'

'That's on top of gibbon *moy* thaughter cigordettes.'

'Hey, they're two totally different things.'

'Are thee, but?'

'Look, I'm not defending her, Ro – even though I think Christian and Lauren have definite questions to ask themselves. As do you and Shadden. My point is that both of those incidents happened, like, *weeks* ago? And since then Honor had definitely turned a corner in terms of her behaviour. We were doing this dance class together.'

'She toalt me. The Cheerdleston.'

'She was honestly like a different person. She'd even stopped talking about killing Sorcha's old pair in their sleep.'

'That's, er, progress, I suppowuz.'

'But now Sorcha's told her no more dancing. And I'm worried it's going to set her back.'

'Sudeka might chayunge her moyunt.'

'She won't, Ro. I'd try to talk her around except I'm on pretty thin ice myself. Her old man put her up to it. Told her she'd made a massive mistake thinking I could be a role model for anyone. And suddenly I'm wondering is he possibly right? And it kills me to even think that, Ro, because being an amazing, amazing father was one of the few things I took it for granted I was genuinely *good* at? I know you're going to tell me I shouldn't think that way.'

He says fock-all, I notice.

There's suddenly an announcement. 'A reminder,' a man's voice goes, sounding pissed off, 'that it is an offence to tamper with the smoke alarms in the toilets.'

I'm there, 'Hey, I'm sorry, I don't want to bring down the mood. It's supposed to be your stag. I'll hopefully cheer up. I think I'll stort drinking now.'

He goes, 'I'll gerr us a couple of bee-ors,' and he presses the Call button.

I'm there, 'What about you, Ro – how's it all going?'

'Veddy good, Rosser. Ine lubben the new job, so I am.'

'You know what I'm talking about, Ro. Do you honestly think you can stay faithful when we're over here?'

'Ine moostard. Ine tedding you, Nudger's method woorks. Hodestly, Rosser, I can go from wodden eddend or the week to the utter wirrout eeben thinking about getting the royut. Long as I do me meditayshidden.'

'And your chanting.'

'And me chanthen – that's reet.'

'So you'll be doing it while we're in Estepona, will you?'

'You bethord beleeb it, Rosser.'

An air hostess arrives. Ronan asks her for two beers. Then he leans forward to check if Nudger is awake. He goes, 'Do you want a thrink, Nudger?'

Nudger's like, 'Yeah – bee-or.'

'Tree bee-ors,' Ronan goes.

She comes back with three cans of Heineken.

Ronan's like, 'Is that alt you hab?'

She's there, 'I'm afraid so.'

Nudger goes, 'Piss. Ine oatenly thrinken it to stop meself soberding up.'

It's wasted on them. It's like feeding sourdough to the ducks.

I open mine. I knock back a mouthful and feel instantly better. The water of life.

I'm there, 'So you're definitely not worried about, you know, being tempted?'

He goes, 'No, Ine not. Ine stayun loyult to Shadden from now on, Rosser. I meant to say, if you want to go out to the tiddy beers and the lap-daddencing clubs and whatebber edelse, you feel free, Rosser. Foyer ahead. I wontherstand that you single feddas hab to do what you hab to do.'

'I've never been into the whole lap-dancing scene, if you want to call it that. Women telling you not to touch them while asking you for credit cord details. It's like being married.'

Ronan loves this line because he cracks his hole laughing, then leans across to the aisle to his friend, Gull, and goes, 'Did you hee-or what the Rosser lad's arthur saying? Said lap-daddencing was like being maddied – a wooban tedding you to keep your bleaten haddens to yisser self while aston you the wholt toyum for yisser crethit keerd!'

I hear this joke being retold back through the cabin, then various people going, 'Who said that – the rubby fedda?' until I hear someone eventually go, 'He's a cadickter, idn't he?' which *should* please me, but weirdly *doesn't*?

Ro goes, 'So what are we godda do, Rosser, while the rest of them are out bleaten whorden?'

I'm there, 'Actually, I've come up with an idea for a game,' and I whip out my phone and stort looking for the file. 'You know when people go on safari, roysh, they all want to see what they call The Big Five? We're talking lion, we're talking leopard, we're talking buffalo, we're talking rhino, we're talking –'

201

'Edephant.'

'Elephant, yeah. Well, I was thinking – okay, maybe this is a stu-pid idea – but we could do our *own* safari? So I spent a couple of nights on the Internet, trying to find out who were the biggest Irish criminals living in Estepona?'

He goes, 'Did you check the Indo website? Palt Widdiams writ a lorra eerticles about the place.'

'I read everything Paul Williams has ever written about the place. And these are the names I came up with.'

I hand him my phone. He reads it, going, '*Griebous Bothily Har-dem. Dangerous Roppie Folan. Fat Frankie Maher. Johnny The Badger Grendon. Andy The Milkman Kinch.* You're arthur putting their pitch-ers in as well.'

I'm there, 'You can also see that I've put little boxes beside each name so you get their autographs as you see them. I was going to print out one for everyone on the stag – that's if the hotel has an actual printer.'

Ronan just stares at my, I suppose, *work* – if you want to call it that? – for a good thirty seconds, then he turns to me and goes, 'You're a bleaten great fadder, Rosser. And doatunt you ebber doubt yisser self.'

So we're all sitting outside a boozer called El Arrecife on the main drag in Estepona – we're talking the whole crew minus Buckets of Blood, who was arrested on arrival in Malaga for causing possibly three hundred yoyos' worth of damage to a smoke detector.

There's a lot of speculation as to what will happen to him.

Gull goes, 'He could end up doing tree yee-or in a Spaddish jayult.'

But Ronan's uncle, Anto – in other words, Tina's brother – goes, 'Would you ast me boddicks, tree yee-or. Thee'll keep him in for a few hours – teach him a lesson – then thee'll lerrum go. Thrust me.'

It's, like, warm out, even though the sun went down hours ago, and the evening air is filled with the whiff of *Jōvan Musk* and *Hai Karate*. We're all, like, seven or eight pints down the road and the group is storting to split between those who are thinking of getting food and those who are thinking of getting their rock and roll.

As usual, I'm thinking of both.

Shadden's brother, Dadden, goes, 'There's a place hee-or that's apposed to do proper Irish cuddy chips!'

And Anto – who's an actual qualified chef – gives me a smile and rolls his eyes.

Kennet goes, 'I doatunt know about you f . . . f . . . f . . . f . . . f . . . f . . . feddas but Ine thinking of g . . . g . . . getting an eardy night. Ine bleaten b . . . b . . . b . . . b . . . b . . . b . . . b . . . boddixed, so I am.'

Before he goes back to the aportment, he gives Ronan a warning as to his behaviour. He goes, 'D . . . D . . . D . . . D . . . Doatunt be habbon sex wit addy quare ones. Do you get me?'

Ronan's like, 'Er . . .'

'Ine thalken about p . . . p . . . p . . . p . . . prosthitutes. You're apposed to be m . . . m . . . m . . . m . . . maddying my thaughter. Doaunt want you p . . . p . . . p . . . p . . . picking up athin.'

'I woatunt.'

'If you *are* wirra hooer, make shuren it's joost a h . . . h . . . h . . . h . . . hadden job you geroff her.'

'I've no inthordest,' Ro goes, 'in addyone but Shadden.'

Kennet seems pleased to hear this, then he focks off back to the hotel, taking one or two of the older ones with him.

A taxi pulls up in front of the pub and Buckets of Blood gets out of the back to huge cheers. He puts his two hands in the air and goes, 'Free the Estepona One, wha?'

I even laugh?

'Happent?' Ronan goes.

Buckets is there, 'Thee let me off with a warden – as to me future behaviour! Ast me bleeding boddicks!'

'Well, you're joost in toyum to get yisser rowunt in!'

I'm already getting the feeling that it's going to be a very long weekend.

My *phone* all of a sudden rings? I check the screen and I see that it's Honor, which is the only reason I answer it straightaway.

I'm like, 'Hey, Honor, is everything okay?'

I hear Gull impersonating my accent, going, 'Hey, Honor, is everything okay?' making me sound like I'm American, then I hear Ronan go, 'Hodor's he's thaughter.'

I'm there, 'What's wrong?' because there's, like, silence on the other end of the phone.

She eventually goes, 'I'm going to focking kill them! I'm going to slit their focking throats while they're asleep!'

I'm like, 'Who? Whose throats are you going to slit while they're asleep?'

The looks I end up getting from the others. Hey, we have our ways on our side of the city and they have theirs.

'Who do you think?' Honor goes.

I'm there, 'Are you talking about Sorcha's mom and dad?'

'He's taken my credit cords away.'

'Your credit cords?'

'Until I learn how to behave myself, he said. He also had my bank account frozen. He's just jealous because an eleven-year-old girl has more money than him, the bankrupt wanker.'

'Maybe hold off on cutting anyone's throat until I get home, Honor, will you?'

'When will that be?'

'After today it'll just be two more nights.'

'I'll try.'

'There's a good girl.'

It's *as* I'm hanging up that I suddenly spot him walking past. I'm there, 'Ro, did you see who that was?'

He's like, 'No, who wad it, Rosser?'

'It was Fat Frankie Maher.'

'Are you seerdious?'

I stand up and I whip out my Big Five checklist. I stare at his photograph. I'm there, 'It's definitely, definitely him.'

I watch him cross the road to use the ATM next to the twenty-four-hour launderette. I'm like, 'Okay, I'm going to be the first to get on the scoresheet.'

I tip across the road. Ronan shouts, 'Be veddy careful, Rosser. Doatunt sneak up on him,' but of course I'm not properly listening.

Which is portly down to me being super-competitive and portly down to me being super-shitfaced.

I walk up behind him while he's taking his money out of the wall and I go, 'Are you Frankie Maher?' and that's when all focking hell breaks loose.

Three or four people appear out of nowhere – they're, like, his *minders* basically? One of them punches me in the back of the head and suddenly the pavement is rushing up to meet my face. One of them kneels on my back and snatches the piece of paper out of my hand, while another one frisks me for presumably a gun.

He's the one who ends up asking all the questions. He's going, 'Who are you? Are you police? *Polícia? Polícia?*'

I'm, like, literally pinned face-down, going, 'No, I'm no one. I swear to God, I was just looking for your autograph.'

One of the other dudes looks at the piece of paper that he grabbed from me and goes, 'The Big Foyuv? This is a bleaten hit list, Frankie. And he's got *your* nayum on it.'

I'm lying there, literally waiting to hear the gunshot that ends my life, when all of a sudden I hear Ronan go, 'He's alreet, feddas – he's wirrus. We're tourdists. We're oaber hee-or on moy stag.'

I hear Fat Frankie go, 'What this list, but?'

Ro's there, 'He's tedding the troot. It's oately a gayum. Collect as maddy authorgraphs as we cadden in the tree days we're hee-or.'

I hear the one who took the list from me go, 'He's got Robbie Folan down hee-or. Griebous. Johnny Grendon. Andy Kinch.'

I'm still staring at the pavement, by the way. I'm practically tasting it. All of a sudden, I hear Fat Frankie go, 'Moy Jaysus, is that Buckets of Blood across the roawut?'

Ronan's like, 'Er, yeah, he's on the stag wirrus,' and then I hear Ronan call him. 'Buckets? Come oaber hee-or – you're wanton.'

Thirty seconds later, Frankie and Buckets are greeting each other like long-lost brothers.

'We did toyum togetter when we were kids,' Fat Frankie is telling everyone. 'I shairt an ould Peter Sellers with this fedda back in me Pat's days.'

Buckets is there, 'I ditn't know if you'd eeben remember me!'

'Remember you? You were veddy fooken good to me back then. I'll nebber forget that. Hee-or, feddas, pick your man up theer.'

I'm suddenly lifted to my feet.

I'm looking at Frankie's face for the first time. I can see where he gets his nickname. His double chins have double chins of their own.

He goes, 'Is this fedda wit you, Buckets?'

Buckets goes, 'He is, Frankie. He's the fadder of the groowum. He's a cadickter, so he is.'

'Is that reet?'

He's asking me.

I'm there, 'I don't know. I suppose that's for *others* to say?'

One of his minders goes, 'The accent on him! Where's he from?'

I'm there, 'Foxrock, originally.'

They're all like, 'Foxrock, originally,' in posh accents.

Frankie goes, 'What are your thressed like that for? Are you into the rubby, are you?'

'Yeah, no, you could say that. I'm a former player. Schools level. Then, later on, I played All Ireland League for Seapoint.'

This clearly means very little to him.

'What's your nayum?' he goes.

I'm like, 'Ross. Slash Rosser.'

'Let me gib you some advice, Rosser – might help lengtidden your life. Nebber, unther addy circumstaddences, approach eer koyunt of people from behoyunt. Do you get me?'

'I get you. I definitely get you.'

'We're like horses, you see – you might gerra kick!'

He takes the piece of paper off one of the other dudes. 'Hab addy of yous gorra a pen?' he goes.

One of them does. He hands it to him. Frankie tells him to turn around, then he signs my checklist, leaning on the dude's back. He hands it to me.

I'm still, like, terrified. My hands are shaking as I take it from him. I'm just there, 'Er, yeah, no, thanks.'

Frankie looks across the road. He goes, 'Where are yous thrinking? El Arrecife, is it?'

Ronan goes, 'That's reet, Frankie.'

Frankie just smiles. He's there, 'I'll join yous for one. I probley owe Rosser hee-or a bee-or.'

I wake up around midday the following day with a hangover that wants me dead. It ended up being some night. Fat Frankie bought round after round and he speculated with his minders how close they'd come to shooting me in the back of the head when Ronan intervened. There was general agreement that it was between two and five seconds.

I think that's why I was knocking it back at twice my normal rate.

I tip out onto the balcony. It's another scorcher of a day. I can see Ro down on the beach. He's got his top off and he's sitting cross-legged, doing his vocal exercises. I can see people staring at him as they walk past.

I send Honor a quick text. It's like, 'I miss u loads xxx ev ok?'

A few seconds later, she comes back to me with, 'There's a poison you can make using five everyday household items that acts in a way that doesn't arouse suspicion.'

I text her back with, 'Maybe just wait until I get back.'

Then she hits me back with just, 'x'.

There's a knock on the door of the aportment. I shout, 'It's open,' and then, a second or two later, in walks Anto, carrying a plate of something that smells incredible.

'I knocked you up one of me speciadity Morden Arhtur Om-adettes,' he goes – I think I mentioned that he was, like, a chef? 'That'll sort out your hangoaber – thrust me.'

He obviously heard me throwing up through the wall. I'm there, 'I don't know if I could hold anything down, Anto.'

He goes, 'There's nuttin like eggs for getting rid of the thoxins. Birra goat's cheeyuz. Spiddach. Few udions.'

He hands it to me. I try a forkful. It ends up being as incredible as it smells.

Anto squints his eyes. 'Is that Ro on the beach?' he goes.

I'm there, 'The one sitting crossed-legged, yeah.'

'What in the nayum of Jaysus is he doing?'

'He's chanting.'

'He's wha?'

'Yeah, no, it's a long story. This omelette is unbelievable, by the way.'

'Gerrer inta ya, Cyntia. You'll be sorthed widdin the hour.'

'Ro says you're doing the food in the Broken Orms these days.'

'I am, yeah. Ine arthur taking over the kitchen theer.'

'And the food is going down very well. I hear lunchtime murders are down by fifty per cent in the pub.'

'Non-gang-relayrit moorders, yeah.'

I have to say, I've always liked Anto. Without him, of course, I wouldn't even *be* here? Because it all storted with Anto. Back in nineteen-ninety-whatever-it-was, we swapped houses as port of a Castlerock College cultural exchange programme known as the Urban Plunge. He came to live in Foxrock and I went to live in Finglas.

I remind him about it and we both have a chuckle.

I'm there, 'You robbed everything that wasn't nailed down.'

He goes, 'I didn't rob athin, Rosser!' and suddenly I'm wondering, did he actually? and I'm thinking that it's funny how your memory can sometimes play tricks.

He's there, 'Your mudder was a teddible nice wooban.'

Like I said – tricks.

I'm like, 'You're wrong on that score, Anto. She was a focking wench – and she still is to this day.'

He goes, 'Then *you* went and roawut me sister – got her bleaten pregnant.'

Ronan spots us on the balcony. He gives us a little wave. And I go, 'I'm actually glad I did.'

He's there, 'There'd be no Ronan if you haddana.'

'All thanks to the Jesuits and their stupid, well-meaning ways.'

That's when Anto says it – totally out of the blue. He goes, 'He's maken the biggest mistake ob he's life, Rosser.'

I'm there, 'Who? Ronan?'

He just nods. He goes, 'He's not rethy to get maddied.'

I'm there, 'You don't think so?'

'Ine not the oatenly wooden eeter. He's ma dudn't wanth him to do it. He's arthur royden half the young woodens in Finglas beho-yunt Shadden's back. Including one ob her broyud's mayuts.'

'Yeah, no, I heard. What was she called again? Something hilarious.'

'It's oately a mathor of toyum befower Shadden foyunts ourra bout her – *and* all the utters.'

'He was doing pretty much the same thing over our side of the city. He's gone through that Orts Block like a pig through Bally-ogan Tip.'

'You're he's fadder, Rosser. You hab to thalk him ourrof it. He caddent maddy the geerdle. Norr if he's stiddle whorden arowunt.'

'He's not anymore, Anto. He thinks he's conquered it.'

'Conquered it?'

'His sex addiction. Supposed. Using – get this! – meditation and chanting.'

'Nudger and he's bleaten Buddhism.'

'I have to say, I was Scooby Dubious myself. But he hasn't been with another woman since he went to live on Lambay Island.'

'There's no wibbin *on* the islunt!'

'Yeah, no, but he hasn't even felt the urge. I have to say, Anto, I'm really proud of him. I'm also proud of myself. I helped him face up to the fact that he had a problem and he did something about it.'

'If you say so, Rosser.'

'I actually wish I'd met Nudger when I was Ronan's age. It might have saved my own marriage.'

Ronan has left the beach and he's standing directly under the balcony. He puts his two orms out in front of him and mimes riding a motorbike. Kennet was talking about us possibly renting mopeds and driving the coast road to Gibraltar.

I tell him we're on our way down.

'The w . . . w . . . w . . . w . . . w . . . way your auld fedda's arthur been tr . . . tr . . . tr . . . treated,' Kennet goes. 'It's a bleaten disgrace, so it is.'

I'm there, 'In fairness, Kennet, he's got away with saying a lot of shit over the years. It's all just finally catching up on him.'

This is us, by the way, on – like I said – mopeds, heading for Gibraltar – we're talking me, him, Ronan, Anto and Dadden. We're having to shout over what sounds like five really loud hair-dryers.

He goes, 'W . . . w . . . w . . . wooden thing your auld fedda is depinitely n . . . n . . . n . . . not is a bleaten sexist. He lubs women. And Ine sayin that as someone who's arthur been thriving him arowunt for the last tree yee-or. You do heerd him thalken to the w . . . w . . . w . . . waithresses in that Shadahan's on the Greeyun – *and* the boords serbing in the Sheddle Burden Bar. He does be t . . . t . . . t . . . t . . . tedding them they're lubbly-looken geerdles and gibbon them compliments when they're able to woork out in their heads exactly what chayunge he's owed. Dud that sowunt like a s . . . s . . . s . . . s . . . sexist to you, Rosser?'

I'm there, 'I wouldn't know, Kennet. I'm no kind of judge.'

Behind me, Ronan gives me a little beep, meaning he wants to talk to me, so I ease off the pedal and let him come level with me.

He's like, 'How's the hagoaber, Rosser?'

And I suddenly realize it's gone.

I'm there, 'Fully lifted. Anto there made me one of his omelettes.'

'Lubbly, ardent thee?'

'Well, it certainly did the trick. Look, thanks again for, you know, stopping me getting executed gangland-style last night.'

'Ah, you werdent to know, Rosser. They're veddy nerbous creatures, you see. Every wooden on that list is libbon in fee-or of he's life. There's criminoddles from alt oaber the wurdled mooben in on their patch. Spaddish, Toorks, Rushiddens. You heert what Frankie said – it's peert of the reason they're all retoyerden to the Middle Deast.'

'It ended up being a good night, though, didn't it?'

'One of the best ebber, Rosser. Did you hee-or what Frankie says to me when he was leaben?'

'No, what?'

'Well, I toalt him I was stoodying Law and he says to me to stick arrit. He says that's what he'd of dudden if he had of had brayuns.

Wouldn't have spent he's life on the rudden – altwees looken oaber he's shoulter. He knows Heddessy, by the way.'

'Hennessy? That wouldn't surprise me at all, Ro.'

'Ah, theer she is, Rosser!'

He's talking about the actual Rock of Gibraltar. It suddenly appears in the far-off distance and we're all excited about seeing it and grabbing a beer or six.

As Ronan says, it's Saturday: 'Tonight's the big nye rowt.'

Up ahead, Dadden storts waving his hand, presumably to warn us about something on the road. Then he storts signalling and he pulls in. We all do the same. And that's when we see what it's about.

Forty, maybe fifty feet ahead of us, on a dirt track beside the road, there's a broken-down moped lying on its side and its owner – a skinny dude in his mid-thirties – is literally kicking the fock out of it and calling it a useless fooken pox of a thing.

'See does this fedda neeyut a haddend,' Dadden goes.

Dadden is actually sound.

Ronan suddenly goes, 'Hee-or, wait! That's The Milkmadden!'

He's trying to say Milkman.

Dadden goes, 'Andy Kinch? It's norr Andy Kinch! No way!'

I whip out my Big Five checklist and I look at the photo. I'm there, 'It *is* him,' because I recognize his sticky-out ears from not only this but also the hundreds of photographs I saw of him on the Internet.

He's basically a hit man, according to the little bit of research I did on him, and got the nickname The Milkman because he always delivers.

'Membor,' Ronan goes, 'we hab to be veddy keerful not to steertle him. Hee-or, Rosser, you hang back this toyum. I'll make the approach.'

The dude is still effing and blinding, bear in mind, and our horts are in our literally mouths as Ronan storts walking slowly towards him with his two hands in the air.

After a few seconds, The Milkman sees him coming and he looks immediately suspicious. You can see his nostrils flaring – Fat

Frankie did say they were like horses – trying to smell whether this stranger who's about to step into his zone is a friend or an enemy.

You can see his hand suddenly hovering over his belt. I presume he's 'caddying' as these people call it.

Ronan keeps walking slowly towards him, step by step, letting him see his hands at all times, no sudden movements, talking softly to him like some kind of, I don't know, Dublin gangland criminal whisperer.

'We oately stopped to see did you neeyut a haddend?' Ronan goes.

And The Milkman is like, 'Just to warden you, Ine caddying.'

I told you.

Ro goes, 'Like I says to you, we pullt in to see could we help in addy way.'

The Milkman gives his focked moped another boot. He's there, 'It's a piece of bleaten shit, so it is.'

Ronan is, like, right in front of him. He reaches out and he touches the dude on the shoulder. And the most amazing thing happens then. The dude immediately calms down.

Ro goes, 'Doatunt woody, Anthy. My about-to-be-brutter-in-law knows all about bikes, keers – athin that moobs. Dadden, hab a look at this, will you?'

Dadden walks forward. We all walk forward and pretty soon he's asking us where in Dublin we're from and telling Ronan he must be off he's bleaten rocker getting maddied, while Dadden works on his bike using only a Swiss Ormy Knife.

The dude turns to me at one point and goes, 'What jersey is that?'

I'm like, 'It's Leinster away.'

'Gimme it.'

'Fock off.'

Ronan goes, 'Gib him the jersey, Rosser.'

I'm like, 'What the fock am I going to wear? I'll burn in the sun.'

'We'll get you a tee-shoort when we get to Gibralthar. He likes the jeersey – gib it to him.'

'One of moy young feddas,' the dude goes, 'is arthur getting mad into the rubby, so he is.'

I'm blaming the IRFU – and Philip Browne specifically – for trying to grow the game beyond its traditional base of eight decent schools.

I take it off and I hand it to him.

'He'll lub that,' he goes.

Ronan's there, 'Do you moyunt if we ast *you* for a fabour, Anthy?'

The dude's like, 'It depends what, dudn't it?'

He's not the friendliest goy in the world. But then, I suppose he wouldn't be in that line of work if he was an actual *people* person?

Ronan reaches into his pocket – he makes sure to do it slowly – and produces his Big Five checklist. He goes, 'Can we hab yisser authorgraph?'

The dude takes the piece of paper from Ronan and gives it the once-over. He goes, 'Where did you see Fat Frankie?'

I'm there, 'He was using an ATM – opposite where we were drinking last night.'

'The fooken doorty-looken doort-boord. He's been toawult I doatunt know how meddy toyums to gerr ourra Spayunt.'

'He *did* mention that he was moving to Dubai – although he said he had one or two loose ends to tie up here first.'

The dude points at me and goes, 'This fedda thalks thoo much. Ine veddy grateful for the jeersey, but. Addyone hab a pen?'

As it happens, *I* do? I hand it to him. He signs Ronan's checklist, then he signs mine, then Kennet's, then Anto's and then Dadden's.

And just as he's finishing the last of them, we hear the sound of his moped storting up again.

'What did I ted you?' Ronan goes. 'Dadden's a bleaten genius when it cuddems to engines, mothors – athin like that.'

The Milkman says thanks and, with my Leinster jersey draped over his shoulder, throws his leg over the bike. He tells us that if we happen to run into Johnny Grendon, aka The Badger, to tell him he's going to put a fooken bullet in his head. Then he puts his foot on the pedal and soon he's disappeared into the distance.

'You met *who*?'

Buckets of Blood and Gull are very impressed.

'Theer's he's signature theer,' Ronan goes, jabbing his finger at his checklist. 'Not tedding you a woord ob a loy. He was pult oaber on the soyut of the roawut – he's moped was arthur breaking dowunt. Am I reet, Rosser?'

I'm there, 'You are, yeah. He took my focking Leinster jersey. I'll be billing Philip Browne for a new one.'

Gull bangs his fist on the table. He goes, 'I fooken toalt you we shoulda gone wit them!'

Buckets goes, 'Arthur the amount you thrank last neet? How were you godda thrive a moped and the bleaten state of you this morden?'

I'm getting the impression that if there was an Irish Gangland edition of Top Trumps, Andy Kinch would be a very good cord to have in your deck.

Gull goes, 'He's kilt thoorty people in he's toyum – that's accorton to Palt Widdiams.'

There seems to be general agreement that this is a lot of people for one man to have killed.

Ronan goes, 'He was a lubbly fedda, but – wadn't he Kennet? Veddy dowun to Eeert.'

Kennet goes, 'Veddy dowun to Eert, yeah – arthur he'd c . . . c . . . c . . . c . . . c . . . c . . . caddomed dowunt.'

We're in Girls, Girls, Girls, by the way, a lap-dancing club on the old Calle Huerta Nueva. Some bird walks over to our table and introduces herself to me as Yelena.

I'm there, 'Yeah, no, Ross.'

She goes, 'Is gute to meet you, Ross. You like private dance?'

'Er . . .'

'What is wrong? You not like me?'

'I do like you. I think you're a ringer for Svetlana Kuznetsova. She's a tennis player in case you're wondering. A big ride.'

'So why you no want dance?'

'It's just I have this issue with paying for something I can get for free *elsewhere*?'

I can tell straightaway that I've said the wrong thing. She suddenly storts *losing* it with me?

'Why you here? You no go to restaurant for food and say, oh, I no pay, I can get better for free at home.'

'Yeah, no,' I go, 'the point is I haven't actually *ordered* any food slash whatever? The only reason I'm even here is because it's my son's *stag*?'

Needless to say, Ronan and the others are all loving seeing me put under pressure. The more they laugh, the angrier Yelena becomes because she thinks I'm ripping the basic piss.

'You come in here and you listen to music,' she goes, 'and you look at girls but you won't pay for anything.'

I'm there, 'It's twenty yoyos for a beer – and this is, like, my fifth.'

'I no care. We are not paid when you drink beer. We are paid for dance. We no dance, we no paid. You understand?'

'I understand and I sympathize. But it's like I said, I've never – as they say – gone professional.'

'Perhaps you just like to look. Perhaps you are pervert.'

'I am a bit, I suppose.'

'Or, no, perhaps you are gay man. And you are trying to hide this secret. That is why you come here. You pretend you like girls but is because you are feggot.'

I go, 'Hey, you don't have to keep talking to me. You're not on the clock here.'

She points at me with one of her freakishly long fingernails. 'You are asshole,' she goes. 'You are big, big asshole.'

And off she goes in a strop.

I turn to the others and I go, 'I actually paid the girl a compliment. Svetlana Kuznetsova – you all heard me.'

Ronan goes, 'Get them in, Rosser! It's your rowunt!'

Anyway, to cut a long story short, it ends up being a cracking, cracking night. We drink a lot of beer and we have a lot of laughs. Occasionally, one or two of the others slip into one of the little rooms for a private dance with one of the girls. If the girl happens to be Yelena, they always come back with the same story.

'Hee-or,' Dadden goes, 'I doatunt know what you said to that brasser but you're arthur getting unther her skin in serious way.

She thalked about you the enthoyer toyum she was daddencing for me. Neertly feel like aston you for me muddy back.'

Gull says pretty much the same thing. 'She's bleaten obsessed wit you, Rosser.'

Anyway, I end up getting up seriously mashed. At one point, very late in the evening, I'm talking to Nudger. Hammered. Making very little sense.

'It's the first day of the Leaving Cert,' I'm going, 'and I'm sitting in the exam hall and I realize I haven't done a tap of work and I literally know nothing. And then everyone storts laughing because I'm sitting there and I'm not wearing any trousers, just boxer shorts.'

Nudger goes, 'Soddy, Rosser, is this a regular dream you have?'

I'm there, 'It wasn't a dream, Nudger. This actually happened. I did it as a dare the first time I repeated.'

Suddenly, Ronan is standing over me, going, 'Rosser, can I hab a woord?'

I'm there, 'Yeah, no, what's wrong, Ro?'

'The feddas is arthur clubbing togetter to buy me a daddence.'

'Okay?'

'But I doatunt want it, Rosser.'

'Why not?'

'It'd feel like I was doing the doort, so it would.'

'I'm not a hundred per cent sure if getting a lap dance is doing the dirt, Ro.'

'Eeter way, I'd radder not, Rosser.'

'But you don't want to lose face in front of the lads?'

'I doatunt want to hoort their feedings eeder. They're arthur putting their hands in their pockets, so thee are.'

'So what are you proposing?'

'Your one is waiting for me in the Room Tree. Anna is the boord's nayum. I'll thisappear for ten midutes – I'll go to the jacks – and you go in and hab the daddence.'

'Ro, it doesn't really do anything for me.'

'It's free, Rosser. Go on – do it for me, will you?'

So I agree. He heads for the old Josh Ritter and I head for Room Three. I knock on the door.

'Come!' she shouts.

So in I go. Anna turns out to be another stunner. This time I'm saying Elena Dementieva.

'Sit!' she goes, pointing at this, like, leather chair. 'Don't worry. I wipe.'

Seriously, I don't know *how* people get aroused in these places?

I sit down and wait for the show to get storted. And that's when she announces that there's a problem.

'Lap dance is ten minutes,' she goes. 'I am finished shift in five.'

I have to say I never expected to meet one who was a clock-watcher.

I'm there, 'I'll take the five. It does very little for me anyway.'

She goes, 'No, I ask my colleague to do instead,' and I know – just know – from the very moment she slips out of the room who it's going to end up being.

Twenty seconds later, the door opens and in walks Yelena.

'So,' she goes, 'you have a change of mind, yes?'

I'm there, 'I just wanted to see what all the fuss was about,' obviously not wanting to tell her that it was a freebie.

She finds a song on her iPod, then sticks it into docking station and the room is suddenly filled with the sound of a song that I don't recognize.

She goes, 'I will show you what all of the fuss is about,' and she walks over to me and sits on my lap, facing me, with one leg either side of me and her love warts jammed in my face.

Like I said, lap dancing has never done anything for me. But I've never had a lap dance like this before. She really puts her back into it, in fairness to the girl, and I can suddenly feel myself becoming seriously aroused.

She's grinding away on my crotch – the usual thing – but it's weird because I can sense that she's actually *enjoying* it? As in, it's obvious to me that this isn't work for her.

'When I see you tonight,' she whispers, 'I like you.'

I'm there, 'I picked up on that. That's half the reason I didn't want to pay you.'

'You don't haff to pay.' She kisses me full on the mouth. She goes, 'There is other room we can go.'

I'm there, 'Okay, is this where you stort trying to sweet-talk my credit cord details out of me?'

She storts unbuttoning my shirt. She goes, 'I don't want credit card,' as she peels it off me.

She stands up and she points at my chinos. 'Take off these,' which is what I end up doing.

She goes, 'Count to one hundred, then follow,' and she disappears through a door to my right.

I whip off my chinos and my boxer shorts as I stort the count. I don't get anywhere close to one hundred, of course. It's more like, I don't know, *fifty*? I walk to the door in just my socks and my Dubes, because the last thing I want is for them to go missing, while carrying just my phone.

I push the door and through it I go with a dick on me like a budgie's perch.

I go, 'Here I come, ready or –' and then I suddenly stop. I notice that it's not a bedroom at all. It turns out I'm outside – on an actual roof.

I'm there, 'Yelena?' because I still haven't copped it yet. 'Yelena, where are you?'

I hear a noise behind me. Yelena is standing at the door behind me. It's either a magic trick or she slipped back into the club by another entrance. She laughs in, like, a *cruel* way?

I'm like, 'Yelena, don't do it! Please – don't do it!'

I make a run for the door, but she's quicker than I am and she manages to slam it in my face and turn the key.

I'm suddenly banging on it with my open palm, going, 'Let me in! Yelena, please! I'm sorry if you felt insulted by what I said!'

But it's no good. I know women well enough to recognize when a situation is beyond rescue.

Fock, though.

I look around me. I spot a plastic bag tangled up in a TV aerial on the roof above me. I reach up and I manage to grab it, then – I can't believe I'm making a pair of plastic underpants – I tear two holes in the bottom, lorge enough to fit my legs through, then I tie the two handles in a bow at the front.

Then I walk over to the edge of the roof and look down. It's a drop of, like, twenty feet to the ground. I sit on the edge, preparing to launch myself off, thinking about all of the nights out in my life that have ended like this and wondering how I've never managed to develop a head for heights.

I end up getting cold feet. But I'm scared of just jumping straight down in case I damage my ankle, so instead I decide to shorten the distance to the ground by sort of hanging off the roof and then *dropping* down? So I turn around and I lower myself over the edge of the roof while holding on to the plastic gutter.

I let my orms go long and I look down at the ground. But shit – my nerve fails me. It looks like a massive drop and I'm suddenly too scared to let go. I'm literally hanging off the gutter, naked except for a plastic nappy, but I can't persuade my hands to open and let me fall.

And that's when I hear the laughter.

Oh, fockety fock!

Yelena has obviously rounded everyone up and told them to come outside.

I hear Ronan's voice go, 'What in the nayum of Jaysus, Rosser?' but I can tell he finds it funny.

I'm there, 'Goys, can you help me?'

Anto's like, 'Joost let go, Rosser. It's oatently about a fifteen-foot throp!'

I'm there, 'I can't. I forgot I'm scared of heights.'

Ro goes, 'Where are you bleaten clowuts, Rosser? Is that a plastic bag you're weardon instead of your jockeys?'

'Goys, my orms are killing me! Do something!'

Then I hear Kennet go, 'Yelena, lub, would you ebber see can you gerrus a l . . . l . . . l . . . l . . . l . . . l . . . ladder?'

Nudger has got his hands on a copy of the *Irish Indo* – one day old. He's reading it when I arrive down to the pool.

'I see your auld fedda's in mower botter,' he goes. 'Bit like you last neet, wha?'

Him and Buckets and Gull are sitting on sun-loungers – half-ten in the morning and already two or three bottles into a day's drinking.

I'm there, 'More bother? As in, more bother than before?'

He goes, 'Some boord's arthur cubbing forward, accorting to this. She woorked in a bank in Dudden Leary. He appadently said, *"Maith an cailín!"* to her when he did a forden cash thransfer in 1981.'

I'm there, 'Give me a look at that!'

He hands it to me and I give it the old left to right. There's a quote from Muirgheal Massey saying that the comment was deeply regrettable and clearly offensive but should be judged within the context of what was acceptable behaviour at the time. However, it says, Senator Sorcha Lalor has described it as clearly port of an historical pattern of behaviour that stretched back many decades.

Then, halfway down the story, there's a paragraph storting with the word *meanwhile* that catches my eye. It's like, 'Dublin City Council has announced plans to rename half of the capital city's streets after women by the end of 2018. The council has asked the public to submit names of women they believe worthy of having streets named in their honour.'

And speaking of Honor. She's suddenly ringing my phone.

I answer by going, 'Hey – is everything okay?'

Nudger mimes drinking a beer and I nod, yeah, I'll definitely have one – breakfast or no breakfast.

Honor goes, 'She has *focking* lost it!'

I'm like, 'Who? Who's lost it, Honor?'

'Your focking wife.'

'I'm just reading the paper here. Are you talking about what she said about my old man?'

'I'm talking about her being a complete bitch.'

'I'm not sure we're allowed to say shit like that anymore, Honor. Look at the trouble your granddad has got himself in. And that was just calling some dead bird a cow.'

'I told her I was sorry for getting that stupid kid drunk.'

'Why did you apologize? I'm not sure that was necessary.'

'Because I was trying to get her to change her mind about dancing.'

'Tactics!'

'Oh, I put on a real show. I cried and everything.'

'It's actually scary the way you can turn it on and off.'

'Anyway, I had her, like, totally convinced that I was ashamed of myself and I told her that I felt I'd turned a corner since I storted dancing.'

'Er, I kind of felt you had as well.'

'And when I asked her if I could go back to it she said, "We'll see."'

'That's good, Honor. At least it's not an actual no.'

'And then that stupid feminist bitch was here last night.'

'Again, if you drop the word "bitch" and just say "stupid feminist".'

'She said that ballroom dancing was sexist because it reinforced the outdated gender stereotype that says men should lead and women should *be* led?'

'Jesus, does that girl ever take a day off?'

'So now my so-called mother is saying she's sticking with her original decision.'

I hear Honor's voice crack. It says a lot that I can't tell whether it's real or another show.

I'm there, 'Honor, are you *genuinely* crying?'

She goes, 'Of course I'm genuinely crying.'

'Okay, look, I'll have a word with her when I get home. See can I smooth-talk her.'

She says thanks, then hangs up.

Nudger arrives back with the beers. 'Was that your young wooden?' he goes.

I'm there, 'Yeah, she's at that difficult age,' pretending she hasn't been like this since she learned to speak. 'It's all ahead of you and Blodwyn.'

He indicates the bottles on the table beside his sun-lounger. He goes, 'Why do you think Ine habbon a last blowout?'

Buddhist my focking hole. I tell him fair focks, though – then I ask him if Ronan has surfaced yet.

He's there, 'He went out to gerra birra breakfast – you know yisser self. There's a place does the Iredish sausages. He went wit Kennet and Dadden. I think Anto's gone wit them as weddle.'

It's a pity he didn't tell me. I wouldn't have minded a plate of something myself.

I go, 'By the way, Nudger, I just wanted to say – you know – thanks.'

He's like, 'What are you thanken me fower?'

'For being such a great friend to Ro over the years. And, specifically, for teaching him how to shut down his sex drive.'

'I know he ditn't get the lap daddence that Buckets and Gull ped fower.'

'That's what I'm saying. He seems to have lost the urge to ride everything that moves.'

About an hour – and three beers later – Ronan arrives back with Anto, Dadden and K . . . K . . . K . . . K . . . Kennet.

'Unbeliebable breakfast,' he goes, then he spots me, lying there, catching a few rays. 'Hee-or, Rosser,' he goes, 'I think you've a birrof nappy theer arthur last neet!'

They all crack their holes laughing, until I end up having to do the same – no choice. It *is* actually funny.

Then he goes, 'You'll nebber belieb who we joost met when we were habben the breakfast. Thee go to this place all the toyum cos thee do the Irish sausages.'

I'm like, 'Who?'

'Johnny "The Badger" Grendon and "Dangerous" Robbie Folan!'

'You're shitting me.'

'Ine not shitting you. Ine not tedding a woord ob a loy.'

He reaches into the pocket of his shorts and he whips out his Big Five checklist and shows it to me. I can see their signatures on it.

'Theeve obviously patched up their diffordences,' he goes, 'because a year ago, they were threatening all sorts against each utter – that's accorton to the *Sudden Day Wurdled*.'

'Did you mention to The Badger that The Milkman was planning to kill him?'

'We were habbon a great chat, Rosser. I ditn't wanth to bring the moowud dowun. In addyhow, as you can see, I've now ticked off fowur of the Big Foyuv. Ine the oatenly wooden of us waiting on joost wooden mower.'

'Who do you need?'

'Griebous Bothily Hardem.'

'How are you going to get him?'

'I've an idea, Rosser – I know where he libs!'

What? The Actual? Fock?

Okay, I've seen some tacky gaffs in my time. I grew up in Foxrock and I live in Killiney – not exactly the good taste capitals of the world. But *Coolock Sur Mer* – that's the name on the brass plaque on the front wall – takes the definite biscuit.

For storters, the front gates are like the Gates of Heaven, twenty or thirty feet high and painted gold. And on top of the pillars either side are two humungous stone swans, raised to their full height.

'He's wife, Medissa, lubs swaddens,' Ronan goes. 'She grew up in Cabra – near the banks of the Royult Caddal.'

I'm there, 'She must *really* love them. Those things are bigger than you or me.'

'He bought this gaff arthur he moordered Nasko Bandalovski – thubble-crossed him – and took oaber he's thrugs importhation bidiness. The Spaddish police says he's responsible for about sebenty per centh of the hedoin cubbing from Afghadistadden into Eurdope.'

'You'd have to say fair focks to him.'

'Thoorty bethrooms, Rosser. He's gorra swibben poowult, snooker roowum and a fowerty-seat cidema. A meerble steercase that's an exact replica of wooden that Medissa lubbed in the Shangri-La Hothel in Abu Dhabi. Cost tree bleaten middion. And a loyumstone founthain, Rosser – in an athrium in the mithel of the gaff.'

'Hey, I said fair focks and I'm sticking to it.'

We both look through the gates. There's a line of fifteen, maybe twenty statues – made of bright white stone – along either side of a long driveway.

'That's the Herdoes' Pardade,' Ronan goes.

I'm like, 'What are they – Greek Gods or something?'

'On the right is Heffo's Eermy – the Dublin tee-um what wudden the Sam in sebenty-six and sebenty-seben.'

'We're obviously talking Gaelic football, are we?'

'On the reet is the tee-um what beat Keddy in the final in two tousand and eleben. Can you see Burden It Barrogan there, look? Diarmuid Coddolly besoyut him! And Cluxton – the bleaten head on him, look!'

'Why have they all got angel wings?'

'Yeah, this cubbing from the madden who libs in a house with tuddets.'

He means turrets. And, like I said, I'm not making any great style claims for *our* kind of people? I heard somewhere that the Vico Road has more stone lions than the Serengeti has actual ones. Three and a half thousand. That's a fact.

I'm there, 'So what's the play here?'

He goes, 'What do you mee-un?'

'Well, we've come all this way. We want to meet the dude, don't we?'

We're on our Tobler, by the way. The others had a few hair of the dog beers for breakfast and then just continued into another day's drinking. But Ronan was determined to spot the last of the Big Five and I didn't want to see him disappointed – not on his stag weekend.

He goes, 'I thought we'd mebbe wait outsoyut until he cuddems out, Rosser.'

I'm like, 'We will in our orses.'

'What's your pladden, then?'

'Okay, in all the years you've known me, what have you learned about Southsiders – as in, what do we lack?'

'Accounthabidity.'

'And?'

'Morals.'

'Okay, aport from accountability and morals, what do we not have on our side of the city?'

'A sense of embaddassment.'

'A sense of embarrassment is right. If we want something, we go and grab it – and fock what anyone thinks!'

'You caddent joost rig on the doe-er, Rosser.'

'Can't I? Well, you just watch me.'

I look for the intercom buzzer and I suddenly realize what Ronan is trying to tell me. There isn't one. These aren't the kind of people who have randomers calling offering to tell them about Jesus or creosote the fence.

Suddenly, a figure appears at the top of the driveway. He's a big dude – as in, like, *ripped*? – and he's wearing a t-shirt, shorts and baseball cap.

I'm like, 'That's not Grievous Bodily Horm, is it?'

Ro goes, 'No, that's he's son – Actual.'

'Actual Bodily Horm! The nicknames are priceless, aren't they?'

Actual shouts at us – the length of the driveway. He goes, 'What the fook do yous waddant?'

I'm there, 'Is Grievous Bodily Horm home?' suddenly very conscious of my Foxrock accent.

Ro goes, 'Jasus Christ, Rosser, no wooden calls him that to he's face. You're making us look like a couple of bleaten abateurs. He's nayum's Roppie Ryant.'

So I shout, 'Sorry, we're actually looking for a Robbie Ryan?'

Actual goes, 'Who the fook are you?'

Ronan decides to take over the talking then, which is fair enough.

'Ine a big admoyrer of your fadder,' he goes. 'Ine just oaber hee-or on me stag and I was hoping to get he's authorgraph. Mebbe eeben a selfie.'

Actual considers this for a moment, then goes, 'Wait there,' and he disappears back into the house.

Ronan is suddenly very excited. He's there, 'Do you think he's gone to geth he's ould fedda, Rosser?'

I'm like, 'Either that or a gun.'

'I caddent belieb Ine about to meet Griebous Bothily Heerm. He's probably me favourdite of the cuddent bunch, Rosser – me favourdite since The Gener Doddle.'

'Take out your Big Five checklist, then. He might just sign it through the gate.'

'Hee-or, can you imagine if he invoyrit us in, Rosser? A few drinks be the poowult. Be some stordee to the ted the utters, wha?'

After a few minutes, a woman appears and storts walking towards us, along the Heroes' Parade, to the gate.

Out of the side of his mouth, Ronan goes, 'It's Medicious Wounding, Rosser. Ine a big fan of hors as weddle. She has a sheet longer than addy of them. Mostly for fighting. Bouncers and shop securdity geerds.'

The only way to describe her is to say that she looks like Teresa Giudice would look like in ten years' time if she was the subject of a *You Won't Believe What Teresa Giudice Looks Like Now* clickbait story and when you hit the link it turns out that she's still actually alright in terms of, like, *looks*?

She reaches the gate and she stares at Ronan through the bars. She goes, 'What do you waddant?'

Ro goes, 'I was saying to your sudden that Ine oaber hee-or on me stag and I would lubben to meet your husband.'

She stares at him for a good long time, then she goes, 'Fook off – you peerda of bleaten jokers.'

And, not surprisingly, we do as we're told.

So it's, like, our last night in Estepona and we're in the Irish bor, May Oblong's, where, after nine or ten pints, we've now moved onto shots. Ronan is horrendufied. He's wearing an L-plate around his neck at the insistence of Dadden, who keeps laying dork hints that before the night is over he's going to tie him up, shave his head and balls and put him on a ferry to Morocco – 'like a proper bleaten stag!'

I'm presuming he's joking. I *hope* he's joking?

There's a hen in the house, by the way. We're talking Kathleen. She's from, like, Kilkenny and she's an absolute cracker. Think Amy Willerton – except an Irish country version with some Chinese letters that don't actually mean anything on the back of her neck – and you're in the right postcode. Her and her mates are swarming around Ronan like pigeons on sick and he's giving them the full blast of his personality.

I don't need to tell you who he reminds me of. I'm talking about me.

'To the institushidden of maddidge!' he goes, holding up a Sambuca – he bought them a full round. 'As that boord in *Fower Wettons and a Funerdoddle* says, "Lub is the addonser – and *you* know that for shewer!"'

One of the Kilkenny birds turns around to me and goes, 'Jaysus, he's a fine thing, isn't he?'

I'm there, 'Hey, I'm his old man, so I'm bound to be biased.'

'I'd say Kathleen now would love to ride him. She says she wants to go out with a bang – you know yourself.'

And all I can do is just smile as I watch Ronan call for another round. Because I know, in my hort of horts, that he'll never cheat on Shadden again.

'Kathleen can try all she wants,' I go, 'but I'm pretty sure she'd be borking up the wrong tree.'

Kennet suddenly appears on my shoulder. 'Your young fedda b . . . b . . . b . . . b . . . bettor not d . . . d . . . d . . . d . . . do the d . . . d . . . d . . . d . . . d . . . doorty on moy thaughter.'

'D . . . d . . . do the d . . . d . . . doorty,' I go. 'It's like listening to focking Morse Code.'

'Ine joost saying. And if he d . . . d . . . d . . . d . . . does do the d . . . d . . . d . . . doort, I'll oately turden a bloyunt eye if it's a hadden job or a blowie.'

'Ronan loves Shadden. You've fock-all to worry about on that score.'

I decide to call it a night. Yeah, no, I've had a surprisingly good time, but I'm actually looking forward to getting home to Honor and – to a much lesser extent – Brian, Johnny and Leo.

I tip over to Ro, squeezing my way past his fan club. He goes, 'Rosser, you cross-dresser! Hee-or, hab a shot!'

I'm there, 'Actually, Ro, I might actually call it a night.'

He just nods and goes, 'C'mere to me!'

He hugs me for a good ten seconds, taps out, then holds me

at orm's length and goes, 'You're arthur organizing an unbeliebable stag for me, Rosser. You're the best madden alreet. The best madden addy fedda who's getting maddied could ebber hope fowur.'

I'm there, 'I'm sorry you didn't get to see all of the Big Five, Ro.'

'Nebber moyunt,' he goes, 'thanks for an unbeliebable stag,' and then he calls over Anto, Buckets, Nudger, Gull, Dadden and Kennet and tells them to raise their shot glasses in a toast to 'the Rosser lad', which they all then do.

It'd nearly give you a big head.

So off I go.

I'm, like, literally two hundred yords from the hotel when I suddenly spot him. It's actually Malicious *Wounding* who I see first? She's leaving a restaurant called Er Terero with two men – one younger, one older. The young man is the dude we saw this afternoon. The older one, I quickly realize from staring at my Big Five checklist all weekend, is the man himself – we're talking Grievous Bodily Horm. He's sort of, like, stocky, in his early sixties, with grey hair, slicked back.

They're about to get into – of all things – a red Citroën Picasso, with *her* driving.

It might be drunkenness. It might be stupidity. It might be the pure love I feel for my son. But I end up shouting at Grievous, 'You're *no* kind of role model! You're a focking disgrace.'

Okay, it probably *is* just drunkenness.

Grievous goes, 'Begga peerton?' meaning, presumably, I beg your pordon.

There's no minders with him. I think I might have read online that he doesn't believe in them.

I'm there, 'I'm just making the point that all my son was looking for was an autograph. Maybe you need to remember that you're only where you are today because of fans like him. And then obviously all the drug-dealing you do.'

Shit, I'm way more drunk than I thought I was.

Actual laughs. He goes, 'That's the sham who was at the fruddent gate eardier on.'

Melissa goes, 'I toalt him to fook off.'

Grievous stares at me and goes, 'Are you a cop?'

I'm like, 'No, I'm not a cop. I'm someone whose son is getting married on New Year's Eve and who's over here on his stag. And it would have literally *made* his weekend if you'd given him your autograph. You're his favourite Irish gangland figure since The Gener Doddle.'

He laughs. Which comes as a definite relief, I can tell you.

He goes, 'The Gener Doddle? That's prayuz indeed. Where is he now?'

I'm there, 'He's in May Oblong's.'

Grievous turns to Actual and Malicious and goes, 'Mon, we'll hab a nightcap.'

Ten minutes later, I walk back into May Oblong's with one of Europe's most wanted drug dealers, his son and his wife, and I don't have the words to describe the look on Ronan's face.

All I *will* say is that there are tears.

It ends up being another long night. They stay for one drink, then another, then another. The Kilkenny girls are totally shoved aside, of course, as me and Ronan end up having the old Deep and Meaningfuls with Grievous, Actual and Malicious, talking about everything and anything – members of the Gordaí they'd like to see dead, members of the legal profession they'd like to see dead, members of the judiciary they'd like to see dead.

Actual says they're planning to relocate to the Middle East, where Interpol can't touch them. They've been looking at properties in the United Arab Emirates. They'd probably be there already except Melissa will miss the house too much.

After a while, I stop seeing them as criminals and stort to think of them as just a normal family, like the Kordashians, except with a thriving heroin exportation business and a long history of violence against the person.

Ronan is in his element, of course. We're having so good a time that I end up having to remind him to get the autograph. Grievous looks at the checklist and goes down through the names, going, 'Prick, prick, prick, prick . . .'

They're a very competitive crowd. I like that about them, and I tell him so.

'Andy Kinch has throyed to kill me twice,' he goes. 'Missed boat toyums. Altwees delibbers, me bleaten howul!'

He signs the page and he hands it to Ro. He has them all now. The Big Five. He stares at the page for a long time. 'Ine godda bleaten frayumt this,' he goes.

And Malicious smiles at Ronan and goes, 'Doatunt be tedding addyone about that gayum, but. In eer loyun, we like to keep a low profile – do you know what Ine saying? We don't waddent bleaten stag peerties at the doe-er evoddy utter day – do you know what I mee-un?'

Ronan smiles back. 'I know what you mee-un,' he goes.

After a couple of hours, she says she's going to take the cor home and Grievous and Actual say they'll foddy her on later in a taxi. Ronan gets dragged up to dance by the girls from Kilkenny and I end up sitting there with just Grievous and Actual, saying thank you to them and also sorry for saying that they were a focking disgrace.

I'm there, 'You are to my son what Brian O'Driscoll is to me.'

It's Actual who goes, 'Who's Brian O'Thrisk Coddle?'

And I end up laughing. For me, one of the greatest thrills of travelling to far-flung, non-rugby places is meeting people who've never heard of Drico and texting him just to let him know. Hey, he's got his three Heineken Cups, his two Six Nations Championships, his one Grand Slam and his four Lions call-ups – and I've got this.

But then I'm thinking, you know what? That's actually a bit *childish* of me? Maybe I'll stop doing it.

I decide to head off again, being seriously, seriously shitfaced at this stage.

Grievous offers me one little piece of advice before I go. It's pretty similar to what Fat Frankie said.

'Make shurden that young fedda fidishes coddidge,' he goes. 'He has brayuns to burden. It's alt veddy weddle looking up to the likes of us – he sees the big house and all the utter thrappings. But there's nutten glamordous about this way of life. It's a doorty, doorty bidiness, Rosser.'

Grievous is a very wise, if dangerous, man.

I look for Ronan to tell him I'm going back to the hotel, but I can't find him anywhere. I'm thinking, it doesn't matter. He'll probably fall into bed in an hour or two.

So I'm walking back to the hotel and – yeah, no, fine – I change my mind and I end up texting Drico after all. I'm just like, 'Sorry for the late text, met a man in Spain tonight and he hadn't a clue who you were, never heard of you, focking hilarious, hope all is well with you.'

And it's just as I'm hitting the Send button that I see a sight that stops me dead in my tracks. It nearly stops my hort, in fact. I'm passing Melissa's red Citroën Picasso. The windows are steamed up and inside someone seems pretty determined to put the suspension through its paces. I hear a male voice grunting and a woman's voice punishing the Amens and the Alleluias. There's a woman's foot sticking through the front window on the passenger side. On the ankle I notice there's a tattoo of a swan.

I look into the cor. I know I shouldn't, but I can't help myself. I have to see it. And then I *do* see it? Through the steamed-up windows, I can just about make them out – my son and the wife of one of Ireland's most wanted men, going at it like the future of the species depends on them.

7. Ross Makes a Discovery – and It is Truly Stunning!

'God forgive me but this Henry FitzRoy sounds like a complete and utter wanker!'

That's what I hear Sorcha – seriously? – say as I walk into the kitchen. She's having a breakfast brainstorm with Fionn to discuss her agenda for the next term in the Seanad, which apparently storts in, like, a *week* or two?

'Who's Henry FitzRoy?' I go. 'And, more importantly, what school did he go to?'

Sorcha doesn't even look up from her laptop. She's there, 'I don't know what school he went to but – Oh! My God! – the more I read about him, the more I actually *hate* him?'

It sounds like either Blackrock or Belvedere.

She goes, 'I can't actually *believe* we named one of the most famous streets in Ireland after a toxic male like him.'

I'm there, 'Which one is FitzRoy Street?' thinking it must be on the other side of the Liffey because I've never actually *heard* of it.

'Sorcha is talking about Grafton Street,' Fionn goes – any opportunity to show *me* up for having a head that's as empty as the Pres Bray trophy cabinet. 'Henry FitzRoy was the First Duke of Grafton. That was all once *his* land.'

Sorcha's there, 'He married a five-year-old girl, according to this orticle I'm reading. And he also killed a man in cold blood.'

'In FitzRoy's defence –' Fionn tries to go.

But Sorcha's like, 'His *defence*?' sounding like she's getting ready to jump down his throat.

He goes, 'We're talking about, you know, the late 1600s here.'

She's like, 'So?'

'I'm just making the point that he lived more than three hundred years ago.'

'Okay, so for you there *was* a time when it was okay to marry a five-year-old girl?'

'I'm saying you can't judge what happened in the seventeenth century by the moral standards we live by today.'

It's great seeing Sorcha put the dude under the hammer like this.

'Or to take the life of another man?' she goes. 'In your mind, there *was* a time when that kind of male aggression was justified?'

I go, 'Yeah, you're out of order, Fionn. I genuinely don't know what Sorcha sees in you.'

He just blanks me and I stort packing Honor's lunchbox for her first day back at school. We're talking orange and duck liver pâté with olive crackers, a peach, a Butler's Mint Truffle Bor and a bottle of San Pellegrino water – still.

Sorcha stands up, puts her two hands on her lower back and storts stretching. She suddenly looks very, very pregnant. The thing looks – honestly? – twice the size it was a week ago.

I'm there, 'Are you okay?' and Fionn says it at exactly the same time.

She goes, 'I'm just stretching my back. But thank you both for being so mandescending. I *have* been pregnant before, you know?'

Fionn tries to make it about work again. He's like, 'Sorcha, I think this issue of the Dublin street names is a very worthwhile one. It does show just how deeply institutionalized gender bias has been over the centuries.'

She goes, 'Thanks for mansplaining that to me, Fionn.'

'But I just think –'

'What? What do you *think*?'

'Well, there needs to be more to you than just this.'

'*Just* this? *Just* the belief that women should have the same rights as men?'

'All I'm saying is this shouldn't be the only thing on your agenda for the new term. You should be using your time in the Seanad to raise your profile for when you stand for election again. I'm saying there are far bigger issues for the people of Dublin Bay South.'

'What, whether or not they can turn right onto Ailesbury Road from the Merrion Road?'

'Well, frankly, yes. That's politics, Sorcha. I'm just concerned that this campaign to change all of these street names is going to alienate half of the electorate. And, yes, Sorcha, I'm talking about the male half.'

'It's actually more of a male forty-eight per cent, Fionn. There's a problem with your mathematics. Your *manthematics*.'

'See, this is what I'm talking about.'

'Fionn, whether you like it or not, my priority in this coming term is to have the name of Grafton Street changed to Markievicz Stree–. . . Ouch!'

Something's wrong.

I'm there, 'What happened? Are you alright?'

'Oh my God,' she goes, 'the baby just kicked me!'

I'm wondering was it the reference to changing the name of Grafton Street? I suspect there'll be a few people on this side of the city who'll want to kick her if it ever happens.

I manage to stop myself from saying it, though. I move over to her, shouldering Fionn out of the way, and I go, 'Can I?'

Sorcha just nods. I put my hand on her stomach. Fionn puts his down next to mine. We stay like that for a good five minutes but fock-all happens and I quickly get bored. I'm there, 'Has it been happening much?'

'The last week or so,' she goes. 'Last night, it was like there was a performance of *Riverdance* going on in there!'

Seeing her smiling for once, I suddenly see an opening. 'Speaking of dancing –' I go, but I don't even get to finish my sentence.

She's there, 'Honor is grounded until mid-term, Ross. And that means no after-school activities for her, including dancing. And don't bring it up with me again. You are lucky to be still living in this house after what happened.'

'That whole giving-cigarettes-and-alcohol-to-other-kids thing happened *before* she discovered the Chorleston, Sorcha. I genuinely believe she's a different person now.'

'I said no and I meant it.'

I go to put the packaging from the pâté into the bin, except it's full. When you've got guns like these, of course, no bin is ever truly full.

Sorcha's there, 'Ross, that bin needs a new bag.'

And I go, 'If God had wanted men to change the bag, he wouldn't have given us the strength to keep pushing the rubbish down.'

It's a cracking line. But just as I deliver it, the doorbell rings and Sorcha stands up. 'That'll be Croía,' she goes. And I decide to change the bin bag after all.

Croía has obviously decided to just gatecrash the meeting because I see the surprise on Fionn's face at the mention of her name. Sorcha goes outside to let her in.

As I'm pulling the old bin bag out, I look at Fionn and I go, 'It sounds to me like the honeymoon period is very definitely over for you.'

He's there, 'Yeah, you'd love to think that, Ross. This is just politics. Sorcha and I know how to separate it from the way we feel about each other.'

'Yeah, no, you keep telling yourself that, Fionn. You keep telling yourself that.'

Croía walks in. Without looking at me, she goes, 'Okay, there is at least *one* too many men in this focking room.'

Sorcha's like, 'Ross was about to drive Honor to school. Actually, Ross, you'd better go and get the boys dressed.'

I'm there, 'Yeah, no, I'm about to – but you told me to change the bin bag first, which is what I'm doing.'

I take the bag outside and fock it into the wheelie bin. When I walk back into the kitchen, Croía is going, 'Look at him there – big, privileged, neo-masculine, woman-hating head on him.'

She's not talking about me, I'm relieved to discover. It's the First Duke of Grafton who's getting it in the neck again.

Sorcha goes, 'He shot a man dead, Croía. It's on his Wikipedia page – look. And this is the *man* whose name we've given to the most famous street in the country?'

'He shot a man dead in a duel,' Fionn tries to go.

Croía just shrugs. She's like, 'Oh, well, if the result was one less gun-toting, macho asshole in the world, maybe he wasn't so bad after all.'

Sorcha goes, 'He also married a five-year-old girl, Croía!'

'Yeah,' Fionn goes, 'he was only nine years old at the time himself. I think we're in danger of losing our sense of historical perspective here.'

Croía storts clapping him in, like, a sorcastic way? She's there, 'Spoken like a true manabler!'

'I'm not a manabler. I'm just making the point that that's what happened back in those days. Children got married. Men fought duels. You can't judge the things people did three hundred years ago by the standard of what we now consider to be correct.'

'*You* can't, Fionn. Or rather you *won't*. Because that would mean having to call out other men.'

'I have no problem calling out other men when I think they're being sexist. Ross will tell you that.'

That's actually true. You wouldn't want to be on a stag with *him*. We're talking zero focking crack.

'Yeah, no,' I go, 'leave me out of this.'

He's there, 'I'm just saying, I've never shied away from telling other men when they've crossed the line – whether we're *in* female company or not.'

'We're so lucky to have *you* on our side!' Croía goes – although she definitely doesn't mean it. 'Another self-humbling male who claims to be a feminist as a cloak for his own psychosexual domination fantasies.'

I laugh. I end up *having* to? Then I pick up Honor's lunchbox and I go, 'Well said, Croía! *Very* well said!'

So I'm, like, driving Honor to school. She's in the front passenger seat – her nose stuck in her phone, as usual – and the boys are in the back, commenting on the driving abilities of various other road users.

'Look at this focking joker!' Leo goes. 'Who let *her* out on the focking road?'

I turn around to Honor and go, 'So – sixth class, huh?'

She's like, 'Hm,' and it's obvious that there's something on her mind. I decide not to ask her about it. I'm sure she'll tell me what it is when she's good and ready – or maybe she won't. Either way, it's her choice.

I should actually write a book: Life Hacks for Parents.

I'm there, 'I can't believe you're going to be eleven soon. This time next year I'm going to be driving you to big school – as in, *actual* Mount Anville?'

She goes, 'Yippity-focking-hoo!' and we drive on in complete silence – aport from the sound of Brian going, 'Women can't drive for shit!'

There's a lot of his grandfather in him.

I'm there, 'Honor, are you worried about going back to school for some reason?'

She's like, 'Excuse me?'

'I'm just wondering is there a reason why you're giving me such a hord time this morning?'

'This is what I'm always like to you.'

'That's not true. We've been getting on so well since I moved back home. You seemed to genuinely miss me when I was in Estepona. And now, this morning, you're back to being a complete wagon again.'

'You promised me you'd ask *her* if I could go back to dancing.'

'I did ask her. I asked her in the kitchen this morning.'

'I heard you. You brought it up, *she* said no and you just accepted it.'

'I didn't just accept it, Honor. I tried to tell her that you were a totally different person since you storted dancing – definitely less of a bitch – but she wouldn't listen.'

'Then you dropped the subject straightaway. I was sitting on the stairs listening to the whole thing.'

'Look, I'm already on thin ice as it is, Honor. The incident with Rihanna-Brogan, the business with Ross Junior – she's having serious doubts about whether I'm the role model she thought I could hopefully be.'

'You didn't make a focking case for me. You just shrugged your shoulders and went, "Oh, well, that's that, then – at least I asked."'

'I don't see what else I could have done, Honor.'

'We could carry on going to dancing and just not tell her.'

'Er, she's grounded you until mid-term. She'll know if we go out.'

'I was thinking, you could tell her you're bringing me to an Alcohol and Tobacco Awareness Course.'

I can't believe she came up with that herself. Sometimes, she seriously frightens me.

I'm there, 'But that'd be lying to her, Honor.'

She goes, 'Yeah, it wouldn't be the first time you've done that. We could tell her it was your idea – to teach me the dangers of giving drink and cigarettes to children. It'd also make her think you're a good father.'

'I'm just scared of what would happen if she found out.'

'Fine. Take *her* focking side, then.'

She goes back to giving me the silent treatment.

'Stay in your focking lane,' Leo shouts at a dude in a silver Peugeot 206. 'You're all over the focking road! What are you, pissed?'

I wind up the window, thinking it might be safer all round. As I do, I hear my phone beep. It's, like, a text message. I check it when we hit the next red light and it ends up being from Ronan.

It's just like, 'Is ev ok Rosser?' and I know it's because I've been ignoring his calls. I didn't say anything to him about what I saw – him being chestnuts-deep in the wife of one of Europe's most dangerous drug dealers – but he's picked up on the fact that *something's* wrong? I couldn't talk to him on the flight on the way back. I couldn't even look at him when I was saying goodbye to him at Dublin Airport yesterday afternoon. And – like I said – I had two missed calls from him last night, which I didn't bother replying to and he knows that's out of character for me because I love talking to him.

We turn into the school cor pork.

'I didn't tell you the full truth,' Honor goes – this comes out of, like, nowhere as I'm pulling up in front of the school.

I'm like, 'About what?'

'I never told you the real reason I wanted to learn the Chorleston.'

'I thought it was so me and you would have, like, a shared *interest*?'

'There's a competition every year – a father-and-daughter ball-room dancing contest for students in fifth and sixth class, called *Strictly Mount Anville*.'

'*Strictly Mount Anville*? That's what I call Milltown Golf Club.'

'I wanted to enter this year. I wanted to win it.'

'Jesus, I love the fact that you're competitive, Honor.'

'Dad, no one likes me. And I know that's my fault for being a bitch. But sometimes it makes me sad that all the other girls look away when they see me coming. Or that, when I walk into a room, they all leave.'

'Is that what actually happens, Honor?'

'All the time. And I just thought if I could win the Goatstown Glitterball, then people might like me.'

I go, 'Honor, you don't have to win things to make people like you.'

As a former Leinster Schools Senior Cup-winning captain, I know I'm talking shit even as the words are leaving my mouth.

She suddenly spots someone through the windscreen. She goes, 'Oh, shit, there's Sincerity.'

I'm like, 'Who's Sincerity?'

'Sincerity Matthews. She won the competition last year.'

Sincerity ends up being this, like, random girl with long, brown hair.

I'm there, 'Is she waving at you?' because she does seem weirdly delighted to see Honor, given that everyone in this school supposedly *hates* her?

'Yes,' Honor goes.

I'm there, 'I thought you had *no* friends?'

'She's not my friend. She's my Buddy.'

'Your what?'

'It's this, like, anti-bullying initiative? Everyone in the school is buddied up with the girl who's closest to them alphabetically in the year register. They think if they give you some randomer to be friends with, it'll stop, like, *cliques* developing?'

'In Mount Anville?'

'Yeah.'

'Good luck with that. So *she's* your randomer?'

'Yeah, we're supposed to, like, look out for each other before school and after school and at lunchtime.'

'She seems kind of delighted to see you, Honor. I mean, *she's* not turning her head or walking away when she sees you coming.'

'It's just an act.'

'Really?'

'She pretends to be nice – oh my God, she has *everyone* fooled – but she's *actually* a bitch.'

'Really?'

'Oh, yeah. Underneath that sweet smile, this girl is, like, way more horrible than me at my worst.'

I'm trying to imagine way more horrible than Honor at her worst and I literally can't.

I go, 'And this is the girl you want to beat in the dance competition?'

She's there, 'No, I want to beat them all.'

'Good answer. Very good answer.'

'But *her* especially.'

Suddenly, the girl is at the front passenger side, waving at Honor with her butter-wouldn't-melt smile. Honor opens the electric window.

Sincerity goes, 'Hi, Honor! How was your summer?'

Honor's like, 'Fine.'

'Hi, Mister O'Carroll-Kelly. I'm Sincerity Matthews. I'm going to be Honor's Buddy this year.'

And I just go, 'Yeah, big deal,' trying to sound tougher with her than I did with Sorcha this morning. I hope Honor appreciates it.

Sincerity goes, 'I love your hair, Honor.'

Honor's there, 'Yeah, it's the exact same as it was last year.'

'Do you want to sit together in the cafeteria at lunchtime? I could introduce you to my friends. They're all *so* nice!'

'I couldn't give a fock either way.'

'I'd love us to be more than Buddies, Honor. I'd love us to be genuine friends.'

'Whatever.'

'Do you want to walk to class together?'

'Just give me a focking moment here, will you?'

She hits the button and closes the window. She goes, 'See what I mean?'

I'm there, 'What! A little! Bitch!'

'You can see why I want to beat her now, can't you? Wipe that smug look off her face.'

'Honor, I wish you'd explained all of this to me sooner. Look, don't worry about your mother. I'll talk to her. Me and you are going to win that competition.'

So – yeah, no – I'm walking along Grafton Street with the kids and I happen to see my old pair slipping into the Westbury Hotel. Of course, it's nearly eleven o'clock in the morning and she'll be due her first pint of Tanqueray of the day.

I decide to follow them in, just to see how they are, although what I really want, if I'm being honest, is to find out when I'm getting my actual money. It's already September.

'Me want Disney!' Brian shouts, as I push the stroller towards the lift. 'Me want focking Disney!'

I'm there, 'We're not allowed into the Disney Store anymore, Brian,' because the famous Jaila is still pacing the floors. 'The three of you are borred for being animals.'

When we get to the first floor, the old pair are being shown to a table in the Gallery. I push the boys across the lobby. Leo is going, 'You pack! Of focking! Fockpuppets!' and people are looking up from their cappuccinos and their Bere Island crab sandwiches as we pass. 'Focking fockpuppet focks!'

The old man is delighted to see us. He stands up and goes, 'There they are. Look, Fionnuala, it's Ross and the future Ireland front row.'

'Fock off,' Brian goes, 'you stupid bald fock!'

Yeah, no, that's the first difference you'd notice about the old man. No wig. And also his voice. Two weeks ago, you could have heard him talking from the top of Horcourt Street. Now, he's basically talking in a whisper.

243

I'm there, 'What are you doing in town anyway? I thought you were supposed to be in hiding?'

He goes, 'Muirgheal wanted to have a chat about some of the latest – inverted commas – *revelations*.'

'What revelations?'

'Oh, they've storted digging up my old letters to *The Irish Times* to use against me. There's one about lady golfers.'

I laugh.

I'm there, 'Didn't you say their smaller brains meant they were more suited to pitch and putt?'

'I actually wrote crazy golf,' he goes. 'But it's any stick to beat me with now.'

He's actually a shadow of the man who, one year ago, stood up in front of a thousand people in the Morker Hotel and promised to lead Ireland into a bright new future.

The old dear ends up *having* to have her say, of course? She goes, 'What on Earth was Sorcha thinking? I thought we were friends. We've known her since she was a child.'

But the old man's there, 'None of this is Sorcha's fault, Fionnuala. I was the one who called Constance Markievicz a cow. I have to take full responsibility for that and keep repeating that anyone who knows me will know that's the *real* Charles O'Carroll-Kelly. Muirgheal is doing a wonderful job as interim leader, by the way.'

The old dear storts making coochy-coo noises at the boys, then – I swear to fock – she goes, 'Aren't they lovely, Chorles? Are these *your* children, Ross?'

I'm like, 'No, I just found them outside Weir's and thought I'd bring them for a focking spin. Of course they're mine.'

'I only asked to make sure. Hello there, little one! What's your name?'

Leo goes, 'You've a head like a bucket of sore cocks!'

Her jaw hits the corpet. I end up just having to laugh.

The old man goes, 'So, Kicker, how did the famous stag go?'

I'm there, 'Errr,' suddenly getting an image in my head of Ronan and Malicious Wounding in the back of her Citroën Picasso, going at it like fighting dogs. 'Fine, actually. Quiet. It was only me, Ro, your mate K . . . K . . . K . . . K . . . Kennet, Shadden's brother, Dadden, then obviously Buckets, Nudger and Gull – oh, yeah, and Tina's brother, Anto.'

'Ronan did a wonderful job for me on the famous Aquatraz. He's given me a – quote-unquote – snag list of potential problems. Pages and pages of things to fix!'

The old dear goes, 'I remember Anto! Is he still a chef?'

I'm there, 'Yeah, no, he's doing the lunches in the Broken Orms.'

'Because I might have a proposition to put to him. You see, I remember, when he stayed with us, he made *the* most wonderful desserts.'

'Okay, you remember that but you have to ask me are *these* your grandchildren?'

'I've been watching the news and seeing all this awful gang violence that's been going on in the poorer parts of Dublin. I've been trying to think of a way that the "What in the Name of FO'CK Foundation" could help to end the cycle of tit-for-tat killings. And I thought, what if I set up a programme where we take these *hoodlums* while they're still young and we retrain them as pastry chefs? I was going to call it Banoffee Versus Gangs. What do you think, Ross?'

'I think all that silicone you've had injected into your forehead over the years has storted to rot your brain.'

I'm about to ask her when she's going to have my five mills for me when Muirgheal all of a sudden shows up. She gives the old man a big hug and goes, 'It's awful what they've done to you. Fionnuala, you must be going through absolute hell as well.'

Brian shouts, 'Here's this focking fockclown again!'

The old dear goes, 'I thought being in prison for a crime I didn't commit was the worst thing that could ever happen to me. That's until I saw the man I love dragged to the floor by this bloodthirsty mob – led by a member of our own family.'

'Did you hear the news,' Muirgheal goes, 'about Grafton Street?'

The old dear looks at the old man, then at me.

Muirgheal's there, 'It's not going to be called Grafton Street anymore. Dublin City Council voted last night to change the name to Markievicz Street?'

The old dear puts her hand over her mouth like she thinks she might be sick.

The old man's there, 'I blame myself. I made the woman relevant again.'

The old dear goes, 'The people won't stand for it! There'll be riots!'

'You're right, Fionnuala. You're as right as a large brandy after dinner.'

'I'm not so sure,' Muirgheal goes, suddenly looking a bit shifty. 'The paradigm has changed. We have to accept that.'

'The what?'

'There's been a shift in the public mood. That's, em, what I wanted to talk to you about, Charles.'

There's something coming. I can hear the sudden change in her tone.

She goes, 'The whole *women* thing is huge right now. And we can't afford to ignore it as a porty.'

The old man's there, 'What are you saying, Muirgheal?'

'All these things that keep coming out about you,' she goes, 'are storting to seriously hurt us. I mean, how many letters to the *Times* did you actually write?'

'It was quite a few over the years.'

'I just saw one that's doing the rounds on Twitter where you said you wouldn't get on an airplane if you saw that the pilot was a woman.'

'I stand by that. I still wouldn't. Unless there was a man sitting in the cockpit to watch her.'

'Unfortunately, you can't say things like that anymore. Building a wall around Cork, restricting the movement of people from Laois, those things are all well and good. But we can't afford to be tone-deaf to the whole women thing.'

Leo shouts, 'Fock you, candyballs!'

She goes, 'I just wanted to let you know that I've completed my internal investigation into the Constance Markievicz tweet.'

'What investigation?' the old man goes. 'That was just some-thing we said to take the heat off me!'

'And my finding, Chorles, is that your attitude towards women is unbecoming of a man who wants to lead this country.'

The old man goes, 'What treachery is this?'

Muirgheal's there, 'I'm sorry to do this to you, Chorles – my own political mentor. But I've decided to challenge you for the leader-ship of the porty.'

Honor rings me at, like, lunchtime to tell me that Week One is going to be the cha-cha-cha. Not surprisingly, I end up having to ask her to repeat herself.

'It's, like, a Cuban dance,' she goes. 'Your feet go cha-cha-cha, cha-cha-cha . . .'

I'm there, 'Hang on, I thought we were doing the Chorleston?'

'Er, it's a different dance every *round*, Dad?'

'Shit, I didn't know that.'

'Have you never even watched the show?'

'Yeah, but it's usually just to see how Tess Daly is looking. And Claudia Winkleman. God, I love Claudia Winkleman.'

'Okay, so the competition goes on until Christmas and it's, like, four rounds. September is the cha-cha-cha. October is the quick-step. November is the foxtrot. And December is the Chorleston.'

'So how long have I got to learn the cha-cha-cha?'

'Two weeks.'

'Honor, there's no way I can learn a new dance in, like, two weeks.'

'Oh my God, Sincerity Matthews is being *such* a bitch to me today.'

'Is she? What's she specifically doing?'

'She asked me this morning if I wanted to copy any of her homework?'

'Okay, I would be *highly* insulted by that.'

'Then *while* I was copying it, she storted saying how she really fancied her chances of retaining the Goatstown Glitterball this year.'

'She's confident, isn't she?'

'Well, you see, her dad is, like, *super* competitive!'

'Hey, I'm pretty competitive myself, Honor.'

'Yeah, but her dad is, like, an actual *winner*?'

'Okay, Honor, you have my attention. What can we do to beat them?'

'Okay, I was thinking we could get, like, private classes from Mrs Leonard. We could do maybe two nights a week and then every Saturday morning as well. That'd be enough for you to learn each dance. Especially if you're as competitive as you claim to be.'

She can play me like her old piccolo.

'Okay, that's it,' I go, 'ring and book the classes.'

And she's like, 'It's fine, I've already done it. Where are you, by the way?'

I'm there, 'I'm in UCD,' because I've decided it's time to have a chat with Ronan – we're talking face to face. 'Actually, I have to go, Honor,' because I suddenly see him walking along beside the lake.

He's with some random girl who looks like Alexis Bledel except with really bad skin. She's laughing her head off at something that he's saying and it's straightaway obvious that she's into him and he's into her.

He'd ride your focking letterbox, of course.

I morch up to him and I go, 'Alright, Ro?' and he's like, 'Rosser? What are you doing hee-or?'

The girl goes, 'Oh my God, who is *this*?' and she looks at me like I'm tinned potatoes.

I stare her down and I go, 'Yeah, acne is God's way of telling you that you're not old enough to have sex yet. Now would you mind focking off, please, so that I can talk to my son?'

Oh, that softens her cough.

Ronan goes, 'I'll gib you a rig in the arthur noowun, Suzadden.' Off she focks.

He goes, 'That was veddy roowut, Rosser.'

I'm like, 'Was it? Who the fock is *Suzadden*?'

'She's a boord in me Constitutioniddle Law class. We're just arthur being at a tutordial.'

'Is that right?'

'Hee-or, I've been throying to get you on the phowunt the last two weeks. Kennet waddants to know can he put anutter thoorty nayums on the guestlist. He forgot there'll be a few of he's freddens getting out oaber Christmas on temper doddy release. That's thoorty-plus guests, Rosser.'

I'm like, 'Thirty-plus guests,' except I say it with a tone. 'Yeah, no problem. No problem at all, Ro.'

He's there, 'Is sometin the mathor, Rosser?'

'Why would you think that?'

'You habn't retordened addy of me calts for the last two weeks. I habn't been thalken to you siddence the stag. And Ine wonthorden did I mebbe do sometin wrong?'

I decide to just come out with it. 'I saw you,' I go. 'I saw you buried up to your focking knackers in Grievous Bodily Horm's wife in the back of her Citroën Picasso.'

He's like, 'Me? That wadn't me, Rosser!'

'Ro, I stood in the street for ten minutes watching you. I was going to nearly tap on the window and compliment you on the length of time you kept it going.'

He just looks away – suddenly realizing that there's no point in trying to shit me here.

I'm like, 'Malicious Wounding? What the fock were you thinking?'

He goes, 'Stay ourrof it, Rosser. You know nutten abourrut.'

'I know all about her husband, though. I've read everything Paul Williams ever wrote about him. What have you got, a death wish or something?'

'It joost happent, Rosser.'

'And what about your chanting and your meditation? I thought it was supposed to cure all of that?'

'It was joost a slip.'

'Some focking slip. Do you know what would have happened if, instead of me, it had been Grievous Bodily Horm – or even *Actual* Bodily Horm – who saw you two going at it?'

'Thee ditn't, but.'

'That's not the point. The point is that you didn't care one way or the other once sex was on the agenda. The point is that even the threat of being shot can't teach you to control yourself.'

'Alreet, I woatunt botter denoying it – the danger added to the trill. Doatunt throy to ted me, Rosser, that you doatunt know how that feels.'

'The husbands of the women *I* sleep with are accountants, barristers, quantity surveyors. There's a big difference between the buzz of trying to finish off upstairs while someone is reverse-porking the Volvo in the driveway and what *you* did. A *big* difference!'

I've obviously touched a nerve with him because he sticks his finger pretty much in my face and goes, 'You're a bleaten hypocrite, Rosser!'

I'm there, 'I'm just trying to give you the benefit of my experience. Look, I came here today to tell you that I can't be your best man slash madden anymore. I'm stepping down.'

'You're not stepping dowun,' he goes. 'You're foyert!' and as he says it, he gives me a hord shove in the chest and I suddenly find myself falling backwards into the actual lake. There's, like, a humungous splash. I'm soaked from head to toe. I end up swallowing a decent amount of it as well.

After a few seconds of flapping around, I manage to stand up and I just stare at him, standing at the water's edge, his face all – I don't know – *defiant*?

He goes, 'I wish the wather had of been theeper – you might of bleaten drowunt.'

Sorcha looks wrecked. With her other pregnancies, she looked, I don't know, glowing. But this time she's got, like, big circles under her eyes. Her skin is blotchy, her hair is dry and scraggly and she looks – you couldn't use the word around her, of course, especially these days – but *bloated*?

I just tell her she looks tired and she says that her and Croía stayed up all night to watch the first of the debates between Hillary Clinton and Donald Trump.

I'm like, 'Who won?'

She goes, 'Hillary, obviously. I don't know why you even have to ask that question.'

'Hey, I don't care either way. I was only going through the motions of conversation.'

'Donald Trump is a racist, a chauvinist and a misogynist, Ross. He kept talking over Hillary the entire time. And yet she *still* won in most people's eyes? What does that tell you?'

'Was Fionn here as well?'

'No, he recorded it and watched it this morning. I think Fionn is having a few difficulties coming to terms with the new *woke* me.'

'I'm, er, sorry to hear that. You should maybe try to get an early night, though. You look wrecked.'

It's, like, half-seven in the evening.

She goes, 'I can't. I've got my speech to prepare for Saturday.'

I'm there, 'What's, em, Saturday again?' wondering has she already told me but I was either not listening or talking over her.

She's like, 'I've been asked to make a speech at the Grafton Street renaming ceremony.'

I'm there, 'That's still happening, is it?'

'Of course it's still happening. I mean, yes, there's been a little bit of pushback from the traders. But it's mostly men who are objecting. Typical of the white, cisgender, male ascendency to turn aggressive when it feels its sense of privilege threatened. As Croía said, it's going to take a period of adjustment – *manjustment* – but it won't be long before the name Markievicz Street just trips off the tongue.'

'Yeah, I'm sure that's true.'

It's not. It's horseshit.

She goes, 'I want you to bring the boys along. And Honor can leave the house – just for one day. This is actual *herstory* we're watching unfold.'

Of course, I've never been slow when it comes to spotting an opening. I'm there, 'Yeah, no, speaking of the boys, do you think your old pair would look after them tonight?'

She's like, 'Why?' immediately suspicious. 'Where are *you* going?'

'I'm going out with Honor.'

'Ross, Honor is grounded until the end of October. You know that as well as I do.'

'Look, for once in my life, I'm going to be one hundred per cent honest with you, Sorcha. I'm taking her to a class.'

'What kind of a class?'

'It's an Alcohol and Tobacco Awareness class.'

'*Excuse* me?'

'She needs to know the dangers, Sorcha. It won't be long until she goes to Wesley.'

'How many classes are there?'

'It's two nights every week plus every Saturday morning until Christmas.'

'Oh my God!'

'What?'

'Does that not seem a bit, I don't know, heavy?'

'She taught Rihanna-Brogan how to smoke. *And* she got Ross Junior shitfaced. I think this would be a good way to show her that what she did was definitely wrong.'

'Well, that does sound very responsible of you. Okay, I'll ask my mom and dad to mind the boys.'

'I'd better go and tell her the good news. The first class storts in half an hour.'

I'm just leaving the kitchen when Sorcha turns around to me and goes, 'What's going on with you and Ronan, by the way?'

I'm like, 'What do you mean?'

'Shadden rang me earlier to invite me to her hair and make-up trial. And she mentioned that you're not Ronan's best man anymore.'

'Er, no, I'm not.'

'She said Buckets of Blood was doing it now.'

'Hey, he's free to ask anyone he wants.'

'Does this have anything to do with those wet clothes you left in the laundry room the other day? And the fact that you had to buy a new phone?'

'Yeah, no, I don't want to talk about it. We're, er, going to be late for this – like I keep saying – Alcohol and Tobacco Awareness course.'

*

Mrs Leonard asks Honor for her music. Honor hands her the One Direction CD and goes, 'So it's, like, the first track.'

The woman slips it into the machine and suddenly we're listening to *That's What Makes You Beautiful* while Mrs Leonard taps out the beat of the song with her hand on her leg. After thirty seconds, she goes, 'This song is perfect for the cha-cha-cha!' and Honor turns to me and smiles because she knows she's done good.

'Okay,' the woman goes, 'there are four basic elements of the cha-cha-cha.'

Honor's there, 'I want my dad to twirl me out and then twirl me back in again. And I want him to dip me. And, at the end, I want to do the splits.'

Mrs Leonard laughs. She's there, 'We can look at those elements the next night. But when you're building a house, you don't build the master bedroom first. Or the kitchen. Ross, what's the first thing you need to do if you're planning to build a house?'

'Bribe a county councillor,' I go.

She's like, 'No, it's lay down foundations. The foundations are the most important part of any major structure. They're the most boring and time-consuming part of the job but without them the whole thing would fall down. It's exactly the same with dancing.'

She tells us both to stand up and follow her into the middle of the floor, which we do, then she stands facing us.

'Now,' she goes, 'there are four basic elements to the cha-cha-cha. Like the Charleston, we have our walking steps. Watch my feet, both of you. Forward, forward, forward – backward, backward, backward. That's it. Do what I do. Forward, forward, forward – backward, backward, backward. Now, for the second element, we want to add some Cuban spirit. So we do the same thing, except this time, we get up on the balls of our feet. Like this. That's it, Honor. Forward, forward, forward – backward, backward, backward. Move those elbows, Ross, and those hips. Okay – stop, stop, stop!'

I'm obviously not doing it right because she stands in front of *me* and goes, 'Your forward steps are bigger than your backward steps.'

I'm there, 'Er, okay.'

'You said you were a kicker on your school team.'

'That's right. Famously.'

'So explain your technique to me.'

'Well, the one I settled on was four steps backwards, three to the side, run my hand through my hair, look from the ball to the posts, then back to the ball, then back to the posts, then back to the ball, hand through the hair again, then run at the ball, then kick the thing.'

'Four steps backwards, then three to the side. And were they all different sizes these steps?'

'No, they had to be the same.'

'Why?'

'Because you have to know exactly where your standing foot is going to be when you strike the ball. That's basic.'

'Well, the cha-cha-cha is no different. When you take three steps forwards, then three steps backwards, you have to end up in exactly the same spot.'

I actually laugh. I just wish everything in life could be explained in rugby terms. It probably could be if people were just willing to make the effort.

'Okay,' she goes, 'let's try it again. Forward, forward, forward – backward, backward, backward. Better, Ross! Forward, forward, forward – backward, backward, backward. That's it, Honor, up on the balls of your feet, like you're a cat! Now, the third element – watch my feet – is the side-step. And it goes side, together, side, together, side. That's it, Ross. Then back the other way – side, together, side, together, side. Your pint hand has popped up again, Ross.'

'Sorry.'

'And the fourth element is the rock step. This is slightly different from the rock step we learned when we did the Charleston. Look at my feet, Ross. Step back like this with your left, weight on the left, then replace your right, shifting your weight in the process. So we step back with the left, replace, right, back, replace, back, replace.'

I'm definitely getting it. Not as quickly as Honor, but then she got her brains from her mother.

Mrs Leonard goes, 'So, when we put it all together, it looks like this. Side, rock step, side, together, step. Rock step, side, together, side. Rock step, forward, forward, forward, backward, backward, backward – cha-cha-cha – rock step – cha-cha-cha – and rock step, side, together, side. Do you think you can remember that?'

My mouth says yes but my face says not a focking chance.

'Don't worry,' she goes, 'by the end of the week you're going to be doing it in your sleep.'

I'm in the cor, having just dropped Honor off to school and – I'm not shitting you – the only thing in my head is *side, rock step, side, together, step. Rock step, side, together, side. Rock step, forward, forward, forward, backward, backward, backward – cha-cha-cha – rock step – cha-cha-cha – and rock step, side, together, side.*

But then the news comes on the radio just as I'm turning right onto the Stillorgan dual-carriageway and I suddenly snap out of it because – yeah, no – the news happens to be about Sorcha.

'Shop owners and traders say they intend to disrupt the renaming ceremony for Grafton Street this weekend,' the newsreader dude goes. 'The Save Grafton Street Pressure Group are unhappy with Dublin City Council's decision to change the name of the city's most famous street to Markievicz Street and will stage a protest at the event on Saturday, when independent Senator Sorcha Lalor – who first raised the issue of the gender imbalance in City Centre street names – is due to cut the ribbon on the first Markievicz Street sign at three o'clock. The chairman of the group, Myles Mulrooney, said he and many other traders had no intention of using the new name.'

Then you hear *his* voice? This Myles whatever-he's-called, going, 'There is a tradition in this city – and it's been well observed for most of our history – that streets on the Southside are named after members of the Anglo-Irish gentry and the well-to-do and that streets on the Northside are named after peasants and trouble-makers. And it works. I've been operating on this street for almost forty years. I pay a high rent and top rates because I want to be on Grafton Street. I don't do it to be on Markievicz Street.'

In the back of the cor, Brian goes, 'That focking prick broke the lights,' and I go, 'Shush a minute, Brian, I want to listen to this.'

Leo's like, 'Fock you – you focking orsehole.'

The reporter goes, 'A number of shoppers we spoke to are also vehemently opposed to the name change.'

Then you hear some woman, who sounds like she might be friends with my old dear – no doubt they found her in the Brown Thomas cosmetics area – go, 'I'm disgusted. Absolutely disgusted. As the song says, Grafton Street's a wonderland. Markievicz Street isn't a wonderland. It sounds like the kind of street that would have a methadone clinic on it and you couldn't leave anything in your car.'

And that's when my phone rings. I check the screen and it ends up being – of all people – Helen. I haven't actually seen her since she got back from Australia. I answer straightaway.

I'm like, 'Helen, how the hell are you?' because I've always been fond of her.

She goes, 'Ross, where are you?' and she sounds – I don't know – upset about something.

I'm there, 'I'm just passing Dunnes Stores in Cornelscourt. What's up?'

'Can you call to the house? Now?'

I'm like, 'Errr,' trying to come up with an excuse because it'd be a pain in the hole to have to turn the cor around. 'Is it urgent?'

She goes, 'It's your sister.'

'Erika? What's wrong?'

'I think you'd better come.'

I end up breaking – honestly – whatever the Cornelscourt to Ailesbury Road land speed record happens to be.

Helen opens the door. It's great to see her, although I'm not sure she one hundred per cent appreciates Brian calling her a focking shitpigeon.

She goes, 'Hi, Ross, thank you for coming.'

I'm there, 'No worries,' giving her a big hug. 'I've missed you. You heard about the old man and his fall from grace? He's taken the wig off at least. And Muirgheal is challenging him for the leadership of the porty.'

She just goes, 'I don't care about your father, Ross. That part of my life is over.'

'I just thought it might be a nice Fock you moment for you.'

'No, fock *you*!' Leo shouts. 'You focking fock!'

Helen invites us into the gaff.

I'm like, 'So what's actually going on?'

She goes, 'Erika is having some kind of –'

'What?'

'I don't want to *use* the word breakdown, but I don't know what else to call it.'

'Er, okay.'

'She's upstairs. Go and see for yourself.'

So I leave her to look after the boys and I tip up the stairs.

Now, I've seen a lot of unusual shit in my time. I'm one of the few people, for instance, who's ever seen the oxygen chamber that Jamie Heaslip sleeps in. Two or three times a year, usually the day after a big game, he invites me round to read Gerry Thornley's match report and player ratings to him through the walls of the thing, while he asks me to repeat occasional words and checks on the performance of his share portfolio on his laptop.

And yet even I'm not ready for the shock that awaits me when I push open that door. The only way to describe it is to say it's like one of those police incident rooms you see in movies where they're searching for, like, a *serial* killer? Literally every inch of wall space is covered with photographs, post-it notes, newspaper orticles, letters, maps and pieces of paper with things scribbled on them. Then there's, like, different-coloured lengths of string connecting various things. I notice Amelie, her face unwashed, sitting on the floor among all the – it sounds like a word but may not be – *debris*? On the top of her dresser and bedside table are plates with untouched meals on them.

Erika is down on her knees, sifting through mountains of paper, looking for something as if her life depends on it. She's goes, 'Fock's sake! I had it in my hand, like, five minutes ago!'

I have to say, I'm immediately worried about my sister. Although that doesn't stop me staring at the three inches of G-string showing over the top of her jeans for about five seconds before I eventually go, 'Hey, Erika?' and she quickly spins around. She has the look in her eyes of a hunted animal. 'I see *you've* been busy.'

She's there, 'I'm trying to figure out what they're up to, Ross. All I know is that it's something dodgy and I just haven't worked it out yet.'

She's talking at, like, two hundred miles an hour, by the way.

I'm there, 'I presume you're talking about *him* and my old dear?'

She goes, 'Look up there, Ross.'

'Where am I looking?'

'That photograph up there. The one of your mother. It was on her website. That's her in Minsk, where she *claims* she spoke at a human rights conference to raise money for the "What in the Name of FO'CK" foundation.'

'Jesus, the state of her – she has a face like a split toe.'

'She's standing in front of a hotel. I found it on Google Images. It's the Minsk Intercontinental. I rang them and they said they'd never heard of any human rights conference.'

I bend down and I pick up Amelie. She's getting huge. 'Maybe the actual conference was in a different hotel,' I go.

Erika's there, 'I rang every major hotel and conference centre in the city and none of them hosted a human rights conference in the last few weeks. And none of them had even *heard* of any human rights conference either.'

'Erika, when was the last time you actually slept?'

'I've been finding out everything I can about this foundation of hers. So here's how she *claims* it works? She goes to a city – always in Russia, as it happens – and she's paid a high five-figure sum to talk to an audience about the experience of being locked up for a crime she didn't commit –'

'Even though she possibly *did* do it?'

'In the audience, we're supposed to believe, are rich businessmen and philanthropists and CEOs of major companies. And they're so moved by her account of her incarceration that they then pledge substantial high five-figure sums – that's according to an interview she did with the *Sunday Business Post* – to help these very obscure charitable organizations that come under the umbrella of her foundation . . .'

'You're talking very fast, Erika. I'm struggling to follow it.'

'Since she was released from prison, she's registered one hundred and fifty charity names. There's a list here, look. The South Dublin/Honduras Clean Water Initiative. The Foxrock and North Cornelscourt Friends of Abidjan. The Foxrock and Deansgrange West Friends of Ciudad Juárez. The Foxrock and South Sudan Joint Partnership to Eradicate Onchocerca Volvulus. Dublin 18 AIDS Awareness. Dublin 18 Hailey-Hailey Syndrome Awareness. Dublin 18 Tree Bark Skin Disorder Awareness. The Give a Child Hope Foundation. Children Without Skis. Banoffee Versus Gangs . . .'

'Yeah, no, I laughed out loud when I heard that last one.'

'These are bullshit charities, Ross.'

'I remember once she did a bake sale in aid of The Foxrock and Mozambique Joint Partnership to Combat River Blindness. But she was looking for a Rehab People of the Year award at the time. Unfortunately, they don't give them out for evil.'

'I checked out that landmines charity she set up. That international body that she claims it's affiliated to has never even heard of her or her foundation. Probably because, like all these others, it's a front for something else.'

'A front for what, though?'

She stands up and goes, 'That's what I have to find out. I need to get my hands on a list of donors, Ross. Can you help me? *Will* you help me?'

She grabs my hand and stares intensely into my eyes. I'm there, 'Of course I'll help you, Erika.'

She doesn't say shit then, just gets back down on her knees and storts scouring the floor again for whatever she's looking for. After one last look at her G-er, I tip downstairs, carrying Amelie with me.

The boys are sitting in front of the TV, telling SpongeBob Squarepants that he's a focking prick of the highest order.

Helen goes, 'Well?'

And I'm there, 'She's lost it, Helen. The girl has lost it in a major way.'

★

Sorcha leans into the microphone and goes, 'It's great to see such an amazing, amazing turnout today.'

Except she must see what *I* can see, which is that the thousands of people thronging Grafton Street this morning are divided between those who are *for* and those who are *against* this thing happening?

You can see it in the placords and banners that people are holding up. Some are like, 'Save Grafton Street!' and 'Constance Who?' but there's others that are like, 'Women – Streets Ahead!' and my own personal favourite, 'Constance Markie-Bitch!' although, now that I think about it, it might not mean 'bitch' in the 'kick-orse' sense of the word. It might be someone who genuinely thinks she's a bitch.

'It is both an honour and a privilege,' Sorcha goes – she's standing on this, like, makeshift stage in the space opposite the Bus Stop Newsagents, 'to be asked to officiate today on what is an herstoric day for our country!'

I notice the famous Croía standing five feet in front of her, clapping at the end of every sentence. Fionn is standing next to her, looking a bit *less* happy?

'Herstoric?' someone shouts. 'You're full of shit!'

I'm relieved to discover that it's not one of my kids. It's some dude standing outside Londis and he ends up being quickly shushed.

Sorcha goes, 'I use the word *herstoric* because what we are here to do this morning is to correct the record of our shamefully gender-blind past and to recognize, at last, the role that women have played in shaping this city, shaping this country and shaping this world in which we live.'

Someone else shouts, 'I'm a woman and I'll never call it Markievicz Street! Never!' and there's, like, more than a few roars of approval.

Every time someone shouts something negative from the crowd, Croía turns around and throws a filthy in their general postcode.

Sorcha's there, 'I understand that this name change is not universally popular. And, yes, dissent *is* important. But what I would ask you to consider is this. For centuries we have been conditioned to accept the Male as Norm principle in our everyday conversations. When something is important, we say it's *man*datory. When something is bountiful, we say it's *man*ifold. When someone is in chorge, we call them the *man*agement. We take these things for granted, just like we take for granted the fact that the streets we walk every day bear the names almost exclusively of men – and not all of them deserving men, as is the case with Henry FitzRoy.'

'What the fock do you know about anything?' I hear someone go.

Okay, that *was* one of mine – Brian, as it happens. I'm there, 'Brian, button it, will you?'

'*You* focking button it,' Leo goes, looking up from the stroller, 'you focking orsewipe.'

Honor crouches down to their level and promises to buy them ice cream if they can stay quiet for the rest of Sorcha's speech. Then she tries to distract them by showing them the cha-cha-cha steps she's learned.

'Don't tell us that Constance Markievicz was deserving,' I hear a woman behind me shout. 'She and her friends smashed the windows in the Shelbourne Hotel. And we're honouring them by naming Grafton Street after her?'

There's, like, a huge round of applause. These would be very much Shelbourne Hotel people. I realize then that the woman heckling her is the old dear's friend, Delma. I'm presuming the old dear is back there somewhere as well, swigging out of her hipflask.

When the applause dies down, Sorcha goes, 'I think the fact that it's a woman saying that shows just how embedded misogyny is in our society. What I would say to you is that you're allowed to think for yourself. You don't *have* to be a stooge for the white patriarchy.'

Someone is suddenly pushing their way through the crowd behind me to try to get to the front. I focking hate people who do that, especially at, like, concerts and shit. I actually turn around and go, 'If you wanted to be at the front, then you should have got here earlier, you focking –' but then I end up not saying anything else because it turns out it's Christian – and with him are Lauren and the kids. I literally haven't seen or heard a word from the dude since he found out that it was Honor who got the little lad gee-eyed.

Christian goes, 'Hey,' and I'm like, 'Hey,' and there's a definite 'This is ridiculous – we played rugby together' vibe between us.

Ross Junior – I swear to fock – hides behind Lauren's legs. And Lauren just glowers at Honor, who suddenly stops practising her dance steps and just glowers back.

'What the fock are you looking at?' Honor goes – she's not scared of anyone. 'Jog on, you stupid bitch.'

'Yeah, jog on,' Brian goes, 'you stupid bitch.'

Lauren turns around to Christian and goes, 'Come on, Christian. I want Sorcha to see supportive faces from up there.'

But he's there, 'I'll follow you on. I just want to have a quick word with Ross.'

And she's bulling. She will never, ever be able to undo the fact that we were on the same Senior Cup team. And I think that kills her. She just rolls her eyes, then continues squeezing and excuse-me-ing her way to the front of the crowd.

Christian goes, 'I was going to ring you.'

I'm there, 'Dude, you don't have to apologize. Even though you did leave your children unsupervised with all that alcohol lying around. I can totally understand why you'd want to point the finger elsewhere.'

He's like, 'That's not why I was going to ring you,' then he looks over both shoulders, leans in close to me and goes, 'What's the deal with that foundation that your old dear set up?'

I'm there, 'I don't know. Erika seems to think it's a front for something.'

'*I* think it's a front for something.'

'Really? Any idea what?'

'No, but Hennessy's building is, like, full of Russians. There's, like, seven or eight of them working on the top floor and no one knows what they're doing. You try to engage them in conversation and they just pretend they don't speak any English – even though they do.'

'Fock! I told Helen that Erika probably needed to be medicated!'

'What does Erika know?'

'I've no idea. She was talking really fast and you know how slow my brain works. You need to see her bedroom, though. She's got all this stuff mapped out all over the walls. It's like something from a movie with Matt Damon in it.'

'Look, it's nothing to do with me. I was just curious, that's all.'

'Dude, we should maybe go for a pint sometime soon. At the end of the day, you know – rugby.'

He nods – he knows I'm talking sense – and says he'll give me a ring, then he follows Lauren, apologizing as he goes, to the front of the crowd.

Sorcha's up there going, 'Today, of course, morks only the stort of the redrawing of the map of our capital city. But for now I just want to say thank you to Dublin City Council for agreeing to make this very courageous beginning.'

She reaches for this, like, rope with, like, a *tassel* on the end of it? It's connected to a curtain covering the street sign above Butler's Irish Chocolates.

The second she does, *the* most unbelievable thing happens. All of the people in the crowd who are *against* the idea automatically turn their backs on her and sit down. And it's, like, definitely more than half.

You can see the shock register on Sorcha's face.

'Pull the rope,' I hear Croía shout.

Which Sorcha does. The curtain falls, exposing the new street sign. She goes, 'It's an honour and a privilege to rename this street . . . Markievicz Street!' to the sound of cheers and boos mixed together.

I notice that Fionn has turned fully around too, and he's staring at the crowd with this, like, *lost* look on his face. And the strangest feeling comes over me. What Father Fehily used to call a moment of profound *revelation*? Maybe it's been happening slowly over a period of months, listening to her old mix tapes – Katie Melua and Gorth Brooks with their tales of woe. But it's like someone has suddenly pulled a tasseled rope and a curtain has fallen in my own mind. And something has been revealed to me and it's this:

I'm not in love with Sorcha anymore.

8. People Can't Stop Laughing at This Incident on O'Connell Street!

Honor asks me if I'm nervous and I tell her no. Which is a lie, because I've been shitting hummus since about two o'clock this afternoon.

She's there, 'Is your stomach okay?'

'Yeah, no,' I go, 'I've got maybe one or two butterflies alright.'

She's like, 'Just pretend that this is a rugby match.'

But it's *not* a rugby match? I'm about to dance the cha-cha-cha in a pair of black trousers that – like a Jurys Inn – have no ballroom. Also, I wasn't expecting a crowd like this. Honestly, I thought we'd be doing this in front of, like, twenty or thirty people. Instead, it's, like, three hundred students plus around the same number of moms and dads. The atmosphere is electric. And I'm talking Leinster Schools Senior Cup quarter-*final* electric?

We're the last to dance. From backstage, we've watched five fathers and daughters do their cha-cha-chas. We're talking Desdemona Burke and her old man, Ed. We're talking Cloud Gorvey and her old man, John. We're talking Annora Finch and her old man, Michael. We're talking Currer Bell Whelehan and her old man, William. And we're talking Sincerity Matthews and her old man, Raymond, who are at the top of the leaderboard after getting two nines and one ten from the judges.

I hear Miss Coleman, the fifth-class teacher who's compering the event, go, 'And now we come to the last couple to dance the cha-cha-cha tonight . . .'

Honor's there, 'Loosen up, Dad! What are you always saying to Johnny Sexton?'

I go, 'To mention me more often in interviews as someone who was a major influence on him growing up?'

'Eat nerves, shit results, Dad!'

'Oh, that. Let's not talk about shitting, though – at least until we get through the next ninety seconds.'

Miss Coleman goes, 'Please put your hands together for Honor O'Carroll-Kelly and her father, Ross!'

There's, like, a polite round of applause as we walk out into the middle of the floor. The crowd is surrounding the dance floor on all four sides. I can tell from the big smiles on their faces that all of the girls absolutely hate Honor's guts but they're all pretending *not* to?

Trust me, as a Mount Anville parent, you get to know the signs.

From the Green Room mezzanine up above us, I hear Sincerity Matthews shout, 'Good luck, Honor!'

And I just think, What a piece of work she is.

The music storts. Like I said, it's One Direction's *That's What Makes You Beautiful.*

I feel so far out of my comfort zone here that I'm actually shaking. But I try my best to channel the nerves and remember the steps. Everything that Mrs Leonard taught us. Every move that me and Honor have been secretly practising on all those Tuesday and Thursday nights, not to mention Saturday mornings.

Side, rock step, side, together, step. Rock step, side, together, side. Rock step, forward, forward, forward, backward, backward, backward – cha-cha-cha – rock step – cha-cha-cha – and rock step, side, together, side.

The ninety seconds feel like ninety minutes until we finally reach the end of our routine. I twirl Honor out, then I twirl her in again, then *she* does the splits, dropping to the floor. And there ends up being a massive round of applause – though that could mean anything.

I pick Honor up off the floor and she gives me a big smile and a hug and, as she does, she goes, 'For fock's sake, Dad!' out of the corner of her mouth, which is the first indication that it might not have gone as well as I hoped.

Miss Coleman – in the Winkleman role – goes, 'Honor, Ross, you looked like you really enjoyed that!'

She's no Winkleman, by the way.

Honor goes, 'I had *such* a good time out there. Oh my God, I'm out of breath. Yes, I really enjoyed it.'

Miss Coleman turns around to me then and she's like, 'Ross, were you nervous tonight?'

And I'm there, 'Yeah, no, I was absolutely shitting it. And I'm saying that as someone who's played schools rugby at the very highest level and would be used to dealing with high-pressure situations.'

'Okay, let's see what the judges thought.'

The first thing I notice is that none of them can make eye contact with us. They say that's a bad sign. I know it's definitely the case with juries.

First up is a woman called Jean – a looker – who runs the 'Broadway Here I Come' stage school at the back of Cinnamon in Ranelagh. She goes, 'Honor, I thought that was a wonderful performance by you. It was confident, it was assured. I think you have a real gift. I thought you were a little wooden, Ross, if you don't mind me saying so. Overall, I liked it, though.'

I'm thinking, fock you.

Next up is another woman, Mena – not great – who is a former Mountie who choreographed *We Live and Move and Have Our Being*, a retelling of the Bank Bail-Out in interpretive dance. She's there, 'Again, Honor, I think you are a natural. What I especially like about you is that you're not afraid to take risks. There were some very inventive moves in there. I especially loved you finishing with the splits. Ross, em, I'm trying to think is there a nice way to put this, you were flat-footed, your timing was a bit off and overall you made it look like hard work out there.'

I'm thinking, fock you, too.

The last judge is some dude called Ryan, who's apparently directing Mount Anville and Blackrock College's modern-day version of *Porgy and Bess*, set in a Direct Provision Centre in Athlone. He ends up totally ripping into us slash me.

He goes, 'Wonderful, Honor. The perfect performance from you. Ross, I have no idea where your daughter got her sense of rhythm from, but it couldn't have been from you, Darling. It was like you were dancing to two totally different songs out there. You were speaking the steps as you were doing them – I saw you mouth

the words, 'Rock step, side, together . . .' – and your hand kept popping up like you were holding a pint of Guinness.'

'Heineken,' I go, under my breath. 'Focking Guinness!'

'I thought you were the weakest dancer we've seen tonight and
you really let your daughter down.'

There's, like, a nervous smatter of applause.

Miss Coleman goes, 'What did you think of those comments?'

I'm there, 'I thought the first two were a bit, you know – *whatever*?
I thought the last goy was being a bit of a wanker, to be honest.'

She ends up nearly dropping the microphone. Hey, I've been
calling it since 1980 and I will go on calling it as long as there are
things to be called.

She goes, 'Er, okay, let's look at your scores.'

The judges take turns to hold up little table-tennis bats with
numbers written on them. Jean gives us six. Mena gives us six.
Ryan gives us three. And I genuinely wish I'd said even worse shit
about him.

Fifteen points puts us at the bottom of the leaderboard. I turn to
Honor and I go, 'I'll do better in the dance-off,' and she rolls her
eyes and goes, 'There's *no* dance-off, Dad. It's over.'

Which comes as a definite relief to me, I can tell you that. I think
to myself, well, at least I don't have to go through that again.

Twenty minutes later, we've changed out of our dance clothes
and back into our civvies, and I'm driving us home. Honor is on her
iPhone, boning up on the dangers of cigarette and alcohol con-
sumption, just in case Sorcha storts throwing questions at her,
while I'm just sitting there, furious with myself.

I blew it and I know it.

I'm there, 'Look, I'm sorry again, Honor. I'm just as disappointed
as you that we're out.'

I'm actually focking thrilled.

She goes, 'Out?'

This is as I'm using the remote control to open the electric gates.

I'm like, 'Yeah, we were eliminated, weren't we?'

She's there, 'There *are* no eliminations, Dad.'

I'm like, 'What?' as I pull up in front of the house.

She goes, 'Everyone stays in the competition. We all get to do four dances. We're bottom of the board. It just means you have to get your shit together for next month. We have to really nail the quickstep.'

The quickstep? Oh, for fock's sake, I think to myself, as she gets out of the cor and walks into the house.

I know I've let her down badly and I think I literally couldn't feel any worse than I do in that moment. But things can always get worse. I know that from bitter experience.

The front passenger door suddenly opens again and someone climbs in, some dude wearing a black coat with the hood up. I end up getting the fright of my life.

I'm like, 'Who the fock are you?'

And that's when he turns and looks at me and I realize that it's Grievous Bodily Horm.

He goes, 'I think me and you neeyut to hab a birrof a chat, Rosser.'

'Thrive,' he goes.

I'm like, 'Where am I driving to?'

'Dudn't mathor,' he goes. 'Thrive. In a nordoddy didection.'

He means towards the Northside. I think that's when the fear *really* storts to hit me? I try to be brave. I think about the dude whose job it is to keep clamping Cian Healy's jeep outside the Shelly and I think that's the kind of nerve I'm going to need if I'm going to get through this.

Grievous says very little, though. I'm the one who ends up having to make all the running in terms of conversation for most of the next half an hour.

'So how are things going over in Estepona?' I go.

He's like, 'Alreet.'

'And, er, what brings you home?'

'Birra bidness.'

'Do you mind me asking what kind of business?'

'You doataunt ast a fedda in moy position a question like that, Rosser – because you might not want to hee-or the addenswer.'

That sends an actual chill down my spine.

I notice a black BMW X5 in the rearview mirror, following very close behind us. 'That's moy young fedda,' he goes, as if reading my mind.

He means it's Actual.

'Take the East Link,' he goes.

I'm like, 'Yeah, no problem,' trying to stay calm. 'So, er, how did you know where I live?'

He's like, 'I can foyunt addy wooden, Rosser. Addy wooden in the wurdled.'

'That's a gift.'

'It is indeeyut a gift. It's why people who go on the rudden from me nebber foyunt addy peace. Do you get me?'

'I do get you. I definitely do get you.'

'Me and Dean hab been foddying you arowunt all day. Ditn't know that, did you?'

Dean is Actual Bodily Horm's *real* name?

I'm there, 'I, er, didn't notice you, no.'

He goes, 'We saw you daddencing wit your thaughter toneet. We boat thought that last fedda was veddy heersh on you. Are you alreet, Rosser?'

'Yeah, no, I'm fine, Grievous.'

'It's just your breeding's arthur going all fuddy since we crossed oaber the ribber back theer.'

I keep imagining I can hear Philip Boucher-Hayes, in his *Crime Call* voice, going: 'This is the last time Ross O'Carroll-Kelly was seen alive.'

I'm there, 'No, I'm fine, Grievous.'

He goes, 'Calt me Roppie.'

I'm like, 'Robbie, then. Yeah, no, I'm fine.'

'I grew up arowunt hee-or, you know? Estepoda is where I lib. But this airdia will altways be howum to me. Turden left up hee-or.'

Which I do. The X5 is still following us.

I'm there, 'It's actually a surprisingly nice area.'

It's not. It's a shithole.

And that's when, out of nowhere, he says it.

'One of yoo-er crew,' he goes, 'roawut moy wife that noyt in Estepoda.'

I'm like, 'What?' *trying* to sound shocked? I'm not sure if he buys it, though. 'Rode her? Why would you think that?'

'Because she's arthur been happy,' he goes, 'and Ine thalken about proper happy, for the past bleaten munt. She's been walken arowunt the house sigging, "I gorra a feeding – that toneet's godda be a good, good neet . . ."'

'That song can get annoying after a while.'

'Veddy annoying. Especially wit *her* bleaten sigging it. I mee-un, you *met* Medissa – you merrur that neet in May Oblong's.'

I'm there, 'I did, yeah.'

'Misser dobble bitch – am I reet?'

'I don't know about that. I like that sort of moody slash pissed-off look. She reminds me of one or two girls I knew from Coláiste Íosagáin back in the day.'

'Doatunt get me wrong, I lub the wooban. We're togetter ebber siddience we were torteen yee-ors owult. But it's veddy reer that she's ebber happy. Eeben Dean will ted you that. Oatenly toyum I've ebber see her *that* happy – mathord of fact – is when she's getting it some wayor edelse.'

'When you say *it*?'

'Ine thalken about the royud, Rosser.'

'I thought you were.'

'When she's playing arowunt – wit someone utter than me. Do you get me?'

'So would that be, like, a regular occurrence?'

'Happens mord offen than I'd liken it to. There's some veddy brayuv and some veddy stupid people out thayor. I meeyun, *she'd* throy it on with addy wooden.'

'Even though she's married?'

The pot is racially profiling the kettle here.

'Dudn't bodder *her*,' he goes. 'She knows I'd nebber touch a hayor on her head. But it's the feddas that make me laugh – the fee-or dudn't stop them saying yes to her, eeben though a lot of the shams she's beeyun with hab thisappeared. Utters hab ended up in wheelchayors.'

Oh, fock. I just keep driving.

I'm there, 'This suspicion of yours, is it based purely on her being all – like you said – happy?'

'Not joost,' he goes. 'I opent the doe-er of the Picasso the foddowing morden and it reeked of sex.'

'Right.'

'Reeked of it, Rosser. So I had a good look insoyut. And on the floe-er, I fowunt two rubber joddies.'

'Two?'

'Yeah.'

'*Definitely* two?'

'Two, yeah.'

I can't tell you how disappointed I am in Ronan. When you sleep with a woman you never want to see again, you're supposed to leave her disappointed and unfulfilled in a sexual sense. That way there's never any afters. This is, like, page one of the manual.

I'm there, 'The whole thing just doesn't add up.'

He goes, 'I've been aston arowunt about you, Rosser.'

'Me?'

'Ine arthur heardon all sorts of stordies.'

'What kind of stories?'

'Joost that you're a birrof a lathies' man.'

'Who were you talking to? Was it Fergus McFadden?'

'Who?'

'He's a rugby player – and a friend.'

'No, I wadn't thalken to him. Pud over hee-or.'

I end up doing what he tells me. The X5 pulls in behind me.

Grievous goes, 'Look me in the eye, Rosser – hee-or, look me in the eye! – and ted me the troot. Did you hab sex with Medissa that neet?'

I'm there, 'Dude, I did not have sex with your wife.'

He stares at me for the longest twenty seconds of my life, then he goes, 'I belieb you.'

Then he opens the door.

I'm like, 'Thank fock for that.'

'But one of yoo-er crew did,' he goes. 'And thrust me, Rosser, I'll foyunt out the troot. And whoebber it was, Ine tedding you now – he's soyunt he's owen death waddant.'

I ring Ronan for, like, the seventeenth time this morning, except his phone ends up just ringing out and it's pretty obvious at this stage that he's screening my calls. I leave him another message – to go with the twelve I left him last night – telling him to ring me back urgently.

Brian, Johnny and Leo are sitting on the floor of their room watching a TV programme called *Football Years – 1999–2000*. It probably goes without saying what kind of football we're talking about.

I'm like, 'Brian, give me the remote control.'

'Fock off,' he goes.

'This isn't suitable viewing. I said give it to me.'

'Fock off, you focking cockfuck orseprick.'

I go to grab it from him, except he sinks his teeth into my hand. I basically scream and Leo and Johnny actually laugh, so out of pure spite I pull the plug out of the wall, then I pull the other end of the flex out of the TV and I stick it in my pocket.

I'm like, 'Now let's see you watch your soccer.'

'You focking prick,' Leo goes, as I'm walking out of the room. 'You fat focking prick with ears.'

I tip down the stairs, quietly congratulating myself on another nice piece of tough-love parenting. And that's when I hear the raised voices coming from the kitchen. It turns out that Sorcha and Fionn are having a serious borney. I listen at the door for about thirty seconds and it's hilarious. They're literally having a row about Daniel O'Donnell.

'He's another toxic male,' Sorcha goes. 'Another misogynistic meat-head who has to prove his masculinity by waving a gun about the place and getting as many women as he can pregnant.'

Daniel O'Donnell? I'm thinking, have I missed something?

I head into the kitchen and I go, 'I've never been a fan of his music, but I thought people generally liked him. I think your granny was actually a fan, Sorcha.'

Fionn's there, 'What music?' pulling a face like he smells bad milk. 'We're having a conversation about Daniel O'Connell.'

'Oh,' I go, 'I thought you were talking about . . . actually, it doesn't matter. Forget it.'

They're both sitting at the table in front of their laptops. I drop the TV flex into the bin.

'Yes, he delivered Catholic Emancipation,' Sorcha goes, 'but that doesn't take away the fact that he was also a rapist.'

Fionn's there, 'An *alleged* rapist. He was never charged.'

'A woman had his baby and he refused to give her any financial support. She ended up being imprisoned for debt.'

'Most historians say there's no actual evidence to sustain the claim that he was the father of Ellen Courtenay's baby.'

And I automatically go, 'I'd love to know what the *herstorians* think about it?' and it's one of those great, great lines that just comes to me in the moment.

Sorcha goes, 'That's actually a good point, Ross. I wonder how many of these so-called *historians* who doubt her account of what happened are men themselves?'

I'm there, 'Probably all of them, Sorcha,' really stirring it. 'God, it makes me sick!'

Fionn goes, 'I just wish you'd run this article past me before you let them publish it. I have a degree in History, Sorcha.'

'Oh, and you think I need your impri-man-tur to express an opinion, do you?'

I'm there, 'What are you talking about anyway?'

Sorcha goes, 'I wrote a column for the Journal.ie about which other men's names I wanted to see removed from the map of Dublin. It was actually Croía who suggested I write about Daniel O'Connell.'

'The piece is full of distortions,' Fionn goes.

She's there, 'He was an alleged sex offender and an alleged dead-beat dad – those are facts. You can also see how much he hated women from the way he treated them. He was having – oh my God – multiple affairs behind his wife's back. Children everywhere! Oh, and he also *killed* a man?'

Fionn goes, 'Sorcha, it was the start of the nineteenth century. Dueling with pistols was a perfectly legal way to settle an argument.'

'He was a violent, misogynistic, gun-loving sexual predator – and I called him out.'

'You called him out? A man who died almost two centuries ago?'

'Irrelevant.'

'I'm just trying to get you to see, Sorcha, that we can't just surrender history to the present. Yes, Daniel O'Connell clearly had some serious personality flaws. But he was still the founding father of Irish nationalism.'

'And what *I'm* trying to get *you* to see, Fionn, is that there are hundreds of Irish women who deserve to have a street named after them more than this toxic, misogynistic, possible rapist, murderer.'

Fionn just sighs. I feel like nearly saying, hey, it's not as easy as it looks, Dude, is it? But then I don't have to say anything. I'm well out of it.

He goes, 'All of this is hurting you politically, Sorcha.'

She's like, 'What do you mean?'

'Not everybody sees the world the way you and Croía do. Some people preferred Grafton Street when it was called Grafton Street. Some people like O'Connell Street being called O'Connell Street. These are the people you're going to be asking to vote for you at the next election.'

'Fionn, I could no more abandon my principles than Aung San Suu Kyi could become a despotic mass-murderer.'

'Have you read the below-the-line comments on your column?'

'I don't read below-the-line comments. As Croía said, who cares what some lonely virgin with a neckbeard thinks about anything?'

'It's not Croía who's going to have to face the electorate. Sorcha, you need to read these comments. You are making yourself very, very unpopular.'

There's suddenly a massive thud upstairs and the entire house seems to shake. Five seconds later, there's the sound of screaming. Either Brian has hit Johnny or Leo, or Leo has hit Brian or Johnny, or Johnny has hit Brian or Leo.

Sorcha goes, 'Ross, are you not supposed to be watching them?'

I'm there, 'I only came downstairs to put the flex from the TV in the bin. They were watching soccer.'

'Can you please go and stop them killing each other?'

I'm just about to go back upstairs when Fionn goes, 'Oh, no! Oh, Jesus, no!'

Sorcha's there, 'What's wrong?'

'There's one comment here I really think you should read, Sorcha.'

'Yeah, I've no interest in what total strangers think of me, Fionn.'

'It's from someone calling themselves Feminist Avenger Thirteen. I'll read it to you.'

'Like I said, I don't care.'

'It says, "Hilarious this woman having a go at Daniel O'Connell for whoring around. I happen to know that she has no idea whether the father of the baby she's carrying is her husband or her Parliamentary Secretary. Hypocrite much?"'

Mrs Leonard is unbelievably supportive.

'Ryan Dorsey?' she goes – at the same time laughing. '*That's* who they're using as a judge? I taught him how to dance and let me tell you – he had two left feet. All he had going for him, in fact, was a pushy mother.'

I'm there, 'He obviously fancies himself as the Craig whatever-the-fock of the panel. He's got one of those faces that you'd never grow tired of slapping.'

'What score did he give you?'

'A three,' Honor goes.

'A three?'

Mrs Leonard just shakes her head.

'Everyone deserves at least a six just for having the nerve to get up there and do it,' she goes. 'That's Ryan, you see. Everything has to be about him.'

I'm sitting on a low bench with my back to the wall.

'It was totally my fault,' I go. 'I let Honor down in a big-time way.'

I notice that Honor doesn't contradict me. The *opposite*, in fact?

She goes, 'He kept *saying* the steps as he was doing them.'

I'm like, 'Don't remind me. I feel bad enough as it is.'

Mrs Leonard's there, 'You're just overthinking it, Ross. It's nothing more than that.'

'And his pint hand popped up again,' Honor goes.

I just shake my head. I'm like, 'Maybe Ryan *is* right. Maybe you deserve a better dance portner. A better father, even.'

Mrs Leonard claps her hands together twice. 'Okay,' she goes, 'that's enough self-pity for one day. Let's go to work.'

I just stand up, then me and Honor follow her out to the middle of the floor.

'Now,' she goes, 'this is probably not what either of you wants to hear, but the quickstep is one of *the* most difficult ballroom dances to master. The good news is that it's also a lot of fun.'

She tells us to stand facing each other, then she sort of, like, arranges our orms so that *my* right orm is high on Honor's back, but crooked at the elbow, and Honor's left is the same, then our other orms are sticking straight out to the side, our two hands holding.

'There's going to be lots of this,' Mrs Leonard goes. 'Keep that elbow *straight*, Ross! *Straight!* And your back, that's it. Like a rod. It feels very formal and very rigid, doesn't it? But with the quickstep, it's your *legs* that are going to have all the fun!'

Honor stares at me in a really, like, intense way and goes, 'Are you following this?' because she knows my attention span wouldn't be the greatest.

I'm like, 'Yeah, no, definitely.'

Mrs Leonard goes, 'The quickstep is fast and smooth – it's a mix of foxtrot and Charleston. It's important to maintain this strong top line – rigid elbow, Ross! – but at the same time appear light on your feet. And we dance it, most excitingly, in four-four time. Honor, have you chosen a piece of music?'

Honor goes, 'I left the CD on the table, Mrs Leonard – next to the CD player. It's, like, *Walking on Sunshine*?'

The woman goes over to the table to stick the thing on, leaving me and Honor still standing there, face to face, in our dance pose.

'They're all talking about me behind my back,' she goes.

I'm like, 'Who, Honor? Who's talking about you?'

'Who do you think? All the girls in my class. They're laughing at me.'

'It's me they should be laughing at, Honor.'

'It's got nothing to do with you focking up the dance. They're laughing at me because of *her*.'

'Are you talking about your mother?'

'It's, like, all over the focking Internet.'

Yeah, no, Sorcha put out a statement basically saying it was a private matter and she wasn't going to allow Internet trolls – hiding behind the cover of anonymity – to distract her from her important work addressing herstorical gender imbalances. That's more or less word for word.

Honor goes, 'Why doesn't she just deny it and say that the baby is yours?'

I'm there, 'Because it might not be.'

'Yeah, so I have to go to school every day, knowing that people are talking about me as soon as I leave the room, saying, "Oh, her mother's a total slapper."'

'Is that what they're saying?'

'Dad, it's Mount Anville. What do you *think* they're saying?'

She's got, like, tears in her eyes. I swear to God, never in my life have I felt as guilty as I do in that moment. And I've got a hell of a lot to feel guilty about.

She goes, 'Even Sincerity Matthews is loving it.'

I'm like, 'Really? What's *she* saying?'

'She came up to me at lunchtime today and she was like, 'Honor, I know you're going through a really difficult time at the moment. I just want you to know that I'm here for you as a friend'.'

'What an out and out wagon!'

'Then she was all, "My mom and dad got divorced when I was, like, seven – so I know a little bit of what you're going through. It's a horribly lonely and confusing time, but trust me, Honor, you *will* get through it. If you ever want to talk, I'm here to listen."'

'Oh, she's a *real* piece of work, isn't she?'

'Dad, I don't want to finish last again this time.'

This unbelievable sense of – I'm going to call it – *resolve* comes over me then? I decide that I will do anything in my power to make sure that doesn't happen. I'd even give up my Leinster Schools Senior Cup medal if it hadn't already been taken off me for doping.

I'm going to practise this dance all day, every day between now and the second round of the competition. I'm going to practise it for eight, ten hours a day – however long it takes – to become great at it.

The room is suddenly filled with the sound of Katrina and the Waves.

'Yes!' Mrs Leonard goes. 'This is perfect!'

And I look Honor dead in the eye and I go, 'I'm not going to let you down again, Honor. I'm promising you now – one way or another, we are going to win that Glitterball!'

I decide, okay, fock it, I can't keep leaving voice messages for Ronan. I'm thinking, he needs to know that Grievous Bodily Horm is on the warpath, so I decide to drive to UCD to tell him to his face. It's the middle of the afternoon and the traffic is pretty heavy.

There's a woman in a black Toyota Corolla who's weaving from lane to lane ahead of us, trying to gain an advantage, but she's just causing a nuisance.

'Pick! A focking! Lane!' Leo goes.

I'm wondering will he grow up to be a driving instructor.

I'm just taking the exit for Belfield when my phone suddenly rings. I answer it and it ends up being Sorcha.

I'm there, 'Hey, what's up?'

She goes, 'I just want to ask you something, Ross, and I want you to be totally straight with me.'

'Okay, let's see what the question is first.'

'Do you think there's a possibility that Honor might be Feminist Avenger Thirteen?'

I actually laugh. I'm there, 'No – not a chance.'

She goes, 'You answered my question without even thinking about it.'

'That's because I don't *need* to think about it? Why would she do something like that?'

'There's lots of reasons she would do it, Ross. She hates me.'

'Hate is a strong word.'

'She *hates* me. And she hates that I'm pregnant and that she's going to have to share her life with another little brother or sister. I was talking to my dad –'

'Your old man. I had a feeling he put the idea in your head.'

'– and he pointed out that this could be her revenge for me stopping her from going to dancing.'

'Keep going.'

'Ross, we've had trouble with her on the Internet before. Remember her trolling all those celebrities? The cease and desist letters?'

'That was ages ago. Last summer.'

'I'm just saying, Ross, that you can't tell me that posting nasty stuff online is out of character for her.'

'I don't see what good it would do her putting the story out there that her mother is pregnant by God knows who?'

'Yeah, it's between *two* people, Ross – it's you or Fionn.'

'You know what I mean. She's already getting a hord time from the other girls in her class, saying you're a –'

'A what?'

'I hate using the word slut, Sorcha, but that's basically what's being said.'

'So you definitely don't think Honor did it?'

'Definitely, definitely not.'

'Well, Croía says it was probably a man anyway. She says I have to ask myself who is likely to feel most threatened by my campaign. Obviously, men.'

'There you are, then. The other thing I would point out, Sorcha, is that Honor is a changed person since she storted this, em, Alcohol and Tobacco Awareness Course.'

'Yeah, we've had false dawns with Honor before.'

'All I'm saying is we're both learning a lot. Did you know that three pints these days is considered a binge?' quoting her something that JP said recently – to general laughter, I should add – in

Kielys of Donnybrook. 'I'm thinking of possibly cutting back myself.'

I'm not.

She goes, 'Where are you, by the way?'

I'm there, 'I've just pulled into the UCD cor pork.'

I'm locking the cor as I say this.

She goes, 'Are you meeting Ronan?'

I'm there, 'Yeah, no, there's one or two things I need to talk to him about alright.'

'Shadden will be delighted to hear that you're back talking to each other. I hope you haven't left the boys in the cor!'

I'm there, 'Of course I haven't left the boys in the cor.'

I have left the boys in the cor. I end up having to go back for them.

She goes, 'Okay, I'm going to go and meet Croía – see what *she* thinks I should do about my private medical details being discussed online,' and then she's gone.

I put the boys into their stroller and we set off for the Law School. The boys draw quite a few stares by calling every randomer we pass either a cockchicken, a fockstick or a tit-muncher.

I find the lecture hall where Ronan's supposed to be. There's some dude at the front – I'm presuming the lecturer – banging on about *mens rea* and *actus reus*, whatever the fock they even are, then I spot Ronan in the second row, listening to every word and taking notes.

I cough one or twice – actually, four or five times – to try to get his attention, then Brian does it for me by shouting, 'Hey, wanker!' and Ronan looks back and sees us at the back of the theatre.

He rolls his eyes, apologizes to the lecturer, then troops wearily up the steps towards us.

I'm doing *him* the focking favour here.

He goes, 'What do you bleaten want?' and at the same time he touches each of the boys on the top of their heads. 'Howiya, feddas?'

I'm there, 'You wouldn't have thought of returning my calls, no? I told you it was a matter of life and death.'

'You were pissing and moaning about your bleaten boat shoowiz getting wrecked.'

'That was in the first few messages I left.'

'Boat shoowuz – that's the foorst toyum thee ebber saw a splash of wathor.'

'Grievous Bodily Horm came to see me.'

Oh, that brings him to his, suddenly, senses. His expression totally changes. He goes, 'Soddy?'

I'm there, 'He was here. Two days ago. Showed up at my gaff.'

'What fower? Dud he know what happint?'

'Not the specifics of it, no. But he knows someone on your stag porty had sex with his wife.'

'How?'

'Because she was walking around with a focking smile on her face for days afterwards apparently.'

'Boddicks.'

'*Boddicks* is right.'

'What did you ted him?'

'I told him he was being paranoid. I told him he had nothing to worry about.'

'Good madden, Rosser.'

'Hey, you're not out of the woods yet. He said he knows his wife well enough to know when she's sourcing it elsewhere.'

'Medissa woatunt say athin.'

'How do you know that?'

'I joost know she woatunt.'

'Well, I hope not, Ro. Because Grievous said he's going to find out which one of us it was – and when he does, that person is dead.'

I've had an idea. Good ones often come to me when I'm lying on my bed and basically thinking about nothing.

I was thinking about the quickstep and how I might get good at it in the short time we have between now and the second round of the competition.

And, like I said, that's when I have one of my famous *brainwaves*?

I find Sorcha's old pogo stick, from when she was a kid, in a box with her My Little Ponies, her Sun Jewel Borbies, about five hundred coloured morkers and her Lolo ball.

I take out the pogo stick and I test its weight in my hand. It feels about right. Next, I go to the wardrobe and I take out one of Sorcha's old maxi dresses – a long-sleeved one with black-and-white stripes that she only wore once because I told her she looked like the focking Hamburglar in it.

I turn the pogo stick upside-down, then I sit down on the side of the bed, holding the thing between my knees, and I pull the dress down onto it. It ends up being a perfect fit, in the sense that the two footrests fit perfectly into the little sleeves, like actual shoulders.

Next, I grab some cushions. Luckily, Sorcha has an absolute fetish for the things. She's constantly buying them. There's always, like, thirty or forty of them on every bed in the house. Removing them to actually get in takes between forty and forty-five minutes every night. These ones are, like, cream-coloured, from before she changed the colour scheme of the master bedroom. I stuff three or four of them into the dress, packing them tightly, so that they fill the thing out.

Next, I grab the Lolo ball. I remove the plastic bit from it, so what I'm left with is just a yellow ball. Using a scissors, I make a hole in it, a little bit bigger than a two-euro coin, then I push the ball down onto the springy bit at the bottom of the pogo stick, which of course is now the top.

Next, I grab a black morker – you can probably guess now where this is going – and I draw a face on the ball. It ends up being a pretty nice face as well. If I had to say it looked like anyone, I'd say Yanet Garcia, except obviously bald as a focking cue ball and with a fatter face.

As a matter of fact, I decide to actually *call* her Yanet?

Then – a nice touch this – I draw a little speech bubble coming out of her mouth. Inside the bubble, I write, 'Oh my God, Ross, you are SO good!' because, being a confidence player, I've always thrived off compliments, even when I'm paying them to myself.

Next, I grab my iPhone, plug in the earphones, stick the buds in my ears and I call up *Walking on Sunshine* on my iTunes and I press Play.

I pick Yanet up and, with my right orm around her, I hold her close to my chest, pull her right orm out to the side – and I dance.

I do it the way we did it with Mrs Leonard last week.

Step, side, close, side. Step, side, close, lock – one, two, three and four. Spin-turn. Step, side, close. One, two, three. Step, side, close, side.

I do it again and again and again and again with Katrina and the Waves on permanent repeat. If I make a mistake, I go back to the beginning of the song and I stort it again.

Step, side, close, side. Step, side, close, lock – one, two, three and four. Spin-turn. Step, side, close. One, two, three. Step, side, close, side.

Yanet is a bit on the light side in terms of weight. She reminds me a bit of Sorcha that summer she had an irritable bowel and had to go off corbs.

Step, side, close, side. Step, side, close, lock – one, two, three and four. Spin-turn. Step, side, close. One, two, three. Step, side, close, side.

This is the way I learned how to kick points. By doing it over and over and over again. Get it wrong, start over. Get it right, try to get it right twice in a row, then three times in a row. Another mistake. Back to the stort.

I end up dancing that pogo stick in a dress around the room for literally hours. When I feel light-headed and I want to stop, I think about Honor's sad face when she told me she didn't want to be last again. So I keep going, beyond the point of exhaustion, towards the point where I stort to really, really hate Katrina and the Waves and wish them actual horm, all the time reminding myself of my promise to Honor.

I will not let you down. We are going to win that Glitterball.

I keep going, even though my legs are screaming at me to stop and my head feels like it's about to explode from remembering the steps.

Step, side, close, side. Step, side, close, lock – one, two, three and four. Spin-turn. Step, side, close. One, two, three. Step, side, close, side.

And eventually, after three, maybe four hours have passed, my body point-blank refuses to dance another step and I lie down on the bed and fall instantly asleep.

*

Bleeeuuuggghhh!!! Bleeeuuuggghhh!!! Bleeeuuuggghhh!!!

Yeah, no, that's the sound of puking and it's coming from the girls' changing room. I'm throwing on my costume – I'm wearing a topcoat and tails, which was Honor's idea – and I'm looking at the other dads, all of us thinking the exact same thing: I hope that's not my daughter spewing next-door.

Raymond rushes over to the door and we all follow him out into the corridor. He hammers on the door of the girls' changing room, going, 'Sincerity! Are you alright in there, Sincerity?' and I only cop for the first time what a completely ridiculous name it is – and I've heard a few beauties in my time.

A second or two later, Sincerity comes to the door. 'I'm fine,' she goes, 'but Desdemona, Annora and Cloud are all getting sick.'

'Cloud?' John Gorvey goes, then into the dressing room he bursts, going, 'Cloud? Cloud?'

We all follow him in.

There's, like, three traps in front of us, all with their doors open, and a girl in a ballgown in each one, kneeling down and hurling her dinner up. I notice that there's sick on the floor and then some on the walls – we must be talking, like, *projectile* vomit here?

Honor, to my huge relief, seems to be fine. She's just sitting there – I'm proud to say – with her game-face on, not letting it distract her, whereas Sincerity is running between the three girls, holding their hair back for them as they take it in turns to vom.

'What's going on?' Michael Finch wants to know. 'Did you eat something, Annora?'

Annora goes, 'I think it must have been . . . bleuuugh! . . . the watermelon punch . . . bleeeuuuggghhh!!!'

Ed Burke is like, 'What watermelon punch?' as he puts his hand on his daughter's forehead to check her temperature. 'You're burning up, Desdemona.'

'There was watermelon punch,' Annora goes, between dry heaves, 'in the green room.'

John goes, 'Okay, who had the watermelon punch? Did you have it, Cloud?'

Cloud goes, 'Yes?'

'You, Desdemona?'

'Yes,' Desdemona goes.

'And you did, too, Annora?'

She's like, 'Yes – bleeeuuuggghhh!!!'

John looks around. 'Did anyone else have it?' he goes.

No one answers.

He's like, 'Mystery solved, then. Where did this watermelon punch come from?'

That's when Sincerity goes, '*I* made it.'

There's a sudden change of current in the room.

'*You* made it?' Michael Finch goes. I heard him say earlier that he was a portner with Ernst & Young, so he'd be suspicious by nature. 'And what did you put in it?'

Sincerity looks at her old man, then back at Annora's old man. 'It was just watermelon, lime and, like, *mint*? I put it through the NutriBullet.'

Sincerity's old man doesn't care much for the accusation. 'What exactly are you implying?' he goes. 'And bear in mind there are witnesses here present.'

'I'm not implying anything,' Michael goes. 'I'm stating it as a fact. Everyone who drank your daughter's watermelon punch has come down with food poisoning. I don't suppose you had any yourself, Sincerity?'

She's there, 'I was going to have it afterwards.'

'Convenient,' John Gorvey goes.

Raymond is there, 'How dare you defame my daughter in such a way? Have you ever heard of Lavelle Solicitors? Because you can expect a letter from them!'

No competition in Mount Anville would be complete without the exchange of threatened legal action. The result of the mother–daughter wheelbarrow race from the school sports day in 2013 is currently the subject of an appeal before the High Court.

I turn around to Honor and I go, 'Okay, let's hit the dance floor.'

You can tell straightaway that the fathers of the sick girls don't appreciate it.

Michael Finch goes, 'What are you talking about? The competition can't go on.'

I'm like, 'Why not? There's fock-all wrong with *my* daughter,' and I end up saying it in a real *Welcome to the Jungle* kind of way. 'It's Mount Anville, my friend. Survival of the fittest.'

Hey, if we'd wanted to protect our daughters from the real world, we'd have sent them to Gaelscoils to talk focking gibberish to each other all day.

Ed goes, 'I think Michael is right. We should seek a postponement.'

William Whelehan, Currer Bell's old man, is there, 'I have to admit, I'm with Ross on this one. It's unfortunate – but them's the breaks.'

I love that expression and I make a conscious decision there and then to use it more in conversation.

Me and Honor step outside, leaving the rest of them to their arguing and their spewing. We head for the backstage area.

I go, 'I have to say, Honor, I really admired the way you kept your focus back there and stayed above the fray.'

Honor's there, 'I actually can't believe that winning means so much to Sincerity that she would try to poison everyone else in the competition.'

'It's a good job *you* didn't drink any.'

'I wouldn't touch anything she made. I wouldn't trust that bitch as far as I'd throw her.'

'That's a good attitude to have, Honor. Always take it for granted that every other focker in the world would cut your throat and step over your dead body if you didn't do it to them first – and you won't go far wrong.'

The competition ends up going ahead but only after a forty-five-minute delay, during which there are threats of High Court injunctions and something called interlocutory relief, then someone else wants to have a sample of the punch sent to a laboratory for immediate testing, but it turns out that the bottle that Sincerity brought it in has somehow mysteriously disappeared.

Throughout all of this, me and Honor remain off to the side, practising our quickstep routine. And I can tell from the expression on her face that she's pleasantly surprised – actually, pleasantly shocked – by the sudden confidence she can see in me.

She's like, 'Oh my God! What have you being doing?'

I'm there, 'I'll tell you afterwards.'

She ends up smiling so hord, she looks like she might burst.

Like I said, the upshot of all the arguments and the legal threats is that the show must go on, but the three pukers will be allowed to compete last to give them a bit more time to recover.

The change in the running order means that me and Honor are first up. And I'm happy with that because I feel pumped as we walk out into the middle of the floor.

'Ladies and gentlemen,' Miss Coleman goes, 'dancing the quick-step to *Walking on Sunshine*, it's Honor and Ross O'Carroll-Kelly.'

The music storts. And then, to cut a long story short, I end up nailing it. Every step, every side, every close. Every kick, every lift, every turn. I do it without thinking, like it's second nature to me, like blinking or breathing. And all without moving my lips to tell my brain what I'm in the process of doing.

The crowd goes literally ballistic at the end – as in, everyone in the audience stands up and storts roaring. It's, like, an *automatic* thing? And two of the three judges – we're talking Mena and Jean – are on their feet as well.

I give Honor a hug and I realize she's crying. And I'm not talking about the pretend crying she does when you refuse to buy her a pair of shoes for seven hundred euros and she rings Tusla to report you for child neglect.

I'm talking about, like, *genuine* tears?

Mena goes, 'Oh! *My* God! What a transformation! When we saw you do the cha-cha-cha, Ross, you were self-conscious, you were ponderous. This week, you led the dance with confidence and real purpose – and, most importantly of all, your legs looked like they were having the time of their life out there! I'm not going to mince my words here. Both of you, that was magnificent!'

Jean is actually in tears as she delivers *her* verdict? She goes,

'Every girl in the world dreams of dancing with her father like that!' and Honor throws her orms around my midriff and squeezes me tight. 'I'm sorry, I'm a little emotional here. You have just set the bar for everyone else in this competition.'

Then it comes to Ryan. He just decides to again be a dick. 'I think it was much improved,' he goes, 'but then you couldn't have got any worse after last week, Darling. One or two missteps from you, Honor. Ross, you didn't always maintain your strong top line. Overall, though, I would say it was quite good.'

I give him the wanker sign while the crowd applauds.

Then we get our scores. Mena gives us a ten. Jean gives us a ten. Ryan gives us a seven.

We tip upstairs to the green room and watch the rest of the competition from there. I'm not being big-headed when I say that no one comes close to even matching our performance. The threats of legal action seem to have definitely given Sincerity the jitters and she ends up pulling out of one of her lifts, then ballsing up her supposedly big ending. Her and Raymond end up getting only two sevens and one six.

After that, the rest of the competition ends up being a bit of an anticlimax, mainly because the three Pukey Lucys are so weakened from spitting chunks that they don't have the energy to do anything strenuous. Cloud actually passes out while doing a triple turn, while Desdemona actually gets sick during her routine, tries to continue anyway and ends up slipping in her own vomit.

We end up getting the highest morks of the night and we finish in third place overall, on 42 points, behind Sincerity and Raymond on 48 and Currer Bell and William Whelehan on 44.

The point is, we're back in the game.

Honor is, like, buzzing in the cor on the way home. She's like, 'Well?'

I'm there, 'Well what?' doing the whole modesty act.

She goes, 'How come you weren't shit tonight like you were the last time?'

I'd want to be careful I don't end up a bit full of myself.

I go, 'I've been practising, Honor. I did, like, five hours straight yesterday.'

She's like, 'I don't understand. With who?'

'Okay, this is going to sound possibly weird, but I stuck a dress on your old dear's pogo stick, then stuffed it with cushions.'

She laughs – of course, she hasn't heard the half of it yet.

I'm there, 'Then I drew a smiley face on her old Lolo ball – you're too young to remember Lolo balls – and stuck it on top. What are you laughing at?'

She's like, 'Are you *actually* serious?'

'Yeah, it's kind of the ballroom dancing equivalent of a tackle bag.'

'Oh my God, you are *so* weird!'

'Then I just danced with it – like I said – for five hours straight. Practising the steps, over and over again. Father Fehily used to say that the secret to success was repetition, repetition, repetition.'

'I'm not knocking it – even though you're a focking weirdo. Dad, we're back in the competition!'

She goes quiet then. I think she's only just realizing what a winner her old man is.

'For the next month,' she eventually goes, 'everyone in school is going to be saying that my dad is an amazing, amazing dancer, and not that my mom is a complete and utter slut.'

And I'm thinking, these are the moments!

'So,' Honor goes, 'the next dance we're doing is the foxtrot. I was thinking we might do it to *Someone Like You.*'

I'm there, 'Is that the Adele song that your old dear used to play on constant repeat?'

'Yeah, that one.'

'Hey, bring it on is very much my attitude after last week.'

We're in the cor and I'm driving her home from school. The news comes on the radio and I go to switch it off, except the first item catches my attention.

'Dublin City Council has announced that it is to change the name of O'Connell Street as part of its campaign to deliver gender balance to the map of Dublin City Centre,' the newsreader bird goes. 'The city's main thoroughfare has borne the name of the political reformer since 1924. However, in recent weeks, the man who delivered emancipation for millions of Irish Catholics has been dogged by historical sexual assault allegations and claims of misogyny and murder. From three o'clock tomorrow, the council has announced, the street will be known as Robinson Street, after former Irish President and United Nations High Commissioner for Human Rights, Mary Robinson. Independent Senator Sorcha Lalor, who recently raised the issue of sexual misconduct allegations against Daniel O'Connell, has welcomed the announcement.'

We're just passing White's Cross when my phone suddenly rings. It ends up being Erika, which is the only reason I answer it.

I'm there, 'I presume you just heard the news as well?'

But it's not about that at all. She goes, 'Why didn't you tell me about Christian?'

She sounds seriously pissed off with me.

I'm there, 'Christian? What are you talking about?'

She goes, 'I met him in Donnybrook last night. He says he's working for Hennessy.'

'Oh, yeah, I meant to ring you about that.'

'He said the building is full of Russians and no one knows what they're doing.'

'Yeah, no, I've just been up to my eyes, Erika.'

'Where are you now?'

'Er, I'm in the cor. I'm just coming up to Foxrock Church.'

'Pull in. I'm two sets of lights behind you.'

So I throw the cor into the bus bay and I wait for her. A minute or two later, she arrives in her silver Jaguar F-Pace. She pulls in behind me and gets out – as do I?

I'm there, 'Dungaree shorts with ankle boots – *very* nice!'

She decides to just ignore this. The girl never could take a compliment.

'Do you have a key?' she goes.

I'm like, 'A key? A key to where?'

'A key to your mom and dad's house.'

'Yeah, of course I do.'

'Give it to me.'

'Well, do you mind me asking why you want it?'

'I want to look at your mom and dad's private emails.'

'Er, do you think that's wise?'

She instantly loses it with me. She goes, 'Your mother burned down my focking gallery and I'm going to find out why!'

I'm like, 'Fine. I'm worried about you, that's all. So is Helen.'

'Gimme the focking key.'

I end up just handing it over. Well, she snatches it from me, then goes to get back into her cor.

I'm there, 'You're also going to need the alorm code – *and* the computer password,' and she just stares at me, realizing that she actually *needs* me for once in her life?

She goes, 'Okay, give them to me.'

I'm there, 'Erika, think this through. What if my old dear is home? Or what if she *comes* home and sees your cor in the driveway?'

Erika goes, 'So what are you suggesting?'

'I'm suggesting that I drive you up there. If she arrives home while you're going through her computer, at least I can stall her by calling her a raddled old soak or whatever other names come to mind.'

Erika knows that this is a better plan than hers.

I'm there, 'Throw the F-Pace into the church cor pork and I'll drive us up there.'

She goes, 'There's no room in your cor.'

'Someone can sit on someone else's knee. I was thinking you could maybe sit on mine.'

'What, *while* you're driving?'

'It's only about a mile.'

'Jesus Christ, Ross. I'll sit in the front passenger seat. Honor can sit on *my* knee.'

'Hey, I'm easy either way.'

So that's what ends up happening. Five minutes later, I pull into the driveway. I leave the boys in the cor and me, Honor and Erika head into the house.

I deactivate the alorm. The code is 1, 9, 2, 5 – the year that Chorlie Haughey was born.

On the hat-stand in the hallway, Honor finds this, like, Russian hat. 'Oh my God,' she goes, 'I love these things!' and she puts it on her head.

I'm there, 'Honor, you keep watch at the window. If either of those two arrives back, you holler, okay?'

She's like, 'Okay.'

Me and Erika head for the study. I switch on the computer, then I type in the password – A, B, B, E, V, I, L, L, E – which is what it's always been. Erika shoves me out of the way, then sits down. She opens Outlook.

I'm there, 'How long is it going to take to read all of their emails?'

She reaches into the pocket at the front of her dungarees and whips out a USB stick. 'I'm not going to read them here,' she goes. 'I'm just going to copy them all.'

I'm there, 'So how long will that take?'

She does some really fast typing, then the answer appears on the screen. Approximately ten minutes.

So now all we can do is wait.

I'm there, 'It's like a movie this, isn't it? One of the *Mission Impossibles*.'

She goes, 'Whatever.'

'By the way, I love your perfume. If you have it with you, I wouldn't mind a little bit, even just on my sleeve there to remind me of you.'

'You need counselling.'

All of a sudden, Honor storts calling from the living room: 'Cor coming! Two cors coming! Her *and* him!'

'Fock!' Erika goes. 'This has still got seven minutes to go.'

I'm there, 'Don't worry, me and Honor will stall them. Here's the back door key. When you're finished, let yourself out and don't forget to lock the door after you. At the end of the gorden, behind the air-raid shelter, there's a section of the wall that *doesn't* have broken glass on top of it? Climb over that, go down the laneway and you'll end up in The Coppings. Send me a text when you're clear of the gaff and I'll pick you up in there.'

I meet Honor in the hallway. I reef the door open just as the old dear – gee-eyed – is trying to get her key into the lock like a blind-folded child trying to pin the tail on the donkey.

'Well, isn't serendipity a wonderful thing?' the old man goes. 'Not only have Fionnuala and I arrived home at the same time, but Kicker is waiting with our beautiful grandchildren.'

'Fock you!' I hear Brian shout from the cor. 'You focking baldy prick!'

The old dear's like, 'Hello, Honor, Dorling,' managing to recognize the outline of her granddaughter even in her drunken state.

Honor goes, 'Hi, Fionnuala – can I have this hat?'

The old dear goes, 'Yes, of course. I bought it *for* you. I picked it up in Minsk.'

I'm there, 'So where have you two been?' just keeping them talking.

They're still on the *doorstep*, by the way?

She goes, 'I just had lunch with the girls!'

I'm like, 'So I can smell.'

The old man's there, 'And I've been in conference with Hennessy all day. Muirgheal has formally submitted her challenge to my leadership of the porty. She's described me as a political liability – quote-unquote. Can you believe that, Kicker? I mentored the bloody girl. And, from Hennessy's initial soundings, it looks like she has enough support in the parliamentary party to win.'

I'm like, 'Bummer.'

He goes to step past me, except I use my shoulder to stop him. He sort of, like, bounces off me. I'm there, 'Yeah, no, don't go in there yet.'

He's like, 'What on Earth is wrong, Ross?'

Totally out of nowhere, Honor goes, 'We want to show you our dancing. We've learned the quickstep, haven't we, Dad?'

Me and Honor take up our stance, then Honor storts singing *Walking on Sunshine* and the two of us stort quickstepping around the gravel while my old pair watch us with a look of utter bewilderment on their faces.

We end up doing the entire routine twice, then I hear my phone beep in my pocket. I pull it out while I'm still dancing as a matter of fact. It's a text from Erika, just saying, 'Done.'

'Anyway,' I go, suddenly stopping, 'we better hit the road.'

The old man goes, 'Aren't you going to come in for a coffee?'

I'm like, 'No, I've just decided I couldn't be orsed.'

I hop into the cor, as does Honor. She goes, 'Thanks for the hat, Fionnuala!'

The old dear looks in the back window of the cor and – this is a direct quote – goes, 'I haven't even got to see these lovely little girls yet!'

As I stort the engine, Leo just goes, 'Fock you, you focking ugly mutt!'

I'm pushing the stroller along Westmoreland Street when Ronan rings. He goes, 'Rosser, where are you?'

I'm like, 'I'm in town. I'm heading for O'Connell Street.'

'O'Coddle Sthreet?'

'Or Robinson Street, as it's going to be in, like, twenty minutes' time.'

'I neeth to thalk to you.'

'Is everything okay? You sound upset.'

'I caddent thalk on the phowunt. What ent of O'Coddle Sthreet are you godda be?'

'Hopefully somewhere near the doughnut stand.'

'Reet, Ine on me way.'

It's nearly ten to twelve when I get there. There's an even bigger crowd than there was on the day of the Grafton Street slash Markievicz Street renaming – except the atmosphere this time is totally different.

There's no one objecting to this name change. Most self-respecting Southsiders couldn't give a fock what anything gets called on this side of the city.

No, the crowd this time is different. For storters, it's nearly all women – we're talking, like, five or ten thousand of them – and the atmosphere feels weirdly angry. I know that Sorcha has been in a fouler ever since the third debate between Hillary Clinton and that

Donald Trump dude the other night, and there's a definite sense from this crowd that she's not the *only* one?

Brian goes, 'Pack of focking –' and I quickly put my hand over his mouth to stop him saying something that might get his orms pulled out of his sockets here.

Leo's there, 'Look at all these stupid focking –' and I slap my hand over his mouth as well.

I'm thinking, I really wish Honor was here to help me keep them quiet. But you couldn't persuade her to cross O'Connell Bridge if the streets were paved with BT vouchers. So she told me to drop her home straight after dance class, where, by the way, we totally nailed the foxtrot.

There's definitely a bigger Gorda presence this time – we're talking two or three hundred of them, forty or fifty of them up on actual horseback, and the street has been totally closed to traffic. There's, like, a podium in front of the big statue of – presumably – Daniel O'Connell.

Sorcha is one of six people who's going to speak this time. And that's when I suddenly spot her. She's standing about twenty feet away from me and she's having – this is too funny – a *major* borney with Fionn in the middle of the street.

He's there, 'I'm just repeating what the Gardaí said. It's a very volatile crowd. You should try to avoid saying anything too incendiary.'

I suddenly notice that Croía is with them. I watch her step in between the two of them and go, 'I've a better idea, Sorcha. How about, for once, we *don't* allow men to tell us what we can and can't say?'

Sorcha goes, 'Fionn, there are things that I want to say and I am going to say them.'

He's there, 'Sorcha, you don't want to be caught up in a riot. Please – just think about the baby. *Our* baby.'

I'm thinking, yeah, no, you don't know that for sure yet, Dude.

Croía's there, 'Sorcha's six and a half months pregnant. She's not terminally ill.'

He goes, 'Will you stay out of my business?'

'Only if *you* check your privilege.'

Fionn ends up suddenly losing it with her. '*My* privilege?' he goes, roaring at her in front of everyone. 'You grew up in Glenageary. Your dad made the *Sunday Times* Rich List last year.'

Croía's there, 'You need to deal with your anger, Fionn. You know you've got a vein in your forehead that's throbbing right now?'

'Sorcha, these aren't your supporters,' he goes. 'This is just a mob – and you're nothing more than a useful tool for Croía and her man-hating hang-ups.'

'Oh my God,' Croía goes, 'he is *actually* visualizing himself punching me in the face right now!'

Sorcha's there, 'If you feel that way, Fionn, then why are you even here?'

He's like, 'Good question!' Then off he storms in a snot.

Sorcha and Croía make their way up to the podium. I notice the other speakers – again, all women – all sitting in a row, getting ready to speak.

It looks like Sorcha's up first.

Jesus, she looks huge, even from down here. She's rubbing her big, swollen belly as she steps up to the microphone.

She goes, 'I'm so happy – as a woman – to see so many of you here on what is another landmork day in the *herstory* of our country. We are very lucky to be living in a time when strong women all over the world are standing up and demanding gender equality as their right. In the next few weeks, the United States of America will have its first ever woman President . . .'

There's, like, roars of approval from the crowd.

'Fock you all!' Brian shouts before I can get my hand over his mouth. 'Pack of stupid fockers!'

Sorcha's there, 'I think we're all looking forward to watching Hillary put that racist, misogynist bully, who openly brags about sexually assaulting women, in his proper place!'

Again, there's, like, roars.

She's like, 'Twenty-six years ago, Ireland did what the United States is about to do in a few weeks' time. We elected *our* first ever woman President – in other words, Mary Robinson. And, as a

297

fellow alumnus of the same school, I am happy to be here on this herstoric day to see this beautiful, beautiful street . . .'

Ah, steady on, I think.

'. . . to see this beautiful, beautiful street named in her honour. In doing so – like the American people – we too have the opportunity to consign a misogynist, gun-loving, alleged sex offender to the dustbin of herstory.'

Someone in the crowd – I swear to fock – throws an actual lasso, we're talking cowboy style, and manages to hook it around the neck of this Daniel O'Connell dude. People stort grabbing the other end of the rope and pulling it.

'Misogynist pig!' a woman shouts, to general cheers.

All of a sudden, I hear a snap, then the sound of thousands of women screaming and I look up to see Daniel O'Connell – all however-many-tonnes of him – falling from the top of the monument, as Sorcha, Croía and the others run for cover.

He explodes into a thousand pieces on the street.

I'm there just, like, shaking my head when I hear a voice beside me go, 'Alreet, Rosser?'

It's Ronan. He looks worried. I can instantly see it.

I'm there, 'Ro, what the fock? What's wrong?'

He goes, 'He's odden to me, Rosser.'

'Who's on to you?'

'Griebous.'

'What are you talking about?'

'Me and Shadden went out this morden. We were looking at cheer cubbers for the wetton. When we were out, he's hebbies turdened up and kicked the doe-er dowun.'

'What?'

'The neighbours said there was tree of them. Medissa mustha toawult him it was me what roawut her. Ine a dead madden, Rosser. Ine a dead madden walken.'

Honor laughs.

'Oh! My God!' she goes. 'She's actually really good-looking!'

I'm there, 'Of course she's good-looking! Do you think I'd want to be seen with a woman who wasn't?'

'Does she have a name?'

'Yeah, no, I call her Yanet.'

'Oh my God, she *actually* looks like Yanet Garcia?'

'That's exactly what *I* thought. That's why I gave her that name.'

'And, like, show me how you do it.'

I give her a quick demonstration of me dancing with her. Honor smiles during the whole thing, then just shakes her head. She loves that I'm an unbelievable competitor.

We're about to leave for Mrs Leonard's.

She goes, 'So you know it's the foxtrot tonight?'

I'm there, 'Bring it on. That's very much my attitude. We're going to win this competition, Honor.'

'Do you promise?'

'I promise. One way or another.'

All of a sudden, I hear raised voices. At first, I think it must the boys in the next room, but then I realize it's coming from downstairs.

It's actually Fionn. He's going, 'You could have been killed!'

'Eugh!' Honor goes. 'It's *her* boyfriend!'

I'm there, 'Yeah, no, they had a massive row on O'Connell Street the other day. Slash Robinson Street. I wouldn't mind hearing this.'

I tip out to the landing and I sit on the top stair, from where I can hear the conversation. Honor sits down beside me.

Sorcha goes, 'Oh my God, Fionn, don't be so melodramatic. So *menodramatic.* I'm not going to apologize for wanting to bring my baby – boy *or* girl – into a world which respects the rights and dignity of women. A world that values their contribution and doesn't place any restraint on their dreams.'

'*Your* baby?' Fionn goes.

'Yes, Fionn – *my* baby.'

'It's not just *your* baby, Sorcha. There's a very good chance that it's my baby too.'

'Well, right now, all we know for certain is that it's mine. And in

case you've missed it, Fionn, I'm the one who's been carrying it for the last seven and a half months. Not you, not Ross. And I'm sorry if – as a man – you find that fact emasculating.'

There's, like, silence for about ten seconds, then Fionn goes, 'When was the last time you laughed, Sorcha?'

That's actually a good question.

She's like, 'Oh, thank you for that. It's really nice to hear a male perspective for once.'

He's there, 'When was the last time you laughed? Or even smiled?'

'I laugh every time Donald Trump opens his big, ugly, racist, sexist, misogynistic mouth on TV.'

'You're not the girl I fell in love with when I was seventeen years old. That Sorcha was kind and compassionate. She thought for herself. She was passionate about the things she believed in. But, above all else, her greatest belief was that people were more important than ideas.'

'Be honest, Fionn, you hate the new woke me because you're threatened by alpha women.'

'What happened to the Sorcha who loved divergence of opinion, who lived for the cut and thrust of honest debate, who hated conformity of thought?'

'Croía has thankfully opened my eyes to the way the world *actually* works.'

'She's shrunk you, Sorcha. You were hopeful and positive and you believed that the world was a good place. But now you're angry and pessimistic. All of the things you believe in can be boiled down to: the girls against the boys!'

'I'm now a gender realist so, yes, I would say I have changed. And I would say it's a change for the better.'

'Maybe, maybe not. All I know is you used to care about the issues that actually affected people's lives.'

'What, a 3fe for Ranelagh?'

'Not just a 3fe for Ranelagh. I remember you telling me you wanted to go into politics to help the poor and the marginalized.'

Honor turns around to me and goes, 'The poor and the morginalized? Er, in Dublin Bay South?'

I'm there, 'Yeah, no, I thought they were all priced out of the area a long time ago. I'd love to know where he's going with this.'

But we don't get a chance to find out because I hear the back door suddenly open and the next voice I hear belongs to Sorcha's old man.

'I don't want to interfere,' he goes, 'it's just that I can hear your voices from the end of the garden – and so can the boys.'

Sorcha's there, 'It's fine, Dad. Fionn has said what he came to say. Now he's leaving.'

I can tell instantly what's going through her old man's head. He's thinking, if Sorcha and Fionn break up here, that leaves the field open for Ross to work his evil magic on her. What he doesn't realize, of course, is that I've no interest in getting back in there.

'If I might be permitted to stick my nose in,' he goes, 'I would say that if your differences are *just* political, then this is nothing more serious than a healthy disagreement of the kind that I'm sure Bill and Hillary Clinton enjoy all the time!'

Sorcha's there, 'All the years we've known each other, Fionn, I never had you down as someone who hated women.'

And Fionn goes, 'I loved you, Sorcha. I really did. But the truth is that Ross got all your best years. And this new version of you is a ghost of the girl I fell in love with twenty years ago.'

The conversation is coming to an end. I stand up, walk to the end of the hall and I open the front door – just to save Fionn the time.

He opens the kitchen door.

I hear Sorcha's old man go, 'If you just sat down and agreed to talk about something else – an issue you *do* agree on. Sorcha, you're meant to be together. Your mother and I have always said it.'

Fionn's there, 'You know what the worst thing is, Sorcha? While you're obsessing over words and pulling down statues of men who died hundreds of years ago, there is evil – *real* evil – afoot in the world. I actually think Donald Trump is going to take the White House.'

'Yeah,' Sorcha goes, 'that's what you'd love, Fionn, isn't it?'

'It's not, Sorcha. It's really not.'

He steps out of the kitchen into the hallway and heads for the door.

Sorcha shouts after him, 'I'll send you a text when I've had the baby. In case you need me to *manterpret* that for you, it means me and you are finished.'

9. You Won't Believe What Yanet Garcia Looks Like Now!

Honor tells Mrs Leonard that I was incredible. And I just shrug, all pretend modesty. I'm there, 'I don't know if I'd use the word amazing. But you did – and several others did on the night – so I might just have to accept that.'

Mrs Leonard goes, 'That's good,' but then she says fock-all else about it. She actually reminds me a lot of Eddie O'Sullivan, in that it pleases her when you do well, but she has zero interest in sitting there for two hours listening to you blowing smoke up your own hole.

She's keen to move on. As are *we*, by the way? It's only, like, three weeks until Foxtrot Week and we've got a lot of work to do.

Honor's there, 'The third dance is the foxtrot. And I want to do it to *Cry Me a River* by Michael Bublé. And I want to finish with, like, three full spins. Then I want Ross to dip me. Also, at the stort, I want him to literally throw me up in the air and catch me.'

I'm thinking, if I'm going to practise doing that, I might need to add a bit of ballast to Yanet. It might mean stuffing a few bags of sugar into those cushion covers.

'Okay,' Mrs Leonard goes. 'Well, first of all, the foxtrot is a smooth, flowing dance, with long, continuous movements that will see you cover a lot of floor space in a short period of time. The thing to remember about the basic foxtrot step is that the side-together steps are twice as quick as the walking steps. So we go, *slow, slow – quick quick. Slow, slow – quick quick. Slow, slow – quick quick. Slow, slow – quick quick . . .*'

My phone all of a sudden rings. I know I shouldn't have it either on or in my pocket, but I'm worried about Ronan. And when I whip it out – yeah, no – it ends up *being* him?

I step into a corner to answer it.

Mrs Leonard goes, 'If you were taking this thing seriously, you wouldn't even have your mobile phone on!'

Seriously. Eddie O'Sullivan.

I'm like, 'Ro, what's the crack?' listening for the sound of him being possibly tortured.

He just goes, 'It wadn't Griebous, Rosser.'

I'm like, 'What?' and this wave of, I don't know, *relief* washes over me?

He goes, 'It wadn't Griebous – what kicked me doe-er dowun.'

I'm there, 'Are you sure? As in, how do you know?'

'I rang Medissa and I ast her sthraight out.'

'Okay, how did you get her number?'

'She geb it to me in Estepona. And I geb her moyun.'

'What did I tell you? Never give Crazy your real number!'

'Doatunt woody – she has me in her phowun unther Peether Meerk in the Idac Centhor.'

'Jesus Christ.'

'In addyhow, listen to what Ine saying to you. I ast her did she teddle Griebous abourrus and she said no.'

'And do you believe her?'

'She said he steerted aston her quest yiddens arthur that night – on account of how happy she was. He does get teddible jeadous.'

'Being married to a woman like Melissa, I can't blame the dude.'

'She towult me the whoalt stordee, Rosser. He thought at foorst it was *you* what roawud her. She toawult him sthraight out that she wootunt hab addy inthordest in the likes of you – in your bleaten sailing gee-er. She said you ditn't look like the koyunt of fedda could sathisfy a wooban.'

'It sounds like she really dissed me from a height.'

'She thought you were bleaten gay, Rosser.'

'Can you just continue with the story? I'm supposed to be learning the *foxtrot* here?'

'In addyhow, Greibous kem to Oyerlunt because he wanthed to look you in the eye and ast you the quest yidden heself. Which he did. And now he's thropped the mathor, accorton to Medissa.'

'Ro, he told me he found two johnnies in the cor. *Two*, by the way!'

'She toawult him that thee must have been stuck on some wooden's shoe when they got in the keer.'

'Okay, *that's* just made me feel sick.'

'It's forgotten, Rosser. Doatunt be woddied addy mower. Ine not.'

'So who kicked your door down?'

'Could be addy wooden. The bleaten scoombags arowunt heeor? You've seen where I lib, Rosser.'

I have. They've got the only Neighbourhood Watch group in Ireland that has a weapons budget.

After a short silence, he goes, 'Look, Rosser, Ine soddy for thrunning you in the lake.'

I'm there, 'It's cool, Ro.'

'It's joost when you said you ditn't wanth to be me best madden addy mower . . .'

'Dude, it's fine. Look, Buckets will do a great job.'

'You're still cubbing, but – to the wetton?'

'If I'm still invited.'

'Of cowurse you eer.'

'Well, I said I'd be there whenever any of my kids made a mistake – and your wedding day will be no exception.'

'Thanks, Rosser.'

I go, 'I better get back to work,' and I hang up, because I'm getting serious daggers from Mrs Leonard *and* Honor at this stage?

I'm like, 'Sorry about that,' retaking my place in the middle of the floor. 'I thought someone was trying to murder my son. The good news is, they're not.'

'Okay,' Mrs Leonard goes, 'let's all stop congratulating ourselves on last week and get back to work.'

So I'm sitting at the kitchen table with my famous rugby tactics book open in front of me and I'm picking my fantasy Ireland team to face the All Blacks in Chicago next week. I'm totally engrossed in one or two selection dilemmas. Would there be a backlash, for instance, if I picked fifteen Leinster players?

And just as I'm thinking, 'Fock the backlash! I'm employed by the IRFU to make the big decisions!' my *phone* rings? I snap out of it and I answer it.

It ends up being my old man.

He goes, 'Hello there, Kicker!'

I'm there, 'You sound in better form. What are you, pissed?'

'It's only midday, Ross!'

'My question still stands.'

'I presume you've seen the front page of *The Irish Times* this morning?'

'I've better things to be doing on a Saturday morning than reading newspapers.'

'If you haven't, I'll give it to you in brief.'

'Make if *very* brief. I'm trying to pick my fifteen for Chicago.'

'They're saying I'm dead in the water, Ross. Pat bloody Leahy. Muirgheal Massey is on course to win the leadership of New Republic, he says. Of the forty-nine TDs who are eligible to vote, twenty have declared their support for her, while only seven have said they'll vote for me.'

'That's shit for you.'

'Well, it looks like your godfather and I are facing a weekend on the phones. Just like the old days, eh?'

'When is the vote?'

'Next Tuesday, Ross. Buswell's at eight.'

'I'll definitely be there. Even if it's just to laugh while Muirgheal wipes the floor with you.'

In the background, I can hear Hennessy going, 'Ask him, Charlie.'

I'm there, 'Ask me what?'

The old man goes, 'Oh, yes, em, do you remember recently, Kicker, you called to the house?'

'Yeah, so focking what?'

'You didn't use the computer, did you?'

'Why are you asking me that?'

'It's just your mother said her email was open and she was sure she'd closed it.'

'So, what, you're accusing me of something, are you?'

'No, I told her I'd just mention it to you. Anyway, better start making calls. See if I can't twist a few arms – quote-unquote.'

He hangs up.

I decide to ring Erika straightaway. But as I'm calling up her number, I get this weird sense that someone is watching me. I look over my shoulder and I end up screaming.

I'm literally like, 'Aaarrrggghhh!!! Jesus Christ!'

Honor is standing at the door of the kitchen, wearing a rubber Donald Trump mask.

I'm there, 'You gave me a fright.'

She goes, 'It's good, isn't it?'

'Jesus Christ, where did you get that?'

'I bought it. For Hallowe'en. I put it on your credit cord, by the way, because I still haven't got mine back.'

'Don't let your mother see it.'

'That's the only reason I bought it. To piss her off. I also have a red sweatshirt that says *Make America Great Again* on the front.'

'It's just she's not in great form at the moment, Honor. Her and Fionn have broken up and we might need to tiptoe around her for a bit.'

'I was thinking I might wear them to the porty tonight.'

'What porty?'

'Sincerity is having, like, a fancy-dress porty in her *house*?'

'Sincerity? I thought we hated Sincerity?'

'We do. She's a bitch. I just want to keep an eye on her.'

'I love that you have a tactical mind, Honor.'

'Will *you* come? Loads of the other moms and dads are going to be there as well. Oh my God, you could go as Hillary Clinton! You could put on mom's red trouser suit and I could lead you around on a dog leash!'

'I'm not sure we should be doing anything to deliberately piss your mother off right now – even though that sounds hilarious.'

'Okay,' she goes, 'I'll go and get my sweatshirt to show you,' and she focks off back upstairs.

I ring Erika. She answers after, like, five rings. She goes, 'Ross, I'm busy.'

I'm there, 'Don't hang up. I was just ringing to find out if there was anything in those emails?'

'I haven't finished going through them all yet. There's 45,000 of them. A lot of them are in Russian.'

'Are you saying there's an actual Russian language?'

'Yes, there's an actual Russian language. I've got a really good friend who studied it in Trinity who's translating them for me.'

Which sounds *definitely* random because I've never really thought of Erika as having really good friends, just women who hated her and men who loved her – like I loved her once.

I'm there, 'So were you right? *Are* they up to something?'

She goes, 'Yes. But I can't say anything over the phone.'

'Can you give me a hint?'

'It's all about what happens after *he* becomes Taoiseach.'

'But he's never going to *be* Taoiseach. He just admitted that himself. He's dead in the water.'

But, by then, Erika has already hung up.

Sincerity greets us at the door of this humungous pile of bricks in Goatstown. She's dressed as a giant cupcake. She takes one look at Honor in the Trump mask and goes, 'Oh! My God! Honor, is that you? That is, like, *so* scary!'

Sincerity leads us into the living room, where I spot Currer Bell Whelehan, who has come as a Ghostbuster. There's no sign of either Cloud Gorvey, Desdemona Burke or Annora Finch, since foul play is still suspected in relation to the watermelon punch.

'Don't eat or drink anything,' I say to Honor out of the corner of my mouth.

And she goes, 'Yeah, do you think I'm stupid?'

Sincerity introduces Honor to some of her non-school friends. She goes, 'Everyone, this is Honor!' as Honor rips off the mask. 'We're, like, Buddies in Mount Anville and – I hope it's okay to say – *friends*? She's also – oh my God – an amazing, amazing dancer.'

I just go, 'Rise above it, Honor. Wait until the competition is over.'

In fairness to Honor, she takes the high road, says hello to everyone, hands me her mask to mind for her, sits down, takes out her phone and storts pasting photographs of her costume on Instagram in the hope of getting an angry reaction from people, especially Sorcha.

'Hello, Ross!' I hear a voice behind me go.

I turn around and it ends up being Raymond – as in Sincerity's old man.

I'm there, 'Raymond – how the hell are you?'

'Fantastic,' he goes. 'Great that you and Honor could come!'

Then he drops his voice and, while barely moving his lips, goes, 'One or two of our fellow contestants decided to boycott!'

I'm there, 'Yeah, no, I copped that. The ones who claimed to be poisoned. If I was you, I'd be highly insulted.'

'Oh, well – will you have something to eat, Ross?'

'Not a focking chance, Raymond.'

He laughs. He goes, 'What about a drink?'

I'm there, 'Yeah, no, I'm fine for everything, thanks.'

'So you don't trust us either, then?'

'No, I don't – and you couldn't blame me.'

'No, I couldn't!'

He actually thinks I'm joking.

He goes, 'Come down to the kitchen. That's where all the grown-ups are.'

There's, like, twenty or thirty moms and dads standing around, drinking Prosecco. None of the adults are wearing fancy dress and I have to say I'm slightly relieved that I didn't let Honor persuade me do that Hillary Clinton thing.

Raymond introduces me to five or six mums and dads whose names I instantly forget. I'm not great at remembering the names of people I have no interest in having sex with and none of the women in the circle are great.

They're talking about – I shit you not – three little boys who got borred from D. L. Kids in Clonskeagh for effing and blinding.

'Oh, those triplet boys,' this woman with a flat face and – God love her – a turned-up nose is going, 'I've heard they're demons – as in, *properly* evil. I've heard they're banned from everywhere.'

It's obvious that no one realizes that their father is standing right here. And it's not everywhere they're borred from, by the way. It's just D. L. Kids, The Disney Store, Imaginosity and Nimble Fingers. They're on a final warning from Hamley's in Dundrum.

Another woman – with no neck – goes, 'I blame the parents. I mean, what were *they* doing while this was happening?'

I get a tap on the shoulder then. I turn around and it ends up being William Whelehan, who's the old man of Currer Bell. It's handshakes and all the rest of it. He goes, 'So have you been practising your foxtrot, Ross?'

I'm like, 'Yeah, no, doing a bit alright. Getting there.'

'I have to admit, with the Financial Year-End coming up, I really haven't had any time to practise our routine,' and I think, yeah, no, I remember fockers like him in school, the Secret Studiers, who told you they hadn't done a tap and then ended up with the points for Medicine in Trinity.

I decide not to let him psyche me out of it, though.

'Yeah, no, pity that,' I just go.

'Currer Bell has us dancing to something by Coldplay,' he goes. 'I think it's called –'

'*Trouble*?'

It's actually Raymond who says it. He's walking around with a bottle of Prosecco in either hand, topping up everyone's glass – I'm like, 'Not for me – seriously!' – and he goes, '*Trouble* is the song that Sincerity and I are dancing to as well.'

William shakes his head and goes, 'Well, you can't be – because I've just said Currer Bell and I are dancing to it.'

'There's nothing to say we can't *both* choose that song.'

'Yes, there is, Raymond. The fact that we said it first.'

It's not long before every other conversation in the kitchen has stopped and everyone is looking in our direction.

Raymond tries to top up William's glass, except he pulls it away. He's like, 'No, thank you.'

Raymond goes, 'Come on, William, it's only a bit of fun anyway.'

'Oh, that's rich,' William goes, 'coming from you.'

'If you've got something to say, you shoud spell it out.'

'I'm saying that three girls got food poisoning from drinking punch that your daughter made. And, while I believed you deserved the benefit of the doubt, I don't anymore. Not now that you've pulled this latest stunt.'

'Don't say another word would be my advice. Because you're going to be hearing from my solicitor.'

'And you will be hearing from mine!'

'Not before you hear from mine.'

'I'll be seeing my chap first thing on Monday morning.'

'Mine works on Sundays.'

'Then I'll go and ring mine right now.'

William storms out of the kitchen, tells Currer Bell they're leaving, then focks off, making sure to slam the front door on his way out.

There's a lot of, like, eye-rolling and head-shaking, then everyone just returns to their conversations.

Someone touches my elbow then. I turn around and it ends up being this woman. She's probably around my age. If you forced me to describe her as being *like* someone, I would have to say she's a slightly less annoying-looking version of Allison Williams, except with a smaller mouth.

She's there, 'Hello, Ross.'

I'm like, 'Er, yeah, no, hi.'

'You don't remember me, do you?'

'Er . . .'

'Don't look so worried. I'm Rosalind Carew. Or just Roz.'

'Your face is definitely familiar.'

I've no idea who this woman is. I'm just giving her that line because she's a looker.

She goes, 'I was in Alexandra College. I used to watch you play rugby.'

I'm there, 'Ah, one of the lucky ones,' and it ends up sounding a bit more big-headed than I intended.

'Well, anyway,' she goes, 'I just wanted to say hello and tell you that Sincerity talks about your daughter *all* the time.'

I'm there, 'Sincerity?'

'Yes. I'm Sincerity's mom!'

I thought Sincerity's name was Matthews. And then I remember Honor mentioning that her old pair were divorced. I'm suddenly being very, very attentive.

I'm there, 'I'm so sorry, er, Roz. I had literally no idea. I thought you were just some random stalker.'

'No,' she goes, 'but that's exactly what I was back in the day! We used to go to all your matches! We were all in *love* with you!'

'That's a lovely thing for me to hear.'

'Oh my God, looking back, we were such idiots.'

'Hey, you've said a nice thing – don't go taking it back now.'

She laughs, even though I'm deadly focking serious.

I'm there, 'So I haven't seen you at the *Strictly Mount Anville* thing.'

She goes, 'I was there both weeks. Watching *you* from the crowd. I wouldn't have believed at the age of thirty-six that I'd still be doing that!'

God, she's a ride.

I'm there, 'It's all getting very serious, isn't it? I mean, I thought the competition in the Leinster Schools Senior Cup was intense! We never had threats of legal action flying backwards and forwards. Except when Gerry Thornley spelt my name wrong in *The Irish Times*.'

'Oh, that's just Sincerity's dad,' she goes. 'He just loves winding people up, that's all.'

'Well, I'm not eating or drinking anything just in case!'

'You'd be right not to!' She laughs, then she goes, 'We're, em, divorced – I don't know if you know that?'

I'm there, 'Yeah, no, Honor definitely mentioned it.'

'But we've stayed good friends. Raymond's remarried. I get on great with his wife, Gráinne. We're actually in the same spin class. It's all very South Dublin.'

'Random would be the word I'd use.'

'Yeah, that's another word for it. And *you* married Sorcha Lalor?'

'Yeah, no, *we're* in the same boat, though. As in we're not actually *with* each other anymore? Separated, but living under the same roof.'

'Yeah, I can't pretend *not* to have seen all that stuff on the Internet.'

'What, about her baby being possibly someone else's?'

'Sincerity was so upset for Honor when that all came out.'

I'm thinking, yeah, she obviously puts on a good act, this kid.

I'm there, 'Is that right?'

'She thinks the world of her,' she goes. 'And I think because they're Buddies, she feels very, very protective of her.'

'That's because a lot of girls of that age are out-and-out bitches.'

'Not Sincerity, I'm relieved to say. She is just the sweetest little girl in the world.'

It just shows you how easily fooled South Dublin mothers can be.

'Anyway,' she goes, 'I'll say hello the next day. When is it – next week?'

I'm like, 'Yeah, the foxtrot. I'm already looking forward to it.'

There's a definite something between us. I can feel it just as surely as she can.

But then Honor is suddenly standing in front of me, going, 'Okay, I am *so* focking bored. Can we go home now?'

There's no sign of the old man. The function room in Buswell's is full. The entire – whatever it's called – porliamentary porty is here. Muirgheal is sitting in the front row. Like everyone else, she's looking over her shoulder, wondering where the old man could be. It was supposed to kick off at eight o'clock and it's already, like, a *quarter*-past?

Eventually, she stands up and walks to the top of the room – to one of the two, I suppose, *lecterns* that are facing the audience. She taps the microphone with her finger to make sure it's on.

'Ladies and gentlemen,' she goes, 'fellow porty members, it's fifteen minutes after the meeting was due to stort and the Porty President is not here. Under standing orders, as the Deputy and Serving President, I am permitted to stort the meeting in his absence. Does anyone have any objection?'

No one says shit, although quite a few are still looking around, obviously hoping against hope that the dude is still going to walk through those doors.

Muirgheal looks down at her speech and goes, 'Thank you for that warm welcome,' which is hilarious because no one even clapped, 'and thank you for everything you do for the porty. As a protégée of Chorles O'Carroll-Kelly, I cannot tell you how much it saddens me to stand before you today and say I no longer believe that he is the man to take New Republic forward. I no longer believe that he is the man to lead us into the next General Election. I no longer believe that he is fit to be the Taoiseach of this country.'

There's, like, a smatter of applause from about half the people in the room.

'In saying that,' she goes, 'I want to pay tribute to the extraordinary foresight that he showed in spotting that there was room in this country for a ninth major political porty. He led us brilliantly into the last election, where we won fifty-one seats, making us the biggest porty in the Dáil. But some of Charles O'Carroll-Kelly's more extreme policies – not to mention his views on women drivers and people from Cork and Laois – frightened other porties out of doing business with us. And now, at a time when we should be providing a vigorous opposition to Fine Gael and their friends in Fianna Fáil, we have allowed ourselves to be distracted by Charles calling the late, obviously great Constance Markievicz a cow. In doing so, he has proven that he doesn't have the political intelligence to lead this party or this country.'

I can't listen to any more of this. I decide to just hit the road. I head for the double doors at the back of the room.

Muirgheal is going, 'Charles O'Carroll-Kelly promised us a new way of doing politics and a break from the cynicism of the past. And there he is, the leader of a porty that owes much of its grassroots support to its principled opposition to water chorges – yet he has won the contract to build and operate the private prison in which non-payers will be jailed –'

I step out of the room. I decide to go for a slash before I hit the road and I tip down the corridor to the thunder room. I push the door. And that's when I hear the old man's voice.

He's going, 'A *girl*! A mere *girl*!'

He's standing in front of the mirror, like he's talking himself up. Hennessy is leaning against the wall a few feet away. And, hilariously, the old dear is in here as well, in the men's room, staring at the back of the old man's head.

I'm there, 'You know they've already storted in there? Muirgheal is calling you out in a major way.'

'Oh, don't worry!' the old man goes. 'I've already read her speech!'

Hennessy laughs.

The old man turns and looks at the old dear. 'Now,' he goes, 'I'm ready!'

I notice she's got – holy shit! – the famous wig in her hands. She steps forward, he bows his head, then she places it on top like she's crowning a king. She smoothes it into shape with her hands, then she kisses him on the lips.

He turns and stares at himself in the mirror. And I watch him – I'm definitely not *imagining* this? – actually grow in size.

'I want you to know,' Hennessy goes, 'I got goosebumps right now.'

The old dear's like, 'Go and kill her!' and she sounds like she means it, like, *literally*?

I follow them out, then down the corridor and back to the function room, where Muirgheal has finished her speech. She's going, 'I propose that we put it to a vote of the porliamentary–' when the old man pushes open the door. The entire audience turns around and there's a definite gasp when they see him standing there. It's Chorles O'Carroll-Kelly – in all his former glory.

He goes, 'Back up the truck, Muirgheal! I'm not gone yet!'

He walks up to the top of the room. I stand at the back, leaning against the wall, with Hennessy on one side of me and the old dear on the other.

He steps up to the microphone. He doesn't even have a note in front of him.

'Ladies and gentlemen!' he goes. 'Of course, you have to say that in the interests of equality, even though there are only two women in this room and only one of them is a lady!'

I can actually *hear* my old dear smiling at him – her Estée Lauder Double-Wear foundation cracking like the ground under Godzilla's feet.

'We are living in a dangerous, dangerous time!' the old man goes. 'A time when free speech is being closed down! A time when the freedoms we fought for are being taken away from us by a new religious elite that calls itself – without any hint of irony – Liberalism!

'Their bible – inverted commas – is political correctness! Their favourite rituals of observance are offence-taking and displays of outrage on social media! And the punishment for those who are considered to have blasphemed against their faith is public crucifixion – such as I was subjected to this summer!

'We, of all people, should be horrified to find ourselves living in this new age of religious puritanism! Many of us here in this room grew up in a country that had the strictest censorship laws outside the Communist world! Where books were routinely banned because they contained ideas that offended the prevailing political and religious orthodoxy! And I, for one, am not prepared to surrender my freedom of speech to a new elite of unsmiling, humourless ideologues, telling us what we can and can't say, what we can and can't think! Exclamation mark, new paragraph!

'People died for my right to stand in front of you here today and say that women can't parallel park! That people from Cork complain a lot! That people from the southern border counties are – for genetic reasons that some would like us not to acknowledge – better line-dancers than the rest of the population! And that Constance Markievicz . . . *was* a bloody cow!'

Everyone laughs.

He goes, 'The right to say these things – right or wrong – is the rock on which true democracy is built! And yet we're living in a climate of fear – fear of being called out for our opinions if they don't chime with the opinions of the moral majority! In such a world, we are all just one contrary view or ill-expressed opinion away from personal and professional ruin! From being forced to sit at home in our dressing-gowns – as I was – without a voice, while Grafton Street ceased to be Grafton Street!'

'Shame!' Hennessy shouts from the back. 'Shame! Shame!'

A few others join in.

'It cannot continue!' the old man goes. 'And it will not continue!'

Hennessy storts clapping, as does pretty much everyone in the room – he's definitely winning them over – except for obviously Muirgheal, and also me. I'm on my phone, looking at Roz Carew's Facebook page, checking out her photos, especially her holiday pics.

The old man goes, 'What we need now, in this era of social media lynch-mob justice, is strong, uncompromising leaders of principle and conviction! Unfortunately, Muirgheal Massey is not that leader! Yes, she *was* my protégée! Which is why it makes me especially sad to have to tell you, the elected members of New Republic, that she has been attempting to form a secret alliance with Fianna Fáil!'

There are literally gasps in the room. I'm wondering is it possibly horseshit, but I see the look of horror on Muirgheal's face and I know she's been well and truly snared.

The old man goes, 'Before you vote on this motion tonight, I would ask you to check your inboxes for an email that my good friend and legal adviser, Hennessy Coghlan-O'Hara, is about to send to you! It contains a chain of correspondence between Muir-gheal Massey and Micheál Martin, in which she discusses with him a merger between our two parties! She promises in this exchange to soften our stance on a whole range of issues, including our posi-tion on leaving the European Union, annual driving test resits for women and building a wall around Cork!'

Muirgheal suddenly loses it. She goes, 'How did you get access to my emails?'

Again, more gasps.

He goes, 'She promised Micheál Martin she would purge the party of what she called extreme opinion, then present our fifty-one seats as a gift to Fianna bloody well Fáil!'

She goes, 'This is dirty tricks from a man who is not fit to be our leader! Let's vote on the motion now!'

The old man smiles. 'To put forward the motion,' he goes, 'you will first require a seconder!'

Muirgheal looks into the audience and goes, 'Who will second the motion? Who will second it?' and she sounds like she's totally lost it now.

No one says shit.

'In that case,' the old man goes, 'your bid to replace me as the leader of New Republic has failed! And now, as leader of the party, I would like to put forward an emergency motion – to have Muirgheal Massey expelled from the party!'

She's there, 'No, you are *not* going to enjoy that pleasure! Because I resign! I quit!' and she storms out of the room, passing me on the way out.

Hennessy shouts, 'Ladies and gentleman, boys and girls, please put your hands together for the next Taoiseach, Mr Charles O' Carroll-Kelly!'

There's this, like, thunderous roar and applause, then they all stort chanting, 'CO'CK for Taoiseach! CO'CK for Taoiseach! CO'CK for Taoiseach!'

I turn to the old dear, who's on the verge of tears – or would be if a 2003 operation to fill in her crow's feet hadn't destroyed her tear ducts.

I'm there, 'He well and truly shafted her.'

She goes, 'That's what happens to people who stand in our way!'

'Don't get too up yourself. I've still got the power to send you to prison, bear in mind. When's my money coming through, by the way?'

'It's not.'

She says it just like that – and with a smile on her face as well.

I'm there, 'Excuse me?'

'I've decided to let Ari's granddaughter have it,' she goes.

'All of it?'

'His entire estate.'

'I thought you were going to fight her for it.'

'Your father talked me out of it. I don't need it. What, another public airing of what happened – people pointing the finger and saying it's blood money? No, if I don't benefit from Ari's death, then people will have to believe me when I say I didn't murder him. Because what was the motive?'

'Well, I still want my five million snots.'

'I don't have it.'

'Then I'll go to the Feds.'

She just laughs. Then, without even looking at me, she goes, 'You must do what you think is right, Ross – just like that silly girl just did.'

So it's, like, ten o'clock at night and the kids are all in bed and – yeah, no – I'm foxtrotting around my room with the lovely Yanet while listening to Michael Bublé on permanent repeat on my iPod.

I know it so well at this stage. Every step, every lift, every facial gesture, yet I'm still practising it, over and over again, because – as Mrs Leonard says – brilliance is five parts talent to ninety-five parts routine.

So I do the routine like I did the routine back in my kicking days. Over and over and over again. Misstep? Stort over. Drop Yanet on her head? Go again, from the top.

Walk, walk, side-together, walk, walk, side-together, walk, walk, side-together, dip.

And just like when I was practising my kicking, I end up becoming totally immersed in it. I can block out everything. The wife I don't love anymore being pregnant by someone else. My old dear trying to screw me out of five million snots. Ronan sleepwalking his way into a marriage that can't possibly last. My other sons having zero interest in rugby. My in-laws living in the gorden. My sister slash half-sister having a possible nervous breakdown.

While I'm dancing, I don't think about any of that shit. I just think about, well, the dance.

I do it again and again and again and again until I'm sweating like a Grand National winner. But even then I don't stop. I just take off my Leinster jersey and my Cantos and do it in just my boxers.

Around and around the room I go.

Walk, walk, side-together, walk, walk, side-together, walk, walk, side-together . . . and then . . .

I throw Yanet up in the air. More impressively, I manage to catch her again. And her smile seems to say, 'You nailed it that time, Rossmeister! Just like you seem to be nailing the entire routine!'

It's a genuinely lovely thing for me to hear. But I don't have time to go patting myself on the back. I just plough on.

Walk, walk, side-together, walk, walk, side-together, walk, walk, side-together, dip.

And eventually, after maybe an hour has passed, my body point-blank refuses to dance another step and I fall face-forward onto the bed on top of Yanet. I lie there, the sweat blinding me, trying to recover my breath, with her underneath me and an expression on her face that tells me I did good.

'Oh! My God,' a voice suddenly goes. 'Is that my Lolo ball?'

Oh, fock.

I look over my shoulder. Sorcha is standing at the door of the bedroom.

I dismount Yanet, going, 'It's not what it looks like!' which I know, from long experience, is the guiltiest-sounding sentence in the English language.

'Oh! My God!' she goes, as she looks at me, standing there, out of breath, sweating, in just my boxers, then I watch the truth slowly dawn on her face. Or what she *considers* the truth? And I can hordly blame her for that because I know it looks like, in a fit of loneliness, I've created a sex doll from bits and pieces of junk I found lying around in her room.

She goes, 'Ross, what the *fock* are you doing?'

And then – oh, fock a duck – her old pair come chorging up the stairs in response to her repeated 'Oh! My God's!'

They burst past her into the room and suddenly they're at the same thing. 'My God!' her old man goes. 'What in hell's name is he doing?'

Sorcha's old dear – Jesus Christ! – reads out what I wrote in the little speech bubble on Yanet's face. '*Oh my God, Ross, you are SO good!*' she goes. 'What on Earth does it mean?'

And her husband's there, 'Well, it certainly clears up the mystery as to all that bouncing around we've been hearing up here.'

Of course, I can't tell Sorcha the *actual* truth here – that I'm practising for Round Three of *Strictly Mount Anville*, so I just have to let her draw her own conclusion, which – from the way she puts her hand over her mouth to stifle a scream – is clearly that I've thrown a dress on her pogo stick, drawn a face on her Lolo ball and, when she walked into the room, I was in the process of boning the result.

'He's like a bloody animal!' *he* goes. 'Can't get through a day without copulating with someone – or some . . . *thing.*'

The penny drops for Sorcha's old dear as well. All the colour runs out of her face. She goes, 'Is that what he was doing – to that ugly thing?'

I'm thinking, you're no focking oil painting yourself, love.

The worst thing is that, in the end, Sorcha ends up actually apologizing to me before she storts backing out of the room. She goes, 'No, Dad, *we* shouldn't have borged in. I'm sorry, Ross. I have to respect the fact that you have needs –'

I'm there, 'This has nothing to do with my needs, Sorcha.'

'We're separated and you're entitled to be with whoever you want.'

'Yeah, I wasn't actually *riding* her?'

But she's like, 'Mom, Dad – come on. We'll leave the two of them to it.'

I ask Christian how much time is left and he tells me it's almost exactly the same amount of time as the last time I asked him – just deduct thirty seconds.

I can't watch. And yet I can't turn away from it either. Ireland are leading the All Blacks by 33–29 with, like, ten minutes to go and I haven't heard Kielys this quiet since a stranger wandered in three years ago and asked why they weren't showing the All Ireland football final.

My nails are all bitten. Christian tells me to have a drink. But I've decided to stay off it this weekend, on account of it being Foxtrot

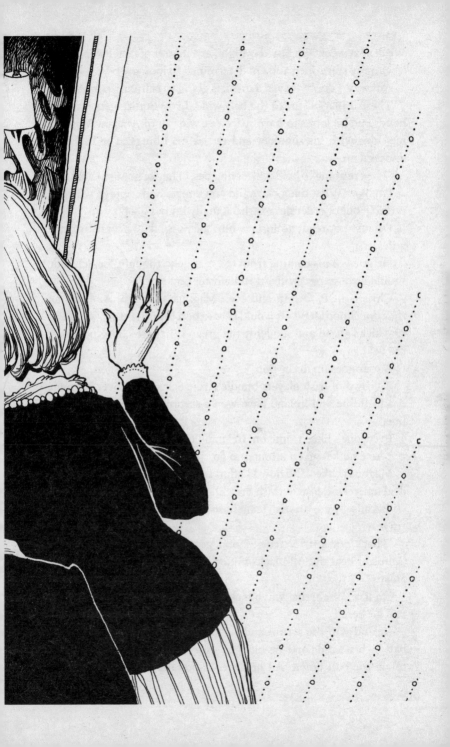

Week next week. On Monday night, as a matter of fact. I want to do it with my shirt open and I'm determined to look my best.

Anyway, I doubt if even a drink is going to calm my nerves.

The All Blacks spread the ball wide. Liam Squire gets it in his hands and he looks to have space out wide until Andrew Trimble hits him with his shoulder and rattles his fillings. The ball gets knocked on.

'They're going to hold on!' Fionn goes. 'They're going to hold on!'

I'm like, 'What the fock would you know about rugby?' which is possibly out of order because he actually knows a lot.

I'm just not ready to forgive him for possibly impregnating my wife yet.

He goes, 'This coming from the man who thought Joe Schmidt should have started with an all Leinster first fifteen?'

Christian, JP, Oisinn and even Magnus all laugh. And just as they do, Simon Zebo – it would *have* to be a Munster man, wouldn't it? – kicks ahead and suddenly the green shirts are chorging down the field.

A roar goes up in the pub.

A crowd of Irish players bundle Ardie Savea back over his own deadball line and Ireland have won a scrum five metres from the line.

Everyone's like, 'Come on, Ireland! For fock's sake!'

There's, like, seven minutes to go.

Magnus is like, 'Sho now I heff to ashk you why ish it shuch a big deal for Ireland to win thish match?'

'Because,' I go, 'an Irish team hasn't beaten New Zealand in, like, III years.'

'That's not strictly true,' Fionn goes, trying to show me up. 'Munster beat the All Blacks in 1978. Have you never seen *Alone It Stands*?'

I'm like, 'Yeah, that was a focking play, Fionn. I'm talking about real *life* here?'

Ireland win the scrum and Robbie Henshaw suddenly has the ball in his hands and he ploughs over the New Zealand line to touch the ball down. All hell breaks literally loose. Everyone in

Kielys is hugging each other and I hear one man behind me say he couldn't be happier even if Seán FitzPatrick ends up getting acquitted of all the chorges against him.

I watch Joey Carbery – a big admirer of mine – step up to add the cheese and biscuits.

You can hear the chant of 'Ireland! Ireland!' echoing around the stadium and the same shout goes up in Donnybrook, Dublin 4.

I'm there, 'What's left?'

'Five minutes,' Christian goes.

I'm like, 'We need another score.'

JP puts his orm around my shoulder. 'Ross,' he goes, 'the lead is eleven points.'

I'm there, 'Exactly. They just need to score a converted try in the next five minutes, win the restort and then they can just wear us down in injury time. We've seen them do it before.'

Oisinn goes, 'Ross, that would require a comeback of Chorles O' Carroll-Kelly proportions!' and he slaps me on the back.

Magnus orders a pint of Carlsberg when he thinks I'm distracted. I turn around to Pat the borman and I go, 'That's the Finnish word for Heineken.'

Pat laughs and pulls him a pint of the Amsterdamage.

After what seems like an hour of waiting, the final whistle blows and all of Kielys goes apeshit. People are crying. They fall to their knees. They hug each other in groups of two, three, four, five people. They're ringing their fathers, their sons, their brothers, even friends they haven't seen in years, to say, 'How are you? How's your wife? I heard you had a couple of kids? You got through the recession okay? Did you see what just focking happened?'

I can tell you this for certain. I'm adding the fifth of November to the list of holy days – Johnny Sexton's birthday (Sexmas), Paul O'Connell's birthday (Pocmas), Ronan O'Gara's birthday (Rogmas), Brian O'Driscoll's birthday (Dricmas) and Garry Ringrose's birthday (Little Dricmas) – when I will refuse to work.

That's if I ever find myself with an actual job again, which I hopefully won't.

Christian thows his orms around me. The whole business of my daughter getting his son shitfaced and me lying to his face about it is suddenly totally forgotten. That's the power of rugby to heal.

But then Fionn walks over to me with his hand out. And I know I should shake his hand because you shouldn't ever leave a bro hanging, especially on a day like today, a day that puts everything into – I think it's a word – *prospectus*?

Instead, I just turn my head away and I go, 'I'm sorry, Dude. You're still dead to me.'

I'm throwing on my tux when I'm suddenly handed a piece of paper – although 'served' I think is the actual *legal* expression?

I give it the old left to right. It ends up being a solicitor's letter, putting me and my fellow contestants on notice that Mr William Whelehan – also acting on behalf of his daughter, Ms Currer Bell Whelehan – has obtained a High Court injunction to the effect that no other participants in the 2016 *Strictly Mount Anville* dance competition except they are permitted to dance to the Coldplay song *Trouble* until the full hearing of a 'passing off' claim brought by the same Mr William Whelehan and that anyone who chooses to ignore the order will place themselves in contempt of court and be liable to a series of penalties, including up to six months' imprisonment.

I screw up the letter and fock it on the floor. I'm not going to let anyone psyche me out of it.

It's Sincerity's old man who ends up making an issue out of it.

He goes, 'Seriously, William? Does winning this thing really mean that much to you?'

William's there, 'Look who's talking! The man who tried to poison us all the last day!'

'Sincerity and I are dancing to *Adore You* by Miley Cyrus,' Raymond goes. 'We were always dancing to *Adore You* by Miley Cyrus. I only said that about Coldplay to wind you up.'

'Yeah, sure,' he goes, getting ready to step into his spats. 'That's easy to say now, once the courts have had their – aaarrrggghhh!'

He suddenly lets this – I swear to God – blood-curdling scream out of him. I've seen men lose ears in rucks and not make the noise this dude makes. All of the other fathers are going, 'What's wrong? What's wrong?' pretending to actually *give* a fock?

He pulls off the shoe – still howling, by the way – and I notice that his sock is basically saturated in blood.

Again, I'm doing my best to remain above it all, thinking, *Walk, walk, side-together, walk, walk, side-together, walk, walk, side-together, dip.*

He looks into the shoe and goes, 'Someone's put a nail through the sole of my . . . Jesus Christ, the pain!'

He pulls off his sock. Holy shit, I think – that *is* a nasty wound. He obviously pushed his foot into the shoe and, at the same time, dragged it across the nail, because there's a wound on the bottom of his foot that's, like, at least two inches long and blood is literally pouring out of it onto the tiled floor.

He's there, 'Who did this? I want to know!'

Ed Burke – as in Desdemona's old man? – goes, 'What do you mean by that? You just stepped on a nail.'

'Stepped on a three-inch nail that happened to be standing perfectly upright?' the dude goes. 'Look! Someone's hammered it in! Which one of you was it? I demand to know!'

All of a sudden, there's a knock on the door. Miss Coleman sticks her head around it and goes, 'Okay, gentlemen – your crowd awaits!'

We all stand up. Except for obviously William.

'I can't dance like this!' he goes. 'I'm going to need stitches.'

Cloud Gorvey's old man, John, gives him a serious filthy on his way out the door. 'Yeah, I remember how sympathetic you were the last day, when our daughters were vomiting. Good luck tonight.'

William goes, 'Which one of you did this? Which one of you was it?'

I meet Honor outside in the corridor. She's like, 'What's going on?'

I'm there, 'Someone put a nail through Currer Bell's old man's shoe.'

'Oh! My God!'

'He's lost about a pint of blood in there. It's funny.'

'Currer Bell's going to be *so* pissed off. They're, like, third overall.'

'I wouldn't shed any tears for them. Serves him right for throwing around solicitor's letters. Let's just concentrate on our performance.'

As it happens, we're on third in the running order, after Desdemona and Ed (25 points) and Annora and Michael (22 points). Everyone seems definitely rattled by the solicitor's letters and the sight of William Whelehan's foot leaking blood like a rare steak.

Everyone except me and Honor.

We're introduced. We walk out into the middle of the floor and I stort unbuttoning my shirt. The crowd, of course, goes ballistic at the sight of The Six. We take up our positions. As we listen to the unmistakable opening bors of *Cry Me a River*, I actually feel like I used to before a big rugby match. I turn to Honor and I go, 'Let's leave nothing out there on the dance floor.'

And she just laughs. She loves seeing this side of me.

Then we hear Michael Bublé's voice. I pick my daughter up, throw her six feet into the air, spinning, spinning, spinning, and then – much to my relief – I catch her again and the crowd goes wild. The ninety seconds fly. I can honestly say that neither of us puts a single foot wrong and it ends up being another standing ovation from the audience and two of the three judges at the end.

Mena goes, 'Honor, absolutely flawless from both of you. Ross, I need to ask you a question – did you ever play rugby?'

I decide not to be a dick about it. I'm in a good mood. I just go, 'Yeah, no, I did.'

She's there, 'Because you hold yourself like a supremely confident athlete. I thought it was rugby alright. You moved with fluidity and style, but also control. Well done.'

Jean goes, 'I thought you two had set an impossible bar for yourselves with your quickstep last month. But there was no drop-off in your performance tonight. I thought that was a faultless routine. And I'm going to tell you something else, going into the final week, you two are going to be real contenders for this title.'

Honor gives me the most incredible hug.

Then Ryan – the dick – goes, 'I have to disagree with the other two. I thought it was all a bit pedestrian, a bit uninspired. Ross, watch your body shape. Honor, you were quite good – but, unfortunately, your father is holding you back.'

We get a ten from Jean, a ten from Mena and a seven from Ryan, the complete and utter bell-end.

'What is *his* focking problem?' Honor goes, giving him daggers from the green room. 'He hates us!'

It's not a bad score, though. Except Sincerity and Raymond end up getting three nines for their routine, which gives them a total of 75. We're in second place, though, on 69, which means we're still in with a shout going into the final round next month.

From the green room, we watch as William Whelehan – his foot wrapped in a bandage made from toilet roll – quite literally limps his way through his routine with Currer Bell, with blood still leaking out of the sides of his shoe and leaving a red slug trail all over the dance floor. It's difficult to watch and most of the audience end up having to actually look away. The two of them end up getting two threes and one two from the judges, which puts them last on 52 points.

William is obviously *not* a happy rabbit? Back in the dressing room, he looks at us each in turn and goes, 'You think *I* can't play dirty, too? Trust me – you haven't heard the last of this!'

Twenty minutes later, me and Honor are walking back to the cor. She goes, 'Six points is going to be – oh my God – *impossible* to make up!'

And I'm there, 'Nothing is impossible, Honor. Ask Joe Schmidt what happened in Chicago last weekend.'

Honor gets into the front passenger seat. I'm about to open my door when I hear my name suddenly called. I look up and I see Roz and Sincerity making their way towards us.

I'm like, 'Hey, how the hell are you?' in my sexiest voice.

Roz goes, 'I just wanted to say hello again.'

Sincerity leaves the two of us to it. She goes around to the passenger side and tries to talk to Honor through the window – which, by the way, Honor leaves *closed*?

She goes, 'I thought you were amazing tonight, Honor!' having to shout to make herself heard. 'I thought Ryan was *so* mean to you! If I'd been a judge, I would have definitely given you ten.'

Honor says nothing, just sticks her nose in her phone.

Roz goes, 'So how *random* is this? All those times I watched you play rugby and I never plucked up the courage to talk to you afterwards. And here I am, nearly twenty years later . . .'

She lets it hang there. Is she looking for me to ask her out? I decide to just go for it. I think I mentioned that she's a serious ringer for Allison Williams except her face doesn't piss me off as much – at all, in fact.

I'm there, 'Hey, I was wondering, do you want to maybe go for a drink sometime?'

And she smiles and goes, 'I'd actually really like that.'

She rhymes off her digits and I put them into my phone and neither of us is able to take the smiles off our faces.

It's, like, half-ten and there's a knock on my bedroom door.

I'm like, 'Come in!'

It ends up being Sorcha. 'I'm sorry to knock so late,' she goes. 'Did I disturb you?'

She seems weirdly stiff. It's all a bit *Downton Abbey*.

I'm there, 'Er, no, I wasn't doing much.'

She's like, 'Can I talk to you about something?'

I tell her, yeah, no, of course she can. I'm there, 'You're up late, by the way.'

She goes, 'Mom and Dad are downstairs and Croía's on her way over. We're going to stay up all night and watch the US election results as they come in.'

I don't know what to say to that. It's like when people tell me how much they love Ed Sheeran – I just feel fock-all inside.

I'm like, 'Hm,' and that's all I can muster up the enthusiasm to say.

'I wanted to apologize,' she goes. 'For walking in on you that night. I should have knocked.'

I'm here, 'It's, er, cool.'

She looks up to see Yanet, leaning against the wall, with a big, happy smile on her face.

'Does she have a name?' she goes.

I'm there, 'Yanet.'

'She actually looks a bit like Yanet Garcia.'

'Yeah, no, that's the look I was going for.'

'Do you want any outfits for her?'

'Outfits?'

'Just so she's not always in the same clothes. There's some of my old dresses in that box over there that I was going to send to St Vincent de Paul. Including the one from Reiss with the slit up the side.'

'Yeah, no, you're fine, Sorcha.'

'You used to love *me* in that!'

This is the weirdest focking conversation I've ever had.

I'm there, 'I appreciate the offer. You seem in good form, by the way. I'm just commenting on it.'

She goes, 'I suppose I'm just excited.'

'About?'

'Tonight, Ross! Do you realize that when the world wakes up tomorrow morning, the most powerful person on the planet is going to be a woman?'

'When you put it like that. Jesus.'

'And not just an ordinary woman. An amazing, amazing woman named Hillary Clinton, who isn't a sexist, or a chauvinist, or a misogynist.'

No, she just chose one for a husband. I don't say that, though. Instead, I go, 'Do you definitely think she's going to win? I'm just making the point that everyone thought my old man was finished and look at him now.'

She's there, 'It was men who brought your dad back as leader of New Republic. There is, like, no way that women are going to be persuaded to vote for Donald Trump.'

I have to say, I've missed talking to Sorcha, even though I'm not in love with her anymore and this is actually a pretty boring conversation.

'I'm sorry it didn't work out,' I go, 'between you and Fionn, I mean. I know you probably find that hord to believe.'

She goes, 'Fionn was in love with the old Sorcha. He didn't even *like* the new me.'

There's suddenly a ring at the front door.

'That'll be Croía,' she goes. 'I hope she remembered the pizzas.' Then back downstairs she goes.

I hop into the sack. I'm actually a bit wrecked. I send Roz a text message asking if she's free on Friday night and she texts back to say yes – what about going somewhere for a bite? She asks me if I've ever been to that restaurant in Ranelagh that serves survival rations with a gourmet twist and I tell her yes and I focking won't be going back. She sends me a smiley face. I tell her that Kielys of Donnybrook does an incredible burger with bacon and cheese, but then she must fall asleep because she doesn't reply.

I fall asleep as well and I end up having this dream where I'm playing for Ireland against the All Blacks in Chicago and we're, like, six points ahead with only seconds to go and I throw a lazy pass to Simon Zebo – I'm still ashamed of it a full week later – which George Moala intercepts and he's running for the posts. And I'm screaming. But then I suddenly wake up and I realize that I'm not screaming at all. The screaming is coming from downstairs. And I'd recognize that scream anywhere.

It's Sorcha.

I hop out of the bed, throw on my clothes and peg it down the stairs. All the time, the screaming is getting louder and more, I suppose, *frantic*?

I push open the door of the living room and I go, 'What the actual fock?' and her old man goes – this is word for word – 'Donald Trump has just taken Pennsylvania.'

Sorcha is, like, hysterical and I notice that she's clutching her bump, as if in pain. I run out to the kitchen, grab the cordless phone and I ring for an ambulance. By the time I make it back into the living room, her old dear is cradling her head and Croía is telling her in a soothing voice that counting is still continuing in Wisconsin, Michigan and Arizona.

I literally shove her out of the way and I tell Sorcha that an ambulance is on the way.

Croía goes, 'We don't need your ambulance – your *manbulance*!' but Sorcha's old man – on *my* side, for once? – goes, 'Of course she needs an ambulance! She's hyperventilating!' and Croía, wisely, shuts the fock up.

Fifteen minutes later, the ambulance arrives. Honor tips downstairs when she hears the siren – as do Brian, Johnny and Leo. I tell Honor that everything's going to be okay and I tell her to bring her brothers upstairs, while Brian calls us all a pack of fockpricks.

One of the ambulance dudes asks Sorcha if she has pain and she says yes. They lift her onto a trolley and they take her outside, with me, her old man and Croía following. Sorcha's old dear stays behind to mind the kids.

The same ambulance dude goes, 'Okay, who's her next-of-kin?'

I'm there, 'I'm her still technically husband.'

But Croía tries to get into the back of the ambulance, going, 'Well, I'm her chief political adviser,' except Sorcha's old man grabs a handful of her coat and pulls her back, going, 'Ross, you go with her. I'll follow in the cor.'

We arrive in Holles Street twenty minutes later. I end up chasing the trolley down three corridors, before it disappears behind a set of double doors and I'm told that I can't go any further and to sit and wait for news.

I whip out my phone and I ring Fionn. He answers on the second ring. He's like, 'Hello?'

He's awake. He probably stayed up to watch the results coming in himself. No focking life.

I'm there, 'Dude, Sorcha's been rushed to hospital. She's in Holles Street. You better come.'

He hangs up. Fifteen minutes later, Sorcha's old man arrives, followed by Fionn, followed by Croía, who storts immediately throwing her weight around, telling the nurses that Sorcha is one of the country's most important feminists and demanding to know what's being done by the predominantly male doctors to help her.

One of the nurses goes, 'Please sit down. We'll call you when we know something.'

Croía's there, 'Could you at least tell her that Hillary Clinton won the popular vote?'

Fionn ends up totally losing it with the girl. He goes, 'Will you sit the fock down and let them do their focking jobs?'

'Well said!' Sorcha's old man goes.

We end up sitting there for ages, with no one saying shit, except occasionally Croía looks up from her phone and comes out with something like, 'Women are going to be waking up this morning, wondering how they're going to explain this result to their daughters?'

I can't listen to any more and I head for the coffee machine at the end of the corridor. Fionn follows me.

I'm there, 'What'll you have?'

He goes, 'Doubt if it matters. I'm sure they all taste equally bad.'

I punch the button for an Americano.

'Thanks for ringing me,' he goes, as the machine belches foul-smelling brown liquid into a cup. 'You didn't have to.'

I'm there, 'I'm a wanker, Fionn. I'm not an orsehole.'

'I'm just saying it was good of you to think of me.'

'We played rugby together. Do you think a single hour goes by when I *don't* think about you?'

And then we end up just hugging each other. It's the hug we should have had last weekend in Kielys after Ireland beat the All Blacks if it wasn't for my stupid pride.

Man, it feels good.

I suddenly notice movement at the end of the corridor. There's, like, a doctor dude, with a serious face, talking to Sorcha's old man and Croía. Me and Fionn run in their direction. I end up winning the foot race.

No surprises there.

I'm like, 'What's the story? How's Sorcha? Is the baby okay?'

The doctor goes, 'Everything is fine with Sorcha and the baby. It was just a bit of hypertension. I can't stress this enough – over the next few weeks, she really needs to take things easy.'

Croía's there, 'Er, with a racist, a misogynist and a sexual abuser about to move into the White House? I don't see how that's even possible.'

I turn to the doctor and I go, 'Can I see her?'

The doctor's like, 'She said the only person she wants to see right now is someone called Croía.'

Croía goes, 'That's me.'

I'm like, 'But I'm her husband.'

Her old man's there, 'And I'm her father.'

And Fionn goes, 'And I'm possibly the father of her baby.'

But the dude's there, 'I'm sorry. She expressly said that she didn't want to see any men.'

I drive home in an actual daze. On the eight o'clock news, I hear Donald Trump say that he wants to be a President for all the people. I'm just hoping that Sorcha is listening. It might help put her mind at ease.

I'm happy that she's okay, but at the same time I'm worried about her. Fionn is right. She has changed since she met Croía and not for the better. It's like when Opal Fruits became Storburst – a lot of us preferred the original.

The old man is on the radio now, saying that the people of America have made their choice, just like the people who voted for Brexit made *their* choice, and that the mainstream media – 'bloody whining liberals' – would just have to get over that fact.

I go through the presets, looking for a decent song. And I do this sort of, like, mental exercise that Father Fehily taught us to do whenever we feel a bit down, which involves basically counting your blessings.

So I'm thinking, okay, I've got a daughter who I've developed this incredible, incredible bond with and we're now in with a chance of winning the Goatstown Glitterball together. I've got a date with a beautiful woman – I haven't even mentioned that she's got humungous jobes – who really likes me and, more importantly, remembers the rugby player I was back in the day. I've got a son who, yes, is about to make the biggest mistake of his life, but at least no one is trying to kill him. I've got triplet boys who are basically thugs, but at least they'll be storting Montessori next year and they'll be someone else's responsibility. I've got the weapon that my old dear possibly used to kill her second husband and I think, when it comes to it, I can still get maybe a million squids out of her for it. And there's at least a chance that I'm going to be the father of another son or daughter after Christmas.

Out loud, I go, 'I am truly blessed!' like Father Fehily taught us to do, then I go to make the Sign of the Cross and I realize that I've forgotten how it goes.

I'm just approaching the roundabout at The Graduate when it hits me. At first it's just a *feeling*? A sick sense that something isn't right – like when I see pictures of Camilla Kerslake with Chris Robshaw, except worse. It feels like the temperature in the cor has dropped and I'm suddenly freezing. I end up having to pull over on Avondale Road and I realize that I'm shaking.

I'm like, 'Oh, Jesus, no!'

I ring Ronan. He answers on the third ring. He's like, 'Stordee, Rosser?'

I can hear wailing in the background. It's Rihanna-Brogan.

He goes, 'Wait'll I foyunt a quiet spot hee-or to thalk. Shadden toawult Rihatta-Barrogan last neet that an eebil, ordinge madden was throying to take oaber the wurlded – this morden she had to ted her that he's arthur succeeding.'

I'm there, 'Ro, that receipt I gave you – for the safety deposit box. Where is it?'

'It's in the kitchen. I hab it hidden insoyut one of them fake Hoyunz Beeyunz caddens.'

He steps back into the kitchen and the wailing kicks off again.

I hear Shadden go, 'Ro, can *you* throy to caddem her dowun? I want to put it up on Facebook that me thaughter is so upset about Doddald Thrump widding the edection that she dudn't wanth to go to skewill this morden.'

Ro's there, 'Ine just looking for sometin for Rosser, Shadden.'

Then there's just, like, silence. From Ronan, I mean. The screaming continues. I hear him moving tins around, then he eventually goes, 'It's bleaten godden.'

He means it's bleeding gone.

I'm like, 'Fock! Fock! Fock!' and I bang the dashboard with my fist.

He goes, 'What's going on, Rosser?'

And I'm there, 'I've just solved the mystery of who kicked down your front door.'

I hang up on him, then I ring Erika.

She goes, 'Where are you?'

I'm like, 'Avondale Road – supposedly Killiney. She has it, Erika. The receipt for the safety deposit box. No wonder she wasn't scared when I told her I was going to go to the Feds. I'm going to drive out to Santry now.'

'What's the point?'

'I want to know for sure that it's gone.'

'Of course it's gone. You have no idea the kind of people they're mixed up with, Ross.'

'Are you talking about my old pair?'

'I'm on my way to see them. I know absolutely everything.'

'Don't go to the gaff without me. I'll meet you in the cor pork of Foxrock Church again.'

So that's what ends up happening. I collect her – she's wearing a short skirt, although that's not strictly relevant to the story – and we drive to the gaff. I ask her once or twice what's going on, but she tells me to wait, so I just drive in silence, taking the odd sneaky look at her legs, wondering is that fake tan or actual.

We pull up outside. I notice Hennessy's cor – his 161D black Beamer – porked in the driveway. Into the house we go, with me leading the way. First, I head for the living room. There's no one in there. But the TV is on – we're talking that Russian news channel that the old man loves – and I notice three champagne glasses and four empty bottles of Veuve Clicquot on the table.

'They obviously stayed up all night to watch the results as well,' I go.

Yeah, no, I thought he sounded a bit pissed on the radio.

I lead the way to the kitchen. And that's where I find them. The old pair and Hennessy. *She's* cooking one of her spinach, bacon and cheddar frittatas, the ugly sow.

It smells incredible.

'Ah, Kicker!' the old man goes. 'You heard the news, I presume! Of course you did! You'll have been following it through the night like the rest of us!'

Hennessy's there, 'It's great news! One of our kind – back in the White House!'

'He means an entrepreneur, Ross! A man who understands business! I've had them all onto me this morning, of course, looking for my – inverted commas – *take* on it! RTÉ. Newstalk. Today FM. Wanting to know would I welcome him to Ireland if I became the next Taoiseach? Of course I would! This is a man I played nine holes with in Doonbeg back in 2014! One or two people actually commented on the similarities between –'

He suddenly stops because Erika has walked into the kitchen behind me.

'Oh,' he goes, 'how lovely to see you, Darling! Is Amelie with you?'

She's like, 'My mom's taken her to crèche.'

'Oh, she's home from Australia, then, is she?'

And that's when Erika says it.

'I know everything,' she goes. 'Everything you've been doing.'

The old man's expression suddenly changes. He's not exactly rattled. He's just serious. He stares at her. So does Hennessy. The old dear carries on cooking.

The old man's there, 'What do you know?'

'I know that the "What In the Name of FO'CK Foundation" is a front,' she goes. 'I know you're using dozens of bogus charities to receive money from Russian companies that specialize in resource extraction.'

The old dear goes, 'A front? How dare you cast aspersions on my record as a humanitarian?' waving the spatula at her. 'Ross, will you have some frittata?'

I'm there, 'Do you honestly think I'd eat anything you focking cooked? Just give me some on a small plate. Only because I don't want to hurt your feelings, you fat focking elk.'

Erika's there, 'I know you've convinced a lot of very wealthy Russians that you're going to be the next leader of this country. I know you're pre-selling them an interest in Ireland's gas, petroleum and peat reserves, as well as lead, copper, barite –'

'Erika,' the old man tries to go, 'there's nothing illegal about any of this!'

'– dolomite, gypsum –'

'These kinds of partnerships between the public, private and philanthropic sectors are the future!'

'– silver, zinc –'

'We're evincing the borders separating politics, business and charity in a way that benefits the planet by alleviating poverty, combating disease and tackling climate change – if you believe in that sort of thing!'

I'm there, 'I have to be honest. I'm struggling to follow any of this.'

Erika goes, 'It's quite simple, Ross. Your mother goes to Moscow and she talks about her experiences as a victim of injustice.'

'Yeah, so-called.'

'A billionaire Russian oligarch is so moved by her speech that he makes a three hundred million dollar donation to Banoffee Versus Gangs. And, in return, our dear father signs a secret deal awarding him the right to harvest one hundred million square acres of Irish timber in Laois.'

Three hundred million? Jesus, no wonder she doesn't need Ari's money.

'Or,' Erika goes, 'she flies to Minsk and she talks about what it feels like to have her civil rights infringed. And, again, another Russian billionaire decides that he's going to donate eight hundred million dollars to Children Without Skis. And, in return, Ireland's future leader promises them the fracking rights to Lambay Island, which he happens to be leasing from the government for a prison he has no intention of ever building.'

'And what about the children?' I go. 'Will *they* get their skis?'

She answers me with just a bitter laugh.

I stare at the old dear. 'You're focking sick!' I go.

Erika's there, 'I've read all of your emails – forty-five thousand of them.'

The old man nods.

'That day,' he goes, staring at me, 'when you and Honor kept us talking at the door, showing us your dance steps, I knew what was going on!'

I'm there, 'So answer me this – who kicked down your grandson's front door to steal the code for that private security box?'

Hennessy suddenly pipes up. He goes, 'That two-bar electric heater could have put your mother back in jail and focking ruined everything. You think these people we're dealing with – the money they stand to make – are going to be held to ransom by a little flea like you?'

'So someone *did* do something to the brakes of my cor that day?'

The old man goes, 'One or two of the private security companies they used may have acted a little, shall we say, overzealously?'

Erika's there, 'They burned my gallery down.'

'There was a chap called Yuri on the team who may have had some anger management issues! I'll buy you a new gallery, Erika! Just like Fionnuala bought Ross a new car!'

I can't believe someone actually *did* try to kill me. I'm so disgusted I end up not even touching my frittata. Two or three mouthfuls – that's all I can eat.

'Even calling Constance Markievicz a cow,' Erika goes, 'was all part of the plan, wasn't it? To create a distraction.'

The old man's there, 'Politics is all sleight of hand, Erika!'

'You orchestrated the whole thing.'

'Except the part where Muirgheal tried to take over the party! I was only supposed to be suspended! But she got a little bit of power and decided she rather liked it! Drunk on all the feminist nonsense that's in the air!'

'Your Russian friends hacked her email account.'

'She was lifting her political hemline to Micheál Martin!'

'So you destroyed her!'

'The only question now is what are you going to do, Erika, with all this information you've collected?'

'I'll give it to Sorcha. She can reveal the whole thing in the Seanad. I'll give her all the emails.'

'You still have them, do you?'

'Yes.'

'Are you absolutely certain of that?'

At that exact moment, Erika's phone rings. She looks at the screen and goes, 'It's Phonewatch,' and she doesn't say shit then for a good, like, ten seconds as it dawns on her. 'They're in my house.'

Hennessy goes, 'You could get into your car, but you won't make it there in time. They'll have your computer and anything else that incriminates us.'

'What if I told you that I had everything stored in the cloud?'

The old man goes, 'They'll find it, Erika! This is what they do! God, I used to think the Irish middle classes were good at burying their shit – we have nothing on these chaps!'

Erika suddenly bursts into tears. I put my orm around her and I pull her close to me. I love the way her hair smells.

She suddenly loses it with the old man. 'You are never going to see me or your granddaughter again,' she goes.

He's there, 'Of course I will! We're family, Erika! I'm doing this for you! And for you, Ross! And for your children! This is what you're going to inherit!'

Erika doesn't want to know about our inheritance. I wouldn't mind him putting a figure on it, though.

She goes, 'When you were with my mom, you were a good person.'

The old dear laughs to herself.

'*No varnish can hide the grain of the wood*,' the old man goes. 'You'll know that quote, Ross – as a keen student of Dickens.'

I've no idea who the fock he's talking about.

Erika decides she can't bear to be around him anymore. She turns around and she storms out of the gaff. I go to follow her, except the old man calls me back.

'Ross,' he goes, 'I've got something *for* you! Something you might be interested in!'

I'm there, 'Is it the five million snots *she* promised me for the two-bor electric heater?'

343

'It's something better than that! I can tell you who leaked the news that Sorcha's baby might not be yours!'

'I don't see how that's better than five million snots.'

'You see, my original suspicion was that it was Muirgheal! I know she and Sorcha have had their differences! So I asked one of my Russian contacts if he couldn't put one of his cyber-security experts on the case! I thought it might be something else to use against her! But do you know who Feminist Avenger Thirteen turned out to be, Ross?'

I'm just thinking, 'Please don't say my daughter.'

'It was that wonderful feminist friend of Sorcha's – Croía Ní Chathasaigh!'

10. This Father-and-Daughter Dance Routine Will Melt Your Heart!

Sorcha is checking herself out of the hospital, even though her old man is *anti* the idea? He's there, 'Sorcha, you heard what the doctor said. You need rest.'

But Sorcha is already pulling on her maternity dress, going, 'I don't have *time* to rest, Dad. Donald Trump is going to be the next President of America and I haven't said *anything* about it on Twitter yet!'

Croía zips her up at the back and goes, 'I tweeted a GIF for you of a little girl crying at a Hillary rally. I thought it was important to put something up.'

'How many Likes and Retweets has it got?'

'Only five Retweets but more than forty Likes. Your runners are here, Sorcha.'

Sorcha steps into her Stan Smiths. Croía bends down to tie her laces for her and that's when she notices me standing at the door of the ward.

'Oh, here comes another one,' she goes, 'to de-*man*-d that you get back into bed and play the part of the frail pregnant woman. You're not acting according to the rules of *manternity*, Sorcha.'

Sorcha barely even looks at me. She's like, 'Whatever you've got to say, Ross, I don't want to hear it.'

She uses the selfie mode on her phone to check her face and fix her hair.

I'm there, 'I think you might want to hear *this*, Sorcha.'

Croía's there, 'I'll drive you to the Seanad. You can think about what you're going to tweet on the way.'

Sorcha's old man goes, 'Darling, please get back into bed.'

'I know who put it out there,' I go. 'The story about Fionn being possibly the father of the baby.'

Oh, that gets Sorcha's interest. She's like, 'Excuse me?'

I look at Croía and I watch her face turn red.

345

I'm there, 'I found out who Feminist Avenger Thirteen is.'

Sorcha goes, 'It *was* Honor, wasn't it?'

It makes me sad that I'm the only one who can see the good in my daughter.

I'm there, 'No, it wasn't Honor. Do *you* want to tell her who it was, Croía?'

Croía – hilariously – tries to go, 'I already did. Some creepy man with big glasses and a neckbeard who fantasizes about hurting women.'

I go, 'Wrong! Feminist Avenger Thirteen,' saying it like I'm turning over a winning poker hand, 'is you!'

Sorcha's face just drops. As does Croía's, by the way. She knows there's not a lot going on with me brains-wise. I'm the last person in the world she expected to discover the truth.

Sorcha's old man's there, 'What the hell is he talking about?'

Croía tries to go, 'Don't listen to him, Sorcha. This is a *manspiracy* to try to turn women against each other. It's exactly the same tactic they used to destroy Hillary and keep her from her rightful place in the White House.'

Sorcha is suddenly looking at Croía differently. 'Okay,' she goes, 'I'm waiting for you to tell me it actually *wasn't* you?'

Croía's there, 'I can't believe we're wasting time discussing this when you've got seventeen thousand followers who are waiting for you to say something on Twitter.'

'Croía –?'

Croía won't even look at her. She storts gathering up Sorcha's bits and pieces and throwing them into her overnight bag. At the same time, she's going, 'We should also use this result as an opportunity to keep up the pressure with regard to the street names. I was thinking Temple Bar should definitely be renamed the Hannah Sheehy-Skeffington Quarter.'

'Croía,' Sorcha goes, 'is it true?'

After a long pause, Croía is like, 'You were wavering. Fionn was in your ear – another toxic male – trying to tell you that there were more important issues than how women are treated by men and *have* been treated for thousands and thousands of –'

'Get out!' Sorcha's old man suddenly goes.

Croía's like, 'I'm not going to take instructions from you . . . or should I say *manstructions*?'

He roars it this time. He's like, 'Get out!'

'Oh my God,' Croía goes, 'you look like you want to hit me. Go on, then, do it – if it makes you feel better and helps validate you as a man.'

But then *Sorcha* says it? She goes, 'Get out!'

Croía's like, 'Can you not see that this is what *they* want?'

'No, it's what *I* want. Get the fock out – I never want to see you again.'

I'm there, 'You heard her, Croía. Hit the bricks.'

Croía totally blanks me. She just stares at Sorcha and goes, 'Hey, I was the one who made you relevant. You were talking about disposable coffee cups before I got a hold of you.'

'You used me, Croía.'

'I helped you put women on the map – literally. The least you could do is say thank you.'

Sorcha doesn't say shit, though. If Croía knows as much about women as she claims, she'll know that this conversation is over.

She finally seems to accept that. She walks past me without even looking at me, then out of the ward she goes. Two or three seconds later, she's back, standing in the doorway with a face that tells me she's about to say something deeply hurtful.

'What the fock are you going to do without me?' she goes. 'Go back to running a clothes shop – like the Basic Bitch that you are and always will be?'

I kick the door with my foot and it slams in her face.

I'm actually tying the laces of my dance shoes when Mrs Leonard tells me that she's figured out who I am.

'Or rather,' she goes, 'who you're married to!'

I'm there, 'You're not one of these people who wants the name changed back to Grafton Street, are you?'

She's like, 'No, I was a friend of her grandmother's. And *you* were the chap who drove all the way to Mayo to collect her.'

Oh my God, that takes me back.

I'm there, 'Yeah, no, I promised her I'd never tell anyone about that.'

What basically happened was this. One Sunday morning, about six or seven years ago, I got a call from Sorcha's granny to say that she'd been thrown off the parish pilgrimage to Knock after drinking a bottle of Horvey's Bristol Cream and telling Father Olapado that he was the antichrist. The woman was murder for the drink and she tended to cross the line when she had a few onboard. Anyway, this was, like, the day after it happened and she had the total fear. She didn't want Sorcha or her old pair to find out, so she rang the only person in the world she knew wouldn't judge her.

I mean, how could I after some of the stunts I've pulled over the years?

I made some excuse to Sorcha and I drove to Mayo to bring her home. Five hours there and five hours back. She told me she didn't think she believed in God anymore – she'd had, like, a crisis in her faith. I cheered her up by telling her some of the things I'd done when drunk over the years – a lot of them while I was on my Ji – and we laughed pretty much the entire way home.

Then we both promised we'd never talk about it again.

'I was on the same pilgrimage,' Mrs Leonard goes. 'The things she'd say when she'd a few drinks on her. She was a gas woman.'

Honor walks back into the room. Yeah, no, she left the CD in the cor and had to go back out to get it.

'The Charleston!' Mrs Leonard goes, suddenly all business. 'Where we all first met! Ross, do you remember the steps?'

I'm like, 'Not a one. But I'll work my hole to remember them.'

'Honor, what song have you chosen?'

Honor's like, '*Supercalifragilisticexpialidocious.*'

'Wonderful!' she goes, clapping her two hands together. 'Oh, we are going to have *so* much fun with this!'

Honor goes, 'I don't want to have fun. I want to actually win.'

God, I love her attitude.

Mrs Leonard's like, 'Where are you in the competition?'

'We're second,' Honor goes. 'But we're six points behind. And one of the judges is being a complete wanker to us.'

'You mean Ryan?'

'He just hates us. Doesn't he, Dad?'

I'm like, 'Yeah, no, the other two judges gave us maximum points for our quickstep and our foxtrot. He gave us two sevens and told Honor that I was holding her back.'

She goes, 'Oh, he just likes to have someone to pick on – like *his* mother picked on him. Oh, I've met some awful Dance Moms in my years, but his was the worst I ever knew: *"Left foot, right foot, left foot! Left foot, right foot, left foot! Are you an imbecile?"*'

I'm there, 'She sounds a bit like my old man when he was teaching me how to kick!'

'A horribly cruel woman. If he made a mistake, she would make him wear his shoes on the wrong feet for the next week – to teach him a lesson. He had to go to school like that.'

'I wonder are we possibly related?'

Honor puts the CD in the CD player.

She goes, 'Mrs Leonard, will you come to watch us in the final round?'

I have to admit, I'm actually surprised when the woman turns around and goes, 'I'm afraid not, Honor, no.'

Honor's hurt. I can see it in her face. I thought the woman liked her.

I'm there, 'Do you mind me asking you why not?' sounding like one of those parents she was just complaining about.

'Because,' she goes, 'I don't like these kinds of competitions. People should dance for the joy of it. It shouldn't be used to turn little girls against each other.'

I'm there, 'It's more the parents actually. Put it this way, there's a lot of solicitors and barristers making a lot of money out of it.'

I suppose Mount Anville will get all that moolah eventually. That's how the South Dublin economy works.

She goes, 'That's why I don't get involved. Too many parents like Ryan's mother, using their children to get one up on each other. Thank you, Honor, for asking me, but no, I won't come.'

Honor goes, 'Fine,' even though I can see that she's totally crushed.

'Now, come along,' Mrs Leonard goes, 'we've got lots and lots of work ahead of us.'

So it's, like, just after six o'clock in the evening and I'm about to go on my date with Roz. I look and feel fantastic. I even give myself a little wink in the mirror at the top of the stairs.

I go, 'You're winning at life, Kid!' and I have to say it gives me a huge boost in my confidence.

I tip downstairs to the kitchen. Sorcha is watching the RTÉ news while the boys are sitting at the table, playing – quietly for once – with their Match Attax cords.

I'm there, 'I'm, er, heading out.'

'Look at this focker!' Brian goes.

Leo's like, 'He's only a wanker!'

But Sorcha doesn't say shit. She's too engrossed in the news. Caitríona Perry is saying that tens of thousands of people across twenty-five American cities took to the streets to protest against Donald Trump's victory in the US election. In New York, a crowd of five thousand people, including Lady Gaga, morched to Trump Tower, carrying banners bearing the message, 'Not my President!'

Sorcha notices me for the first time. She mutes the TV.

'It makes me feel *actually* nauseous,' she goes, 'to think that *he's* going to undo all the amazing, amazing things that Barack Obama did for the world.'

I try to do the glass half full thing.

I'm there, 'It might not be as bad you think. Do you remember that time in *The West Wing* when John Goodman took over from Jed Bortlet? At first you thought he was a dick. Then after two or three episodes, you kind of got *used* to him?'

She looks at me with this look of just, like, disgust on her face. She goes, 'Are you *actually* suggesting that they're the same thing?'

I'm like, 'I suppose not.'

'One is a TV show, Ross, and the other is real life.'

I don't know what's upset her more – Donald Trump winning the election or Croía using her like she did. Either way, she's in foul form.

I go, 'Anyway, like I said, I'm heading out.'

She's like, 'Where are you going?'

'Just – like I said – out.'

'Do you have a date? Sorry, I shouldn't have asked you that.'

'It feels weird telling you this, but – yeah, no – I do have a date.'

'I noticed you were wearing your *Acqua di Giò*. It's a bit early for a date, isn't it?'

'She has to get home early. She has, like, a daughter.'

'Oh.'

'It's actually the mother of a girl in Honor's class.'

'Like I said, it's none of my business.'

'I don't know if you remember Rosalind Carew?'

'Went to Alexandra College? Played hockey for the seconds and was Deputy Head Girl?'

'Er, possibly.'

'*That's* who you're going on a date with?'

'Yeah.'

She doesn't say anything for ages. I can see she's jealous. 'Like I said,' she goes, 'you're a free agent.'

She puts her hand on her swollen belly then and goes, 'What kind of mother am I going to be to this baby, Ross?'

I'm there, 'The best mother in the world!'

I have to say it. She's upset.

She's like, 'How could I be? I've got three sons who've been borred from every toy shop and play centre in this city and a daughter attending an Alcohol and Tobacco Awareness programme.'

'She's not,' I suddenly hear myself go.

I say it just because I want to give her some *good* news? You could call it a crumb of comfort.

She's there, 'What do you mean?'

I'm like, 'When I told you that Honor was going on a course to learn about the dangers of giving cigarettes and alcohol to children, it was one of my famous little white lies. I've been bringing her to dance classes behind your back.'

'Excuse me?'

'We entered the *Strictly Mount Anville* dance contest, Sorcha. We're actually in second place with just the Chorleston to go!'

She's like, 'Oh! My God!' but not in a good way.

'For what's it's worth,' I go, 'that's also the reason I threw a dress on your pogo stick and drew a face on your Lolo ball. I wasn't using it as a sex doll. I can't tell you what a relief it is to finally be able to tell you that.'

'I can't focking believe this!'

'You focking prick!' Leo goes.

I'm there, 'I hoped you'd be genuinely pleased.'

She's like, 'Pleased? That you both lied to me – again?'

'Sorcha, you wouldn't believe the change that has come over the girl since she entered this competition. If you could only see us dance together. I think she's actually turning into the little girl you always dreamed of having.'

Sorcha just shakes her head. 'Don't say another word,' she goes. 'Just go on your date.'

And Brian's like, 'Focking orsehole.'

Roz asks me if I've done much dating. I presume she means since the separation and not while I was married.

'In fairness to me,' I go, 'I've mostly been concentrating on being an amazing father to my children. I've had one or two dates,' and I think about Jaila with her Venti Lattes and Hedvig with her horndog of a husband. 'To be honest, the two or three dates I've had since the break-up have been pretty disastrous.'

She laughs and goes, 'Same with me. I've been on Tinder a few times.'

'Stop – the scrapings of the barrel.'

'There are some seriously weird people out there, aren't there? There are so many assholes on it who don't even want a conversation with you. They want to skip straight to sex. I'm old-fashioned in the sense that I really need to get to know someone before I progress to that level.'

'Hm.'

She laughs and slaps me on the side of the orm. She's like, 'You're so funny the way your eyes went to the door there! You're actually hilarious!'

I just laugh along – what else can I do? I go, 'How was your burger?'

She's like, 'Yeah, it was good. It's just I wasn't that hungry. So this is, like, *still* your local, is it?'

She's talking about Kielys.

I'm there, 'Always was. Always will be. In twenty years' time, you'll see me up at the bor there, reminiscing about the player I could have been if I hadn't been such a piss-head. Maybe even bragging about my own kids – how *they* could have played for Ireland, just like *I* should have?'

'Sincerity said you've got three little boys,' she goes. 'What are they like?'

'Very annoying.'

'You don't mean that!'

'I do. I honestly thought they'd be more into rugby, but they've got literally zero interest. They're triplets, by the way.'

'Oh my God, did you hear about those triplets who got banned from D. L. Kids and –?'

'That's them, Roz.'

'What?'

'They're banned from D. L. Kids because they can't stop focking and blinding. They're banned from everywhere. *They're* my children.'

She puts her hand over her mouth. She goes, 'Oh my God, I am *so* sorry!'

I'm there, 'That's what I meant when I said they were annoying.'

'Well, at least you've got Honor!'

'Yeah, no, that's true.'

'She's *such* a sweet little girl.'

'She certainly has her moments.'

'You get on so well.'

'She's very like me in terms of wanting to be a winner and doing whatever it takes to achieve that end.'

'I told you that Sincerity absolutely adores her. Do you know what she said to me last night? She said she'd love to see Honor win the Goatstown Glitterball.'

'That's mind games. Because she knows we're breathing down her neck.'

'It's not mind games! Although the competition has become pretty vicious, hasn't it?'

'That's the South Dublin professional classes for you.'

'Raymond is convinced that one of the other fathers is going to sabotage him. Currer Bell's dad thinks *he* put that nail through his shoe.'

'There's one or two think your daughter poisoned their kids as well.'

'Sincerity wouldn't do something like that!'

'Let's just change the subject. I've got, like, a grown-up son as well – we're talking Ronan.'

'Yeah,' she goes, 'Sincerity said Honor talks about him all the time.'

'He's getting married on New Year's Eve. Clontorf Castle. I've tried to talk him out of it. Not the venue. The getting married bit. I don't want to see him make the same mistake I did.'

'I got married *way* too young.'

'I'm sorry, I never even asked you – what position did your husband play?'

'He actually never played rugby.'

'Jesus – how did you two ever meet?'

'We've known each other since we were kids. Our families go way back. It's a long story.'

I'm there, 'Protestants!'

She laughs. It's funny because it's true. 'What's wrong with Protestants?' she goes.

I'm there, 'Hey, nothing. Father Fehily, my old schools coach, used to say Protestants were the same as Catholics. They just talk to God on a different network.'

Again, she laughs. But then she suddenly says that she has to go home. I'm disappointed because it's only half-nine and the reference to Father Fehily was actually my way of bringing the conversation around to my schools rugby career and her memories of it. But she says she doesn't like to be out after Sincerity's bed time and I just have to accept that.

I pay the bill, then we head outside to Hailo two taxis, one to Goatstown and one to either the Vico Road or town – I haven't made my mind up yet.

She goes, 'Can I just say, that was such a nice night. Do you mind me saying, you're actually a lovely, lovely guy?'

What I like about this girl is that she totally *gets* me? And when I say 'totally gets me', I mean she's completely taken in by my act.

She goes, 'I can see where Honor gets it from now.'

I'm there, 'You definitely don't fancy heading into town, no?'

'I'd love to, but unfortunately I can't. I'd love to see you again, though.'

'Yeah, no, that'd be great.'

Then she suddenly leans in and she kisses me. She tastes of jojoba lip gloss and elderflower tonic. Luckily, I've no objection to either. We end up kissing for a good five minutes until her phone beeps to tell her that her taxi is ten feet behind her.

She whispers in my ear, 'That was worth waiting nearly twenty years for!' and then she gets into the back of the taxi and tells me to text her. I tell her I will and for once I actually *mean* it?

My taxi arrives a minute or two later. I tell the dude to drop me into town but then I change my mind and tell him – yeah, no – I'll head home instead. It might be a sign that I'm possibly maturing, but I really, really like this girl. Maybe I'll wait till about midnight and send her a text, asking her what she's wearing – see can I steer her down that route.

Half an hour later, I'm home. I let myself in and I tip down to the kitchen with the intention of grabbing a stick of Heinemite and bringing it up to bed. I have to say, I end up being surprised – although shocked is *more* the word? – to find Honor and Sorcha sitting together at the kitchen table.

Sorcha is working on something on the Singer sewing machine

that her granny left her, while Honor is playing *Supercalifragilistic-expialidocious* on repeat on her iPhone.

I'm like, 'What's going on?' but I don't say it in, like, a *bad* way?

Sorcha – without even looking up – goes, 'I'm making Honor a dress for when you do the Chorleston together.'

I end up being just, like, speechless. Honor shrugs and mouths the words, 'I don't know,' at me – presumably she means she doesn't know what the fock has gotten into her old dear.

Sorcha goes, 'Show me that picture again, Honor – the one of Julie Andrews and Dick Van Dyke.'

Honor turns her phone around to Sorcha.

'Oh my God,' Sorcha goes, 'I could make a jacket like that for you, Ross! There's a dress in your father's room, Honor – I saw it when I was getting the sewing machine – and it's exactly the same design. Vertical stripes. Pink, white, orange and yellow.'

Honor's there, 'I'll go up and get it.'

As she's passing me, Honor whispers, 'She just came into my room and storted being really nice to me.'

Of course, understandably, I'm concerned.

When Honor goes upstairs, I sit down at the table next to Sorcha – this is without even getting my beer.

I'm there, 'It's, er, nice to see you two getting along so well – random, but nice.'

She goes, 'I've been neglecting the things that matter the most, Ross.'

'Specifically?'

'My children. Honor. The boys. This little one inside me. I got distracted by what I *thought* was important? You know, I read online earlier that thirty thousand people have signed a petition calling for Markievicz Street to be changed back to Grafton Street – and I actually didn't care.'

'I don't think Markievicz Street was ever going to catch on. It's like trying to get people to call Lansdowne Road "the Aviva Stadium". It's like – fock off!'

'So I went into Honor's room and I sat down on her bed and she looked up from her phone and she said, "What the fock do you want?" like she does. And I said, really calmly, "Tell me about your dancing." And she did. And the excitement in her voice, Ross! She's found something she genuinely, genuinely loves. And you were right. She's, like, a totally different person. I think she's finally becoming the little girl I hoped would not only be my daughter but also my best *friend*?'

'I'm delighted for you. I'm not being a wanker.'

'I've decided to take some time away from politics. Maybe a year. I want to have my baby and actually reacquaint myself with my children. Does that make sense?'

'It'll definitely take a lot of pressure off me, Sorcha. I have to say, being a stay-in-bed husband has been a lot horder than I *expected* it to be?'

'Hi, Honor!' Sincerity goes, waving to us across the cor pork. 'Good luck tonight!'

I'm just like, 'Rise above it, Honor. Just smile and wave.'

Sorcha goes, 'I always thought Sincerity was a lovely little girl!'

I'm there, 'Yeah, no, looks can be deceiving. Tell her, Honor.'

Honor goes, 'She poisoned Desdemona Burke, Cloud Gorvey and Annora Finch.'

'And then her old man put a nail through Currer Bell Whele-han's old man's shoe,' I go.

Sorcha's like, 'Oh! My God!'

She's been away from the gates of Mount Anville for so long, she's forgotten that the backstabbing is as vicious as a day in West-eros. I open the boot of the cor and Honor takes the dress out of it. I pick up my suit bag and sling it over my shoulder. Sorcha takes the bag with our shoes in it and my straw boater, which she sewed a band of material onto, so that it matches my pink, white, orange and yellow striped jacket.

I'm there, 'You two head inside. I'll, er, follow you in,' because I want to go and say hello to Roz.

Yeah, no, we've seen each other, like, three or four times at this stage, although we agreed to keep it on the down-low for now – just for the sake of the kids.

I tip over to her as she's locking her cor. I'm all, 'Hey, how the hell are you?'

And she's there, 'I'm very well, thank you,' grinning like a chimp with the keys to the monkey nut store.

I think she genuinely feels that she lucked out when she met me. And, likewise, I actually love the way I feel when I'm around her. We've been for, like, two or three romantic meals – excluding the one in Kielys – and there's talk of us possibly going to Rome in February for Valentine's Day slash Ireland's second match in the 2017 Six Nations.

I've ridden her twice.

I'm there, 'I just wanted to say, you know, I hope your daughter does well tonight. And when I say well, I obviously mean just okay!'

Sincerity pipes up then. She goes, 'Thanks, Mr O'Carroll-Kelly. I'd love to see you and Honor win, though.'

I'm just thinking, I bet you would, you little focking sociopath.

She sees her old man arrive in his brand-new seven-serious and she goes, 'Oh my God, there's my Dad!' and she goes pegging it over to his cor.

I'm like, 'Anyway, I'll give you a ring, okay?'

She goes, 'Yes, please do!'

Honor and Sorcha are waiting at the door of the school for me. Sorcha's there, 'Were you talking to Sincerity's mom?'

I'm like, 'Er . . .'

'You can tell me, Ross. I'm not going to be the psycho ex-wife.'

'I was talking to Roz, yeah.'

It's, like, the second week in December, by the way, and there's a real Christmas feeling in the air.

We walk into the building and Honor suddenly lets a squeal out of her. She goes, 'Oh my God, there's Mrs Leonard! She came! She came!'

The three of us walk over to her, except we realize at the last minute that she's actually talking to Ryan – the judge who, for some reason, *hates* me? She's going, 'So *this* is what you're doing now, is it? I don't remember you being so good a dancer as to make you fit to judge others.'

'Well,' he tries to go, 'I'm also writing and directing. I'm doing Mount Anville and Blackrock College's joint production of *Porgy and Bess*, set in a Direct Provision Centre in Athlone.'

'And how's that mother of yours?'

'Oh, she's, em, still the same – the same old Ailbhe.'

'And what kind of judge are you? Are you like her?'

The dude looks like he's about to burst into tears.

He's there, 'In what sense, Mrs Leonard?'

She goes, 'In the sense that your mother thought bullying was the way to bring out the best in people. Are you the same? Or do you give criticism in a way that's designed to encourage people's confidence? I'll be interested to see which it is.'

She leaves the dude looking – I swear to fock – about six inches shorter. Then she spots us standing there. She tips over to us.

She goes, 'Good luck tonight!'

Honor throws her orms around her and goes, 'I thought you didn't believe in competitions like this!'

'Well,' the woman goes, 'let's just say that every now and then I meet a student I can't help but take a special interest in.'

I introduce her to Sorcha. The woman goes, 'Hello, Sorcha. I was telling Ross, I knew your grandmother.'

Sorcha's like, 'Oh my God! You're *that* Mrs Leonard!'

She's there, 'Shall we sit together?' and off the two of them go after wishing us luck one last time.

Me and Honor head for the dressing rooms.

I'm nervous – but nervous in, like, a *good* way? I'm the last of the six fathers into the room. Raymond Matthews greets me with a handshake. He's like, 'May the best couple win!' because the general feeling is that me and Honor are the only ones who can catch him and Sincerity now.

I stort changing into my dance costume.

William Whelehan goes, 'Be careful putting your shoes on, Ross.'

And Ed Gorvey's like, 'And don't drink anything his daughter offers you.'

Raymond tries to rise above it. He opens his locker. And that's when I see it – a massive bowling ball, which is about to roll off the top shelf onto him.

He's not *aware* of it, though? He's looking over his shoulder at William and Ed, going, 'You lot really need to get over your –'

The bowling ball falls from just above head height onto his right foot, landing on it with a sickening thud.

He lets out a roar. It's like, 'Aaarrrggghhh!!!'

I'm thinking, it's got to have broken a bone or two.

He sits down, clutching his foot and howling. There's no doubt who he blames.

'This was you!' he goes, staring straight at William.

William goes, 'You can prove that, can you?'

'I'm going to sue you for common assault –'

'And I'll countersue for defamation.'

'I'll increase the charge to attempted murder and conspiracy to fix the results of a . . . Jesus, I think my big toe is broken!'

I throw on my stripy jacket, stand up and, very coolly, I go, 'Like you said, may the best couple win!' Then I head for the backstage area.

Honor is standing there in the dress that Sorcha made her, practising her steps, totally ignoring the other girls. She looks amazing. I can't tell you how proud I am of her focus.

I sidle up to her. I'm there, 'Don't get too excited, but Currer Bell's old man just took out Sincerity's old man with a bowling ball.'

Honor's like, 'Excuse me?'

'He reckons he's broken his big toe. But it's like Father Fehily used to say – forget about the other team, just concentrate on your own performance.'

I'm happy to say, she doesn't need to be told.

The other fathers arrive into the backstage area. Raymond is limping heavily. Sincerity goes, 'Oh my God, what happened?'

He's like, 'I'm not saying another word,' staring at William, 'until I've spoken to my solicitor.'

There ends up being a lot of just waiting around. The running order has been decided to let all the couples who have no actual chance of winning go first, before Honor and me and Sincerity and Raymond face off against each other in what is basically the final.

Miss Coleman tosses a coin to decide which of us will dance last. We end up winning.

Me and Honor keep practising in the wings, not even bothering to watch the other dancers. They're losers and we have no interest in them. Sincerity, on the other hand, watches each and every one of them do their thing, saying shit like, 'Cloud is *so* graceful!' and 'Annora has done *amazing* work on her core strength!'

At the same time, her old man is applying an ice pack to his foot to try to bring the swelling down. Eventually, it's their turn to perform. He puts on his sock, then his shoe – his face twisted in pain.

Then out he limps with his daughter and they dance the Chorleston to *Those Magnificent Men in Their Flying Machines.*

Again, we don't bother watching, although it's impossible not to hear the comments of the judges. Jean asks Raymond if he was in pain out there and Raymond says that he doesn't want to say anything that might prejudice a future civil case. She says she thought the routine was hugely ambitious and that Sincerity is without a doubt the most natural dancer in the competition, but that Raymond was unfortunately way off the pace tonight. Mena says she agrees – Raymond was a bit flat-footed, a bit tentative, but Sincerity chormed the audience, as she has every single time she's danced. Ryan says he'd prefer to focus on the positive aspects of the performance and he thought they both did wonderfully well.

They end up getting three sevens, which gives them 96 points overall. I turn around to Honor and I go, 'What are we on?'

'We've got 69,' she goes. 'Which means we need 28 points to win.'

I'm there, 'Okay, this needs to be our best performance of the competition.'

Outside, we hear Miss Coleman go, 'Our final dancers this evening . . .'

Just as I'm getting ready to walk out, Honor grabs me by the hand and goes, 'Dad, whatever happens out there tonight –'

I'm there, 'You don't have to thank me, Honor. I've had the time of my life.'

'I wasn't going to thank you. I was going to say, we better beat that focking bitch.'

'Oh.'

'Dancing the Chorleston,' Miss Coleman goes, 'to the tune of *Supercalifragilisticexpialidocious*, will you welcome please, Honor O'Carroll-Kelly and her father, Ross.'

We end up getting the biggest roar of the night. And as soon as the music storts, the audience can't resist clapping along. They love us. And they're, like, fully entitled to because we end up, like, totally smashing it.

We're totally in the zone. I remember having matches like that when I played for Castlerock College – and later on for Seapoint in the All Ireland League – where I didn't need to go looking for the ball, because it seemed to always come to me. Or I didn't need to go through my usual pre-kick routine, because I could have put the ball between the sticks wearing focking clogs.

We totally nail the two hordest ports of the routine – the bit half-way through where we stand back to back, with our orms linked, then I have to bend down and flip her over my back so she ends up facing me.

The crowd actually *gasps* when we do it?

Then, at the end, where I sort of have to get down on my hunkers and Honor has to step on them and do an actual backwards flip. Again, we nail it, nail it, nail it.

At the end, everyone in the audience is on their feet, as are all three judges. I catch Sorcha's eye. She's just in, like, floods of tears.

I bend and I hug Honor. She squeezes me so tight, it's like she's never going to let me go. I laugh. I'm there, 'You said you wanted people to like you, Honor – listen to that!' and it actually brings me back to my Leinster Schools Senior Cup days.

Next, it's the comments of the judges.

Jean goes, 'I loved it, loved it, loved it! It had so much energy and so much personality. I don't think it was the best dance you've done, but I certainly think it was the best dance of the night.'

Roars.

Mena goes, 'I agree with Jean. You set an impossibly high bar for yourself with your quickstep and your foxtrot. But that's to take nothing away from this performance – it was fun, it was lively, you took risks, which paid off. It was wonderful.'

Next, it's Ryan. I'm expecting him to have a pop and I'm actually getting ready to call him a focking bell-end when he goes, 'There is only one word for what I've just seen and that word is sublime. I want to mention something that I haven't given you enough credit for up until now. And it's this. You two have this amazing bond. You clearly adore each other, but it's also like you have this extraordinary symbiosis. When you dance, it's almost as if you're the same person. To see a parent and their child interact like this –'

Shit, his voice suddenly cracks.

He finally gets his shit together and goes, 'You have charmed us all!'

Again – roars. Then we move on to the all-important scores.

Jean holds up her bat. She goes, 'Nine.'

Fock.

Mena holds up her bat. She's like, 'Nine.'

Shit.

I turn to Honor and I'm like, 'Are you doing the math here?'

She's there, 'For us to win, this needs to be a–'

'Ten!' Ryan goes.

Honor just screams. There's a possibility that *I* scream as well? The audience goes totally bananas.

We're just, like, hugging each other and we're both crying. Then the other girls and their parents – even those carrying injuries – run out into the middle of the floor to say fair focks to us.

Miss Coleman walks out, holding this humungous glass trophy, then goes, 'As is the tradition, I'm going to ask last year's winner to present this beautiful Dublin Crystal trophy to the new champions.'

Sincerity, all smiles, takes the trophy from her.

Miss Coleman goes, 'Ladies and gentlemen, boys and girls, the winners of the Goatstown Glitterball for 2016 – Honor O'Carroll-Kelly and her father, Ross!'

The crowd goes mental. Sincerity goes to pass the trophy to Honor. But as Honor goes to take it from her, Sincerity – smiling – lets go of

it. And the entire audience gasps as it falls to the floor and smashes into a million pieces.

So it's, like, ten o'clock in the morning and I'm lying in bed when I get a text from Roz. She says that Sincerity is terribly upset about what happened last week and that she wants us to know that it was a genuine, genuine accident.

And I'm thinking, yeah, I'm sure it focking was.

I suddenly become aware of voices downstairs. I could be wrong, but it sounds like Erika and Helen.

I hop out of the bed, throw on my clothes and tip downstairs. I walk into the kitchen and I was right – it *is* them? Sorcha and Honor are there as well.

I'm there, 'Hey, Erika. Hey, Helen. Is Honor telling you about the dance contest and how that little bitch tried to ruin our moment of glory?'

And that's when I notice that Honor's crying. As a matter of fact, they're all crying.

I'm there, 'What's going on?'

It's Honor who answers. She's like, 'Erika and Helen are moving away.'

Sorcha goes, 'I feel awful, Erika. I haven't been there for you for the past few months. And I feel like, if I *had* been, you wouldn't be leaving.'

Erika shakes her head. She's there, 'It wouldn't have made any difference, Sorcha. I have to get away – from *him*.'

At first, I think she means me – at the time, I happen to be checking out her bazoos, through force of habit – but then I realize she's actually talking about the old man.

I'm like, 'Hang on, this is all news to me. Where are you going?'

Helen's there, 'Australia. To my sister in Adelaide.'

I go, 'But not for good – as in, you're coming back, aren't you?'

'I put the house up for auction, Ross. Barry Conroy thinks I'll get a great price for it with the way the market is. There'll be no reason to come back. Nothing to come back for.'

Erika goes, 'Mom only came home to try to persuade me to

move out there with her. I could open another gallery over there. Somewhere that Charles and your mother can't hurt me.'

I'm there, 'But I'll miss you – both of you.'

'Yeah, my eyes are up *here*, Ross.'

'Sorry. I'm saying I'll miss you, Erika – and Amelie.'

Shit, I suddenly realize that *I'm* crying now?

I'm there, 'When are you leaving? Please say after Christmas.'

Erika's like, 'This afternoon, Ross.'

'This afternoon? But that doesn't give us any time to say goodbye.'

'So we'll have to say it now.'

She gives me a hug and I end up totally losing my shit. I'm, like, bawling, going, 'I loved having you as my sister – even if I was always a bit weird around you.'

I know I'll never be able to smell *Chloé* perfume without getting an instant horn.

She goes, 'Thank you, Ross. For going to Argentina to find me. For persuading me not to give Amelie up for adoption. And for talking me into moving back here. You'll always be my brother – weird or not.'

She says goodbye to Sorcha then. She hugs her and goes, 'If you ever go back to politics, Sorcha, go after the real enemies. Find out everything you can about Fionnuala's foundation.'

The most hortbreaking moment is when she says goodbye to Honor. Because Honor goes, 'I thought I'd always have you as an auntie.'

Erika's there, 'I'll still be your auntie. We can Skype all the time.'

'Ever since I met you, I wanted to be just like you.'

'I'm not a role model for anyone, Honor.'

'You totally are. You're a bitch and I've always loved that.'

'Honor, you have the best mother and the best father in the world. They're your role models. Be like them.'

And then, sixty seconds later, I'm watching them drive away and I suddenly feel like a humungous hole has opened up in my life.

I hug Sorcha, then I hug Honor, then I hug Sorcha again. And then I decide, fock it, someone is going to focking pay for this.

I head outside and I hop into my cor and I head for Foxrock, angry enough to do something genuinely stupid.

He ends up not being home. *She* is, though? I find her in the kitchen, three fingers into a bottle of Bombay Sapphire at, like, twelve o'clock in the day. Her blood must be about seventy per cent proof. I must remember not to cremate her when she's gone. They'd have to drop sand from helicopters to put her out.

She goes, 'Merry Christmas, Ross!'

It's still, like, a week away.

She's there, 'And to think where I was this time last year. Trying to maintain my sanity in that prison by doing Nigella's Christmas Dinner for a hundred other inmates.'

She's horsing into a bowl of Kalamata olives – something to line her stomach.

She goes, 'What's wrong? Why are you looking at me like that?'

I'm there, 'Erika's moving to Australia. Because of what you did to her.'

'I didn't do anything to her, Ross. It was a business associate of your father's who took a sledgehammer to a nut.'

'And now she's moving away – to get away from the two of you!'

She pops an olive into her mouth and goes, 'I hope she's taking that awful mother of hers with her?'

I'm genuinely lost for words. I'm actually convinced in that moment that she is, without a shadow of a doubt, *the* most evil woman in the world. I turn around to leave and that's when I hear this suddenly, like, *choking* sound coming from her?

When I look at her again, I notice that her face is red and her eyes are popping. It's obvious that an olive has got lodged in her throat. She's suddenly got her two hands up to her neck and she's hacking away, trying to dislodge the thing.

I literally freeze. I just stand there – in shock at first, but then I stort watching her with this, I don't know, weird fascination as she struggles for air.

And in that split-second – yeah, no – I'm going to admit it, I think, what's the play here? Do I save her life? Or do I let the Kalamata olive do its thing?

She hits the deck then and I watch her face turn a weird shade of grey. She's kicking her legs wildly and stamping her feet on the Canadian maplewood floor and she's trying to say something to me, which I presume is, 'Help!' or something along those lines.

I'm thinking, wouldn't the world be a better place without her in it? With her no longer around, wouldn't the old man go back to being the father that Erika knew and the husband that Helen loved?

She's pounding on her own chest now, desperately trying to loosen the thing, but it's obviously wedged in there pretty tightly.

I'm thinking, will anyone even miss her? Wouldn't it be better all round if I just stepped out of the room here and let nature take its course? Then I could do what she did to Ari. I could tell the Feebies that I walked in and found her dead on the floor.

And I decide, yeah, no, that's what I'm going to do.

But then something – or rather *someone* – shoves me from behind and sends me sprawling across the floor, and then I hear the old man's voice going, 'She's choking, Kicker! Can't you see that your mother's choking?'

He grabs her and he drags her to her feet. Then stands behind her, puts his orms around her front and performs the – whatever it's called – *Hindlick* manoeuvre on her? Three times he does it and suddenly the olive shoots out of her mouth and across the room like a focking bullet.

The old dear storts throwing up then – it's mostly gin, it has to be said. The old man tells her it's okay, she's safe now, then he looks at me and goes, 'What in the name of Hades were you doing, Ross?'

The old dear manages to get enough air into her lungs to go, 'He was going . . . to let me die . . . He looked . . . in my eyes, Charles . . . and he smiled . . .'

The old man doesn't want to believe it, of course. He goes, 'I expect you were in shock, Ross! You were in shock at the thought of your mother potentially choking to death! But you were just about to leap into action when I walked through the door! Isn't that right, Kicker?'

But I don't give him the answer he wants to hear. As a matter of

369

fact, I don't say shit. I just go, 'Have a nice life, the two of you,' and I walk out of there.

So it's, like, three days before Christmas. Sorcha and her old pair have taken the boys out to some carol service in Dalkey and I'm just, like, lying on the sofa, in my Cantos with the loose elastic, eating Quality Street and chatting to Roz on the phone.

She goes, 'So am I going to see you before Christmas?' because the girl is definitely, definitely keen.

I'm there, 'Yeah, no, that'd be good.'

'Sincerity is spending tomorrow night with her father and his wife. Do you want to come here for dinner? I've got a goose.'

'I'd love goose – and whatever else is on offer.'

'It'll just be goose.'

'Are you absolutely certain of that?'

'Yes, I am!'

It won't be. She's filthy. *And* she can't keep her hands off me.

I'm there, 'How's *his* foot, by the way?'

She goes, 'He broke four bones in it – including his big toe. He says he's bringing a private prosecution against Currer Bell's dad for assault.'

'And isn't Currer Bell's old man already suing *him* for putting that nail through his shoe?'

'That's Mount Anville parents for you!'

'Imagine what it'll be like when they move to the secondary school!'

She laughs, then she goes, 'Anyway, Sincerity was telling me that the school is having a new Glitterball trophy made.'

'Yeah,' I go, 'this one's going to be fibreglass – shatter-proof, apparently.'

'She still can't understand how it happened.'

'Hm.'

'She said she thought Honor had it in her hands and then all of a sudden –'

This weird, I don't know, *feeling* comes over me then. It happens very suddenly. I'm suddenly thinking . . .

'Ross?' she goes. 'Are you listening to me?'

I'm there, 'Sorry, I missed that.'

'I said Sincerity thinks Honor might have let the trophy fall on purpose.'

'Roz, I'm going to have to, em, ring you back, okay?'

I hop up from the sofa and I peg it up the stairs – taking them three at a time. Into my room I go. I throw open the wardrobe and I pull out the box from Sorcha's red Magimix food processor, where I saw the thing a few months ago. It's not there. I stort pulling out other boxes and looking inside those. Again, nothing. I look under the bed, in the bottom of the wardrobe, all the wardrobes, behind the curtains – still no luck.

Holy fock.

I wander down the landing to Honor's room. I knock on the door and I hear her go, 'Oh my God – *what*?' which is her way of saying, 'Come in.'

I stick my head around the door. I'm there, 'Hey, Honor.'

She goes, 'What do you want?' and this is without even looking up from her phone.

I'm like, 'I just wanted to see what you were up to. They say you should always check in with your kids – and know what they're doing.'

'I'm trolling Laura Whitmore.'

'Oh, that's good – as long as I know. By the way, Honor, did you know there's a *Strictly South Dublin* dance competition that me and you could enter as the winners of the *Mount Anville* one?'

'No interest.'

'I just thought, you know, it was good fun – and it definitely helped us bond, didn't it? You actually stopped being an out-and-out bitch to me for those few months.'

She finally looks up from her phone. She goes, 'The only reason I wanted to win was to see the look on that stupid knob's face when *she* didn't. And I did that. End of story.'

I'm there, 'Your mother's bowling ball is missing.'

I decide to just blurt it out like that, to see her reaction.

She doesn't seem shocked at all. She actually laughs.

I'm there, 'Your old dear had a bowling ball. It was another one of her fads. She bought it around the time I first met her. She used it twice, then focked it into a corner along with her rollerblades and her ladies' golf clubs.'

She goes, 'Great story, Dad!'

'I saw it a few weeks ago. It was in a box. And now it's not there anymore.'

'Is there a focking point to this conversation and are you going to get around to it this side of Christmas?'

'I'm wondering, by any chance, was it the bowling ball that broke Sincerity's old man's toe?'

'What you really mean,' she goes, fixing me with a cold, hord stare, 'is did I put that bowling ball in her dad's locker, knowing that it would fall on top of him as soon as he opened it?'

'I was trying to come up with a better way of phrasing it – to hopefully stay on your good side – but basically, yes, that's what I'm wondering.'

'Next, you'll be asking was it me who put that nail through Currer Bell's dad's shoe?'

'Shit, I hadn't even *thought* about that one. That's how much I always try to see the good in you.'

'Then you'll be wondering was it me who dipped a rotten chicken breast into the watermelon punch to make all the other girls sick?'

'Jesus Christ.'

'Then you'll be asking me did I drop that Glitterball trophy on purpose just to see the look on that stupid bitch's face when it smashed into a million pieces?'

'And did you, Honor?'

'How would you feel if I said yes?'

'I suppose I'd be, yeah, no, disappointed in you.'

'Oh, please! What did *you* do to win that stupid rugby trophy?'

'That stupid rugby trophy happens to be called the Leinster Schools Senior Cup. And that was just a little bit of doping, Honor.'

'Was it illegal?'

'Yes, but I never deliberately injured anyone. Well, I did, but it was always in a way that was within the rules – sometimes borderline.'

'Why are you so upset?'

'I don't know. It's the first thing we've ever done together as a father and daughter. I'd love to think we won it because we were the best dancers in the competition. I suppose now we'll never know.'

'Look, Dad, if you want to know whether I made all those girls sick and injured Currer Bell and Sincerity's dads, just ask me straight out.'

'Did you?'

She looks me dead in the eye and she goes, 'Of course not, Dad!'

But, of course, I know she's lying.

As I'm walking out of the room, she goes, 'You *should* be actually pleased.'

I'm there, 'Pleased? Why?'

'Because I've turned out more like you than *her*.'

She's talking about her old dear. And even though I know she's right, I realize it's not something to be celebrated.

Sorcha tells me to ring Ronan and ask if him and Shadden and Rihanna-Brogan want to come to us for Christmas dinner. She says they've got a wedding to plan and it might take some of the pressure off them.

He answers the phone by going, 'Rosser?' and I can instantly tell from his voice that something is wrong.

I'm like, 'Ro, what's going on?'

He goes, 'She's hee-or, Rosser. She arthur cubbing to Oyerlunt.'

'Who? Who are you talking about?'

'Medissa. She came oaber to do her shopping for the Christmas. She's arthur rigging me. She waddants to see me.'

'*See* you? What for?'

'What do you think? She wants the royid.'

'Tell her to fock off. Tell her it was One Night Only. No further dates will be added at this time.'

'She says she's in lub with me. She says no one's ebber mayud her feel the things I mayud her feel that night in Estepona, norr eeben Griebous.'

'You focking idiot.'

'I know what I am, Rosser.'

'Mister Two Condoms – it focking serves you right for showboating!'

'Ine apposed to be getting maddied in just oaber a week.'

'Look, just tell her to fock off and to never ring you again.'

'I caddent.'

'What do you mean, you *caddent*?'

'She's blackmailunt me. She says if I doatunt meeth her, she's godda teddle Griebous abour us.'

'Oh, for fock's sake.'

'Ine apposed to be maddying Shadden. We've the bleaten choorch reheersiddle tomoddow, Rosser. And she's wanton to see me toneet.'

'What are you going to do?'

'Ine godda hab to royid her.'

'Don't ride her.'

'I've no bleaten choice *but* to royid her.'

'Where is she staying?'

'The Greshoddum.'

'The what?'

'The Greshoddum.'

'Again.'

'The Greshoddum.'

'Again.'

'The Greshoddum.'

'One more time.'

'The Grehsoddum.'

'Okay, Ro, what I *think* you're trying to say is The Gresham. Cough twice if that's right.'

It just saves a lot of time that way. He coughs twice.

I'm there, 'Okay, I'll go and see her. Ro, you just focus on the rehearsal tomorrow, okay? I'll see you at the church.'

'What are you going to do, Rosser?'

'I don't know yet.'

'Are you godda royid her yourself?'

'I will if I have to.'

I hang up on him, then I go outside and I hop in the cor.

I'm just, like, shaking my head the entire way into town. I thought being the father of the groom was going to involve maybe collecting funny stories for my speech from some of his associates and maybe one or two of the Community Gordaí who've tried to frighten him straight over the years.

I didn't think it would involve, well, *this*?

I ask for her at reception. 'I'm looking for a guest called Melissa something-or-other,' I go. 'She's as rough as guts.'

They instantly know who I'm talking about. The receptionist phones her room, then she hands the phone to me.

Melissa's like, 'Who's dis?' and I tell her that it's Ronan's old man. She laughs like I've said something funny, then she tells me to come up to her suite.

She's waiting for me at the door. She doesn't invite me in. 'So dis is who he sends?' she goes. 'He's ould fedda who thresses like a bleaten sailor.'

I'm like, 'My son is getting married, Melissa. You need to accept that basic fact.'

She goes, 'I doatunt cayer if he's getting maddied. I just want to hab sex wirrum.'

'But he's already told you he's not interested.'

'Ine in lub wirrum. And I hab to warden you, Ine used to getting what I waddant.'

I decide then it's time for me to do what I do best. I decide to make her fall in love with me. I lean against the doorframe and I give her one of my looks. I'm like, 'You know, you're a very attractive woman, Melissa.'

She's not, by the way. I don't know what the fock Ronan was thinking.

I'm there, 'You could have any man you want.'

Again, she couldn't. She genuinely couldn't.

She laughs. She knows where this conversation is going. She's suddenly serious then. She leans forward and she kisses me on the mouth. She tastes of minibor.

'Take off your shoort,' she goes.

I laugh then? I'm like, 'My shirt? What, here in the corridor?'

She nods. So I do what I'm told. I've no problem doing it either. I've been doing a surreal amount of sit-ups lately.

She suddenly hits me the most almighty slap across the face.

She goes, 'You teddle your son that if he's not hee-or by noyun o'clock toneet, Ine godda tedddle Griebous eboddy ting.'

Then she slams the door in my face.

I tried, I think to myself. At least I did that. I stort making my way back towards the lift slash elevator. I'm putting my shirt back on and wiping the lipstick from my mouth when I suddenly become aware of a figure standing at the far end of the corridor.

I don't even need to look twice to know that it's Grievous Bodily Horm.

'Okay,' I hear myself go, 'this is not what it looks like!'

He's there, 'Ine shewer there's a peerfectly iddocent expladation as to why you're leabon my wife's hoteddle roowum with your shoort open. You've stiddle gorra birra lipstick theer, by the way.'

He points at my left cheek. I thank him and wipe it with my cuff.

'So let's heerd it,' he goes. 'But foorst let's go somewayer a little mower proyvit.'

He indicates a door to his left, which leads to the fire stairs.

He's like, 'Somewayer with no secure doddy cammer dodders.'

He pushes the door and I have no choice but to walk through it, into this, like, concrete *stairwell*?

In my head, I'm going, 'Think, brain – just think.'

'Hab you addy idea,' he goes, 'how many people I've kiddled?'

I'm there, 'I'd say it's a fair few, Grievous – and that's not me blowing smoke up your hole.'

'Accorten to the *Sunday Wurdled*, it's well into thubble figgors.'

He looks down the stairs. I'm guessing he's trying to, like, calculate how much damage he could do to me by pushing me down the first flight. So I decide it's time to stort trying to talk my way out of this.

'Yeah, no,' I go, 'the thing is, Grievous – and I know you're going to genuinely laugh at this – the entire thing is a hilarious, hilarious coincidence.'

'I know the troot,' he suddenly goes. 'It was your young fedda what roawud her. It was Ronan – the doorty hooer.'

'It wasn't him. I swear on my mother's life. And my father's.'

'Nebber moyunt *their* loyuvs, Rosser. We're thalken about your bleaten life hee-or. And if you doatunt ted me the troot now, Ine godda thrun you down evoddy floyt of stayers in this hoteddle. Do you get me?'

'I get you.'

'I know who it was, Rosser. I joost want to hee-or you confeerm it. So ted me the troot – who roawud Medissa?'

'It was me.'

'You?'

'Me. I rode her. In her cor. They were my johnnies you found on the floor. I used both of them as well. Two johnnies.'

'You're cupboarding for him.'

'I'm not covering for him. I rode her in Estepona and I just rode her there now as well.'

'You must have been bleaten quick. Ine oatenly arthur watching you getting into the lift foyuv midutes ago.'

'I am quick. Anyone will tell you that.'

His face for some reason *softens* then? He goes, 'I admoyer you, Rosser.'

I'm there, 'Did you say you admire me?'

'Most feddas in yoo-er position would have gibbon their son up at this stage. You're not eeben afrayut.'

'Oh, I am afraid, Grievous. I'm focking terrified. But I'm still not giving him up. I rode your wife. I loved it – and so did she.'

'You've more cuddidge than addy fedda I ebber met.'

'Hey, I might even ride her again.'

'Stop saying you roawud her, will you?'

'Okay.'

'Ronan woatunt be touched, Rosser. You hab me woord. Medissa would nebber forgib me if I did athin to him. Between me and you, I think the wooban's in lub wirrum.'

'Er, good.'

'In addyhow, I like him. Ted him to make shewer he fiddishes coddidge – Ine letting him away on that condishidden. He could be a solicidodder wooden day – helping the likes of me to stay out of jaiyult.'

'That's, er, where the money seems to be alright.'

'But I hab to hab me rethribution, Rosser. I hab to hab me powunt of flesh – utterwise, me competitodders will think Ine arthur gone soft. Do you get me?'

'I could give you money. My old man is good for it. Or I could cut out the middle man and just give you the code to his safe.'

'Do I look like I neeyut muddy?'

He does. He dresses like a shop security gord from the 1980s.

I'm like, 'So what do you want from me?'

'I wanth to hit you,' he goes. 'Just wooden punch is alt.'

I nod. I'm like, 'Okay, one punch. But not in the –'

I'm about to say the word 'face' when the punch suddenly arrives out of nowhere. It cracks me full on the bridge of the nose. My eyes stort watering, I can hear a bell ringing somewhere in the distance and I can feel myself about to fall backwards until I'm suddenly grabbed by the front of the shirt.

'Doatunt fall dowun the stayers,' he goes. 'I'll keep a hoawult of you hee-or until your head clee-ors.'

It takes a minute or two. I'm going to have two black eyes, not only for Christmas but also for Ronan's big day.

'Mon,' Grievous goes, 'let's go and hab a Christmas thrink – joost to show there's no heerd feedons.'

Sorcha puts her hand over her mouth when she sees me. She goes, 'Oh my God, what happened to your face?' because – yeah, no – I've got two big, angry bruises under my eyes.

I'm there, 'Don't worry about it. It was, er, rugby-related.'

She's like, 'Oh my God, are you and Rob Kearney *still* fighting over that Aeroccino?'

'Yeah,' I go, deciding that it's easier to lie to her. 'But don't worry, it's all sorted now.'

Which *is* actually true, by the way. Rob explained the whole thing to me a couple of weeks back, when I ran into him in Base Pizza on the Merrion Road. It turns out the Leinster players had been passing the thing around for months. It was actually Devin Toner who stiffed Rob with it and he thinks Sean Cronin originally passed it on to Dev. I think Ian Madigan was the one who had the thing first. He only used it once, stuck it in the dishwasher and flooded the circuitry.

Anyway, after a bit of pushing and shoving, me and Rob decided the whole thing was ridiculous and there'd be nothing more said about it.

'Rugby,' Sorcha goes, shaking her head.

I'm there, 'You say that like it's a bad thing.'

'You've got the church rehearsal tomorrow – and you've got two big black eyes for it.'

Yeah, no, it's the day before Christmas Eve, by the way, and I'm watching TV, wondering what I'll wear for my date with Roz tonight. And by that, I obviously mean which Leinster jersey?

Sorcha is fussing around the room, straightening the Christmas cords on the mantelpiece, then moving baubles from one branch of the tree to another. I can tell there's something on her mind.

'I noticed you got a cord from Croía,' I go.

There's a woman on it dressed as Santa Claus, showing off her bicep. She's got a good set of guns on her, in fairness to the woman.

Sorcha goes, 'She just wanted to let me know she was sorry about the way things turned out. And that she's working with Muirgheal Massey now.'

I'm there, 'That's hilarious.'

'I think she's persuaded Muirgheal that she was done down by the cisgender, white, male patriarchy.'

'Those fockers again, huh?'

'Ross, can I talk to you about something?'

I'm like, 'Er, yeah,' meaning make it quick, because I'm going to need to stort getting ready for my date soon.

She sits down on the sofa beside me, her two hands on her big, swollen belly. She goes, 'Ross, I heard something. It was the night of the *Strictly Mount Anville* dance contest.'

I'm like, 'There's no proof that it was your bowling ball, Sorcha. Or that Honor poisoned those other girls. She looked me in the eye and denied everything and that's good enough for me.'

'Okay, I have no idea what you're talking about, Ross. I was going to bring up what Mrs Leonard told me.'

'Oh?'

'She said that Gran got thrown off the parish pilgrimage to Knock for being drunk and that you drove all the way to Mayo to collect her.'

'Yeah, no, that was years ago.'

'But you never told me?'

'The woman was embarrassed. She got shit-faced. She told a black priest he was the devil.'

'And you did that for her, Ross?'

'Your granny was a great old bird. I liked her a lot, Sorcha. Even if the drink brought out the definite racist in her.'

The most random *thing* happens then? She puts her hand on my leg, leans forward and kisses me on the cheek. And then she keeps her face close to mine, leaving me with very little choice but to turn my own head and kiss her on the mouth. We end up doing that for, like, a minute or two.

I'm there, 'Is this a mistake?' putting other people's feelings first for once – if I give Sorcha the old hot and sour now, there'll be none left for Roz later on.

She goes, 'I want you to move back into our bedroom, Ross.'

I'm like, 'What?' because this comes at me straight out of left field.

She's there, 'I want us to get back together.'

I'm thinking, oh, shit.

She goes, 'Oh my God, your face! Do you not want to?'

And I'm there, 'Er, yeah, no, I do,' even though it's not actually true. 'I'm just wondering, you know, what's changed? Was it just the granny thing?'

'It was everything. It was the amazing transformation I've seen in Honor.'

'Keep going.'

'And the way you helped me see the truth about Croía. Over the last few weeks, I've realized something, Ross. I still love you.'

Shit. Shit. Shit.

I'm there, 'I'm still a total wanker, though.'

She goes, 'I know.'

'I just want to make sure we're not making a massive, massive mistake here.'

'How you do feel about me?'

'Yeah, no, I've definitely still got, er, feelings for you.'

'Let's go upstairs! Let's go upstairs right now!'

Her old pair have taken the boys into town to see the moving crib and Honor is in her room, trying to provoke celebrities on Twitter.

I'm there, 'Are you definitely sure?'

She storts pulling at the buttons of my chinos. Being pregnant always made her horny. She goes, 'How sure do I seem to you?'

I'm suddenly, like, conflicted.

There's so many reasons *not* to do this? She's carrying a baby that possibly isn't mine. I don't love her anymore – at least I don't *think* I do? And Roz has a goose.

But, on the other hand, Sorcha is the mother of the majority of my children. The two of us living under the same roof but leading separate lives is not a recipe for long-term happiness for anyone, especially Honor, Brian, Johnny and Leo – plus the new one, whether it turns out to be mine or not. Me being back in her bed at least simplifies things.

I'm genuinely torn. I don't know the right thing to do. But, at the same time, I'm as hord as Crumlin here. So I make no objection as she takes me by the hand and leads me up the stairs for fifteen minutes of fun – and what the future holds beyond that, who even knows?

Epilogue

I'm late. They've already storted the rehearsal when I arrive. The priest is showing Kennet the point in front of the altar where he's supposed to hand Shadden over to Ronan, and Kennet goes, 'You b . . . b . . . b . . . b . . . b . . . bethor be ready for t . . . t . . . t . . . t . . . teeyors, Fadder. It's godda break me bleaten heert – gibbon me b . . . b . . . b . . . b . . . b . . . beaurifuddle thaughter away.'

The priest just smiles – an absolute pro – even though he's obviously thinking, I hope this stuttering focker doesn't have much more to say – I'm supposed to be saying Mass at midnight.

He turns to Ronan and goes, 'And who, may I ask, is your best man?'

Ronan goes, 'Buckets of Blood.'

It hurts a bit. I'm going to admit that.

The priest is like, 'Hello, Buckets.'

Buckets is there, 'Howiya, Fadder?'

'*You'll* have the rings, will you?'

'No, I'll ted you what's godda happen, Fadder. Ronan's young wooden, Rihatta-Barrogan, is godda hab the rigs. She's godda walk up the oyult with them on a velbit cushidden, Fadder. Then she's godda haddend them oaber to you, Fadder.'

I just smile to myself. Buckets *has* this. I sit down in one of the pews towards the back of the church. The reason I'm late is because I rang Roz to apologize for my no-show last night. I told her that me and Sorcha had decided to have one last crack at the whole happy-ever-after thing. She made some joke about a goose dying for nothing, but I could tell she was upset.

Sorcha is meeting Fionn for coffee in Dalkey. It'll probably be Idlewilde. She says she wants to tell him herself about us being back together. She knows I always meet the goys in Kielys on Christmas Eve night and she doesn't want me to tell him the news because she thinks I'd rub his nose in it.

I definitely would rub his nose in it.

The priest suddenly goes, 'And is the father of the groom here?'

And Dordeen is like, 'Him? He's probley at howum, woodying about how much this is alt costing him – tight bastoord. Soddy, Fadder.'

I go, 'Yeah, I'm actually here, Dordeen,' and everyone turns around.

Ronan goes, 'Howiya, Rosser?' and I watch the shock register on his face as he notices my two black eyes.

Shadden's there, 'Moy Jaysus – what happened to you, Rosser?'

I don't answer. Ronan excuses himself and storts walking down the aisle towards me. His mouth is open.

He goes, 'Was it Griebous dud it?'

I'm there, 'No, it was a bit of rugby banter in Kielys between me and a dude from Gonzaga, which spilled over into violence, which spilled over into handshakes, which spilled over into pints all round and an agreement to respect each other's traditions and way of life. In what other sport would you get it?'

He just stares at me. Like Frank Sinatra, he's shooby-dooby-dubious. Again, he goes, 'Was it Griebous, Rosser, what dud it to you?'

I'm there, 'Ro, drop it. You're getting married. All you need to know is that you and him are quits.'

'Are you saying you took a baiting for me?'

'It wasn't exactly a baiting. It was more of a decking. He decked me. I let him on the understanding that that would be the end of it.'

He stares at me for a long time.

Kennet goes, 'What the b . . . b . . . b . . . b . . . b . . . b . . . bleaten heddle is g . . . g . . . g . . . g . . . going odden?'

And Ronan – out of nowhere – goes, 'I caddent maddy you, Shadden.'

I'm like, 'Ro, shut your mouth. You're nearly over the line.'

But he turns around and he shouts it the length of the church, 'I caddent go troo wirrit. I've been caddying on behoyunt yisser back, Shadden.'

One of the bridesmaids goes, 'Doatunt you deer thrag me into it!'

I presume it's Lorrayunt. She's a focking disgrace, by the way. She looks like an extra from a zombie movie who did her own make-up on a moving bus.

Ronan confesses to everything, though. He goes, 'Ine soddy, Shadden. I've been doing the doorty on you all oaber towun.'

The priest goes a bit *Four Weddings and a Funeral* on us then. He's like, 'Is this true, Ronan? *Have* you been doing the dirty all over town?'

Shadden bursts into tears and buries her head in her old dear's – let's call a spade a spade here – pyjama top.

Kennet points at Ronan and goes, 'G . . . g . . . g . . . g . . . g . . . get the f . . . f . . . f . . . f . . . fook owra hee-or. I ebber see you again, I'll do bleaten t . . . t . . . t . . . t . . . t . . . t . . . t . . . toyum oaber it.'

Ro goes, 'Ine soddy for ruining yisser life, Shadden!' and he runs out of the church with tears streaming down his face and Shadden's old dear telling me, for some reason, that it's all my fault.

I run after him, but he's faster in his Nikes than I am in my Dubes and he manages to outsprint me in the cor pork of Lidl.

I whip out my phone to ring him – and that's when I notice the twenty-nine missed calls from Fionn.

I ring the dude as I'm already running back to the cor. He answers straightaway. I'm there, 'What's wrong? Is it Sorcha?'

He goes, 'Her waters broke in Idlewilde!'

'Jesus!'

I'm suddenly worried about their floor. I don't know why. It's probably just nerves.

'Ross,' Fionn goes, 'get here quickly! She's already at ten centimetres!'

I hop into the cor and I drive across the city. Except the traffic going over the East Link ends up being shit and it takes me, like, an hour to get to the hospital.

I just throw the cor up on the kerb and I race inside. I ask for her at the desk and they tell me the ward. I take the lift to the third floor, then I race down the corridor. As I turn the corner, I spot Sorcha being pushed towards me on a bed, totally out of the game.

I go, 'Sorcha? Are you okay?'

One of the nurses pushing her goes, 'Sorry, Sir, could you step out of the way, please?'

I'm there, 'I'm her husband. I just want to know how she is.'

'She's fine. It was very quick. She's sleeping now.'

'What about the baby?'

'He's a little bit premature, but he's fit and healthy.'

'*He?*'

'Yes, your wife gave birth to a little boy.'

'Can I ask you a random question? Does he look like me?'

'You can decide that yourself. He's through there.'

She points to a door at the bottom of the corridor. Slowly, I make my way towards it. I'm so nervous, I can actually hear my breath come out all uneven.

I push the door and in I go. The room is dork. Fionn is in there. He's standing with his back to me, staring through this giant window into this, like, incubator, where a tiny little baby is sleeping.

Fionn's shoulders are going up and down. As I walk up beside him, I realize that he's crying. I'm like, 'Hey, Fionn.'

And he goes, 'Hey, Ross.'

He's actually sobbing his hort out. At first, I think it's because he's found out that it's mine after all. But then I stare at the baby for a good thirty seconds, and I notice his weak, moley eyes, and I know in that moment that Fionn is the father.

Acknowledgements

Thanks as always to everyone on Team Ross: my editor, Rachel Pierce; my agent, Faith O'Grady; and the artist, Alan Clarke. Enormous thanks to Michael McLoughlin, Patricia Deevy, Cliona Lewis, Patricia McVeigh, Brian Walker and everyone at Penguin Ireland. A special thank you to Hannah Keane for the character of Sincerity. Thanks to my family – Dad, Mark, Vincent and Richard – and my wife, the wonderful Mary McCarthy.